# Fallen Crown

W MILLION

STOMILL BOOKS

Copyright © 2022 by W Million

All rights reserved.

No portion of this book may be reproduced in any form without written permission from the publisher or author, except as permitted by U.S. copyright law.

This book is a work of fiction. The names, characters, and establishments are the product of the author's imagination or are used to provide authenticity and are used fictitiously. Any resemblance to any person, living or dead, is purely coincidental.


Model: Dane Peterson

Photographer: J. Ashley Converse Photography

Editing: Red Adept Editing Services

# Bellerive Royals

## Series Order

**All the books in the series are interconnected standalones.**

Fake Crown

Scarred Crown

Heavy Crown

Fallen Crown

## Chapter One

### BRICE

Women love me. It's some sort of chemical reaction caused by my smile, my toned, tattooed physique, or my princely status. I've never questioned a woman's innate attraction; I've accepted it as my lot in life. They love me, and I love all of them.

But judging by Maren Tucker's glare across the conference table, I still won't be counting her among my fans anytime soon.

"With all due respect, *Your Highness*, we're not putting together this charity adventure race team for a lark. We want to raise money, and we want to have the efforts of the team taken seriously." My title oozes false sincerity. If we were alone, she wouldn't bother to pretend. Her tongue is acidic, and I've been on the receiving end of her poison more than once. One of a thousand reasons I'd never want her tongue caressing mine. She'd ram it down my throat and laugh as I choked.

"With all due respect, *Ms. Tucker*, if you want publicity for this team, and if you want the producers of the streaming service to spotlight Bellerive, there is no one better to be on it than me." As I finish speaking, I scan the conference room to make eye contact with the other board members from the Alzheimer's Society who are witnessing this exchange.

"That's a valid point," Tim Eggleston says. "Being able to lobby the island's wealthy for donations, suggesting they get behind Prince Brice, especially given the family connection to the disease, would be very beneficial. We can't discount that. His high profile balances the lack of experience."

The reminder of my father's diagnosis causes me to flinch slightly. While my father's situation is well-known, I'm hopeful the coronation for my older brother, Alex, as king of Bellerive and his appointment to the island's Advisory Council will move along laws to assist my father and give him greater choices about the quality of his life. I've seen what this disease does to people, and I wouldn't wish it on anyone, let alone my father. A slow decline until he bares almost no resemblance to the father who raised me.

"We need a team member who will take this seriously," Maren says.

"We'll consider the offer, Prince Brice. It's generous of you to donate your time to training and fundraising for our organization and the race." Tim surveys the room and takes a deep breath. "We're in danger of going over our allocation for tonight's board meeting, so we'll revisit this at the next one. We have about a month before training needs to commence."

Maren opens her mouth to protest, but the other members seem to be done with the conversation. She must really hate me to argue my involvement in front of her colleagues. Especially since I'm going to win. Only a fool would turn down the publicity and built-in fundraising. Not to mention the elevated profile our team would have on the documentary-style program funded by InterFlix, the biggest streaming service on the planet. As the director of the Bellerive's Alzheimer's Society, Tim is not an idiot. Everyone likes money, and including me on the race team is a license to print it.

The board members rise from their seats, and eight of them file out. Maren is the last one to leave her spot at the table. Outside the door, my security detail awaits. If she's got something to say to me that she'd prefer no one else hears, her window is short.

"The other team members have done an adventure race before. They understand the training required to do well. They're committed." She tucks her long dark hair behind her ears, and her blue eyes, the color of ice chips, meet mine.

"I'm a fast learner." I give her a suggestive glance meant to annoy. "I can master this. Learned all kinds of skills for all sorts of situations over the years."

"The *skills* you've learned have nothing to do with a ten-day adventure race." She scowls. "I guarantee it." With a huff, she gathers her papers into the folder in front of her. "You only became serious about being a real benefactor to the society when your father was diagnosed. Before that, you were an on-paper, just-for-show, throw-money-at-it guy."

Acidic. Burns right through me. She's got me wrong, but it *feels* right to her and maybe a bit to me too. Throughout my life, I've been the third in line to inherit the throne. Pending a large disaster, there was never any chance of me ruling, and I've been given a long, often indulgent, leash on royal matters. No one has ever had to take me seriously, and I've never cared either way. My brothers have had much different experiences. Alex has the full weight of the monarchy on his shoulders, and Nick has been suffocated by it. Me? I've enjoyed the privileges without the same heavy lifting. Being an afterthought, the punch line to a joke, just made me work harder to be liked.

There are few people who'd dare to dislike me so publicly. If anyone can get away with obvious scorn without social or political repercussions, it's a Tucker. Funnily enough, her billions are inherited, just like mine.

Her complete distaste for me isn't a surprise, but the longevity is. We went to high school together, although she's a few years younger than me, and she couldn't stand me then either. Joke's on her because I also don't enjoy her company. Stuck up. Entitled. From one of the oldest families in Bellerive, she's a trust fund baby who parades around Bellerive. Pretty but ineffective.

"Remind me again how many boards you sit on? How many of those are you throwing money at without putting in adequate work?"

Her nostrils flare, and I wish there was a tally on the wall. Direct hit. One point for me.

"I'm on five, and I work hard for every one."

"Work hard?" I raise my eyebrows. "You flounce around the island attending cocktail parties and suggesting other people open their wallets." I'm tempted to ask her what else she opens to get their money, but I'm too well trained by the Bellerive Royals PR team to let that one fly. From what I've heard, her husband is also a waste of space, and I wouldn't be surprised if she sought fulfillment elsewhere. I might hate her, but I'm not stupid enough to comment. Too many people walking around recording private conversations for me to give anyone but family my *real* opinions.

"I'm training the team." She breezes past me and out the door. "And I won't allow the board to put you on it."

Convincing her isn't my problem. Tim can overrule her later, but I follow close on her heels anyway. "This cause means a lot to me. I'm passionate about raising money to find interventions, ways to support people with the disease."

She keeps walking, and I clench my fists while I stay beside her. My two security guards are behind us. Depending on what I'm doing, there are always one or two burly men in attendance.

"You might not understand what it means to be passionate about anything," I say, "but it means someone will go to any length to get what they want. I want on this team."

"Passion is overrated." She whirls on me with her meeting folder pressed to her chest. "Getting the job done and done right is far more important than *passion*." She spits out the last word, but the action feels put on, as though she's trying to provoke a reaction from me.

"To succeed, passion and results go hand in hand. If you don't have them both, well, you're doing *something* wrong. I'm sorry that hasn't been your experience, but I promise you, it's *always* been mine."

"Has it?" Her shoulders relax. "In my experience, women are incredibly adept at pretending passion to stroke the ego of their partner—in any situation. Easy to make a man believe the two go together when a *panting production*"—she gives me a coy smile—"is all that's required. Something to think about, *Your Highness*." She turns on her heel and sails out the front door.

Goes to show how little she knows me. Any woman faking shit is only hindering her own satisfaction. I get off either way.

Jag, my main security detail, lets out a low whistle. "You want to work with that?"

Working with her is the price I have to pay for what I want. A spot on the team. By the time we leave for the race, it won't be me wishing I'd stayed out of the event, it'll be her.

If someone is nice to me, I'm nice in response. Be a dick to me, and the attitude I whip out will be bigger. Much bigger. Get a measuring tape. I dare you.

She wants to block me from participating, and I won't let her win. She's about to get a reminder of how influential the royal family can be.

## Chapter Two

## MAREN

After a disastrous board meeting, the last thing I'm after is more bad news. Unfortunately, I booked the appointment with my divorce lawyer, who is also my cousin, for today, since I was already in the area. After some quick retail therapy for another pair of running shoes, I make my way to Caitlin's office in the center of Tucker's Town.

I glide through reception and take the stairs to her office. It's three flights, but I need to let off some steam before I broach another subject that'll make me extra salty. Fucking Enzo leaving Bellerive and heading to America at the first sign of trouble. Trust me to fall in love with and marry a man who's a worse husband than my father.

Caitlin's secretary, Pam, rises from behind her desk when I open the stairwell door. Her broad smile spreads across her weathered face. "You're one of the few people who doesn't take the elevator. I hear you'll be off on another adventure race soon. When was the last one? Six months ago?"

A dark cloud descends over my mood. I shouldn't be surprised when people bring it up as though I'll be participating. For years, I've trained and raced with my teammates, and I thought I'd race until I died. The exhilaration is addictive. Or it was. Six months ago, I believed a lot of things that turned out to be untrue.

"Taking this race off," I say. May never race again.

"Still not recovered from your injury?" Pam asks.

The tightness in my gut is almost unbearable, and a hand strays to my stomach. "Just decided to lead in a different way. Is Caitlin available?"

"She's on the phone, but you can go in. Her mother called."

Perfect. Caitlin and I can be in foul moods together. I rap my knuckles on the door before entering her spacious office. She rotates her chair away from the ocean view. Her blond hair is in a messy bun, and her glasses are perched on her nose. Whatever her mother is saying causes Caitlin to grimace and roll her eyes at me.

Her mother is my father's sister, and while my generation is privileged, we're aware of the silver spoon lodged in our mouths. Most of my siblings and cousins are doing their best to avoid the spoiled or entitled titles. Caitlin does a lot of pro bono work across the island, and I spend my time supporting charities and promoting fundraisers designed to make people's lives better.

Every race I've done since I was a young teenager has been in support of a charity, and we've always met or exceeded our fundraising goal.

My father's generation of Tuckers didn't even realize the table was set for them, let alone acknowledge the spoon feeding them. I'm sure you can imagine how that's worked out. We've been battling their self-centered attitudes for years.

Caitlin holds up a finger. "Mom." She lets out an exasperated sigh. "Mom. I have to go. I have a client." Her lips purse. "That's none of your business, but yes, they are a paying client." She winks at me.

Once she hangs up the phone, her shoulders slump. "Why can't they just be normal?"

"I blame our grandparents," I say.

"At least our grandparents thought they were fighting to maintain the Tucker name through the assets they acquired and the things they did. Our parents sold off everything, kept the money, and seem obsessed with amassing more wealth."

"Mine are still silently seething that King George wouldn't give them an honorary title." I sink into the chair across from her. "They really thought they had a chance of throwing my sister at Prince Alexander when he was on the hunt for a wife."

"Thirsty doesn't look good on anyone. Doesn't matter how much money you've got."

Secretly, I was happy my older sister wasn't interested in luring Prince Alexander, and that was before the debacle with Denmark and his hasty marriage to a foreigner. Between Prince

Nicholas and Prince Brice man-whoring around the world since they were teenagers, and Prince Alexander's notoriously icy attitude, the royal siblings could battle the elder Tuckers for the dysfunctional title.

"Have you given any further thought to filing for divorce?" Caitlin plants her elbows on the table.

"I'm not filing." I drag my purse onto my lap as a shield. "He can be the quitter. That's not me."

"At least let me formally file the separation documents. It'll give you more options and an easier path to divorce eventually. If you two reconcile, then those documents mean nothing, anyway." She gives me a searching look. "You seem better since you went on the meds. Maybe you should reach out to him."

"I'm also not doing that. He blamed me for the…" Even thinking the word causes my stomach to roll. The meds might have evened out my emotions, but they haven't erased my memories. "Then when I couldn't get over it fast enough for his taste, he left the country to give us both *some space*." I throw my hands out. "That wasn't what I needed. Maybe if he stayed, I wouldn't have needed the medication."

Caitlin doesn't say anything, but her eyes soften in sympathy. She's poured herself into her work, and if she wants the life I tried to build for myself with Enzo, she's never given me any indication. When her parents suggested she put herself forward for Prince Alexander's wife search, she'd laughed in their faces. Her relationship with her parents is a tad more confrontational than mine. Must be the lawyer in her.

"If you don't want to divorce him, then one of you needs to reach out."

When Enzo and I got married right out of college, I never thought we'd be here at twenty-five. Maybe I should have. There was no one in the world more fun to be around than Enzo when times were good. He dominated any room he walked into. The epitome of tall, dark, and handsome. When he approached me at the campus bar, I became a puddle at his feet. My husband was built for fair weather—sunny skies and warm air.

Rain isn't his thing. Any time life got rough, he was never quite there. Missed a train, got sidetracked by something else, or showed up but was just a touch closed off. Nothing was ever so dire that I wondered if I could really depend on him. Turns out I should have taken all those tiny rain clouds as a sign he wouldn't be able to hack the big storms either.

I loved him so much I overlooked his shortcomings, but the moment the door clicked shut on our house and silence surrounded me, they all came rushing to the forefront. What kind of man leaves their wife when she's at the bottom of a pit of despair?

"I'll contact Enzo when I can be sure he's no longer a selfish bastard," I say. "Might take a while. I think the selfish and bastard parts are quite ingrained."

"God, Maren. Just divorce him." She throws up her hands. "No one but you will see it as a failure. As quitting."

Lots of people around Bellerive will see it as both. Bringing an American to the island as my husband was enough of a hubbub, especially since Enzo's job involved becoming social media famous. Not that he didn't work hard. Between his gaming videos and his online workout channel, he put in a lot of hours. His flexibility meant he could, if he wanted to, travel around the world in support of my various charities. And he did, for a while.

But the Tucker family is steeped in old, elitist money and a mountain of history on this island. Expectations abound. Enzo didn't fit in anywhere in that sense, but he did try, at first.

The truth is, we'd already been fraying when I agreed to train and travel to that last adventure race. It was a race we'd conquered three years before. Only thirty percent of teams ever finished. We knew we could do it again.

Enzo loved my sense of adventure when we met, but there was no doubt he resented me when he arrived at my bedside in Chile.

My mother has always said I have a wild heart, and she was shocked Enzo managed to break me down into marriage. To live in Bellerive, we had to be wed. Didn't feel like breaking to give in to the life he said he wanted. The one he painted with pretty words and empty promises. Us, together, on the island paradise I called home. Bending, maybe.

I was definitely broken by the time he left.

"Look, if that's all you asked me here to talk about, I have another appointment I need to get to." There's nothing else on my calendar, but I'm itching for a run. Since I broke my ankle,

I've had to start building the distance from scratch, and I'm finally gaining that sense of accomplishment I've been missing.

"That's not actually why I called you." Caitlin winces and rubs her face. "Your mom asked me to check in with you. She's worried about you agreeing to train the race team you were once part of. She wasn't sure you were being honest with her, and you finally seem like yourself again."

"Other than Prince Brice trying to horn his way onto the team, everything will be fine. No one needs to worry. I'm not racing; I'm training them."

"Prince Brice?" Caitlin's eyebrows almost disappear into her hairline.

"Can you imagine?" I let out a chuckle as I stand. "Talk about a disaster."

"The country would eat that up. You'd raise a lot of money."

"And we'd potentially put my teammates' lives in danger. He has zero training."

"You'd be one of the best to train him. Everyone has to start somewhere."

She's gone from attempting to gently talk me out of taking on this task to stroking my ego. Before my accident, my team was one of the best in the world. I have no doubt I could train Brice if I thought he'd take it seriously. Having watched him from afar since we were teenagers, I'm certain he doesn't have a serious, dedicated bone in his body. The only thing he's ever seemed to put his full effort behind is getting drunk with his brother, Nick, and dumping scandals on the king and queen.

Although I can't see King Alexander being the same indulgent presence on the throne, I'm not willing to stake anyone's life on Brice's ability to see something through properly.

"No," I say. "The fourth needs to be a woman. Keep the team balanced. Prince Brice would probably back out at the last minute and leave us in the lurch."

"The Summerset Royals are many things, Maren, but they aren't quitters. Especially with the media focus on this race and with his dad's involvement in the cause. But if your objection is truly more about balance, then I'd go see Melody Winter. She lives out in Padget Bay. She's into hiking, rock climbing, long-distance running. She'd be an excellent candidate to fill your shoes."

Now this is what I really needed. Another person to present at the board meeting as a viable option. While the Winter family isn't as well known and won't draw the same fundraising power, not having to train someone from the ground up is a definite asset.

As I head for her office door, Caitlin says, "And if your mother asks, tell her I tried very hard to convince you not to do this."

"So hard." I laugh as I open the door.

# Chapter Three

## BRICE

If you ain't cheating, you ain't trying, which is exactly why I invited Tim and Cheryl from the Alzheimer's Society Board to the royal estate for a grand tour a week before the adventure team vote. One thing I've learned about Maren during our various interactions is that she likes to win, just like me.

"As you can see," I say, "we have lots of buildings that could be used to store equipment or that can be renovated for a particular purpose. We have the boat launch straight into the ocean for paddling practice. If I was a team member, I have no doubt my family would throw the full weight of their support behind me and the cause."

"King Alexander has approved this?" Tim gazes around the huge empty barn.

No, he hasn't. Has no idea I've even suggested it. Or that I want to be part of the adventure race team. I might have slid the word *donation* into a conversation the other day. While Alex will ultimately have the final say, finances and facilities are who I'll have to speak to about my plans. My oldest brother has more than enough to worry about between negotiating the referendum laws, teaching Rory how to be royal, and raising my niece.

"It won't be a problem," I say.

Cheryl shifts on her feet. She's been uncomfortable since she arrived. I invited her because she's the one most likely to side with Maren in a vote. The less dissention at the table next week, the harder it'll be for Maren to stick to her disapproval. My skills might not be on par with other team members, but I bring money, influence, and a lot of potential media attention. Normally, that last one is a negative, but I'll milk that cow if it's the only advantage they'll accept.

"What do you think, Cheryl?" I ask.

"You're being very generous." She crosses her arms. "But Maren has a lot of experience training teams. She's raced for years, and if she thinks there isn't enough time to train you, I can't, in good conscience, put the other team members in danger to stroke your ego."

That's very candid, if inaccurate. I can see why she and Maren get along. "Which I could completely understand if I'd never done any of the adventure race skills. But in Patagonia, I took a wilderness first aid course; in Wales, I paddled extensively through the Snowdonia region; and in Kalymnos, Greece, I've rock climbed. While Ms. Tucker would love to paint me as a novice to anyone who'll listen, it's far from the truth." A day or two of all those activities hardly makes me an expert either, but I'm hoping my bravado will steer them away from digging too deeply. I'm capable of mastering those skills even if I haven't yet.

"You've done all that?" Cheryl narrows her shrewd gaze.

"I've done all that, and if I took more time, I could probably come up with other relevant skills I've acquired. From watching the other seasons of this show, I'd say adaptability coupled with a will to win are the most important character traits. I have both in abundance, and that's not all I bring to the race table." I gesture to the space around us.

Cheryl and Tim exchange a glance, and I decide not to press any harder. At least I've countered Maren's amateur narrative, and by the time I've finished the tour and alluded to all the money and exposure I could throw behind the event, I'm confident next week's vote will fall in my favor.

After our tour finishes and as soon as they're both ensconced in their vehicles, I make a beeline for Alex's wing of the palace. Since I've now promised something I'm not sure I can deliver, I need to secure some support in that area too.

At the door to Alex's suite of rooms, Kane, my brother's head of security, holds up his hand.

"Quick chat with Rory," I say. "Five minutes. Tops."

Kane checks his watch. "Nap time ends in ten minutes. Come back then."

"Oh, come on. She'd see me if you told her I was here."

"King Alexander's orders. Rory has been very tired. She's not to be disturbed during Grace's naptime."

I turn around to head back to my wing of the palace, and I slide my phone out of my pocket to fire off a quick text to Rory. More than one way to get access to my sister-in-law. As I go through the main foyer, Nick comes from the direction of the kitchen, and he's eating a scone.

"Have you talked to Alex about the state of the assisted dying law or whatever we're calling it?" Nick asks.

Like always, Nick's tone whenever he brings up the law is vaguely disapproving. Although he's agreed to go along with the referendum outcome, and he's okay with our father having choices and options, he's not completely on board.

"Nothing," I say. Last time I booked a meeting with Alex to discuss it, he said he'd tell me when there was news. The longer it takes for the law to be finalized, the trickier it might be to have our father qualify for it. Unlike Nick, I am fully behind the creation of assisted dying legislation. Already, our father is experiencing a surprising number of memory issues. Makes me wonder if our parents hid the diagnosis even longer than they've let on.

"How long are you in Bellerive this time?" I ask.

Nick and Julia have been spending so much time in Tanzania lately that I'm never completely sure when they're in the country or out of it. Their uniform initiative to help send girls to school is a passion project for them, and Alex has opted to let them run with it rather than forcing them to engage in more outreach here at home.

"A few weeks," Nick says. "I heard through the Tucker grapevine that you're trying to get on the Alzheimer's charity adventure race team? What the hell is that about?"

"That just happened this morning," I mutter. The Tucker grapevine is extensive with deep roots across the island, and Nick is friends with Maren's older brother.

His question about why I'm so keen isn't one I want to dig into. At the moment, I've got more time on my hands than I likely should, and I could ask Alex for more Bellerive work. But I need something that's going to occupy my body *and* mind. When left to my own devices, I spend far too much time stewing over our father's diagnosis, his downward spiral, our impending loss. While I might be okay with the concept of assisted dying, and I might even believe it's an important choice for our father to make, the reality of him making it is hard to consider.

"Have you run this past Alex?" Nick asks.

"Well." I squint at him. "Rory seemed like the better person to speak to."

"Still makes the best cream tea." Nick chuckles and shoves the last bite of his scone in his mouth.

"Seems unbelievable that she bakes while nursing Grace," I say.

Alex could not have chosen someone more opposite to him, but they work. There's no doubt our brother, who was once so rigid and hard to read, loves her deeply. As the eldest, he was always the most likely of the three of us to get married, but I never thought he'd marry for love. With Nick and Alex paired off, and already an heir to the throne, the pressure to do any of that is completely off me. I figure I've got years to coast before anyone bothers to wonder why I've never married.

One woman for the rest of my life is a big nope. My heart is too wild to be tamed by just one. I've sampled all the flavors, and none have enticed me to limit my menu. Why drag something casual into a long-term arrangement because that's what society expects? Much better to let other people fall fast and hard while I stand on the sidelines laughing. Nick and Alex seem happy enough now, but I've seen them both at rock bottom over a woman. That'll never be me.

My phone beeps, and I do a fist pump to see Rory has texted me. She's been a great addition to the family.

"Must be the queen," Nick says with a grin. "I'm supposed to meet Jules to go look at suppliers for the J.J. Bellerive Foundation. We're trying to keep everything as local to Tanzania as possible, but I feel like we're getting hosed on a few of the items."

"Good luck. The two of you have ATM written on your foreheads. Cha-ching," I say before I head toward Alex's wing again.

"Isn't that your Vegas motto?" Nick calls after me. "And you're the one who needs the luck!"

This time when I get to the door, Kane lets me in without even a murmur of protest. Rory must have come out with the big queen energy when she woke up, which she would have done if he'd told her I stopped by in the first place.

When I knock on the door to the main bedroom suite, Rory tells me to come in. I stride into the room, hell-bent on securing her help to bring Alex around to my newest plan.

"Whoa. Whoa. Whoa." I skid to a halt and hold up my arms to cover my face.

"It's a boob, Brice. With a baby attached to it. I know you've seen a breast before—lots of them if the rumors can be believed."

"Yes, but I came in here to prevent Alex from murdering me, and I fear I've stumbled into something sure to get me murdered."

"There is now a burping cloth covering my breast. You're safe." Slowly, I lower my arms, and Rory's green eyes are tired but amused. "Such a wimp. My boobs are currently glorified bottles."

"Murder, Rory. Fratricide. No one wants that." I fall into the armchair opposite the one she's in near the fireplace that isn't switched on. "Do you happen to know Alex's plans for the outbuildings on the estate?"

"No," Rory says. "But you could ask Alex yourself, and then you'd know."

"I wanted to borrow one for the next..." I calculate the length of time between now and the race. "Six months. For a charity race."

"Nick told me he'd heard you were vying for a spot on Bellerive's adventure race team. What's that about? Isn't it on InterFlix? That's huge."

Fucking Nick selling me out. "Do you think Alex has heard that as well?" In theory, I came to ask Rory to break the news to Alex and ask for the use of the outbuilding closest to the water's edge for storage and whatever else we can cobble together quickly.

"Does Alex need to approve your participation? Is the race dangerous?"

*Yes and yes.* "Queen Aurora, I am trying to defer to your wisdom."

"And I'd like to stay happily married. Go talk to your brother. I am not your go-between." She peeks under the cloth to stare down at Grace, my niece, as though I've been dismissed.

I must say, she's become a lot more assertive since she became a queen and a mother. Posey still enjoys my nonsense, and since her boyfriend has become one of my best friends over the years, I could work that angle. Posey has Rory's ear about anything she wants, and I have Brent's. It's the long way around, and I much prefer a shortcut.

"Go talk to Alex." Rory lets out a deep sigh. "Actually"—she holds up a finger—"explain to me why you want to do it."

I ease my hands over my face and lean my elbows on my knees. It would be easy to give her the pat answer, the one I'll likely give anyone who asks from here on out. My father has Alzheimer's, and it's a cause close to my heart. But that's not why I want to do it. Or at least that's not the driver.

"If I tell *you* the truth, will you talk to Alex?"

"You don't think you can talk to Alex about it?" Her green eyes soften.

"I don't want to." Alex has Bellerive. Nick has his project in Tanzania with Jules. I want this race, but I'm not in the mood to have my dedication or skill set questioned, which is exactly what Alex will do. Most of the time, he isn't critical on purpose; it's just his nature.

Maren Tucker, on the other hand, takes great delight in picking holes in me. She'll be one person who'll never get the real reason I'm keen to do this.

"Tell me," Rory says, and she gives my foot a gentle kick with her own.

"I'm afraid Alex won't get the law for Dad sorted in time, and I'll be stuck watching our father deteriorate while Alex and Nick are consumed by other things." I peer at the blanket covering Grace. "Other people."

Silence sits between us, but I can't make eye contact. That's more candid than I intended to be, but there is something about Rory's softness that draws out an answering tenderness in other people.

"You want use of the outbuilding, and you want permission to participate?" Rory readjusts Grace under the blanket. "I'll mention it to Alex, but I'm sure he'll want to speak to you about the risks involved."

"I'll be trained," I say. "Maren Tucker is training us, and she's been doing these races since she was a kid."

"Maren Tucker." The name rolls around Rory's mouth. "Isn't she the Tucker who doesn't like you?"

"Correct." I bark out a laugh. "Being on the team serves a third purpose. She doesn't want me there."

Rory readjusts herself under the blanket and brings Grace to rest against her shoulder before she starts patting her on the back with rapid taps. "I'm no expert on parent-child relationships." She tips her head at where Grace is curled onto her shoulder. "But sometimes being there for someone you love is all you can do, the best you can do. Don't bury yourself in this race and miss out on time with your dad."

"It's a healthy distraction and a good cause." But it also gives me a chance to be away from the main house for hours at a time, to leave the estate to train when our father's noticeable decline wears on my soul. My mother is already discussing the modifications to their suite of rooms that will need to be made to keep my father safe as the disease progresses.

"I'll chat to Alex." Rory cradles Grace in her arms and wipes her mouth. "Baby snuggles?"

"Oh, go on then." I rise and take Grace from her, wedging her into the crook of my arm like a rugby ball. "If I'm going to be the favorite, fun uncle, I need every advantage over my competition."

"Tattooed bad boy Prince Brice cradling a baby." Rory digs her phone out from the side of the chair. "Hold still. PR will be so pleased I remembered to take a photo they can release to the public."

I chuckle and give her a grin while raising Grace so her tiny face is visible. "As long as they hashtag it *Nanny Brice*, I'm all for it."

Rory snorts as she closes her phone. "I'll let them know. Seeing you holding his daughter might soften Alex a little too."

"I'm winning all over the place." Stealing the hearts of the public, softening my brother's tough outer shell, and becoming this little one's top contender for uncle of the year. As long as the Alzheimer's Board votes me onto the race team, I'll be on my way to carving out my own sliver of happiness. A new adventure awaits.

## Chapter Four

## MAREN

In front of me on the conference table is an impressive list of Melody Winter's athletic and wilderness-based accomplishments. After Caitlin's suggestion, I went out to Padget Bay and met with Melody to see whether she'd have time to commit to the racing team. Her response wasn't enthusiastic, but she agreed to let me put her forward as a candidate. While I didn't make her any promises in either direction, I'm confident. To keep the team balanced and to lead with experience, she's the best choice. Many, many racing teams have three men on them, but I won't be giving Brice or anyone else that tidbit of information.

Brice doesn't stand a chance once I get talking, even though he must have told everyone at the palace he was vying for a spot. Otherwise, I'm not sure why the royal PR machine would have kicked into high gear. They released a photo of Brice cradling the heir to the throne this week, and if that isn't outright manipulation of the public, I don't know what is. The whole island was buzzing at the sight of Brice looking so comfortable with the tiny baby. Given his playboy image, it was a good move to make him more palatable for any upcoming opportunities.

Shame he won't be getting any.

"And our final item," Tim says, checking his agenda. "Prince Brice has offered to be the final member of the race team, and unless—"

"I have an alternate candidate." I rise from my chair, and I circle the conference table, giving everyone, including Brice, a copy of my candidate's accomplishments.

"Oh, perfect," Brice says, and he takes out his own folder. "Thought it might be overkill, but I've got a list of mine too." He follows me around the room, handing out his own sheaf of papers. "Some light reading." He plucks Melody's sheet from the table and flips it over. "This is... well. Single sided. But it's something, isn't it?"

When our gazes connect across the table, he has the audacity to smirk.

"I think my fellow board members will find that Melody's skill set aligns directly with what's needed for the race. An extensive resume isn't necessary, just the right one. She's a fantastic athlete, and she's female."

"Her biological sex doesn't really matter, does it?" Brice rocks back in his leather chair.

"A balanced team is a better team," I say.

"Team New Zealand, Team Australia, and the top-rated team in the USA would disagree with your assessment. They've only ever had one female on any of their winning teams." Brice raises his eyebrows over the top of Melody's piece of paper.

It appears someone used all their spare royal time to do some research. Or he made someone else do it. Seems more likely. If he was truly a worthy opponent, this battle of wills might be fun.

"That's true," I admit. "Training a balanced team to victory would be quite an accomplishment. With Melody, we can make that happen."

"Oh," Brice says with what has to be a mock confused expression on his face. "I thought the point of the race was to raise money for charity, not to stroke your ego as a coach."

"All right," Tim says, holding up a hand. "Why don't we all take a few minutes in silence to look over the qualifications of our two candidates. Maren, I'm assuming you've spoken with Melody, and she's interested in participating?"

"She is," I say. Interested is the wrong word, but I'm not going to risk my chances here. "With her, we'd have a chance at the prize money, which we could add to the donation pile."

Brice doesn't contradict me; he merely raises his eyebrows in a way that suggests he doesn't believe me. Truthfully, the team with Melody or Brice probably doesn't have much chance of winning.

While everyone else looks through Brice's stapled pages, I stare at him across from me. He tosses Melody's single sheet, and it flutters onto the table's surface. With his gaze locked with mine, he mouths *so light*. I can feel my jaw tighten at his cocky attitude. Men who get everything they want through charm and charisma are no good to society. He'll be a terrible team player. Incapable of compromise or taking direction. I know his kind. I married his kind. The best when the wind is at their back and awful in a headwind. Let us all down when we need support the most.

"Well," Tim says after turning the final page of Brice's document. He takes in the other board members. "Should we put it to a vote?"

"Before we vote," Cheryl says, "I want to be clear that Maren will train the team regardless of the outcome."

I resist the urge to rub my face and heave out a sigh. If there was one vote I expected to receive, it was Cheryl's. We had a long chat two weeks ago over a glass of wine about Brice's complete lack of suitability. She's not the only one I took for a drink on the sly, and perhaps other people will see Brice as all shine and no substance, and I won't need her. If I was petty enough, I could probably win by refusing to train Brice. Competent coaches are few and far between.

"Ultimately, the most important thing is the cause. We're raising money for Alzheimer's, and I'll train the team either way." It pains me to admit that, and part of me really wants to be a petty bitch and slap my palm on the table and say if he stays then I go. But I'm too well trained for an outburst. My family might be full of title diggers and wealthy do-nothings, but decorum is central to the family's image. We can't appear to care about any of it because we're above such trivial concerns. If only image was reality.

"All right," Cheryl says, giving me one last long look. "Let's vote."

"All in favor of Prince Brice, raise your hand," Tim says.

Every single hand at the table except mine, but including *both* of Brice's, goes into the air.

*Cocky bastard.*

Tim declares Brice the victor, and everyone pats Brice on the back on their way out the door, and once again, we're the last two left in the board room.

"It appears we'll be working together after all, *Coach*."

"So it appears, *Rookie*." I tuck my papers inside my purse and slide it over my shoulder. He's not going to see an inch of my anger and frustration. "Training starts tomorrow morning at four at the marina. You need your own gear. If you're late, we leave without you."

"My own gear?" Brice gathers the papers strewn around the conference room.

"And if you don't have it, I and the rest of the team will be waving to you from the water as we get as far away from you as we can." I give him a saccharine sweet smile. "That clear enough for you?" If he was anyone else, I'd give him a list of things to bring.

Before he can answer, I shift past him and out the door. A run or a session at the rock climbing center or a long SUP through the canal are the only things that'll calm my fury.

Another male getting exactly what he wants with minimal effort. Must be a joy to be a man in this world.

---

I arrive home hours later covered in sweat to find my mother lounging on my couch, taking in my ocean view with a white wine spritzer in her hand. She must have helped herself to my supply. Bringing her own would be out of the question.

"Can I help you with something, Mother?" I drop my keys on the side table and tuck my purse between the table legs. From the workout bag on my shoulder, I take out a towel to mop my brow. Sweat equity in any form means nothing to my parents.

"I can't drop in on my middle child?" She eyes me over the side of the couch. Her shoulder-length dark hair is the same shade as mine, except hers comes from a bottle now.

With an older brother and sister and a younger brother and sister, I'm smack-dab in the middle. Sometimes it amazes me she had all of us close together because she doesn't seem to have much interest in parenting. Once, when I was drunk, I asked her, and she told me she loved babies. The moment a baby became a toddler, her interest waned. That's what nannies were for, apparently.

"You can, and you do drop in, but never without a reason."

She sips her wine while I get myself a glass, and when I sink into the couch on the opposite end, she turns up her nose in disgust. "Aren't you going to shower?"

"No." I take a sip of my drink. Little rebellions are necessary in private because I never make them in public, even if I feel them.

"I heard from Cheryl that Brice Summerset has joined the race team. You'll be training him?"

Traitor Cheryl already filled my mother in on the results of the vote. While I never discussed Brice's potential involvement with my mother, I'm not surprised she found out. One of the perks of being independently wealthy is that my mother's job can be gossiping 24/7.

"You've always been very close with the members of your race teams."

Two of my siblings would likely argue that I'm often closer to my team than I am to my family. Though that wouldn't be completely fair. I'm close with Nathaniel, my older brother, and Sawyer, my older sister, but I have less in common with Gage and Ava, even though we're all within a few years of each other.

"If you have to end up divorced, snagging a royal on the rebound wouldn't be so terrible."

"No one is getting divorced." I snort and shake my head.

"I'd have to check the rules on a royal so far down the line of succession getting involved with a divorcee, but I can't see why it wouldn't be possible. King Alexander found a way to legalize his bastard child and marriage to a foreigner."

I wince at her phrasing before setting my wine on the coffee table and putting my head in my hands. "Mother, if King Alexander ever heard you say that, he'd banish you from the island without a second thought. Have you heard how he talks about his wife?" While I might think the whole arrangement is convenient and scandalous, there's no doubt King Alexander would wage war for his wife. He's already gone to war against the Bellerivian press more than once about libelous or slanderous articles they've written about Queen Aurora. I can only imagine what he'd do to Celia Tucker if he heard her speaking ill.

"Who's going to tell on me? You? I think not." She takes a last gulp of her wine and sets her glass on the table. "Have you spoken to Caitlin about filing the separation paperwork?"

My parents never liked Enzo, and as soon as he fled the country while I was still sick and recovering, that was the final strike against him. They might not have been the most loving and dedicated parents while I was growing up, but the small island mentality of protecting your own still runs through them. We're fractured and close all at the same time. A mass of contradictions.

"Marriage is a commitment I take seriously," I say.

"Clearly, he doesn't." Mother rises and removes a lipstick from her purse, lining her lips while she peers down at me. "You've always hated to lose, but digging into your own unhappiness isn't any way to win either." She sails past me to the door. "Besides, Prince Brice is no poor woman's prize. No shame in panning for that gold." She winks at me as she opens the door to my top-floor apartment and disappears in a puff of expensive perfume.

Guess Mom and Dad are still angling for that royal title after all. The target for their firing squad just became me. *Awesome*.

## Chapter Five

## BRICE

At three thirty in the morning, Jag drives into the marina parking lot on the outskirts of Tucker's Town with the SUV loaded with equipment. Since Coach Tucker was a sore loser and didn't want to give me any indication of what to bring, I went overboard. There is nothing she can ask me to give her that I haven't got somewhere in the oversized SUV. Finding it might take a minute, but I can guarantee it's in here. Paddles, life jackets, safety equipment, water, electrolytes, first aid kit, water shoes, a cushion for my butt or knees, and the list goes on from there.

When I arrive, there's a lone vehicle in the parking lot. The Mercedes-Benz G-Class isn't the most expensive SUV someone could own, but it doesn't exactly scream money conservative. Has to be Maren. Arriving half an hour early was supposed to guarantee I'd be first and be able to watch the others roll in. A good first impression. An indication I'm taking this seriously, despite the lies Maren has probably already fed them.

They've all been racing together for years. I went down that internet rabbit hole last night before bed trying to determine exactly how tough it'll be to win some respect. Discovering Tucker's misstep in their last race, one that put her in the hospital, should have made me happy. Something to tease and goad her about when she's, undoubtably, riding my back over the next six months. Instead, a strange queasiness stirred in my stomach at the notion of her being hurt. A worthy opponent shouldn't have such an obvious weakness. One accident isn't going to soften me to her when her dislike of me is so clear and sustained. I've never done anything to deserve her distain, but I receive it, nonetheless.

Jag gets out of the SUV first and approaches the other car. The driver's window rolls down, and he exchanges a few words with the driver. Bellerive is the safest place in the world for me usually, but one can never be too careful. The referendum on assisted dying has stirred up strong feelings in people, and my family is a big force in legalizing it.

Maren exits her vehicle, and she points up the road to Jag and makes a few other motions, which look like instructions or directions. He nods his head along with her and then glances down at his feet.

Not willing to wait any longer, I get out of the SUV and wander over to hear what they're discussing.

"It's about 8 to 10k in total," Maren says when I get close enough.

"Should have brought my runners," Jag says.

"If it's vital for you to be near, you can always trail us in the vehicle," she says.

"What's going on?" I check my watch. There's still twenty minutes until everyone else should arrive.

"We're going on a run," Maren says. "I hope you brought the right shoes."

They're on my feet, if she cared to look.

"We train two components at a time some days. Never know what you might face on the racecourse. A quick run, and then we'll paddle out with the rest of them."

A run isn't a big deal. I've been jogging around the estate to clear my head since Dad's diagnosis months ago. "Where's everyone else?"

"They'll be here at four thirty." She gives me a sly smile. "Need to grab anything before we get started?"

*Four thirty?* She either expected me to be late or deliberately gave me an earlier start time. The sun hasn't even begun to peek out of the horizon, and the streetlights are still on. She's got a headlamp perched on her forehead, but I didn't bring one of those. There's a flashlight somewhere in the back, but I'm not running with that clenched in my hand. The run wasn't on the itinerary she gave me.

I tug my lightweight sweater over my head and pass it to Jag. My T-shirt rises with it, the morning breeze off the ocean causing goose bumps to rise across my skin. Maren glances away. She really does hate every part of me.

"You following?" I ask Jag.

He nods and climbs into the driver's seat again. Maren tips her head toward the sidewalk and begins a light jog. We stride beside each other for a minute in silence, but the longer we run, the faster she seems to be going. The changes in pace are subtle, but as we ascend the first hill, I realize how flat the royal estate is. My breathing is coming out rough, and my chest is tight. But there's no fucking way I'm stopping. Jag can pick me up off the sidewalk and rush me to the hospital if I collapse, but I'm not giving Maren the satisfaction of besting me on the first day.

I grit my teeth and increase my pace to match hers. Her breathing is elevated, but her strides are long and easy, as though she runs like this every day. I've never run at this pace for a sustained amount of time. Apparently, I've been too easy on myself. After today, that stops.

We run in silence, partly because there's no way I could speak even if I wanted to. But the longer we go, the more I realize I won't be able to keep up. The best I can hope to do is nip at her heels as she weaves us through the narrow, sleepy streets of the villages along the coast of Bellerive on the outskirts of Tucker's Town.

Why is it so fucking hilly? I swear to God she picked the most difficult route. If we'd gone toward the city, I'm convinced it would be flatter. When we make a left-hand turn, and I spot the hill on Warner's Road that I'd never attempt at a walk, let alone a run, I let out an audible groan.

"You okay back there?" Maren huffs out, her voice filled with false sweetness.

"This the best you got, Tucker?" I grunt out. It's a taunt I can't follow up because if this is the start of her torture, I'm in trouble. My goal is to make it up the hill without stopping or without walking, and I'm not sure I can do it. She's already putting an increasing amount of distance between us, and my sense of competition as well as my temper are flaring in response. It's one thing to wish I wasn't part of the team. It's another to sabotage me on the first day. This is an ambush, meant to cut me down to size, and I won't let her do it.

Jag rolls down the window of the SUV and leans out the side. I raise my hand to him. "Don't! Not a word." The vehicle could be in park for all the ground I'm covering right now, but I'm still jogging, and even if it kills me, I'm getting to the top without stopping. My quads are screaming in protest, but I'm almost there.

When I crest the hill, Maren is jogging in place, and she glances at her watch. She makes a *tsking* sound and shakes her head. "Bit slow, I'm afraid. Back down we go to the marina or we'll be late to meet the others."

She turns on her heel to descend the hill, and I follow her, my legs so wobbly I'm afraid I might skid down on my face.

Jag cheers me on while he inches along the road beside me. Someone will die today, and I'm starting to think it'll be me.

"You've got this, Your Highness," Jag calls when I get to the bottom of the hill and start the agonizing journey back to the marina. Maren is so far ahead, I can't even see her anymore. The brutal pace she set leading up to the hill has murdered my legs. They are jelly, and I have no idea how I'm going to stand on a SUP board for however long we paddle for next.

She's an evil genius, and as much as I hate her right now, I have to respect an opponent who doesn't play fair. Means I won't have to feel bad about whatever I plan in retaliation. Today will not go unanswered.

When I stumble into the parking lot, there are four familiar faces watching me, Maren and her three ex-teammates who are now my teammates. All of them are from wealthy families with diverse cultural backgrounds who can trace their family's arrival back hundreds of years. Bellerive only tightened their immigration borders about a hundred years ago when it became apparent the island could only hold so many people comfortably. Now, it's incredibly difficult to gain permanent citizenship. While we're in the same social circles, I don't know any of them well.

Given the amount of training I've been warned about, avoiding formal employment must be the key to putting in the hours. Paxton Smith is short with tan skin and close-cropped brown hair. By contrast, Riker Grant is a tall Black man with a broad smile and athletic build. Both men are in their thirties. The final team member is Wren Jones whose pale skin has to be a liability under the full force of Bellerive's sun. Her red hair is piled into a messy bun on the top of her head, and she keeps glancing at Maren as though she's already worried about our coach.

The paddleboards are stacked against the main building, and a glow is starting to seep across the horizon. Being out on the ocean in the dark didn't seem safe to me, but at least the sun is rising now.

Each person grabs a board, and I'm left with the one on the bottom. Brent and I have taken these out for a lark before but usually in sheltered inlets or coves. The ocean isn't white caps, but it's choppy. While everyone else slides their board into the water, paddles past the breaking water, and rises onto their feet with no issues, my gut clenches at what's ahead for me.

Wobbly legs and choppy seas aren't a great combination. At some point, I'm going to fall in. Gritting my teeth, I climb onto the board and paddle out to everyone else. At least the paddling part is mostly arms and back. The team is stretched out in a line, stabilizing themselves as though it's second nature. I sit for a beat with my legs dangling in the water. Feels good to have my runners off after Tucker's first effort at torture.

"To Tucker's Point Hotel and back?" Maren says.

"That's probably five or six kilometers out and then the same back. Too far for me today." Wren glances from me to Maren. Like me and Maren, Wren is in her mid-to-late twenties.

"It's not like you to want to do less." Maren frowns, and her gaze narrows.

"And it's not like you to come out of the gate at a sprint when a walk will do just fine."

This is a battle of wills I'm not opposed to witnessing. I've never been part of an organized team before, and figuring out the dynamics will be important to besting Maren and establishing myself.

"Fine," Maren says. "We'll go to Walker's Line and back."

Wren dips her paddle into the water and strokes forward without saying a word in response. At least not all of them enjoy the idea of my suffering.

With both hands pressed into the board, I manage to get to my feet. But I'm no sooner up than the rocking motion of a bigger wave causes me to drop to a push-up position on the board while the rest of the team balances with ease. At least I didn't tumble into the water, but my muscles are groaning at the sudden movements.

"Balance," Maren calls out in a lilting tone that grates on my nerves.

"No shit," I mutter as I rise to my feet again.

Maren strokes out ahead of the rest of us in a long, even pattern suggesting a lot of experience. Not long later, in a move that I'm sure is designed to show off, she actually turns around on the board and observes me and the others as we paddle toward her.

Another swell comes out of nowhere, and this time, I'm not prepared. Before I can drop to my knees or fall flat, I'm knocked off the board. I hit the water and tumble in the darkness for a moment before I orient myself to the surface again. When I emerge, Wren is beside my board, and she helps me back on.

"Balance," Maren calls over her shoulder again.

When I rise to my feet, Wren checks my positioning and gives me a few pointers on where to put my feet. Not that it matters. The muscles in my legs are already seizing up from the run.

"Epsom salts and a hot bath when you get home," Wren says. "You're part of the team now, and Maren is only riding you because part of her wishes she was racing."

And she hates me, but I'm not going to say that out loud if she hasn't admitted that nugget to her teammates. I'll pick my moment to make her look petty. Today isn't it. Her pettiness is already obvious.

"Knocking me down a peg or two is just a bonus," I say.

Wren chuckles. "She is competitive. Wouldn't want any of us to believe you're better than her."

If I have a say, that's exactly what they'll believe by the time we're done with the race. Another wave hits the side of the SUP and tips me into the ocean. When I pop my head back up and wipe the water off my face, from up ahead, I hear Maren call back, "Balance, Your Highness."

*Screw balance.* I hoist myself onto the board again. I might not be a winner today, but if I tilt my life enough in the direction of training, it won't take me long.

---

Posey dumps more Epsom salt into the bubble bath, and I breathe a sigh of relief at the hot, almost scalding water surrounding me. My entire body aches. Maren Tucker knows how to wreck a man. The run killed my legs, and the paddle murdered my arms and shoulders. There are muscles I didn't even realize worked on my body that are screaming, and I'm not a complete fitness novice. I jog around the estate, play tennis with Nick, lift some weights with Alex.

"Call Brent," I say to her when she perches on the bathroom counter near the sink.

"He's training." She sets her phone beside her on the granite.

"This bath shit isn't going to cut it." Though I do feel better than when I attempted to ease myself in. Posey agreed to help me preserve my reputation as tough enough to do this race, so I've protected her nonexistent modesty with swim shorts. While Posey might roll her eyes at my manhood, Brent wouldn't be so keen on me flashing it at the woman he's head over heels in love with. And safeguarding my bromance with Brent is just as important as easing my sore muscles.

"He's not some magical guru. He'll probably tell you to use a heat and ice combo and go see a masseuse." Posey examines her nails.

"The team is rock climbing this evening. I'll bet I can barely climb out of this tub unassisted let alone scale a fake mountain. Call Brent. Brent will help me."

"Unless Brent is going to fly here and loan you his body, Brent can't help you. You and your exhausted muscles are on your own. I can't believe you tried to keep up with Maren on a run.

In high school, she was one of the fastest runners on the island. She took part in international track meets."

"She fucked me over yesterday, and not the fun kind. She rode me hard and put me away wet."

"Accurate," Posey says with a sly grin. She glances at her phone. "He texted me back with the name of a cream for muscles. I'll see if I can get it from the pharmacy after work."

"After work is too late. Give the name to Jag. He'll get it for me."

Posey picks up her phone, and her fingers fly over the keyboard before she sets it back down again. "Do you want to hear what else Brent said?"

"I already texted him all my revenge plans," I say.

"This message makes more sense with that context," Posey says. She holds up her phone to read. "'Don't do anything that'll compromise the team's respect for you or her, or it'll put a damper on the adventure race. Any revenge should happen outside training hours.'"

"He's such a team player." I let out a long-suffering sigh. "Those plans were good."

"He *was* the team captain for Northern University's swim team."

"All right, tell me what else you know about Maren Tucker. I read she was in some sort of accident during her last adventure race."

"Broke her ankle and sustained some other injuries, I gather. That's why she's not racing this time," Posey says. "That's common knowledge."

"How does her husband put up with her?" I lean my head back against the tub.

"He doesn't," Posey says. "I heard he left the island after they had a fight. She was still recovering from her injuries. A *scandal*."

I stare at the wall across from me. Hadn't heard that. No matter how much I disliked someone, I wouldn't be able to leave them to fend for themselves while they were recovering from injuries that put them in the hospital. There's being an asshole, and then there's *that*.

An island-fleeing fight has to be extra juicy, and it just might be my ticket to exacting some revenge in private or public. Whether Maren settles down or continues to try to punish me for some unknown slight will determine if I use whatever information I dig up. Some ammunition would be nice to hold, even if I never use it.

"Can you find out for me?" I ask. "More about her accident, more about her deadbeat husband?"

"I could, but do you really think it's right to use her personal tragedy to appease your wounded ego? She was injured. Her husband left her. Rubbing salt in those wounds just makes *you* an asshole."

Based on what I know now, I'd put money on her husband being, quite literally, the worst man in history. What kind of person leaves their partner when they need them the most?

Not a single piece of me cares if Maren Tucker believes I'm terrible. Unlike her husband, I don't owe her any loyalty. Using her personal *tragedy* against her will only reinforce what she already believes. It's not as though I'll be stooping lower. She set the bar, and I have no trouble sinking to it.

"I may not use the information," I say. "But I want it."

## Chapter Six

## MAREN

Prince Brice walks into the climbing center in a black tank top and shorts, tattoos and muscles on full display. There's no bodyguard today. I may harbor an intense dislike for the prince, but I can't deny his attractiveness. Light-brown hair, eyes that are more golden than brown, and a wide smile that toes the line between playful and cocky. Women have flocked to him like a magnet ever since I was old enough to notice. Fools, all of them.

The Bellerive Royal men are blessed by a genetic combination that renders each of them different but no less beautiful. Of course, the easy-breezy life Prince Brice lives doesn't exactly lend itself to premature wrinkles and gray hairs. Training for this race just might give him both.

As he makes his way toward me, I'm surprised at how fluid his gait is. Between the run and the long paddle, he should be stiff and sore. While he *looks* fit, I didn't actually expect him to *be* fit. All gloss and no substance. A flash of annoyance sparks in me that anything about him is surprising.

"All right, Tucker," Brice says when he gets close enough. "What's the latest torture disguised as training?"

"A little run and a small paddle are hardly torture," I say as I gather all the clips and harnesses we'll need to rock climb the hardest wall in the back room of the center.

"Is 10k is a little run to you?"

"Eight." I throw our harnesses over my shoulder and head for the area I already reserved.

"Ten," he says, and his jaw tightens as he falls into step beside me.

It *was* ten, and I cock my head, trying to decide whether he's that good at judging distances or whether he typed our route into a map app and had the distance displayed for him. Likely the latter. Though his ability to *almost* keep up with me for as long as he did yesterday caused me to push myself harder than I'd normally be comfortable with, given the state of my ankle.

"Getting a taste for rock climbing today," I say.

"Done it before."

"Yes, I'm sure you've done it all before. Left no feat of athleticism untouched." A day here or there of some activity in a foreign country arranged for PR purposes hardly counts as real experience. He doesn't want to be seen as an amateur, and I don't intend to treat him like one. Arrogance on the course will put everyone in danger, so he might as well face his ignorance during training. Luckily, I have no problem arranging a few hard knocks.

"I never say no to adventure," Brice says.

"I have no doubt 'no' isn't in your vocabulary." There are photos all over the internet of him saying "yes" to all sorts of things. I open the door to the final room and sail through without holding it for him.

He grabs it with a grunt. "Everyone should live their life through a 'yes' lens instead of a 'no' one. Why limit the possibilities?"

"Not all experiences or possibilities are equal or"—I give him a long look—"worthy of my time." Although it bothers me to hear him claim a philosophy so close to mine—too close to something I once said to Enzo in a crowded bar. *"To be alive is to be challenged. Seeking out the next adventure is the best part."* My wiser, more knowledgeable self, cringes at my naivety. Not everything in life should be a *yes*. Some experiences are best left as a firm *no*. Save yourself the pain.

"Spoken like someone who hasn't experienced nearly enough joy." His hands are on his hips, and he's surveying the giant wall in front of us.

His comment reverberates through me. When was the last time I experienced unadulterated joy? Not once since Enzo left, and even before he ditched Bellerive, I can't put my finger on our final good day. In Chile, my fall wasn't just physical.

"Where's everyone else? Or did you give me a starting time thirty minutes before the team again?"

"Today was trainee's choice." Though Wren tried to pick rock climbing, saying she thought I needed to be supervised with Brice. Something about me committing murder, which I won't do, at least not literally. Metaphorically murdering him doesn't bother me in the slightest. Which isn't what I told her, obviously. Coaches don't pick favorites or the opposite of favorites, which is what he is. "Each team members has a different training goal for today."

"I could have picked my own goal too," he says.

"Oh?" I pass him a harness that needs to be put together. "What do you know about what it takes to race?"

"I've seen all the seasons." He holds up the harness and stares at the buckles and straps.

"Bit like watching your team play in the NFL and feeling like you could step into the quarterback's shoes during the Super Bowl." I slip into my harness and begin buckling myself in. "You're no Tom Brady."

"Don't you mean Nathan Fa'avae?" He weaves one of the straps through the wrong buckle, and I glance up at the high wall.

Naming one of the best adventure racers in the world isn't exactly an incredible accomplishment. Two minutes with a search engine would have given him that, and if he's truly watched all the seasons, the winners are always featured heavily. He drags the strap out and tries another loop.

"Need some help?" I ask.

"Depends." He glances at me before drawing the strap taut in the wrong place. "Are you going to be helpful?"

"Since I'd prefer you didn't die today, yes." I tighten my own harness.

"Limiting it to today isn't a resounding endorsement, but since I don't want to fall"—he glances at the top of the wall—"a hundred meters to my death, I'll take the help."

"Seems you're terrible with size *and* distance." I close the space between us, and this time, the faint odor of eucalyptus reaches my nose. He's used some kind of rub for his sore muscles, and a zip of triumph shoots through me. The run and paddle weren't as well tolerated as he wants me to believe. "Perhaps a basic measurement class is needed." I tug on the straps around his waist, and I'm keenly aware of how close to his groin I'll have to work to get the harness together correctly. Perhaps taking it all apart to showcase his ignorance was a bad idea.

"I'm much better at judging size when I'm looking down at it."

"I'm sure everything seems much bigger from above." If we're talking about his dick, I can easily counter that one.

"Once I've grasped it, I'm pretty confident about the size."

*Gross.* He's definitely referencing his dick. Or who knows what other body parts on other people. Keeping my head down, I make short work of the harness, and I wedge the final strap into the right loop, yanking it tight. When I glance up, he's staring down at me with amusement. His reaction takes me by surprise since he seems to dislike me almost as much as I detest him.

"By the end of this, you're either going to love me or hate me even more."

"Shall we make a bet? I know which side I'm on." To change my mind, he'd have to become a totally different man.

"I *am* a gambling man," he says. "What would we wager?"

"Not a clue. There's nothing I'd ever want from you." The idea of owing him something if he somehow managed the impossible causes my heart to kick. I don't want a scrap from him, but more importantly, I don't want him to lord his victory over my head either. Gloating would ensue, there's no doubt. Prince Brice would not be a gracious winner. The good news is that he'd have to get me to admit my opinion had changed, and I'm very good at hiding my truth.

"We'll see," he says with a cocky smile. "I tend to grow on people."

"Like a fungus."

"Ah, yes. The fungal infection—which reminds me. Didn't the Tucker family try to latch on to the Summersets recently? Your older sister, Sawyer, went on a date with Alex, didn't she?"

"While he was not-so-subtly wife-hunting?" I cock an eyebrow. As if he thinks he can infer *my* family is the problem. "She declined. A happy miss for her," I say.

"Yes, I'm sure Celia and Jonathan Tucker were delighted."

*Ugh.* This is what he does. Gloats. My parents' desire for a title is fuel to use against me. How he believes anyone could think the mess his older brother made of his multiple engagements is anything but a lucky escape is beyond me. In the right circles, what Alex did is an open secret. None of us would ever confirm it to the press, but we all know. Two engagements, a royal baby out of wedlock. The story Alex fed to the press is utter nonsense. If Brice was smart, he wouldn't be rubbing my parents social clawing in my face. Unlike most Bellerivian families, the Tuckers have enough money and clout to go nuclear.

We're at an impasse. Both of us in our climbing gear, glaring at each other, and neither of us seem to be willing to break the standoff.

"Oh, you're here," Wren says from the doorway. "What a coincidence! I opted to train climbing today too."

"We were just about to start," Brice says.

"Excellent," Wren says. "I'll join you." She strolls past Brice and blatantly examines his harness. "Maren give that to you in pieces?"

"Yes," Brice says, and he slides a glance my way.

His expression is hard to read, but if he's surprised my teammates know me well, he'll soon understand the bond we share. Once you've been through an adventure race together, anticipating a teammates' actions or reactions becomes second nature. Beyond the racing, we enjoy each other's company. Though I've been enjoying Wren's attitude a lot less since Brice joined the team. He doesn't need to be babied; he needs to be toughened up.

"Good for you getting it together properly." Wren already has her harness on, and she strides to the far station, the easiest starting place.

"Yes," Brice agrees, his amusement returning. "I sure showed her."

"Why don't you climb this route first?" Wren says. "Maren can guide you and check your form, and I'll be your belay."

"I'm sure Tucker will enjoy my form," he says.

I press my lips together to avoid snapping back, which is what Brice wants. If I can't keep my retorts focused on training, I'll undermine my authority as the coach, and I've worked too damn hard and earned every scrap of my knowledge to look like a fool.

Wren hooks Brice up to the ropes, and he approaches the wall, examining the placement of the holds. When he goes to reach for the first one, Wren cringes but doesn't say anything.

"You want to maximize your static reach." I release a deep sigh and go to the wall to demonstrate how to straighten his posture and rise on his toes to get a good grip. "Otherwise, your arms will get tired quickly."

He gazes at me wordlessly for a beat, and I can't tell if he's taking me seriously or not. Then he says, "Any more tips, Coach?"

"Don't over grip the handholds. Keep your hands relaxed and light." I demonstrate, and when Brice grasps the rock just above our heads, I slide my hand under his to check the tension in his wrist. His skin is warm and smooth against mine. "Yeah," I say, "gentle like you're cupping an egg or a light bulb and trying not to break it."

"I tend to prefer my grip firm," he says with a smirk.

"Not a surprise that your primary concern is your own satisfaction." I give him a mild look and keep my voice pitched low.

"My own satisfaction is always a concern," he says, leaning close enough that his breath stirs the tendrils of dark hair that have escaped my ponytail, "but it's never my *only* one."

I can feel my jaw tighten at his obvious innuendo, and my heart kicks at his proximity. An unexpected awareness electrifies the space between us, and when our gazes connect, his expression shifts from brimming with amusement to one laced with curiosity.

"You're not as immune to me as you'd like to believe," he whispers.

"Everything okay over there?" Wren calls to us.

"Peachy," Brice says. "Tucker was just explaining how to achieve satisfaction"—he glances at Wren—"when climbing new heights."

Wren's concerned gaze seeks mine, and I shake my head in response before stepping away from the wall and Brice. His comment about me not being as immune as I'd like is far too close to the truth. Whatever zipped between us isn't something I'll be allowing to happen again. For one, I'm married. And two, Brice Summerset is the last man who would ever tempt me. Talk about jumping out of the frying pan and into the fire.

## Chapter Seven

## BRICE

For the next two hours, my climbing skills are picked apart by first Maren and then Wren. When one explains a technique, and I don't immediately pick it up, the other interjects with a different explanation. There's an ease and a shorthand between them that probably shouldn't surprise me, but it does. A few times, Maren even laughs at Wren's sometimes eccentric instructions.

By the time we're on the last climbing section, my muscles, which were already sore from Tucker's torture yesterday, are screaming in protest. I've hidden my discomfort so far, but I'm not sure how much longer I can prevent it from being obvious. There's no way I'll be the first person to suggest quitting, and neither of them seems to be losing enthusiasm for correcting my mistakes. Holding in my sigh of resignation, I stare up at the wall of the last section where the handholds are farther apart and a whole lot smaller. *What a joy.*

Joshua, the owner of the climbing gym, peers into the room. "Maren Tucker," he crows. "I saw your name on the booking calendar, and I couldn't believe it. You're back training?" He wanders into the high, open space. His family, who are central figures in Bellerive's Filipino community, own a slew of gyms and fitness centers across the island.

"Coaching," she says, and there's a pink tinge to her cheeks. She holds up her index finger to me and Wren, and then she makes her way to him at the door.

"She'll warm up to you," Wren says once Maren appears to be out of earshot. "She's had a tough year, and she's not great at letting people in under the best circumstances."

If she'd made that claim yesterday, I'd have said hell had a better chance of freezing than Maren Tucker did of deciding I wasn't a complete waste of space. Even earlier, before Wren showed up, Maren made her dislike for me clear.

Then at the rock wall, when she touched my wrist, an unexpected spark jumped between us. Nothing I'd ever act on, but it was the first indication I've had that I could alter how she sees me. Perhaps she doesn't hate me for some perceived slight or flaw in my character. Perhaps she hates me for the way I make her feel.

And that? Well, I know how to handle women who want me but can't admit it, even if I'm slightly disappointed she's turned out to be one of them. No need to hate the popular kid just because he's popular.

"I'm not worried about what Tucker thinks of me," I say. The last two days of training has made it clear I'll have to work hard to keep up with the team. While I've always been the peacemaker between my elder brothers, I do have a competitive streak. Normally, I'm winning ladies, not races, but I enjoy the idea of this new challenge. So different from anything I've ever done before. "Tell me what I can train on my own without her interference."

"Interference, huh?" Her lips twitch. "Most would call it coaching, especially with the amount of knowledge Maren has of the races and the rigors of them."

"I would appreciate Maren's skills if she was riding something other than my back." I flash her my most charming smile.

"I'm starting to see why the two of you don't get along." Wren shakes her head.

"We only need to tolerate each other for the sake of the race." I cross my arms. "She's married anyway, and I try my best not to be a home-wrecker." Out of the corner of my eye, I watch for her reaction at the mention of Enzo, the absentee husband.

"I notice you didn't say you *weren't* a home-wrecker."

"Can't help what you don't know," I say. Or don't get around to asking. A few women have proven to be slippery with the details of their life. A consequence of being rich and moderately famous—sometimes people can't resist my magnetic pull, and they're seduced by the idea of one night with a royal. For some, forbidden fruit tastes much better than whatever they've got lying around at home. Who am I to deny their desires? My life isn't theirs.

"You can train your body as much as you want here in Bellerive," Wren says. "Take yourself to the brink of exhaustion, but you'll never match the mental toughness needed on the course. If it's bad weather, train anyway. Climb the stairs, run the hill, bike up Mount Juniper. There'll be a lot of low points, but you gotta battle through those to get the highs."

I can't decide if she's telling me I'm already not doing enough or if she's just trying to give me a reality check. Either way, I file away her suggestions. Jag and I are going to be getting extremely fit over the next six months.

"That what happened to Tucker at the last race?" I ask. "Not mentally tough enough and made a mistake?"

Wren's expression closes, and I realize I've gone about ten steps too far. Since she's proven to be my sole ally, pissing her off will only make training more miserable.

"Whatever gossip source you've tapped doesn't know what they're talking about," Wren says as Maren and Joshua wander back to us. "She hurt herself saving me from my own stupidity."

Her revelation causes me to rock back on my heels. Maren took the fall for a teammate?

"I can tell from your expression," Maren says to Wren when she's close enough, "that Prince Brice is being his normal charming self."

Wren doesn't answer but instead eyes Maren and Joshua, who are both decked out in climbing gear, including helmets. "Not liking the look of this," Wren says.

"Maren says her ankle is better." Joshua proceeds to hook himself up to the ropes, and he motions for me to clip in too. "You're my belay. Maren and I are racing to the top."

Beside me, I can't hear the whispered words between Maren and Wren, but I can tell the bad mood I put Wren in has only increased with Maren's decision to climb the wall.

While they argue in lowered voices, Maren attaches herself to Wren's rope. "I've got a helmet, and you're my belay," Maren says as she heads toward her section of the wall. "I'll be fine, Wren."

"Prince Brice, you want to count us down?" Joshua asks as they both chalk their hands. "From five."

I glance at Wren, who releases a long-suffering sigh. Maren checks over her shoulder and makes a "hurry up" motion with her hand. With that, I count down from five, and as soon as I call one, they're off, spiders up the wall. Both of them are so fluid and natural, it's hard to decide who to focus on, but without realizing it, my eye is naturally drawn to Maren, who leaps and scrabbles for hand and footholds without a flicker of fear. Either she really trusts her belay or she doesn't care if she falls. When she makes one final, daring leap to tap the buzzer at the top a half second before Joshua, a tiny flare of pride at her athletic prowess lights in me.

Joshua and Maren sit at the top of the wall, laughing and chatting to each other, but I'm mentally following their paths up the wall again. They never stopped to assess where to put their hands or feet. Pure instinct seemed to guide them.

"They do that a lot?" I ask.

"Used to," Wren says. "Before Maren's fall. Wasn't sure she'd ever have *that* in her again." The hint of a smile tugs at the corners of Wren's lips. "Impressive, isn't it?"

It is, and as Maren and Joshua have us lower them back to the ground, I ponder what I need to do to match what I've just seen. "Why didn't you ask him to be on the team?"

"He only enjoys climbing," Wren says. "That's the problem with most of the athletes on the island. They enjoy training one discipline only. To truly succeed at adventure racing, you have to excel in multiple areas, and most people don't have the time or the inclination to do it."

"Makes me a rare breed," I say.

"The rarest," she says. "Adventure racing is not for the faint at heart."

The only weakness in my heart lies behind the palace gates with a man who now needs to be reminded to eat his meals. He's taking the medication that's meant to slow the progression, but if this is slow, I can't imagine how he'd be unmedicated. The reminder of what awaits me at home makes me reluctant to leave the gym.

Joshua gets called away, and Maren and Wren embrace in a long hug that brims with something I can't identify. Relief, maybe. Whatever happened to Maren during their last race has obviously had an impact on the team's dynamics and on Maren's mental state.

I haven't figured out how to leverage Maren's weaknesses, and the annoying part is that she was a good coach today. While I can chalk some of her attitude and patience up to Wren's influence, it doesn't change how much knowledge she relayed to me and also how strong of a competitor she is, even when she's not at the top of her game.

"Tomorrow," Maren says to me as she loops her arm around Wren's shoulders, "we tackle Mount Juniper on mountain bikes. Meet at Caspian Car Park after dinner—at seven."

As I'm unbuckling my harness, Seth Rockton enters with a group of guys I've been to Macao with before on a few stress-relief vacations. Not my stress—theirs. Third in line to the throne is all the perks without the pressure. No worries for me.

Seth comes over to me and locks his hand with mine before tugging me into a half hug. "I heard you were on the adventure race team," Seth says.

"Had nothing better to do," I say. "Why not, right?" Out of the corner of my eye, I swear Maren rolls her eyes while she gathers her equipment.

"It's for a good cause this year," he says. "Looks good on paper."

"Plus," I say, "I figured there'd be some hot women who didn't mind getting dirty."

Maren lets out a retching sound, but Seth doesn't seem to notice. Makes me smile to realize she not only heard me but gave me a reaction.

"Only you'd be able to pull women while competing in a long-distance race," Seth says.

"It's truly a curse to be this irresistible." I grin when Maren throws her harness over her shoulder and strides out of the room in an obvious huff. Too fucking easy to get under her skin today.

"Shame she's married." Seth watches Maren leave. "Always been a bit of an ice queen. Would've loved a chance to heat that up."

His comments about Tucker almost roll off me, but I can't quite shake my annoyance with Seth. "We should grab a beer soon," I say as I check my watch. Tonight is a dinner for No Child Hungry, an initiative to make sure every school-age child in Bellerive has access to a healthy breakfast each morning. "I have to get going."

"You ever need a climbing partner, let me know."

Since I'll be building a wall on the estate as soon as I can get the materials shipped to Bellerive, his offer means I won't have to ask for other help or rely on Jag as my belay.

"I'll call you," I say as I head for the door.

Other than the Alzheimer's events, the No Child Hungry charity is the only one the entire family supports with not just our money but our time too. I just hope my muscles don't stiffen up before the end of the night or that no one wonders why I reek of a eucalyptus muscle rub.

Maren Tucker might consider me a fool or a thousand other negative things, but I won't allow any of it to be proven true. Whatever she throws at me during training, I can take it. She won't get the best of me.

# Chapter Eight

## MAREN

Sawyer, my physiotherapist and my older sister, makes a *tsking* noise as she examines my ankle. It's swollen, as I suspected it would be given the run and SUP yesterday and my ill-thought-out race to the top this afternoon. Admitting any weakness isn't one of my strengths. I'll push myself to the brink and tumble over the edge before I admit failure.

"No heels tonight," she says.

"I have to go for an hour. It's not an event where flats are appropriate, and I already have my outfit picked out." Cocktails will be an hour of drinking and circulating to talk up the charity. Dinner will be a two-hour affair, but at least I'll be seated for that part. As soon as dinner is done, my commitment is over.

"Flats are always appropriate." Sawyer takes a heating pad out of the warmer, wraps it in towels, and lays it across my ankle.

"You keep using this in ways it's not ready for, and it might never be up for the challenges you enjoy."

The last day or so, I've gone beyond my current limits, but I needed to prove myself. Now that I've done that, I can step back and focus on coaching rather than participating. Letting someone like Prince Brice beat me at race events I'd normally be able to accomplish while half asleep wasn't going to happen. Old habits are hard to break. Ignoring my body in favor of obsessive training is what got me into this mess, at least in my personal life. Enzo might have left me, but he accused me of leaving him first, of not being as invested in our relationship as I was in my team, in my races.

"Have you changed your mind about racing?" Sawyer sinks into the chair beside the physio table. She runs a hand along her shorn head. Last month, she allowed her long dark locks to be shaved off in the center of Tucker's Town after being part of a group that raised an obscene amount of money for cancer.

I shake my head at her question, but I don't meet her gaze. The truth is, I'm not sure how I feel about racing. Right after my accident, I would have jumped back into it with both feet if they'd been working properly, and not because I was ready to face what happened on the course. Sometimes the old adage about getting back on the horse isn't about overcoming fear but rather about avoiding the idea of it at all.

The more time that lapsed without being able to train, the more uncertainty seeped into me. While I missed training, I wasn't sure I still had the edge I needed. Today at the climbing wall, I beat Joshua to the buzzer, but the race wasn't like it used to be. Before my accident, I never questioned whether I'd get to the top of the mountain first, navigate the hairline turn in slick mud, or swim through ice-cold water without getting hypothermia. Up the wall today, I couldn't get my head cleared. Each time I leapt for a handhold, I was certain Wren would take my full weight when I misjudged it.

I never used to doubt myself about anything, and now I doubt everything.

"I haven't changed my mind," I say. "Just a bit of training while I'm coaching. I'll cut back."

"You gotta let yourself heal, Mare."

It's not like I've never hurt myself before. You can't engage in extreme sporting events and remain uninjured, but the consequences have never been so dire. I'm convinced that anyone who has ever had a brush with death is forever changed by the experience. Impossible to avoid.

"I'm getting there," I say. More than anything, I wish that felt true.

---

The No Child Hungry charity dinner is always a lavish affair, and it pains me to arrive in plain black flats like some kind of old lady. While they might be more comfortable and better for my ankle, they don't lend the same sense of authority and sophistication that I'm used to coating myself in before I arrive at one of these things.

Because the universe hates me, Prince Brice is the one on the door greeting donors and important people with King Alexander, Queen Aurora, and their infant heir, Grace. Since I'm on the board of this charity with his brother Nick, Brice's central role at the door is a surprise.

"Your Highness." I give my rookie the shallowest bow I can muster while in public, and my pale-pink dress touches the floor. The receiving line is one of the only places where a formal bow is expected, and I purposely dipped much lower for the king and queen.

"Coach Tucker." His lips twitch with amusement. "You seem a bit shorter than normal tonight. Did you shrink an inch or two?"

More like three without my heels, and the fact he's noticed, given that most of our time together has been spent in running shoes, is extra annoying.

"Same height as always," I say. "But we've already established you're not good with size."

"True. When everyone else seems small in comparison, it's hard to judge with any accuracy." He places his hand on his heart. "Being above average is a cross I gladly bear."

"Yes," I say. "You're such a martyr."

"When you're at the bar, ask for the Brice special," he says before I can scoot away. "You won't be disappointed."

"Oh, I'm aware of the Brice special," I say. "I've heard about it all over the island for years."

"As you should," he says with the hint of a smile. "It's damn good."

"Strange," I say, over my shoulder. "That's *not* what I heard."

"Perhaps you should get your hearing checked." He lets out a chuckle, and the warmth in it is surprising. He's enjoying our verbal parry and riposte. Am I?

"What's that? I didn't quite catch it." I place my hand next to my ear as I continue deeper into the crowd. No point in dwelling on whether our mutual digs at each other are amusing or frustrating. The smart angle is absolute indifference.

At dinner, I'm seated next to a Montgomery who asks far too many questions about Enzo and his extended business trip overseas. That's the official lie Enzo and I agreed on after my parents insisted they needed something to tell people. Anyone who understood Enzo's job would realize it's impossible for him to have to be anywhere but with me for this long, but the people who've turned their nose up at my husband don't stand a chance of comprehending what a social media influencer does. Lying to them is easy.

Sometimes I consider revealing everything, explaining in detail how he let me down to every socialite who asks, but then I'd have to admit what happened. The only thing that would get me is their pity or some trite, meaningless comment about my youth, as though that somehow shields me from grief. I've gotten enough of that from my own family.

Dinner finishes without too much pomp and circumstance, and I weave my way toward the exit, satisfied I've fulfilled my duty and quite exhausted from the last three days of trying to kick Brice's ass and, instead, kicking my own. Ahead, the queen steps into my exit path, a sleeping Grace nestled against her.

"Maren, right?" she says with a broad smile.

We've met before at other fundraisers, but I'm sure she's introduced to lots of people around Bellerive. Since she didn't grow up here, it must be a tad overwhelming to be expected to remember everyone's name. That's one thing the former king and queen had in spades—they were raised here and neither of them ever seemed to forget a face. Part of me wonders how long the king was slipping before people realized it wasn't age leaving rust marks on his memories but something much more sinister.

"Queen Aurora." I offer a half curtsey even though I don't technically have to.

"Oh, it's—" She flushes. "No need for that. I just wanted a quick word with you about Brice. How is he doing so far? There have been a lot of calls for Epsom salts and some sort of special muscle rub that Brent recommended." Her brow is furrowed.

The baby stirs in her arms, and a vise circles my abdomen. Before I can gather a response, King Alexander appears at her elbow.

"Do you have the donation? I can't seem to locate it," he says to her.

The tiniest grimace flashes across her expression, and she shifts the baby, trying to get into her pocket.

Someone draws Alex away, and I'm left watching her struggle to maneuver the baby and dig something out of the bejeweled outfit she's wearing that must have pockets. Other than a burp cloth that resembles a shawl, she doesn't have a purse.

"Would you like me to help?" I offer. "Dig it out of your pocket?"

"If you could take Grace for a second, that would be fantastic." She holds the baby toward me, and on instinct, I accept her.

As soon as she's in my arms, Queen Aurora's sigh of relief is audible.

"Carrying her around all night has been exhausting. I should have told Alex, and he did take her for part of dinner. But I'm trying so hard, you know? PR said the optics were better if I held her. The *optics*. Listen to me. Such an old-fashioned sentiment, don't you think? That *I* have to be the one with the baby."

The whole concept of royalty is old fashioned, but I'm not going to be the one to drop that truth bomb when she's in over her head. Not sure what she thought she was marrying into, but if my family is steeped in tradition, her new one has traditions layered with actual societal rules.

"Why I was trusted with the donation, I have no idea." She riffles around in what appear to be deep pockets.

Grace wiggles, and I stare down at the sleeping figure in my arms, and my heart contracts. She's such a gorgeous little thing with a tuft of blond hair and sweetly puckered lips. The handover didn't phase her at all. She's still sound asleep.

There's something about the smell of new babies that's intoxicating, as though the world is rife with possibilities. For not the first time, I understand my mother's preoccupation with these tiny bundles. Celia Tucker has never been shy about her desire for grandchildren. All of us have been hearing about it since we were teenagers.

"Do you mind holding her for a moment longer?" Queen Aurora asks. "I just need to get this to Alex, and I can get to him and back a lot faster on my own." She worries her lip and glances around. "Or perhaps I should find family or staff."

"I can hold her," I say, but the vise around my abdomen is tightening. In my head, I do the math, what might have been mine. What will never be mine.

She purses her lips and seems to consider the decision for a moment, and then she flashes a smile at someone over my shoulder, and the tension eases out of her. "Back in a sec."

Grace stirs again, and I sway gently, willing her to stay asleep. There are other people milling around us, but it could be just the two of us. Contentment and sadness mingle at the weight and feel of her cradled against me.

"Well, look at you," Brice says at my shoulder. "Never would have pegged you as the mothering sort. Maternal instincts would be something to scoff at, I'd expect."

The comment is a bullet to my heart, and tears prick at the back of my eyes. I steel myself, the same way I've been doing for months, ever since the accident. It takes a moment before

I'm sure I can speak without him realizing how deeply his words struck.

"Kids aren't my thing. No idea why anyone would want that weight of responsibility." The band around my abdomen has migrated to my chest, and it's so constricting, I can barely breathe. "Here." I pass her to him, and he takes her as though he's held her a thousand times. Maybe he has. Maybe the PR photo wasn't fake. "I have to go."

For the first time all night, I'm grateful for the flats as I practically flee the benefit, my dress fluttering behind me. No one tries to stop me or intervene in my escape. The memory of Grace, heavy in my arms, makes my stomach ache. A bud that will never bloom.

In the car, I sit with my hands on the steering wheel, willing myself not to cry. With a glance at the clock, I see it's too early to take my medication. The sadness that's sweeping over me isn't new, but I'd forgotten its fierceness.

On autopilot, I realize I've driven to my house rather than my apartment. From the driveway, I stare at the security lights that keep it lit. A picturesque two-story stucco house with no ocean view but a garden fit for a family. When Enzo and I picked it out, we had so many plans. So much hope for the future.

*Stay or go? Stay or go?*

I throw the car in reverse, and this time, I keep myself focused on making the right turns to get me to my top-floor apartment with the ocean view. It's not mine, technically. The Tucker family owns it, but when I couldn't drag myself out of my pit of despair after Enzo left, my parents packed me up and brought me here. They thought the view might help.

It didn't, but the medical intervention my older sister, Sawyer, and my older brother, Nathaniel, arranged did. Clinical depression isn't solved by someone telling you to snap out of it or offering you pretty things or packing up their bags and leaving you behind.

I go through the motions of getting ready for bed, and as I lay staring at the ceiling, tears leak out of my eyes and onto my pillow.

When my phone rings, I contemplate ignoring it. Answering it never gets us anywhere, but there's still part of me that longs for what we once had, that wishes he'd just come home.

"Hello?"

"Hey, M," Enzo says, and his words are slurred like they always are when he's had one drink too many and remembers he has a wife.

The deep timbre of his voice, coupled with the nickname he gave me years ago causes the tears to fall faster. "You're drunk."

"And you're crying." An accusation. "Gage told me you were getting better. *You* said you were getting better."

"Better isn't linear," I say.

"I don't even recognize you anymore," he says. "How do we get past this?"

*Not by leaving the country*. But I've said that so many times even I'm tired of hearing it. Doesn't change his response, make him want to come back.

"You're not the only one who's lost something," he says. Bitterness. So much fucking bitterness.

Comparing who's lost more has never gotten us anywhere either. We're both losers in that scenario, and he's so focused on his feelings that he never acknowledges mine. Maybe he thinks I do the same to him. We haven't had a civil conversation in months.

"Are you ever coming home?" We've danced around this question, but my conversation with Caitlin is fresh in my mind. Since he's drunk, he'll be honest. The one benefit of him calling when he's had one drink too many with his buddies is the lack of filter.

"Yeah. Yeah, M. I'm gonna come home. I don't know when. I don't know. Our vows mean something to me. I just—I need time to process everything. We need some time to regroup."

*Regroup.* Doesn't that imply there's more than one person? A group. A team. But it's just me and just him. Separate. Grouping with no one. I curl into a ball on my side, and I listen to him breathing through the phone line.

"Do you want to come to Boston for a while? Maybe a change of scene'll help us."

"I can't right now." The words are tight in my throat because I know what's coming next.

"Please tell me you're not back fucking training." Enzo releases a huff of air into the receiver. "You promised you were done. Wasn't what happened enough?"

Tears run in rivers down my face, and I can't speak, can't explain. Racing is in my blood, and while I have no idea if I'll ever work up the nerve to compete again, I can't let it go. Training and medication are the only things that have made a dent in my depression. He doesn't understand what he's asking, how low I sank, how hard I'm scrambling to keep my head above water.

In the first few months after my fall, I told him I wouldn't race anymore. At the time, I thought it would appease him, keep him in the house, on the island. But he left anyway, too far away to see me waving my arms as my head sank under the water.

"It's late," I say.

"M."

"I have to go."

"I love you, Maren. You know that, right?"

"I can't." My voice is thick with tears. "I can't."

And then I hang up the phone and cry myself to sleep.

# Chapter Nine

## BRICE

As soon as my father was declared incompetent for the purposes of ruling, before Alex was able to take over, my mother instituted a schedule for him. Since Alzheimer's often operates on a first in, last out system, his short-term memory is likely to be impacted before his long-term memory wavers too badly. She wanted the schedule to get far enough into his brain that it would provide some grounding for them both as he became more confused and forgetful. Magical thinking, likely, but we do what we can to cope.

Yesterday when I visited him, he asked me three times in the space of an hour what I was up to later. Each time I mentioned the adventure race, he asked me similar questions—not identical but close enough. Information isn't sticking on a regular basis.

Today, his balance is off, and I've been following him around their suite of rooms to make sure he doesn't fall and break something. Since he retired as king, his decline has become more noticeable, as though he was somehow holding himself together or his position tethered some part of him to the here and now in a way he no longer has. Or maybe I'm spending more time with him, and I'm seeing things I should have seen before. Things I suspect Julia's mother saw, things I know my mother pinpointed as more than mere forgetfulness.

"Alex has had the baby." My father arches his brows in my direction, looking for confirmation. He does this a lot now. Information he thinks is correct but can't be completely sure and has to be verified.

"Yes," I agree. "They've called her Grace."

"I've met her?" He frowns, and his eyes flick back and forth as though he's searching for a memory.

"You have." He sees her almost every day, but I know better than to pile on extra details.

He gives a satisfied nod and settles into a wing chair near the fireplace.

My mother is due back from running her errands in a few minutes. I tried to beg off being the one to watch Dad, but she doesn't like asking staff when he's still very coherent, if forgetful, sometimes confused, and a bit off-balance. But every time I look at him, I picture the other Alzheimer's patients I've seen and interacted with since I became a patron of the Alzheimer's Society. He doesn't get better. He only gets worse. Some patients decline with a certain sweetness, and others burn bright with rages. No two people are exactly the same. There's no way to know who he'll become as the disease ravages him. My dad and not my dad all at the same time. The man who raised me is trickling out, one lost memory at a time.

There's a knock on the central door to my parents' suite of rooms, and before I can call for whoever to come in, Alex pokes his head in the door.

"Mom's not here?" Alex says by way of greeting.

"Errands. What's up?"

Alex enters the room and shuts the door behind him. He runs a hand through his hair and releases a deep sigh.

I'm tempted to push for whatever is bothering him so much that he sought our mother. They've had a rocky year between Alex's almost wedding to a Denmark princess and my mother's initial stubborn attitude about Rory. All seems to be well there now, but Alex isn't one to seek advice from Mother. Even with our father's memory issues, Alex is more likely to ask Dad's opinion on something rather than our mother's. After all, Dad's long-term memory is largely unaffected still. He and Dad drew even closer after Dad's diagnosis. I suspect Alex covered some of Dad's day-to-day shortcomings before the truth came out.

"We voted on the final version of the law today," Alex says, and he glances at our father who has fallen asleep in the wing chair.

My heart migrates into my throat, and I can't speak. I just nod at him to continue. Part of me is desperate for Dad to have the option to use it, but another part of me is like Nick and wants to cling to any grain of hope I can find. Either way, I lose my father, and I'm keeping the wall of grief at bay by not thinking about any outcome too deeply. Right now, my father is here. Someday, he will not be.

"He'll qualify, I think, if we can get Dr. Bennett to put the medical paperwork together this week. Then it has to be reviewed and confirmed by a second doctor. Finding one who'll agree with Dr. Bennett shouldn't be a problem. Dad has to sign the right to die forms in the presence of a lawyer."

I clear my throat and hope my expression doesn't portray my conflicted feelings. Agreeing that it's the right thing for our father to have the choice in how his life ends is one thing, but setting the final steps in motion is another.

"When?" I manage to get the single word out around the lump in my throat, and I hope Alex understands my meaning.

"He has to go before he's lost the ability to consent. Given that the disease tends to take recent memories first, and there's already decline there..." He runs a hand through his hair, and when he meets my gaze, I see the conflict in him too. "Soon. It would have to be soon."

I slump into the chair across from Dad, and I take in his sleeping form. My gaze roams over the planes and angles of his face, trying to memorize every detail. In some ways we're lucky, maybe, that there's so much evidence around the island of the life he's lived. Pictures, videos, speeches, and the three of us. None of that makes the sharp ache in my chest any easier to bear.

"Second thoughts?" Alex asks.

I grip the back of my neck while I consider what this desperation creeping into me means. Laying my forearms on my knees, I glance at Alex. "Don't tell Nick. This is what Dad asked us to do for him, and I don't want my uncertainty to bolster our brother's."

"Is that what you're feeling?"

"What are you feeling?" I counter.

"As though there is no right answer." He sucks in a deep breath. "Slow or quick or somewhere in between, the awfulness is still there, at least for us. But if we do what he's asked, then at least maybe it's not there for him." He runs his hands from his temples down to his chin. "Rory and I have talked about it a lot. No matter what, I can't get what I truly want—a healthy father. That's not an option before me on the table."

I release a deep sigh and place my head in my hands. He's right, but even that doesn't lessen the chasm opening inside me. As a kid, whether we were in trouble or not, we always knew our father would shield us as best he could. Bellerive and its people were important to him, but I never doubted that we were too. Sometimes I felt like Alex and Nick were a bit *more* important, but that meant less pressure for me. Hard to be angry about that.

The door to the suite of rooms opens, and my mother rushes in. Her brown hair is loose around her shoulders, and she's carrying a pharmacy bag. She could have easily gotten a staff member to pick those things up. What's happening to Dad isn't easy for any of us.

"I have to go." I push myself up from the chair and head for the door my mother just came in. "Training." The bike ride up Mount Juniper doesn't start for another hour, but I'll happily arrive early to avoid hearing Alex tell my mother the news. No doubt she's as conflicted as me and Alex.

"Brice," Alex says.

"Just let me know the details when they're sorted," I say, as though those details won't wreck me, and then I close the door to my parents' rooms.

---

It's raining, because of course it is. My mood is foul, so the weather might as well match it. The windshield wipers on the SUV are removing water at the highest setting, and we're sitting in the parking lot waiting for everyone else to arrive. We're early, but my bike, which is attached to the rear hatch, will be soaked. Not that it'll matter. In minutes, my whole body will be soaked in the downpour.

"This doesn't seem safe to me," Jag says. "Slick, slippery road. It's still daylight, but it'll likely be dusk on your way back down."

I'm not convinced we'll make it to the top during daylight. Apparently, he has more confidence in my biking and physical fitness than I do. If there's one thing I've learned this week, it's that I am not nearly as athletic as I believed. There is not a single muscle on my body that doesn't ache on some level.

"Wren says we have to train in every condition to prepare for the race. Have you watched the show? It's not going to pause for some rain." Though I'm not eager to get out of the car and face this weather tonight. My head isn't in the right space.

A Mercedes-Benz parks beside my Rolls Royce Cullinan, and annoyance flares in me. She'd have to be the first one to arrive after me, not Wren or Paxton or Riker, who I could pretend to be jovial and good natured with. The one who grates on me in ways I find annoying and enjoyable in equal measures.

Riling her up and listening to her either bite back or storm off is a pleasure, but her dismissive attitude of me grates on my nerves. Last night, she practically tossed Grace into my arms before she fled the benefit. Read that all wrong. The way she'd been swaying with my niece as though the two of them were locked in their own little world had spread an unexpected warmth through my chest. *Tucker as a mother*. The mere suggestion ended up horrifying her.

Could have been what caused the rift between her and her husband. He wants kids, and Maren would rather not. Makes sense to me. Though I have no desire to get married or ever settle down, spending so much time with Grace has made me wonder whether Alex could really be angry if I had a kid with some woman out of wedlock. I mean, he almost did it. He's not that much of a hypocrite.

Another grandchild would please Mom and Dad—and my brain stalls on my father's name. He'll never meet any children I manage to have.

There's a knock on the car window, and I realize everyone is on their bikes, getting soaked in the rain, waiting for me. Here early and still late. Won't live that down.

From the seat beside me, I grab my helmet. When Jag makes to get out with me, I hold up my hand. I can get my bike off the rack myself. There's no need for him to get soaked. He's going to follow us in the SUV.

Within thirty seconds of getting out of the vehicle, my light-gray shirt is almost black, and it's plastered to my chest. The water is running off my helmet and down my face in rivers that make it hard to see, but I follow the group toward the hill, my muscles primed for protest with the first downward stroke of my legs on my mountain bike.

Tucker is in the lead, Riker and Paxton are two across behind her, and Wren is on my left, paired up with me. She must really think she needs to babysit me. A bike up Mount Juniper, even in this shitty weather, isn't insurmountable.

When she tries to make small talk over the torrent of rain, I can barely hear her, and I'm not in the mood to chat anyway. Normally, I'll talk to anyone about anything, but I can't cope with the superficial filler tonight, and I won't mine my grief for someone who is practically a stranger.

Jag creeps along behind us with his hazards on to keep anyone from running into us in the downpour. Water kicks up with the tires, soaking whatever parts of me the rain doesn't naturally trickle into. It occurs to me that this might be the most miserable I have ever been in my life.

Wren appears to tire of my nonanswers, and she pulls ahead of me, happier to bike alone than to have my hostile company. Can't blame her. I can hardly stand myself tonight, and that's rare. I'm a fucking good time, normally.

The group is getting quite far ahead of me, and I'm regretting my asshole attitude because it's becoming harder and harder to pedal. My leg muscles groan with each stroke.

"Your Highness," Jag calls from the open window over the pounding rain. "You've got a flat tire."

A flat tire? *Fan-fucking-tastic.* Might explain why it's been getting progressively harder to get up the hill, other than the fact we're ascending a freaking mountain. I climb off the bike, and I hold the seat, staring at the deflated tire. I don't have a spare.

Jag has thrown the SUV into park, and he's standing beside me now. "You know how to change it?" he asks.

"Not a clue. You?"

"A car, sure. But a mountain bike? Not a chance."

I release a deep sigh, and I hoist the bike onto my shoulder, carrying it back to the rack. Instead of standing out here in the rain, we might as well drive to the top of the mountain, wait for the rest of the team at the rest center to see if anyone can fix my tire before we go back down. If not, I guess my training is a bit easier tonight. Won't hear me complain, though I'd been hoping this ride would serve as a positive distraction. Instead, it's just soured my demeanor even more.

Once I've secured the bike, I get into the SUV beside Jag, and we sail up the mountain, past the rest of the team, and we park outside the rest center, facing the crest of the hill.

It's not long before Tucker appears with a scowl so deeply ingrained in her face that I fear it might be permanent. If it wasn't for the spark that jumped between us the other day at the climbing gym, I'd believe she really hates me. Doesn't matter what she thinks or feels, I'm not willing to play the game today.

Before she gets to us, I'm out of the car and walking toward her. Despite her obviously shitty attitude, I'm prepared to explain my flat tire and lack of preparedness. Even if I'd had a spare tire, I've got no idea how to use it.

"Took the easy way, huh?" Tucker yells over the pounding rain as I approach.

"Not exactly," I say, and a familiar flare of annoyance ignites. Would it kill her to let her guard down an inch? "I got a flat tire."

Paxton, Wren, and Riker crest the hill and head into the shelter of the rest area after throwing us a few raised eyebrow glances. No one in their right mind would choose to be out in this weather, but Tucker hasn't made any move to go inside.

"You should have waited," she says. "Someone would have doubled back for you. We don't leave teammates behind."

"But I had a vehicle, and it's fucking pouring. You expected me to hang tight and wait for someone?"

"Where's your spare tube for your tire?" She holds out one hand while her other brushes water off her face.

"I don't have one," I admit.

"You need to be better prepared. There won't be an SUV to take you up a hill on the course."

"Not like you've helped with preparedness. It's like a fucking game to you, to see if you can catch me out."

"Hasn't been hard to highlight your inexperience," she says as she storms toward the rest area.

"You always make the right choice? Never made any mistakes?" My tone is deliberately antagonizing as I follow her. "We both know the truth."

She whirls on me with tense shoulders and a raised finger, but instead of saying anything, she just stares at me.

I run my hands across my face to clear my vision. Almost looked like there were tears in her eyes. Normally, my digs elicit anger. Tears of rage? When I examine her again, any hint of sadness is gone.

"I don't know why you wanted to be on this team," she says, "but it's not too late to back out."

Wren, Paxton, and Riker come out of the rest station and head to their bikes, ignoring me and Tucker.

"We can find someone else. If you can't stick with the team during training and you can't rely on your teammates for help, you might as well just go home."

"It'll be too dark if we don't leave soon!" Wren shouts from the parked bikes. The three of them are already back on, ready to ride.

I go to the back of the SUV, and I unhook my bike. Jag is out of the vehicle at my side.

"Your Highness, does Ms. Tucker have a way to fix your bike?" he asks.

I ignore him while I grab my helmet out of the back, buckling it up and pushing my bike toward the group.

"That's not safe," Tucker calls to me when she catches sight of me. The other three have already started back down the mountain. She gets off her bike, letting it fall to the ground to stand in front of me. "You'll wreck your bike or hurt yourself."

"You wanted to see commitment—here's commitment." I let my bike fall to the ground beside hers. "I can't win with you."

"Going down the mountain in these conditions on a broken bike doesn't make you a hero; it makes you a fool."

"I suppose you'd be more than capable of recognizing one of those." The words are out before I've even thought about what I'm saying. It's a comment meant to wound, but I'm not even sure who I'm referring to—her or her husband. Whatever happened at the last adventure race, Wren didn't make it sound as though Tucker had been a fool.

She glares at me, but there's a tinge of something in her expression that looks a lot like hurt, and all the anger drains out of me. My attitude, at least tonight, has very little to do with her, but she's bearing the brunt of it. An apology is on the tip of my tongue when Riker, Paxton, and Wren crest the top of the hill again behind us.

"Prince Brice," Wren calls. "Tomorrow is another day. Mare—we have to get down before it gets too dark. We're not leaving you behind. It's too dangerous."

"Go home," she says to me before she picks up her bike and slides onto the seat. She bikes over to the rest of the group and makes a circling motion with her hand, leading the way.

I shake my head and pick up my bike out of the mud. It's filthy, and the torrential rain has brought a chill to my bones without the exercise and adrenaline to combat it.

After I've secured the bike onto the back of the SUV, I climb into the rear and sit there for a moment, letting the heat Jag is blasting thaw the ice in my veins.

"Trail them down the mountain with your hazards on. She might not want me to be part of the team, but we've already determined she can't stop me."

"As you wish, Your Highness," Jag says. "We'll watch a YouTube video tomorrow and figure out how to change that tire."

"Tomorrow is another day," I agree as I stare out the window. It's the kind of comment meant to bring someone comfort, but for me, knowing what might be on the other side of tomorrow, it no longer does. One of these tomorrows will be my father's last.

# Chapter Ten

## MAREN

The tea slides down my throat, and the conversation between my mother and my sisters goes on around me at my parents' lavish oceanfront house. My enjoyment of trivial island gossip is nonexistent, especially since I've been the source of it more than once. Even if they were discussing something serious, I'm not sure I could follow. Enzo's drunken phone call and Brice's strange behavior are playing on loops in my brain.

Enzo's actions have become normal, almost routine. He gets drunk and calls, and I end up in a thought spiral about our marriage. While I know I still feel something for Enzo, the amount of hurt between us is literally and figuratively an ocean, and I don't know when either of us will be willing to swim across it to figure out our situation.

But Brice Summerset has got me mixed up for other reasons. After seeing him at the fundraiser in his typical jovial, *everyone loves me* mood, his shift in attitude during last night's bike ride was jarring. In all the times we've spent together, I've rarely known him to be deliberately cruel or foolish. Once, in high school, and that wasn't even toward me. Left a lasting impression that I'm starting to wonder if I need to shake.

The effort he's put in during the other training sessions hasn't gone unnoticed. For my money, I'd have thought the guy would walk his bike up the mountain rather than taking the ride, just to prove he could. His behavior last night made me question whether I'd been reading him wrong in the other training sessions. Maybe he really doesn't have the grit and perseverance needed to be on the team.

Enzo has made me doubt all my instincts where men are concerned. He's proof that I can be swayed by a pretty face, can assign men character traits they don't possess. I can't decide if that's what's happening with Brice.

"Did you hear what Mom said?" Sawyer nudges me with her arm.

I glance up from where I've been staring into my empty teacup and blink.

"The former king appears to be on the cusp of getting his assisted death," Mother says. "A lawyer in Caitlin's office is drafting the legalese to get George to sign."

"Caitlin would never tell you that," I say.

Ava, my younger sister who is home from Northern University on break, flicks her dark hair. "It wasn't Caitlin. I overheard someone at the bar last night talking about it."

"All rumor and conjecture, then," I say.

"Except I called some of my sources and had it confirmed today," my mother says with a sly grin. "Where the royals are concerned, one can never have too much information."

Although the leak might not be coming directly from Caitlin's part of the law office, I should call her later to let her know. If the king is poised to use the assisted death law, the news will spread like a wildfire across the island.

"Speaking of royals," my mother says. "Have you made any progress with Prince Brice?"

"He's becoming a much stronger athlete," I say, deliberately misunderstanding her.

"Athlete," my mother scoffs. "Only you would find that an attractive trait."

"Not only her," Ava says. "I like athletes too." She grins like a Cheshire cat. "Basketball, lacrosse, swimming, football... So many talented athletes at Northern."

"If Maren isn't going to pursue Prince Brice, perhaps she can set up a meeting for you, Ava? He's a bit older than you, but it might help balance you out."

I suppress an eye roll at my mother trying to tame my youngest sister. Sawyer practically raised Ava, and any rebellion my mother senses likely has more to do with Sawyer's do-gooder personality and drive to help people than to do with my mother.

I'm not even sure my mother rates on Ava's radar most days. But Sawyer? Ava loves to get a rise out of our older sister.

"Based on what I've seen, he's got no interest in settling down. I'd be sending her into a disaster area," I say.

"Besides," Ava says, "I have more than enough hot men at Northern. The whole royal thing isn't appealing."

"That's weird," Sawyer says. "Didn't your last boyfriend call you princess?"

Ava chuckles and shrugs. She takes an exaggerated sip of her tea. "No harm in role-playing. Maybe when I'm as old as you, I'll have my boyfriends call me queen."

Sawyer's face scrunches up, and she shakes her head while she pours herself more tea.

"I would have suggested Sawyer for Prince Brice, but given that she wouldn't go on that one date with King Alexander, and now she's got this awful haircut." Our mother gestures at Sawyer's shorn head. "I can't expect miracles."

"You already are expecting a miracle," Sawyer says, not at all offended by our mother's behavior. We're all used to Celia Tucker. "Trying to get Maren, who would have to get divorced, together with a royal, who appears to have no interest in commitment, is exactly that. A miracle. A really warped one since you'd be hoping for Maren's deep unhappiness to accomplish it in the first place."

"She's already deeply unhappy," my mother says, waving her hand at me as though I'm not also sitting in the room. "Enzo was never much of a man."

"Here, here," Ava says, lifting her teacup in a mock salute.

I have a suspicion she laced her tea with bourbon.

"Enzo is a complete and utter shit," Ava says. "But Sawyer is right. She's still married to him."

"Easy to fix," my mother says. "He fled the country. Been gone for a few months now. No sign of a return. Cut him loose. Move on."

I'm so tempted to ask her why she never cut Dad loose in the same cavalier fashion. Calling out my terrible marriage doesn't shield her from her own. The first time I realized my father frequently cheated on my mother, I was appalled. Abandonment is one thing, but cheating to me then, and maybe even now, seems so much worse. What's the injustice scale in a relationship?

It's not as though I don't know why my mother has stayed. Sawyer asked her once, and she said she'd rather be with my father than be alone. For a long time, marriage was a philosophy I couldn't stand, which might have been why everyone was so shocked when I agreed to tie myself to Enzo. When I was younger, I equated marriage to misery.

But I was certain Enzo would never be Dad. And he hasn't been, but he isn't better than Dad either. For all my diatribes on my father's wandering eye, when my mother has needed him, when one of us kids has needed him, he's dropped everything to be there. He's selfish and selfless in a weird combination that makes it hard to hate him. In trying to escape one fate, I created another with Enzo, which might be far worse.

"I'm not cutting him loose," I say. Though part of me wonders what I'm holding on to. It doesn't feel like Enzo is holding on at all anymore. It's me, in the middle of an ocean, clinging to the life raft of our marriage, hoping Enzo will materialize beside me.

"Futile," my mother says. "Any man who books a plane ticket off the island rather than weathering a storm is no man at all."

"That's very gendered," Ava says. "Any *partner*."

My mother ignores Ava and sips her tea while staring at me. Whatever she's expecting me to say, I've got nothing. Defending Enzo is pointless because I'm also angry with him, which makes it hard to figure out whether there's still anything positive between us. Most of the time, I'm happiest when I'm not thinking about him at all.

Then something Ava said clicks into place. "When did you say you heard about the lawyer getting involved with the former king, Ava?"

"Last night at Wino Wine Bar," my mother answers for her. "King Alexander and the Advisory Council just finished hammering out the language of the law yesterday. Must be trying to rush through George's paperwork."

My heart sinks. Brice would have known when he showed up to bike last night that his father's days were even fewer than he'd realized. If there's one thing I understand, can relate to on a deep level, it's grief. Crushing, drag-me-under grief. The reminder makes the emotion sweep over me again, the tide rushing in, but thankfully with my meds, the sensation no longer knocks me off my feet.

My phone chimes in my purse, and I dig it out. There's a text from Wren saying that Brice is begging off practice tonight. I stare at the screen while my mother and sisters chat around me. Without giving myself time to think it through, I text Wren back and drop my phone into my purse.

"I need to go," I say, rising to my feet. "We have practice in an hour."

"Your ankle." Sawyer nods toward my foot.

"Will be just fine." I hitch my purse onto my shoulder. "We're running hills tonight, but I'm just working the stopwatch. No need to panic. I heard you the other day. I need to rest it." My bike ride up Mount Juniper will remain my secret.

"You're not overtraining again, are you?" My mother scans me with a worried frown. "You've never quite regained the weight you lost when Enzo left."

"I'm off," I say. "The tea was hot. The company was good. Until next time." I wave to them all before I make a beeline for the front door. As I'm leaving, Nathaniel is arriving, and he breaks his stride to take in my appearance.

"You all right?" he asks. Between Gage, my youngest brother, and Nathaniel, my oldest, there's no question who is the most sensitive. Nathaniel can spot a chink in someone's emotional armor at one hundred paces. Gage couldn't spot the dent an inch from his face.

"Did you know that the law for the assisted dying was firm now?" While I knew this was coming based on the referendum result, the legalization feels quick, even though it's taken them months to lay out the parameters.

"Yeah, I heard." Nathaniel's blue-green eyes soften. "I didn't think you'd be so thrown by it."

"Not thrown," I say. "Just... Surprised. One of those things that was slow and then quick." A chill runs through me, and I rub my arms. If that's how I feel as an outsider, I can't imagine how Brice must feel. He probably has lots of people around to support him if the tabloids have even a grain of truth to them, but I can't ignore what may be happening in his life. Anyone else on my team would rate a visit, and while some of my negative feelings about Brice's breezy lifestyle might seep into training, there's no room for that today.

"The Summersets must be spinning," Nathaniel says. "Can't even imagine." He rubs his palm across his forehead. "Is Dad around?"

"Haven't seen him," I say as I back away toward my waiting SUV. "Did you text him?"

"Ignored me," Nathaniel says. "You going to train?"

"Coach," I say because I know how much he worries about me. Maybe even more than Sawyer. "A quick stop first."

"Tell Brice..." Nathaniel gives me a helpless look. "There really aren't any good words, are there?"

I shake my head and squeeze the straps of my purse. Of course Nathaniel would understand where I'd be going based on my question. He understands how much racing and my teammates mean to me, and Brice is now included in that bubble, even if I didn't want him there in the first place.

"But I guess you know that, don't you?" he says.

Tears prick at my eyes, and I turn from him with a wave to duck into my vehicle. I toss my purse onto the passenger seat, and I sit for a beat staring out the front window. Maybe going to see Brice is a bad idea, given my own close and recent relationship with grief, but part of me thinks that's exactly why I have to go. There are no good words, but it doesn't mean you don't try.

I hit the button to start the SUV, and I turn out of the Tucker estate toward the palace.

## Chapter Eleven

## BRICE

My bottle of tequila is half full. I could look at it as half empty, but that would be fucking depressing, and who wants that? Turns out, Truth and Tequila isn't as much fun when I'm the only one playing. Posey is in Michigan with Brent, Alex is with Rory and Grace, Nick is likely having grief sex with Julia, and my mother is holed up with my father in their suite of rooms, pretending everything is fine when it's decidedly not.

For a guy who's normally surrounded by a lot of people, I couldn't find a single person in my contact list that I actually wanted to be around. The only people who might understand how I'm feeling have someone else to lean on. At least I've got my Gran Patron Platinum to keep me company.

"Just one shot," I say to Jag, who is stationed by the door of the barn where I've had a climbing wall installed. "One. You don't even have to tell me a truth first." He's got no idea how the game actually works, I don't think. Or maybe he does because he simply raises his eyebrows and doesn't answer me.

Propped up against the wall is the mountain bike he helped me fix this morning while we watched a series of YouTube videos on changing a tire tube. Not the most fun I've ever had, but it was better than thinking about what was happening at the lawyer's office.

"Your Highness," Jag says, touching his earpiece, "Ms. Tucker has just entered the estate."

"Tucker?" My vision is slightly blurry, and the idea of seeing her is equal parts appealing and unappealing. Why would Tucker be coming here when there's practice—and then I remember I texted Wren half an hour ago to say I wouldn't be attending. I groan. "Drunk on a…" I squint at my watch and give up when the date won't come into focus.

"Monday," Jag fills in for me.

"Fuuuccckkk." I collapse on the spongy ground, the remnants of my bottle of tequila between my legs. She'll never let me live this down, and there's no way she'll go easy on me. The thought should be unappealing, as though her attention is a nuisance. Might be the alcohol, but I'm not really annoyed.

"Should I send her away?" Jag asks.

"No." I run my hands along my face and then lie back to stare at the vast ceiling. "No point. One way or another, she's going to think I'm an irresponsible idiot. Might as well let her see the proof." She can call me on my shit. No one else is around to care.

"Do you want me to speak to her before I let her in?"

That would be the easy way out. Let Jag smooth over the rough edges between me and Tucker. Have him tell her about my father. Might not make any difference to her. Seth was right the other day—she's an ice queen. Death is probably the tiniest blip on her radar. The way she went up the climbing wall, there can't be too much Maren Tucker is afraid of. She walks through life daring it to come at her. Even though it galls me to admit it, there's something admirable in her attitude.

Except I'm fairly certain something I said the other night punctured her tough outer shell. I stare at the roof with narrowed eyes as I try to remember exactly what I saw. Were there tears? Or was it simply the rain? Seems impossible that Maren Tucker would lower her guard enough to be hurt by anyone, let alone me.

"Your Highness," Jag says. "Ms. Tucker has arrived."

I don't sit up to greet her, and with the spongy floor meant to soften any falls, her progress toward me is silent. Or at least I expected her to approach me.

"You had this built?" she asks from near the climbing wall.

With a sigh, I rise on my elbow and swig from the bottle. "Yep."

"Hmm." She runs her hand along the wall, and there's a palpable longing emanating from her.

"I can't belay you. I'm drunk. Jag can. He's had some practice." I gesture to where Jag is still standing at the open door, trying to ignore me and Tucker.

She motions to her flowing, knee-length dress in a seafoam green. "I'm good. Another day when you're sober and I'm dressed for it."

I roll onto my stomach, and I cross my arms to lay my chin on them. Then I remember my tequila, and I bring it around to sit on the ground beside my elbow. "Why don't you like me?"

"Should I like you?" She arches an eyebrow.

"We hardly know each other. There's no reason for you not to like me."

"You don't like me. And the same could be said."

Christ. Do I really tell her that I don't like her just because she doesn't like me? Makes me sound like I'm five. Even drunk me can recognize that truth. "You're very prickly."

"As opposed to just being a prick?" She leans against the climbing wall, keeping her distance.

"Want to play Truth and Tequila with me?" I ask.

"Probably not. What does it entail?"

"We ask each other questions. Impossibly hard questions."

"Like why did a prince want to join an adventure race team?" She stares at me for a beat. "Is this the part where you drink?"

I open the bottle and sit up to take a swig. With the bottle cradled in my hands, I say, "Your turn. Why do you hate me?"

"Hate is a very strong word. One I don't use lightly. I don't hate you."

"You gotta drink. That's a nonanswer." I hold the bottle out toward her.

"I don't like cheaters," she says.

"You ain't cheatin', you ain't tryin'." I wink at her.

She recrosses her arms and lets out a frustrated huff. "I don't mean cheating at trivial things. I mean in relationships."

Pretty rich coming from a family where her father is a notorious philanderer. I wouldn't be at all surprised if Jonathan Tucker has spread his seed much farther than his five children with Celia. "Daddy issues, huh? I got those too."

We're both quiet for a minute, and then her implication actually clicks in. "You think I cheated on someone? I'd have to be exclusive with someone to cheat on them, and maybe you don't know this, but that doesn't happen with me."

"High school," she says as though that's enough of a clue.

"High school or not, I've never cheated on anyone." I shrug and take another swig from the bottle.

"Presley Cook," she says. "I heard all about it."

"That should be your first clue. Unless you're the one it happened to, you don't know what the hell you're talking about. Yeah, I dated Pres for about five minutes in high school. Longest five minute of my life, which is why I don't do that anymore." Presley was my girlfriend for most of high school, but the other part is true enough.

"You cheated on her, and she broke up with you."

"That's some grade A bullshit." I gesture toward her with my bottle. "You should have to drink for even letting that lie come out of your mouth."

"I was at that party. I saw her. I heard her telling everyone, and I was in a car home with her later."

For Tucker to build her entire estimation of my character on a lie from ten years ago is something else. The temptation to not even defend myself is pretty strong. What the fuck do I care what she believes?

But it's not like this conversation is a one-off. We're going to be spending a lot of time together, and maybe setting her straight might make her reconsider her other opinions on me too. At the very least, this confrontation is a nice distraction from other wounds I'd rather not be prodding.

"If she said that," I say, "and if I ever heard that rumor, I was too proud to admit the truth." I stroke the label on the tequila bottle. My old friend. "Pres was my first everything, and it wasn't me who cheated."

Concern and confusion mingle in Tucker's expression. She seems to be searching her memory for something. "But I saw you leave that party with Felicity. Presley was Caitlin's friend, and she cried all the way home about how you'd slept with Felicity at the party and then broke up with her."

"Right events. Wrong order. I was a vindictive prick. Your veiled comment earlier might have been on the nose." I touch a finger to the side of my nose before taking another drink. "Sure you don't want some?"

"Not a fan of tequila," she says.

"Should have known." I swirl the bottle before tipping it back again.

"You broke up with her and then slept with someone else the same night."

I assess how much tequila I have left, and I don't answer her nonquestion. Her voice was flat with disapproval, and I already admitted my shitty behavior once. Pres messed with the bull, and she got the horns. Or rather, Felicity got my horn.

"You're proud of yourself," she says with a scoff.

"I'm not not proud of myself." I grin at her across the space between us. My attitude is partly alcohol and partly the urge to get under Maren Tucker's skin. Who'd be proud of what I did? But I was an eighteen-year-old punk who'd had his heart broken. My only power move, as far as I could see it then, was what I did. Being with Felicity hadn't even been fun, and I'd promised myself two things after that night. The first was that there'd be no more girlfriends, and the second was that sex couldn't be completely meaningless. Took some trial and error for me to be sure that second one should stick.

Tucker got the important part of the truth. I'm not a fucking cheater, and I can't imagine ever doing that to anyone because I understand how terrible it is to be on the other end.

"Still hate me?" I squint at her.

"I'm reevaluating my stance on Brice Summerset," she says. "Though being proud of hurting someone is never a good look."

"I will take your opinion under advisement."

"Now you sound like your brother."

"Heard that before, have you?"

"I sit on a board with King Alexander. He's rather fond of that phrase when he really wants to tell someone to fuck off."

That elicits a chuckle out of me, and I nod before pressing the bottle to my lips again. Alex is Alex wherever he is.

Tucker wanders over to me, and she crouches in front of me in a practiced move given she's in a dress. We're eye to eye, and she searches my face. "You can't run hills when you're this drunk."

"I am aware," I say.

"Do you want to talk about your dad?"

"Not even a little bit." I'm not sure that's true, but I can't imagine what I'd say to her. There isn't anything *to* say. The time for protesting or long-winded espousals on my feelings was months ago, before we agreed to go along with this for Dad's sake. Hell, months ago, I was a driving force behind legalizing this. And it's not even that I'm uncertain now. I just wish it wasn't happening, not that it can't happen.

"Okay," she says.

Her response draws my gaze from the bottle to make eye contact, and the depth of understanding I read on her face is surprising. Her siblings and parents are all still alive. What would Maren Tucker know about the rawness of a grief like this? The loss of possibility, of a future I'd always imagined. All the things my father will never know, never witness. Tears prick at my eyes, and I glance away while clearing my throat.

"You're going to be late," I say.

"Do you want to be alone?" She rises to her feet and smooths down her dress.

"What would you do if you stayed?" Having her here has been an unexpected and not unwelcome distraction from my terrible, no-good, very bad day.

"I have a change of clothes in my vehicle. If you were serious about Jag belaying, I could give your wall a shot."

"And I'd just watch you climb?" I narrow my eyes as I consider my options. Drink alone or drink here while watching a not-unattractive woman perform daring feats of athleticism.

"Or talk to me. Or say nothing." She takes my bottle of tequila from my hand. "Drink some water."

"Boo!" I laugh and stagger to my feet. When she tries to help me stabilize myself, we end up mere inches apart. On impulse, I smooth down her dark hair with both my hands and plant a slobbery kiss on her forehead. Although I don't mean for it to be anything more serious, her breath catches at the contact, and an unexpected warmth spreads across my chest at her proximity. She smells like peaches, as though she bathed in them.

Instead of letting her go, I draw her into my chest, and she comes willingly, wrapping her arms around my waist in a reciprocal hug. "You may be a party pooper, Tucker, but you're just the right hugging height." I rest my chin on the top of her head and release a sigh.

"Glad I can be of some service."

"Well, if you're talking about servicing me—"

She punches me in the side and steps back. "Do you want me to stay or not?"

"Jag," I call to my bodyguard at the door. "Tucker needs a belay."

A hint of a smile tugs at her lips before she heads for the door to grab her things. It's only when Jag comes to my side that I realize Tucker took what was left of my tequila.

"She come here to ream you out?" Jag asks.

I stare at the door, at the way her absence has caused something inside of me to shift back into a sadness I've been holding at bay. "The opposite," I say. "I think she came to comfort me."

Tucker reappears dressed in a tiny pair of spandex shorts and a sports bra, and I silently congratulate myself on opting for ogling the hot woman rather than sipping my tequila alone.

For the next two hours, she climbs different routes up the wall, and at one point, she lets me call out a color for her to use next from my spot lying on the spongy black floor. She doesn't ask me again about my father, and she even laughs a few times when I give her an impossible transition that she, annoyingly, makes possible through her sheer boldness. There's isn't a leap she won't take, and nine times out of ten, she makes them.

She's a study in contrasts. Uptight and rigid and free and fearless. A mystery that suddenly feels worth solving.

## Chapter Twelve

### MAREN

What I'm doing is dangerous, but I can feel something inside me coming back to life, and part of me wants to grasp that sensation with both hands. For a while, I was so low, I wasn't sure the highs would ever return.

For the sixth night in a row, I'm headed to the royal estate where Brice and two of his bodyguards wait. They'll belay us, and we'll climb.

Seems simple enough, right?

But the fluttering in my stomach tonight as I drive through the gates makes me wonder if I'm inching toward a flame I won't be able to control. Previously, I've kept Brice's easy familiarity at bay through an icy, impenetrable front. Yes, I believed he cheated on Presley in high school, and that colored my view of him, but my dislike was more than his resemblance to the worst part of my father. To me, he always felt like too much—too loud, too confident, too attractive—as though he was making up for some deficit inside by trying to be everyone's friend.

I'm not sure what my opinion of him is morphing into, but it's changing—rapidly. Brice Summerset isn't all gloss and no substance, but I'm not sure what exactly lies beneath the surface.

When I step through the barn door, Brice is already there in a red tank top and black shorts. His tattooed biceps are more defined than they were even a week ago. For him to become more attractive hardly seems fair. His light-brown hair is mussed, as though he's been running his hands through the short strands while he waited. On his feet are the shoes he'll take with him on the adventure race. I told him yesterday he should start climbing in them, and today he has them on.

Goose bumps of anticipation rise across my skin.

Enzo doesn't want me to race anymore, and I've told him I'm only training my replacement in the terse text messages we've exchanged. Training is what the group of us did earlier when they went for a ten-kilometer run along the hilly, looped course while I called out their times per loop.

Coming to the barn isn't about training Brice or getting the team ready.

I've never considered myself a liar, and after I hurt myself, I tried to be honest with Enzo. Even as guilt and grief dogged me, I tried to tell him that I needed the training, maybe even the racing. He didn't want to hear it, and I craved his support so badly I was willing to say anything to get it. Now when we speak, I skirt the truth out loud while something inside of me is unfurling, blooming in a way I wasn't sure would happen again.

For the first time since my accident, training isn't just soothing. It's exciting.

"I had them change all the handholds today." Brice gestures toward the wall. "You seemed a bit bored last night, so I asked maintenance to make the routes more challenging."

*Bored?* Must have been my guilt showing through that I sent Enzo's call straight to voicemail and texted him that I was at a charity event. I was on my way here, and I didn't want to explain what I was doing or why. None of the answers are easy when Enzo and I are so far apart.

Tonight, Brice and I are meeting later than normal because Brice had to attend a meeting about the palliative care center being established in an old, run-down, ocean-view mansion the committee is looking to convert. Not sure if he offered to take point on that initiative for the family or he was assigned it. Either way, I wasn't sure what sort of mood he'd be in when I arrived. But he seems the same as he's been all week. Not buoyant or down—level—as though he's got a tight grip on whatever emotions are going on below the surface.

"I like a challenge," I say while I scan the new routes.

"Hmm," Brice says. "As do I." A hint of a smile plays at the corners of his lips.

I set my water bottle on the ground at the starting point to the farthest wall and grab a harness. Instead of taking the other end of the wall, which has been our pattern—start outside and work inside—Brice puts his things close to mine. All week it's been as though we've needed the distance to warm up to each other, and when we reach the middle to switch sides of the wall, there's a cordial politeness between us.

The change in the routine we've established gives me an opening to ask him about his day or to question his choice in start position, but I enjoy that we mostly climb in silence. In every other situation, he's often the center of attention, and it's refreshing to realize he doesn't always have to be switched on and performing for an audience. We exist in the same space, and it brings me a strange comfort to glance over and see him climbing, together but separate. Sometimes he'll ask me how to tackle a particular handhold or transition, but otherwise, we forge our own routes.

His shoulder brushes against mine as he comes to my side to stare up at the handholds and footholds. "I want you to teach me how to do what you do."

"I don't know what you mean." I half turn to meet his gaze, and just like almost every other time we've made eye contact in this space, the searing intensity in his light-brown eyes makes my gut clench.

"I want to learn how to switch off the fear. You climb like you don't care if you'll fall."

"That's not—" I bite my lip and stare at him. If he only knew. "I just don't think about the fear. I focus on the next handhold."

He gazes at the wall with his brow puckered.

"On the course, you have to be able to accurately weigh the risks and rewards, or else someone can get hurt. Especially if you're the team leader."

"Is that what happened with you and Wren when you were hurt?" He turns from the wall to face me.

"Are you asking me how I hurt myself?" Talking about the logistics of my injury is easy enough. The aftermath is the hard part.

"When we first started training together, I asked Posey to find out what happened to you," he says. "Not much printed in the press about your accident."

His admission catches me off guard, and I'm not sure which piece to address first—that he sent Posey Jensen after me or that he scoured the press in Chile to find out the details.

"You asked Posey Jensen to dig up information on me?"

"I don't deal well with people who don't like me." He shrugs as though his admission is nothing. "I don't think Posey found out anything, if that makes you feel any better."

"It doesn't." My family might be fractured in places on the inside, but on the outside, we're a brick wall. Come for one of us, and you come for us all. It's the best part about being a Tucker. We're everywhere on the island—generation after generation—and we don't feed each other to the gossip mills. "You could have asked me. It's not like what happened is a secret." My stay in the hospital is the part my family worked to suppress. NDAs and money locked down anyone who treated me there and when we got back. I could never figure out if my parents were protecting me or the Tucker image in Bellerive.

"Wren seemed a little uptight about it," he says.

"You asked Wren too?" This conversation is slowly raising the hackles I'd thought were lowered for good.

"If I'd asked you a few weeks ago, would you have answered?"

"I would have told you to mind your own business," I say as the door behind us opens, and Jag enters with Gary, another guard on the property. Rather than giving him what he's asked for, I hook myself onto the rope and nod at Gary that I'm ready.

"You're not going to tell me." Brice releases a long-suffering sigh and steps into his harness.

"Apparently, you only wanted the information to use against me." I survey the wall and pick my handholds, beginning my climb. "Information warfare."

Within minutes, Brice is climbing below and beside me. He's not a sure enough climber to catch me before I reach the top.

"You need to see it from my point of view," Brice says.

"Oh? Seems like a childish point of view if your main concern was whether or not I *liked* you."

"Everyone likes me."

"Impossible," I say. "There will be someone who has met you and doesn't like you. Statistically speaking, that's the truth."

"You got those stats handy? Would love to see some evidence of your *non*research."

"I'm busy beating you up the wall." I gauge a difficult transition, and I make the leap, hanging off the wall by one hand for a moment. "I'll have to dig them out for you later." I grunt as I correct myself. "All my research is focused on you. So, it's a bit narrow."

"That's bullshit. Anyone I like, likes me. Vice versa."

"That's friendship. You're describing friendship." I shift my weight to take me a little farther from his climbing line.

"I *do* have a lot of friends."

"Really? Or are they acquaintances? Who have you talked to about your dad?" I'm prodding a wound I know he doesn't want to touch, but to me, as someone who's been in the pit of grief, it's a valid question. After my injury, I realized how few people I could actually depend on. It's not a great feeling.

There's a long beat of silence, and I'm not sure he's going to answer. Maybe I went too far. The two of us seem to be locked in silence or combat, and there hasn't been too much in between.

"Nothing about the situation changes if I talk about it," he says. "Let's just climb."

"Your Highness—" I say.

"Don't." His voice is tight below me. "You've been calling me Brice all week. I'm not sliding backwards with you. I just don't want to talk about it."

I reach the top of the wall, and I sit on the ledge, waiting for him to catch up. He grunts as he pulls himself over the edge, and we stare out at the vastness of the barn side by side while Gary and Jag chat down below, our ropes in their hands.

"We were coming down a cliff edge," I say. "Not far. To save time, because we'd been gaining on the lead team, we made the decision to free climb. We'd done it before. So many times before and at greater heights. Should have been easy." I take a deep breath. "Wren lost a handhold, and when I grabbed her to help her back on, my foothold crumbled under me." The memory snakes down my spine. "She made it back on. But I didn't. I fell, and I didn't get back up." The impact of hitting the ground, the sound of my ankle snapping, and the taste of blood in my mouth comes back to me in a flash.

"Spooked you?" He glances at me, but it's more curiosity than concern in his gaze. I'm alive and functioning, so how bad could it have been, right? He'll never know.

"Changed me," I admit.

"Not your first injury, was it?" He searches my expression, and I have no desire for him to realize the external injuries weren't the problem.

"No, it wasn't." I twist on the ledge to pick my handholds and footholds for my descent.

"Tucker, why isn't your husband on the island?"

His question catches me by surprise, and I pause my climbing to consider my answer. "He's away on business."

Brice lowers himself over the edge above me, and he makes his way down until we're almost level. "You don't want to tell me—say that. I'm not some geriatric you're sitting beside at a charity dinner. We don't have to be friends, but I think we should at least be honest with each other."

His declaration that we don't have to be friends shouldn't cause such a tightening across my chest, as though the notion bothers me. It's true enough. Just because I've always been close to my racing teammates doesn't mean Brice and I will ever achieve the same level of comfort with one another as a participant and coach.

He passes me, and even if I should leave it alone, I can't.

"Nothing changes if I talk about it." Talking doesn't bring Enzo back or make what happened any less terrible or make my reality any less permanent.

"Fair enough." He glances up at me, and the frustration that had crept into his voice earlier is gone. "We'll just climb."

When we're both at the bottom, Brice grabs his things and motions for Jag to follow him, and he's back to his side of the barn.

For the next hour, we climb in silence, neither of us inching any closer to the middle like we normally do, and when I leave at the end of our session, it's not with the sense of fulfillment I've grown accustomed to.

At home in my apartment, I text Enzo, but he doesn't respond, and the hollowness of my life echoes around me.

## Chapter Thirteen

## BRICE

Along with the group workouts, Tucker and I have fallen into a pattern of training together without the rest of the team for the last few weeks. I don't think she's telling my teammates; I know I'm not. If she was, I'm sure Wren would have made an appearance, and we no longer need her as a buffer. Truth be told, I like it better when it's just the two of us.

We rarely talk about anything that isn't related to training, but ever since I asked about her dipshit husband, I've glimpsed hints of sadness in her that tug at something deep inside me.

She isn't an ice queen like Seth claimed, even though I didn't refute it at the time. Her outer shell is tough, but underneath lies something far more fragile, and every time she lets me get a peek of it, this intense desire to take on the world streaks across my chest. Thankfully, the feeling subsides, or her guard goes back up before I can morph into the Hulk. My inability to do anything for my father must be causing me to overcompensate by being protective of Tucker. Only logical explanation for this sudden flare of feeling.

"Earth to Brice," Brent says from the pool edge where he's been teaching me to be a more efficient swimmer. "More or are we done?"

"We're done." Not that he's likely to be upset—I haven't been the best student. He's run me through some drills and breath control exercises to prepare for any deep dives or underwater tasks on the racecourse. I hoist myself out of the Olympic-sized outdoor pool, grab my towel off the bench, and follow him toward the changerooms.

"You're pretty quiet. How are you doing with everything with your dad?"

"Fine." Not quite accurate. "I've known for months."

Brent holds open the changeroom door. "Posey said Nick's having a hard time, and I thought maybe you might be too. If you're not—cool. But if you are—"

"I support my father's wishes." That's my mantra, even as fear and sadness occasionally seize me. Before my father began a noticeable deterioration, he was clear on the outcome he wanted. Having born witness to so many Alzheimer's patients, I understand how varied the decline can be. My father doesn't want to know what his path would look like; he has no desire to walk it.

"You can support his decision and still feel—"

"Nah," I say, and I pop open my locker to retrieve my clothes. "No point in dwelling on what's coming." My phone is on the top shelf of the locker, and when I check it, there's a text from Posey. "Posey wants to meet up?"

"She told me she's got information on Maren Tucker. Are you two still at each other's throat? Thought maybe you were done with your crazy revenge plot."

His words linger in the air around me, and I stare at the text message. The smart choice would be to tell Posey I don't want her information, that it doesn't matter anymore. But I've never been great at making the smart choice when the wrong one is staring me in the face. One more shot, one last card hand, one final bet. Moderation and I aren't really friends.

Instead of answering his question, I text Posey back that I'll meet her at the estate in half an hour. Knowledge is power, and while I'm sure I don't need to wield anything over Tucker's head right now, I can't guarantee we won't flip back. Just the other night we could have easily slid back into combat mode if I'd let her. Whatever Posey has to tell me might not even matter or be important in the slightest. Tucker already told me about her fall. What else could there be?

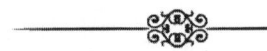

---

When I get to my suite of rooms, Posey is already there lounging on the couch with a latte in her hand. "Where's my boyfriend?"

"Said something about grabbing dinner and meeting you at your place?"

"Oh," Posey says, and her shoulders collapse.

It always amuses me to see how much the two of them still crave each other's company. Nick was always going to be a sucker for Jules, but the closeness Posey and Brent have as well as the loyalty Rory and Alex have shown each other never ceases to amaze me. I've enjoyed lots of women, but I've never sought one of them out as though it was at the top of Maslow's hierarchy of needs.

I pour myself a whiskey and swirl the liquid around in my glass. Technically, I have a team training and then likely something with Tucker later on—though whatever we do, it'll be a last-minute decision. We seem to be engaged in a game of chicken in regard to who texts who first about training together. Nothing is arranged in advance.

On the way to the estate, I fought with myself over whether finding out whatever Posey has to tell me is the right move. My gut knows the answer.

"So," I say. That's all I can bring myself to utter. To ask outright feels like a betrayal of the truce Tucker and I have been building the last few weeks. My curiosity is burning too bright for me to reject whatever Posey has to say.

"It's a doozy," Posey says. "Are you sure you want to know?"

I stare into my glass and then down the rest of the liquid. Whether or not I want to know isn't the issue. *Should* I know?

"Will it make me think less of her?" That's the line in the sand I've decided to draw. If Tucker will still look the same to me after, Posey can tell me.

"Definitely not. Might help you understand her a little better." Posey breathes out a deep sigh. "But I probably wouldn't tell her you know. The information fell into my lap the other night at Wino Wine Bar, but it's not common knowledge. Not by a long shot."

That much I know. Despite my own digging, I got nowhere. I set my glass on the bar. "Tell me."

"As you know, Maren fell in Chile and was injured. Everyone seems to know that much. The part that's been kept hush-hush, and I totally get why, is that Maren's fall caused her to have a miscarriage."

"Holy shit," I say, and I sink into one of the armchairs across from the couch.

"Yeah," Posey says. "And then her husband left her."

That wasn't my first thought. My first thought was my comment to her at the charity dinner a few weeks ago when she held Grace. My exact words won't come back to me, but I know I teased her about her mothering instincts—or rather, lack of them. I wince.

"Jesus," I mutter. Any coherent thoughts are gone. It's no wonder Tucker isn't keen to share the whole truth. Why would she want to bare her soul to the stranger she hated a few short weeks ago? "Was it the fall or the miscarriage that made her no longer want to race?"

"No idea," Posey says with a shrug. "The loose lips closed up pretty quick the other night. If I hadn't been listening so closely, I wouldn't have even caught what I did."

Tucker doesn't appear to be afraid of climbing or at least not climbing in a controlled environment. Her reluctance to be on the team again must be linked to the loss of her baby. My stomach dips at how much of an idiot I've been. Here she is dealing with this huge loss, and I'm firing verbal BB gun shots thinking I'm so clever.

"To be clear, I told you this information so you *wouldn't* use it against her."

I level her with a glare.

"Do not act offended with me." Posey points her finger in my direction. "You've been ultracompetitive with her from the get-go."

That's true, but for her to insinuate I'd use Tucker's miscarriage as a way to gain an advantage is low. Only someone really terrible would—"Is that why her husband left the island?"

"If I had to guess, yes. The timing fits, but that really is a guess. I have no idea. Has she said anything about Enzo?"

"Nothing truthful."

"Just tread lightly. I know you're going through some things too, even if you don't want to talk about it, but keep your relationship professional or whatever the hell you call your situation." She drains the rest of her latte and drops it in the garbage can beside my chair.

Order and instructions have never been my thing, and her advice is likely falling on deaf ears. Ideas are rotating around my head, and they are definitely not professional in nature.

Although her family is big, I've heard they are highly dysfunctional. Other than hiding what happened to her, who knows how helpful they've been. Tucker doesn't need a colleague or another training buddy. She needs a friend, and luckily, I'm a friendship expert.

---

We're running hills, which is hands down my least favorite type of training. Sweat is pouring off me because Tucker decided the heat of the day was a good opportunity to see whether she could reduce our will to live. Before, thoughts like that would have made me happy. Now I'm cursing myself for not being able to shift my outlook on her fast enough.

*Friends. Friendly. Tucker is my buddy. One of the guys. This torture is fun.*

As I come down the hill, trying to keep myself from falling on my face as my legs wobble underneath me, I call out, "Wanna hear a joke?"

"Me?" Tucker frowns and checks her clipboard.

She rarely runs with the group, but she always runs with me. I haven't been able to decide what that means.

"Yes, Tucker. You." I huff out a breath as I turn to stare at the top of the hill again. It's possible she'll boot me in the butt to make me start moving again. Honestly, she probably should. These wobbly legs aren't going to be made better by this brief pause.

"Is it a good joke?"

"Terrible. But that's the beauty of it. It's so bad, it's good."

She raises her eyebrows and marks down Wren's time as she circles around us and heads back up.

"Two guys walk into a bar," I say. "The third one ducked."

A hint of a smile tugs at the edges of her lips, but she doesn't acknowledge me.

"No?" I try to catch her gaze. "What will the terminator be called in his retirement?"

"Dad jokes? Really?"

"The Exterminator."

"That's a terrible joke," she says, and then she shoos me toward the hill. "We only have so many training days left."

"Don't remind me of the calendar," I say as I start to jog up the hill. "It scares me because its days are numbered."

"At least that one was clever," she calls to me, and I can hear the smile in her voice.

Each time I pass her for the next hour, I have another joke I've remembered at the ready. On my last tour around her, Tucker finally cracks.

"What does a sprinter eat before a race?" she asks me.

I wrack my brain for the answer, but if I've heard this one, I can't locate it. She's got my attention, and I tip my head to get her to continue.

"Nothing," she says. "They fast."

My delight is genuine, and I can't help the laugh that roars out of me. Underneath all the prim properness, Maren Tucker has a sense of humor, and she even knows some dad jokes. As I head back up the hill for my final run, there's a lightness in me I don't expect. With every step, I see a flash of her grin, broad and happy, and I vow that I'm going to see that grin a hell of a lot more over the next few months.

While we train together, I'll no longer be the guy who adds to her misery. Instead, I'm going to try my best to ease it.

# Chapter Fourteen

## MAREN

The ocean breeze lifts the ends of my hair as the team paddles along the coast. It's one of those days where I can't help feeling grateful to be alive. Between the sun, the breeze, and the cool ocean water below, it's a perfect day.

"Everyone good?" I call back to the group.

Varying shouts of agreement float up to me, Brice being the loudest, of course.

We're halfway through training, and we've settled into something resembling a friendship. Though I've never asked Brice, my mother says they've set a date for George's... I don't even know what to call it. Three weeks to the day before Brice leaves to compete. Sometimes her ear to the ground is helpful.

The timing, had anyone asked me, could not be worse. The last thing he'll need in a mentally and physically grueling race is to be battling grief too. Intense grieving while isolated from his family and while promoting the Alzheimer's Society for an international audience is a recipe for disaster. InterFlix is already advertising the season he'll appear on, but there's a part of me that worries the focused attention will eat Brice alive. Grieving in private was hard enough, but to do that publicly? I can't even imagine.

Just as Brice predicted when he asked to be selected for the team, donations to our charity race have poured in, from Bellerive, but also from all over the world. There appear to be no borders to Brice's friendship. Unlike other years where we've practically had to go door-to-door to raise money for a cause, the press has been loving Brice's pursuit of athletic excellence in the face of his father's diagnosis. Radio appearances, TV spots, and articles have littered the internet. The advanced promotion has created a certain fervor over the upcoming season that I've never witnessed before. InterFlix must be ecstatic. When we applied and they accepted, they thought they were merely getting skilled racers, and instead, they've gotten a prince and international playboy. Quite a deal for them.

Wren appears at my side, paddling in the same rhythm as me to keep pace. "InterFlix arrives on the island today for the promo videos?"

It's a rhetorical question. They're interviewing everyone, including me. While I'm not racing, I've agreed to be part of the support team that will be available at each refuel station in Fiji. Initially, I didn't want anything to do with the actual race activities, but I'm unreasonably concerned about Brice with the timing of everything. Maybe I'm projecting, but seeing him so low once before makes me believe George's death will hit him hard. Harder than he might realize. Even if he supports the reasons behind George's decision, deep grief is something no one understands until they experience it. You can try, but anyone's empathy can only extend so far. The hole you can fall into is vast and lonely.

"I was thinking," Wren says, "that we should organize a mini adventure for the prince soon. Make sure he's race-ready or at least on track to being race-ready."

The thought had occurred to me too.

"Tucker!" Brice calls from the rear. "Where can you find an ocean with no water?"

Ever since we started training together separate from the team, he's been treating me like I'm one of his buddies. "No idea," I say.

"On a map." His chuckle bounces off the cliffs we're paddling beside.

He loves his dad jokes, and it's nothing for him to swing his arm around my shoulders now and draw me against him as though we've been friends, rather than mortal enemies, for years. Wren has commented on the switch that seemed to flip between us. I blamed the change on the natural evolution of team camaraderie. Spend enough hours with someone, and at the very least, you get used to them.

A sense of teamwork or the hours we've spent together aren't what's shifted us closer.

The wound in me responded to the wound I saw opening in him the night drunk Brice asked me why I didn't like him. At a surface level, he's a good-looking, rich man-child with an easy-breeze attitude. Every other previous interaction had only hardened that perception. Prince Brice was the open book who didn't take anything seriously. Not guarded or particularly deep.

But that night, I saw hints that his protections are invisible but present, and there's a part of him that very few people see. The realization surprised me enough to lower the walls I've built, ones designed to keep the kind of man I thought he was out. Even two and a half months later, I don't know who he is, but I understand he's not who I've believed him to be.

"Very clever, Brice," I say, and I glance over my shoulder to catch him grinning.

"His attempts to get you to laugh are getting progressively worse," Wren says, her gaze following mine. "It's been nice to see the ice thaw between you two."

Maybe the coldness between us has thawed a bit, but Brice is an iceberg, and I recognize the danger he poses. It's not what's on his surface that attracts me; it's what lies beneath. The urge to know him, beyond the superficial, is stronger than I like. So far, I've resisted. My life is already complicated enough without forming any attachment to a prince. Realizing he's not exactly who I believed him to be isn't the same as knowing he's the *right* kind of man.

"I could take him on one of the routes we've done before," Wren says. "A two- or three-night camp out on the island."

Wren's idea is solid and likely the best plan. Brice, Wren, and Jag on an island adventure shouldn't make envy spiral down my limbs. In terms of preparation, Brice and Wren becoming closer teammates is good for the race, and if she wants to show him how to rough it across the island, I should be happy I don't have to.

"Yeah," I say. "You should work out the details with Brice. I can map out the course for you."

"Excellent," Wren says. "What time is your InterFlix interview?"

"After dinner," I say, and I try to hide my grimace. Although I've never been on the show, I'm familiar with the probing nature of their interview questions. It's part of the reason I hesitated to even be part of the support team. My emotional wounds are healing, but the edges are still raw and tender. If they prod too hard, I worry about the aftermath. Not to mention what Enzo is going to say when I finally tell him I'm going to Fiji. I don't know if being a crew member is a compromise, a concession, or in open defiance of what Enzo wants me to do. I'd have to talk to him about it to know, and I'd rather live in ignorance until the last minute. Probably tells me all I need to know.

"If you need to talk after..." Wren leaves the thought unfinished.

"I'll be fine," I say, and I remember what my therapist said about that word during our first session. Feelings Inside Never Expressed—the word is a coping mechanism meant to keep people out. She wasn't wrong. "One interview won't derail me."

---

Hye Jin, the producer tasked with interviewing me, layered her questions in such a way that I didn't even realize she was prying my scabs up until they were already oozing. By the time my two-hour interview block is finished, I'm exhausted, and when Brice texts me to see whether I want to train, I leave his message unread.

The camera crew is gone from my apartment, and I'm left alone with the ocean view and too much time to contemplate whether Enzo was right all along. Maybe I shouldn't be doing any of this anymore. Hye Jin didn't know about my miscarriage, but she seemed to sense there was a bigger reason why I'd turned to coaching rather than racing. A shark sensing blood. Going on the InterFlix show is like throwing chum into the water. With Brice on the team, we're a focal point. How deep will the show or the press be willing to dig?

I'm drifting to sleep on the couch when there's a knock on my apartment door. Instead of getting up, I lie still for a moment to see whether whoever it is will go away.

My phone vibrates on the coffee table, and when I check the message, I groan. It appears Brice isn't taking my *unread* response very well.

*I'm impossible to ignore, Tucker. Answer the door.*

I roll off the couch and grab the blanket from the back to wrap around my shoulders before I head to the door. While I could ignore him, I'm well acquainted with his persistence. The last time I disregarded a text from him, he sent me emojis and memes until I was forced to respond.

When I open the door, Brice scans me with narrowed eyes. "Are you pawning me off on Wren?"

"What? No." His question feels so out of left field given my state of mind that my response is automatic.

"Why is she the one offering to take me on a three-day backpacking trip around Bellerive that you're planning?"

"Can we talk about this tomorrow?" I run my fingers along my forehead. There's a vague pressure behind my eyes that signals an oncoming headache. My ability to give Brice a coherent response is hindered by my lingering unease about my interview coupled with my emotional exhaustion.

"Do you have a headache?" He leans against the door to my apartment.

"One's starting."

"Take anything for it yet?"

I shake my head.

He slips past me without asking and heads to my kitchen. He's only been in my apartment one other time when we met here to go for a run.

I'm too tired to follow him, and I go back to the couch and lie down, hoping he'll take the hint and leave. There's some banging of cupboards, the water in my fridge clicks on, and then Brice is standing in front of me with a glass of water and a bottle of pills.

"Do you need these or these?" He has my prescription bottle in one hand and a package of aspirin in the other.

"You went through my stuff?" My cheeks heat, and I sit up with a huff. I snatch both from him and set them on the coffee table.

"You have a headache. I was trying to help. It's not like I was in the kitchen searching the internet for why you're taking those."

I rub my fingers in circles on my temples and rip open the package and toss the pills into my mouth, using the water to chase it. He can look up my medication if he wants on the internet—doesn't matter to me. Personal boundaries clearly mean nothing to him. I lie back on the couch and tuck the blanket around me. I'm hoping he'll take the hint.

Rather than leaving, he sits at the other end of my couch and props his feet on my coffee table.

"I'm not in the mood, Brice."

"Can't say I've ever heard that before." A hint of a smile tugs at the corners of his lips.

"Proud to be your first." I point to the door with my finger. "And on that note..."

"I don't want to go on a three-day camping trip with Wren." He stretches out and laces his hands behind his head, closing his eyes.

"So don't go."

"But I agree with her that I should go on a mock adventure race and that Bellerive is the safest environment for me to practice. Given that I am a prince and that—" He opens one eye to peer at me. "Don't tell Maren this, Tucker, okay?"

I let out a deep sigh. Part of his schtick is to pretend as though Maren and Tucker are two different people. Poor Maren is always the heavy, and Tucker is his buddy. Today, I have no interest in being either.

"Uh-huh," I mutter.

"I have no idea what I'm doing on this adventure race. Each part I can handle. Throw them together and, well, perhaps not so great."

"You're not that bad," I say.

"That sounds almost like—" He pretends to think. "A compliment." He leans across my body to put his wrist against my forehead. "Doesn't *feel* like a fever..."

"Just tell me what you want," I say. "Hye Jin, the producer for InterFlix, sliced me open, and I just don't have the energy for this right now."

"She did what?" He's still stretched across me, and he stares down at me, all hint of teasing having vanished.

"It doesn't matter," I say.

"No," he says, and his hand settles on my hip. Even through the blanket, my skin heats at the contact. "It matters. If she said something to upset you, it matters."

I'm unsure what I should even say or admit. "She was trying to talk me into racing again. Said it would be a great comeback narrative."

Brice eases away from me and lets out a slow breath. "But you don't want to race anymore."

The truth isn't nearly that simple, partly because every day, the answer changes or shifts. If Enzo was supportive, it might feel easier to be sure, but he isn't.

"I'm not even certain I should go to Fiji at all."

"Not even on the support team?" He frowns. "Why not?"

"You were right about how much excitement would revolve around your involvement with the show." It's the closest I can come to saying I don't want them to dig too deeply into my life, discover the truths I want to keep buried.

He gazes out my oversize windows to the ocean stretched out before us, and he doesn't say anything for a long time.

"If I'm going to be out in the wilderness of Bellerive," he says, "I don't want Wren to be the one guiding me. I want it to be you."

"Wren's your teammate, and—"

"She's too nice," he says with a hint of impatience. "I want someone who's going to force me to be better, to step up. Someone who has no problem calling me on my shit. If the point is to prepare me, I want to know I've been prepared."

Normally, he's full of jokes and laughter, and to hear him say something like this that reveals more of himself causes another flare of interest to ignite in me. But more than that is the realization he values me in a way I never would have expected when we were sitting across from each other at the conference table months ago.

"I'll talk to Wren," I say. "I'll take you."

## Chapter Fifteen

## BRICE

Nick wanders into the kitchen as I'm planning and packing my meals with Joyce, the head cook, for my three-day camping trip, which starts in about an hour. It's ridiculously early, and it would be unusual for Nick to be awake, but jet lag after his last trip to Tanzania, coupled with our father's circumstances, means he's more of an insomniac than a solid sleeper of late. Normally, I'd offer to be a sounding board for his worries, but every time I talk to him, his fears become mine. I get dragged down. Tucker notices and says something, and then I feel guilty for bringing my drama into her life. Leaning on her is not in the plan. She gets the best of me. I refuse to tarnish the few glimmers of happiness I see in her with my family's circumstances.

Joyce nudges me and passes me the last of Rory's scones in an airtight container with a wink. I tuck the present deep into my backpack. Another perk of being the *former* third in line to the throne is that I'm Joyce's favorite royal. She'd never admit it, but I know it's true.

Tucker gave me a packing list, and scones aren't on it, but there's no way she'll question my decision once she tastes one. If Rory hadn't married my brother, I would have been first in line to sponsor a full-time bakeshop.

"Where are you off to?" Nick asks as he opens the fridge and peers inside. "Really? The scones are all gone? Every last one? The palace has become a bunch of savages. She just made them yesterday."

"Tucker and I are going on a three-day cross-island trek," I say while Joyce makes herself busy, away from Nick's grumbling complaint. I could get the container out of my bag and give him one, but I'd rather see the delight on Tucker's face once she's had one and realizes there are more.

"You didn't even leave me any coffee?" Nick rattles the pot I just emptied into the thermos I've attached to my backpack.

"Not sure how you expected me to know you'd be up at five thirty in the morning." I run my finger down Tucker's neat scrawl. She passed me the list last night after we went for a run.

"I must be getting old," Nick mutters. "Jet lag used to be nothing, and I never depended on coffee to stay alive."

Not touching that one since we both know there's a lot more going on than that.

"Get your supply issues sorted out in Tanzania?" I ask.

"Close enough, I think," Nick says. "Feels like I hardly see you anymore. What's going on with you and Maren Tucker?"

"Nothing." I fold the packing sheet and tuck it into the pocket of my shorts. Maybe I'll get to the front entrance early. "She's my coach."

But if she wasn't married, I sometimes wonder if it would be more than that. There's an undercurrent brewing between us that I'm a lot more comfortable with than I should be. She was the person I butted heads with. Then she became my coach, and we're inching into something else. I have a lot of women as friends, and sometimes there's an unacknowledged sexual tension, a *what-if* that could go somewhere but rarely does. For me, a friend is a friend.

With Tucker, it's chemistry, but it's something else too—something I can't quite put my finger on. The only thing I know for certain is that I like how much she challenges me in what I say, in how I act, in how far I'm willing to push myself. Being third in line to the throne with a plethora of friends, I've rarely met anyone who prodded me to be more than I already was. Initially, her attitude toward me was a point of frustration, then her haughtiness amused me, and now her drive to be the best is propelling me deeper into the racing world. No matter what we train together, she dares me to do better. I don't want to just survive this adventure race experience; I want to thrive.

"Nate told me Sawyer was initially worried about how hard Maren was pushing herself. Does she train too or just coach?"

I lean against the counter and cross my arms, taking in Nick's comment. Her family has been worried about her? At least her older brother and sister, anyway. Should I have noticed something other than her underlying sadness? Up until the InterFlix producer prodded her too hard, her grief was mostly the faintest outline around her.

"Why would they be worried about her?"

"She had that accident," Nick says, and he flicks on the coffee maker after filling it. "Nate mentioned that her ankle was in pretty bad shape."

Those pills she takes aren't directly related to her ankle, and I wonder if the ankle is the family's smoke screen for what's really going on. Doesn't take an internet search to recognize Prozac. "You ever meet her husband?"

"Nope. Watched a few of his YouTube videos out of curiosity once. The workout ones, not the videogame ones. Very fit guy." Nick grabs a mug from the cupboard above the coffee maker.

At his comment, I glance at my biceps and flex them. It's not like fitness is hard.

"The whole family was pretty wary of her marrying him. He's been over in the US for a while now, I think. You've probably heard all about it. Some sort of business opportunity."

"The guy makes YouTube videos," I say with a scoff. "What sort of business opportunity would take him away from his injured wife for months?"

My tone gets Nick's attention, and something like delight enters his hazel eyes. "Have you got a crush on a married woman?"

A crush. Makes me sound like I'm back in elementary school. "Tucker and I are buddies. I have a lot of respect for her racing skills."

"Buddies." Nick laughs. "Tell me what any of your other friends' partners are up to other than Posey and Brent. I'll wait. Go ahead." He makes a "go on" motion with his hand.

"Training has eaten up a lot of my time lately."

"You can go feed your bullshit to someone else. What's her cup size?"

*34B, if I had to guess.* I run my palms along my cheeks and sigh. Fine, so I've noticed. I'd never deny she's an attractive woman. Attractive might be too mild of a word.

"On a more serious note," Nick says, "I know your philosophy has always been that you aren't responsible for someone else's marriage, but if something happens between you and Maren Tucker, Bellerive will never forget. That's a scandal with a capital S. Is that really something you want to invite in here given everything else we're dealing with?"

"We're buddies," I say through gritted teeth. It's not like I'm so hard up for female company that I *have* to have Tucker. Self-control is a thing, and while I've never been big on exercising it, I'm sure I *can*. Besides, her shitty attitude toward me was the direct result of a misunderstanding around cheating. Even if I was tempted, she wouldn't be. She's not the type.

"Just wanted to make sure there wouldn't be any buyer's regret," Nick says as he pours himself a cup of coffee and takes a sip. "You know, like that tattoo on your back."

"It's grown on me," I mutter. Drunk me thought the Chinese characters were a good idea, but I've since had them mostly covered over. Someone has to look closely to find them.

"More like grown *with* you," Nick says with a laugh before heading for the door. "Some mistakes are more permanent than others."

Once he's out the door, I stand with my back pressed into the counter, and I'm aware of Joyce's presence on the other side of the kitchen, assessing inventory before the rest of the staff arrive. My chat with Nick has cut into my preparation time, but I was almost ready anyway.

"What do you think, Joyce?" I'm not sure why I'm asking, because Nick has it wrong. Nothing is happening between me and Tucker, and there won't be. He's not reading the situation right, but it's hard to explain what we are to each other. A comfort, maybe.

"You always say you should take your happiness where you can find it," she says. "You've seemed happy since you started training for this. Not a false happy. A real happy. If it's the racing, that's wonderful. Truly wonderful that you've found something separate from this place. You're going to need it, I think. But if she's the cause of your joy, be careful. Joyous and careful. A broken heart at a time like this or a scandal..." She makes a tutting noise.

"Neither of those are going to happen," I say. "The training is what I enjoy. Her company is merely a bonus." Even saying that seems strange. Funny how quickly a perspective can shift.

Maren Tucker's company is a bonus. I let out a little laugh. Unbelievable but true.

"Good luck on your adventure. I hear King Alexander has allowed you to go without a bodyguard? Better be careful."

Alex did agree. Unorthodox, and I suspect Rory had a hand in convincing him I'd be safe with Maren after we had a chat in the corridor one day about how much I needed to unplug from everything going on with Dad. I had a feeling she'd go to bat for me, even if I didn't explicitly ask her to. She's good like that.

"I'm always careful," I say with a grin before I pick up my backpack and head for the door.

---

We're picking our way through Bellerive's northern national park, which is also a temperate rainforest, for the first leg of our three-day adventure. Rather than taking the well-worn paths, Tucker got permission a few years ago from the National Parks Commission to take alternate, harder routes mapped out for the race team. Only problem is the ground is fucking slippery with moss since they haven't gone this way for almost a year.

I lose my footing again, and I curse as I almost go down. "Don't say it," I grumble before Tucker can come out with her typical sing-song "Balance, Your Highness," as though she thinks she's funny. Now that we train so much together, sometimes it *is* funny, but now is not one of those times.

She glances over her shoulder and grins. Catching her amusement dismantles the annoyance that's been building in me with each slick step. At least she's enjoying herself, and warmth spreads across my chest. I suck in a deep, appreciative breath.

"I love the air out here," Tucker says as she navigates her way through the underbrush.

"Damp and fresh," I agree.

"You ever come out here?"

I consider her question for a beat. Of course we've been to this national park, but the last time I remember being here was for a ribbon-cutting ceremony over new bathrooms at one of the campsites.

"Not really," I say. "We grew up this weird mix of sheltered and worldly."

"I have no idea what that means," she says.

"You wouldn't. You were busy running all over Bellerive, quite literally."

"My mother was very free-range, and my father was very nonexistent unless we got hurt."

"How'd you end up in adventure racing?" We've spent so many hours together, but we're never truly alone. Our conversations have always been tempered by the reality of other ears within range. Jag or someone else is often tailing us, ensuring my safety, even though I'm not sure why anymore. With Grace, the line of succession is even further from me than before. When Nick and Jules have kids, I'll be another level down. Maybe letting me do this without Jag is Alex's way of acknowledging the new reality. My place in the monarchy is even less necessary than it was before.

"Mrs. Hayes—do you remember her from St. George's Middle School? She put together a junior adventure race team when I was eleven. Since I was a good runner, she asked if I wanted to train for it. The rest is history. I started, and I never really stopped."

We walk in silence for a few moments with Tucker holding some branches so they don't slingshot into my face. There was a time when she definitely would have released them, perhaps with a gleeful cackle.

"You never answered my question," she says.

"You had a question?"

"The worldly part of your claim, I can understand. The royal family has probably been to every country in the world. What did you mean by the sheltered bit?"

"This," I say, gesturing to the forest around us. "I could play on the estate, and if something was tied to school, I could participate. But to go out into the wilderness and camp? Without security? Without five hundred contingency plans in case someone wanted to kidnap or murder me? Didn't happen. A bit less restrictive at university in London, but I'm never truly alone. Not that it's ever bothered me." That much is true. I am a people person whether by choice or design.

"I think we must be opposites," she says.

"You don't say." I can't keep the sardonic tone out of my voice.

"I enjoy silence and my alone time."

"I'm learning to appreciate silence." Our nights where we climb in the barn, there's a companionable quiet between us, and there's a similar comfort when we run or bike or paddleboard together. We don't have to talk—we can just exist together. Not sure I've ever had a friendship quite like that. Where something in me is comforted by the mere presence of someone else without a single word having to be exchanged.

"And I'm learning to appreciate inane chatter." There's a hint of amusement in her voice to take the sting out of her words.

"Don't forget the dad jokes."

"That would be the inane part." She hops over a little creek of water and points to a particularly slippery rock to warn me. "What is your obsession with dad jokes, anyway?"

"Practice. Embarrass my own kids when I'm a dad." I'm halfway over the creek before I realize what I've said. Not exactly something I imagined telling Tucker, let alone anyone. Her shoulders tense, and I wince at my stupidity. Bringing up kids around her is something I try to avoid. "Forget I said that."

She turns around, walking backward in the little clearing we've come to, and instead of pain or whatever else I might see, she seems curious.

"What?" I ask, a hint of challenge in my tone. I'd be a good dad.

"Mr. I-don't-do-commitment wants a baby?" Her look is definitely tinged with disbelief before she turns back around to lead the way.

"Don't want the wife or the girlfriend or whatever," I clarify. "Just the kid."

"Well, I suppose anything is possible nowadays. Let me know how the birth goes once you've figured the logistics out."

"Obviously I could hire a surrogate. Not much fun in that for me."

"Oh, my God. Did you really just say that?"

"You cannot fault my honesty."

"You're aiming to knock up some poor, unsuspecting woman? You realize you'd have to share custody. Make support payments—possibly to mother *and* child. The whole thing."

"Logic has no place here, Tucker. A man can dream."

"Dream of impregnating a woman on purpose but also by accident."

"Alex did it," I say.

"I'm not entirely sure what happened between King Alexander and Queen Aurora, but I'm certain it's not the mess he fed to the press."

"Not really supposed to discuss that mess with outsiders," I say. Alex would remove my head from my shoulders for putting Rory back in the line of fire since things have finally settled down.

"It's not like people don't know."

"There's knowing, and then there's *knowing*." If anyone should understand how loyalty and family structure works, it's Tucker. Her family closed ranks around her after her accident, and they're feeding everyone the lies about Enzo's job to save face.

Tucker stops to consult the map in her bag, and when she glances up, she says, "I've never met a man who wanted a baby more than he wanted a woman."

"Oh," I say. "Did I give you the impression I'd be quitting women?" I give her a wolfish grin.

"Of course." She shakes her head. "What was I thinking? You'll continue to enjoy your buffet."

"I'm not sure I understand the point of marriage," I admit. "Why did you get married?" It's a question I've been wondering for months, especially since the state of their marriage would be my worst nightmare, but I've never felt I had the right to pry.

"He fed me pretty words and promises made of Turkish delight." She folds the map and avoids eye contact. "And maybe I fed them to him too."

The reference to *The Lion, the Witch, and the Wardrobe* is not lost on me, but I'm trying to work out what she means. Nothing good, anyway. They were lying to each other? Poisoning each other?

"We need to walk faster," Tucker says as she sticks the map into a side pocket of her backpack. "While we'll set up tents in the dark on the course, I'd rather not teach you how to do it the first time by flashlight."

Before I can say anything in response, she's leading the way through increasingly dense underbrush, and a strained silence settles between us. As we walk, I curse myself for daring to bring up Enzo. If there's one subject guaranteed to sour her mood, it's him. She even handled the baby talk better than I expected. For the rest of our trip, I'm not saying a word about him.

Truthfully, I'm happier when we pretend like he doesn't exist too.

# Chapter Sixteen

## MAREN

We've trudged almost forty kilometers through the rain forest, and when we emerge, we're at the edge of a farmer's field on a cliff overlooking the ocean. It's prime real estate in Bellerive between two national parks, but Victor Tucker has set up a seasonal campground closest to the cliff's edge, and he farms the rest with cattle. It's low season, and the campground isn't normally in use. Since he's my father's cousin, I called and asked if we could spend one night on the property. It's a regular pit stop when my team is training.

I open the side gate that Victor keeps unlocked for us when he knows we're coming, and I lead us through the field toward a campsite near the block of washrooms and showers Victor had built on the property.

While we've walked, my mind has been all over the place. Hearing Brice talk about wanting to become a father left tiny papercuts all over my subconscious. Enzo had really wanted to be a dad too. Not more than he'd wanted me, or at least I hadn't thought it was more than he wanted me. Another thing I'm not sure about anymore. Even if we can make our relationship work, our life together might never be what he once envisioned.

Despite the chaos in my brain that my chat with Brice caused, having a real conversation with him was refreshing. Each of his responses revealed another layer I never would have suspected.

I lower my backpack onto the grass, and Brice drops his with a thud before he collapses beside it.

"Forty fucking kilometers," he says.

"It'll be more like fifty fucking kilometers during the race, and that'll be just to keep up. If you want to win, sleep has to be cut."

"One thing I will not be cutting is my food intake."

"Wise choice," I say as I unhook his tent from the side of his backpack. It's a fancy pop-up tent, but it's tiny—room for him and likely his backpack but not much else.

Brice watches me adjust the built-in supports, and he groans as he gets off the ground to come help me. "Suppose I should learn this," he mumbles.

It doesn't take long to get everything secured, and we stand side by side, staring at the ocean view where the sun is starting to slip beneath the horizon.

"Guess I'd better get mine set up," I say.

"Help?" Brice asks while he unlaces his hiking boots.

"I could put it together with my eyes closed," I say. "I've had the same tent since I was fourteen."

While Brice digs around in his pack for something, I slide the contents of my tent bag onto the ground. Automatically, I count the tent poles, and I frown. Tipping the bag upside down, I riffle through the parts, and then I sit on my haunches in disbelief. I'm missing one of the central poles.

"Do you need to close your eyes to get started?" Brice teases.

"I'm missing a pole," I say, and I wrack my brain to figure out how this is possible. Then I remember Ava coming to my house just after Enzo left and asking to borrow my tent. At the time, I never expected to need it again. Enzo was supposed to come back, and I was supposed to be done with risking life and limb for a thrill. Turns out neither one happened.

"My sister," I mutter.

"Sawyer? She seems like the type who'd put everything in its place."

"Ava."

"Ah," Brice says, and he doesn't make the same claim about my younger sister.

Ava's reputation around the island as being a bit of a scatterbrain is well earned. I used to think she put it on to annoy Sawyer, but I'm wondering whether it was ever an act or if she pretended for so long that it became the truth. In any event, I'm sure she went camping with whatever athlete she brought to Bellerive and didn't bother to pick up all the pieces of my tent before leaving one of the island's national parks.

"Does a tent work when its missing one of its central poles?"

"As a method of annoyance or suffocation, maybe." I stare at the pieces of my tent, and not for the first time, I curse the emotional stupor I fell into months ago. If I'd been in my right mind, I never would have agreed to let Ava have the tent. It's not like our family can't afford to buy one.

"Do I dare say it's just a tent?"

"That would be like me telling you all tequilas taste the same."

"That bad, huh? How can I help?" Brice crouches at my side.

"Hire a hit on my sister? I recommend a tent pole as a murder weapon."

He runs his hand along the top of my head and down my back. The gesture is just the right weight against my body, and for some reason, his silent comfort brings a lot more reassurance than I'd expect.

"Who knew camping was so in-tents?" he says.

A burst of laughter escapes me at the unexpectedness of his dad joke. It shouldn't surprise me. He seems to have one for every occasion, but with his hand still lingering on the small of my back, the moment feels strangely intimate, as though we've been like this a million times before. I lean my head against his shoulder, and his lips press against the top of my head. He is effortlessly affectionate, and warmth spreads across my body in response.

"The good news," Brice murmurs, "is that my tent is technically a two-person one."

I glance at the tiny whisp of fabric not far from us. We'll have enough room in there for two sleeping bags, and I suspect we'll have to use our backpacks as footrests or pillows to fit everything in. Cramped is an understatement.

"And," Brice continues, "Joyce gave me the last of Rory's scones this morning. You have not lived until you've had an Aurora Summerset scone."

My stomach rumbles in response, and Brice leaves me to grab a container from beside his bag. He pops it open, and the smell of butter and raisins hits my nose, and my mouth waters. Until this moment, I hadn't realized how hungry I was. Protein bars and electrolyte drinks only get me so far.

He picks one up, and instead of passing it to me, he takes a big bite. "Quality check," he says around his mouthful.

I laugh and try to weave around his hand while he pretends to block me from getting one.

"I'm not sure yet," he says, and he takes another bite, batting my hand away from the container. "Wouldn't want you to get sick when you're leading us through the wilderness."

"Come on, Brice. Please." I try to dip around him.

He takes another bite, and he holds the container high enough I can't quite reach it. When I go onto my toes and try to swipe it from him, my chest connects with his.

"I think you were in the middle of begging," he says, and he glances down at me with a flirty smirk. "You may continue."

"Oh, my God," I say, and I shove his chest. "First the dad jokes and now the sexual innuendoes."

"There was nothing sexual about my comment," he says as though my suggestion is ludicrous. He takes another bite of scone. "But if you want to take it that way—I don't mind when a woman begs there either."

Heat floods all kinds of places that have no business getting hot, and I ignore him while I go to my backpack to dig out my food.

"It was a joke, Tucker," Brice says from behind me.

"I know," I say, but I can hear the strain in my voice. Of course he was joking, but my body reacted as though he wasn't, which is bad for so many reasons. Affection is fine, but the sexual tension is wrong. I shouldn't feel it.

"Come here," he says. "I don't know if Maren lets you eat sinfully delicious sweets like these, but we won't tell her."

To prove that his comment and my reaction doesn't matter, I drop my food on top of my bag, and I peer over the edge of the container before selecting one of the remaining scones. I'm sure the atmosphere around us has cleared, and I silently congratulate myself on playing it cool as I bring the scone to my lips. But when I glance up at Brice, he's riveted by my action. My lips part in surprise at the intensity of his gaze. The air crackles around us, as though me biting into a scone is the most erotic thing that's ever happened.

"Just let it slide in there," he murmurs. "You won't regret it." His voice is rough and quite possibly the sexiest I've ever heard him sound.

A little flirting is okay, isn't it? It's not like any of this means anything to him, and I'm married. The teasing and the touches and this insane tension between us isn't foreplay. They're harmless exchanges between two people who'd never act on whatever this is.

Except when his gaze slides to mine, I'm not sure about any of what I've just told myself. His light-brown eyes have darkened, and my breath hitches at our proximity. If I stepped even a little bit closer, I could brush up against him, and not only do I think he'd let me, I think he'd welcome it. The realization is so surprising that I take a step back, as though his rapt attention has stung me.

I take a large bite of the scone, hoping I look as unattractive as possible, and I turn away while I chew. We can pretend that flare of feeling didn't happen. *I'm* going to pretend it didn't happen.

"Tucker," Brice says to my back. "I feel it, but I'd never act on it. Okay? You'd hate me for it, and I don't want that."

"We're oil and water," I say, partly because I'm surprised by his blunt honesty. I've never met a man who said exactly what they thought with no hint of embarrassment or uncertainty. We had a moment, and he's not the least bit uncomfortable acknowledging it. But I am. His easiness with whatever is brewing between us is terrifying.

"Nah, we're not oil and water. I used to think that too, but it's not true."

We're far enough apart now that I can turn to face him without wanting to either brush myself against him or run away. The two instincts are there—the desire and the fear. But I don't ever want to become my father. Enzo and I might be going through a rough patch, but marriage is for better *and* for worse. You can't just pick the half that suits you.

"So what are we, then?" I tip my chin in defiance.

"Oil and balsamic vinegar."

"It's the same," I say. "They repel each other. Globs of vinegar sit in the oil. They don't mix."

"Sure, they *can* be separate. But when they're mixed properly, they complement each other. The tastes—" He makes a circular motion around his mouth with his index finger. "Mingle, and it's delicious when it's done right."

My heart pounds in my chest, and a cool sweat breaks out under my arms. How can him describing oil and balsamic vinegar be sexy? What is wrong with me?

"I'm the oil, of course. Since I have a much smoother personality." He grins at me before taking another bite of scone.

"And I'm the bitter bite." I roll my eyes and try to pretend this whole exchange is annoying.

"Were you raised a heathen with no palate?" He picks up another scone and offers it to me.

As much as I'd like to resist, he's right that the queen's baking is unparalleled. I finish the last bite of the one I have in my hand, but I hesitate to accept another.

"Balsamic vinegar is not white vinegar. They're nothing alike," Brice continues. "Balsamic vinegar has a rich, complex sweetness, and the tartness is … merely superficial."

There's so much sincerity in his tone that it makes my chest ache. There are layers upon layers upon layers to this man, and each one I reach intrigues and scares me more. I take the scone from his outstretched hand, and he searches my expression.

"The oil is made better by the vinegar, that's all you really need to understand."

It's the strangest and best compliment anyone has ever given me. Since I'm not really sure how to respond, I bite the scone and let the sweetness of his presence seep into me.

---

Brice shifts onto his side in his sleeping bag beside me, and the full moon shines through the open flaps of the tent that are being lifted once in a while by the ocean breeze. Camping out has always been a balm to my soul, and I wasn't sure how it would be with Brice.

Rather than our conversation earlier inspiring awkwardness or more tension, we've been subdued and comfortable around each other, as though we cleared the air.

But we haven't.

Since we've settled into the tent, the air has grown thick again, as though we're both waiting for the other person to speak. It's a game we often play from who will text who about training to who will end our training session first. We're in a weird competition to care both less and more than the other person. I recognize it, but I have no idea how to solve it. Maybe this is just how we function. Oil and balsamic vinegar.

We're packed into his tiny tent like sardines. Sleeping on top of each other would likely be more comfortable than being wedged in here shoulder to shoulder. Or back-to-back, which is how we are right now. Neither of us sleeping. Listening to each other breathe.

"You awake, Tucker?" Brice asks.

"Yes," I whisper. He must know. It's easy enough to tell when someone is really sleeping or just pretending to.

"Tell me something you've never told anyone else."

Instead of keeping my back to him, I rotate around to face him, and he does the same, as though both of us were looking for the other to crack the door.

"Something I've never told anyone else?" I pretend to think about it seriously. "Royalty is overrated," I say. "Don't tell the Summersets. They'll freak out."

He lets out a soft chuckle, and we're close enough for his breath to stir the strands of my hair that have fallen over my cheek.

"You've told someone that before."

"It's true. I tell a lot of people that one."

We stare at each other in the moonlight, and the faint scar on his forehead, just above his right eye keeps drawing my attention. I've noticed it before, but it's rare for me to have a chance to examine him without it being weird.

"How did you get that?" I ask.

"What?"

I run my index finger over the scar, and his brow wrinkles. The brief skin-to-skin contact sends a thrill from my finger down along my body. To think I once believed he was merely a pretty face.

"Nick," he says. "I said something about Jules, and he punched me." He lets out a little chuckle. "We were young and drunk. I think he really wanted to punch Alex. Family ring left a permanent reminder to think before I speak." He hesitates for a moment and then says, "Of course, I have to be looking in a mirror to be reminded, so I forget a lot."

"Maybe you should just carry a mirror in your pocket to consult before you speak."

"I have probably heard worse ideas."

"You don't seem so sure." The easy teasing is familiar. We're rarely combative anymore.

"Maybe I should just carry around a smart-ass who doesn't mind correcting me."

"That idea is definitely worse. I'm heavy. A mirror is not."

Brice digs his arm out of his sleeping bag and flexes his bicep. "Nobody is too heavy for me."

I can't help laughing at how he didn't bother to stroke my ego by saying I wasn't heavy. Instead, he caressed his own. Typical.

"I've been trying to get used to that sound," he says, "but I don't hear it often enough."

"You'll have to work on being funnier."

"That's a Maren comment. Tucker thinks I'm funny."

We fall into a companionable silence, both of us with half smiles on our faces. It's a moment I could live in, quite happily, forever.

Brice asked me to tell him something I've never told anyone else. I didn't think I had anything to say, but as we lay there scanning each other's faces, I realize I might, and the realization makes my stomach clench.

I never used to think I was anything like my father, but as I take in Brice's features, my heart flutters, and I worry that the apple hasn't fallen far enough from the tree.

---

It's dark when we reach my vehicle after our final leg of our three-day trip. Last night, we were both too exhausted to do anything other than eat and then fall into a deep sleep, but when I woke this morning, Brice had his arm flung around my middle. We didn't talk about it, and he acted as though it was no big deal. Maybe to him it wasn't.

But each of these micro-actions feel like we're inching across a tightrope. If I tumble, I'll fall into a space I swore I'd never occupy. A moral dilemma Brice said he'd never push me into or ask me for looms before us.

In some ways, our burgeoning connection is unfathomable. A few months ago, there wasn't anyone I disliked more than Brice Summerset. He was too much of everything and not enough of something. How wrong I was.

For the last three days, we've had our phones off. A complete disconnect from the real world. While competitors are participating in the adventure race, they aren't allowed access to any technology. A map and a compass are the only navigational tools allowed.

When we climb into the car, I turn on my phone, and it chimes with a bunch of missed messages and voicemails. I have three texts from Enzo—the first mundane and the next two worried. I didn't tell him I was going into the wilderness with Brice. Wouldn't matter who I went with. Enzo wouldn't have approved. He's certain I should be done racing, and while I'm not sure I have it in me to race, I *need* the training.

"You okay?" Brice asks as he clicks his seat belt into place.

"Fine," I say, and I cringe at the inauthenticity of using that word.

Brice pats my knee and seeing his hand on my leg makes me realize I might be letting these familiarities slip by because I miss having someone do these things. Enzo was always affectionate, and I haven't had anyone touch me, sexual or otherwise, in months. It's no wonder Brice's attention feels good.

As I drive Brice back to the estate, I consider my options. I can keep sliding down this mountain with Brice, one sure to break my heart one way or another, or I can let go of my pride and try with Enzo. A real effort.

My heart thumps as I drive through the estate gates. Giving Enzo another chance is the right thing to do. The grown-up choice.

Brice grabs his things out of the back of my SUV, and before I can drive away like the coward I am, he comes to the driver's side and places his forearms on my window ledge.

"I'll see you tomorrow?"

"Mmm-hmm." There's a tightness across my chest, but I can't keep ignoring my husband and letting whatever this is with Brice expand across my life. I'm married.

*I'm married.*

And I will not become my father.

He hoists his backpack onto his shoulder, and he gives me a wave as he heads toward the main entrance. I sit for a beat in the vehicle, working up the nerve to make the call.

Then I turn the SUV toward my apartment, and I dial Enzo's number.

"I was getting worried," Enzo says. "What have you been up to the last few days?"

"Really busy with some charity things." Not a complete lie. The race *is* for charity. "I was, um, thinking about taking you up on the offer to come to Boston."

"To stay?"

I can't read his tone, but I forge ahead anyway. "For a week or so, if that's okay with you."

"Yeah," he says. "It's your apartment too."

Technically, it's a Tucker family apartment, and my parents were not happy when I said Enzo would be staying there while we worked out our issues. They think he's a freeloader, but can you really call someone that when they're literally part of the family?

"I'll be there tomorrow," I say. "I'm booking my flight as soon as I get home."

One way or another, I need to figure out if what I'm starting to feel for Brice is real, or if I'm a deeply lonely and unhappy woman clinging to any sign of affection.

# Chapter Seventeen

## BRICE

At the ocean's surface, I let out a gasp and suck in a deep lungful of air. "This is bullshit."

Brent chuckles from the paddleboard he's keeping within my reach. "You have to release a little bit of air when your lungs get tight."

We're working on breath control at an inlet cove on the eastern side of the island. There's a lot of reef around here, and the water, even far out, isn't as deep as you'd expect given that Bellerive is an island in the middle of the North Atlantic Ocean. Riker and Paxton suggested this spot during training this week. Training Tucker hasn't been running.

My frustration isn't so much about my insufficient lung capacity but rather about my complete lack of concentration. Brent has given me the same advice three or four times now, and each time, I get halfway down to the stupid brass key on the sandy ocean floor and forget to let out my air. My brain has been a muddled mess as the days on the calendar flip by. Tucker has been gone a week, and my father is one week closer to no longer being with us.

I hang on to the end of the board with one hand, and I wipe my face with my other one. After our three-day camping trip together, I wondered whether I'd freaked Maren out with my casual flirting. We'd already been dancing around each other, so I thought facing the tension head on was the best thing to do. Be honest. Lay out my cards. She's fucking hot, and I would totally sleep with her. But I wouldn't do that, because she'd hate me for it. Honest. Up front. No bullshit. Get the awkwardness out of the way.

Turns out I should have gone with the head-in-the-sand approach. Impossible for me. Maren wasn't ready to face the fact there *is* something between us. Whether it's merely pent-up sexual frustration or something else, we'll likely never find out. But I certainly didn't expect her to go work out her frustrations with her fucking good-for-nothing husband.

Just the thought causes me to clench my jaw.

"You'll get it," Brent says.

"I don't understand why she'd go to Boston for a week," I burst out. "Or longer. She's still not back. He left her. He left." I fling out my hand, flicking the water in annoyance.

Brent rears back on the board. "That's...unexpected. Okay." He draws out the last word. "Is there something going on between you and Maren?"

"No." I turn onto my back and rest my head on the board, and I float, sculling with my hands to keep myself level. "I just think it's dumb that she gave in first."

"If no one gives in, nothing ever changes," Brent says. "She married him. She must love him."

The thought causes a wildfire of anger to rage across my body. "He doesn't deserve her. He's a fucking coward." The opposite of Tucker in a way that actually matters.

Brent doesn't say anything for a long time, and I'm fine with that because wallowing is my favorite pastime this week. The one text message I sent to her went unanswered. Took all my self-restraint not to send a flurry of follow-ups. At one point, I checked the flight times to Boston. What the fuck would I have done in Boston? Clearly a moment of mental instability.

"Want to go get a bottle of tequila?" Brent asks.

"No."

"There *is* something going on between you and Maren," Brent says.

"I don't want to talk about Tucker." There's nothing happening between us, or nothing serious anyway. She's married, and I don't do commitment. It's not like I can offer or even want to offer her some sort of alternative. If she was single, sex would be a definite possibility, if not a certainty. I'd be unable to resist finding out whether the energy that hums between us is just as good in other places and situations. Or perhaps *all* the places and situations. Just the thought sends my imagination into overdrive.

Under different circumstances, my curiosity would have completely fucked up our friendship and adventure race training. Past experience tells me it's almost impossible to revert to friendship once that line is obliterated. Even though I'm not much for repeats, since that often leads to a gray relationship area, I can't imagine being a one and done with Tucker. Maybe I should be grateful she's off-limits.

"I bought Posey a ring," Brent says. "Took Julia with me."

I push off the board to tread water and so I can see him better. They've been together for years now, and while there's no doubt they're committed to each other, I'm a bit surprised he's bought a ring. "Thought maybe you two weren't going to do the whole marriage thing."

"Had to wait until I was sure Posey was ready." He squints into the sun.

"How do you know she's ready?"

"She's brought it up a few times since Nick and Jules got married—'Someday when we get married' and things like that. Never happened before, so I figure it's a good bet."

"Congratulations, man." The whole concept still feels foreign to me. How can anyone ever be certain they could spend their entire life with someone else and never get bored? Or fall out of love? Or wish for something else? While my parents have been relatively happy, I've seen a lot more of the opposite. Many of my friends who got married young have already given up on their "starter" marriages and are either married again or in new relationships.

None of my friends have been in a marriage as shitty as Tucker's, and she's clinging so hard she went to Boston to try to work things out when it's clear to me he's not worth her time or energy. At her lowest, he left. That's one situation where I'd wholeheartedly support walking away.

We return to shore, and Jag meets us on the beach to help with carting everything back to the SUV.

"I appreciate you coming to visit," I say to Brent.

"Posey thought you could use some bro time," Brent says. "Besides, any excuse to see her is good enough for me. She didn't have to ask twice."

"You'll be ramping up your training for the last Olympics soon. After that, you're moving here?"

"That's the plan," Brent says. "Coach the local swim team. Try to figure out how to make use of my MBA. Convince Posey that kids are fun."

"Won't have to talk her into that one too hard," I say. "Grace is converting us all."

"Is she?" Brent leans against the SUV while I open the rear door. "*Grace* has converted you?"

"My thoughts on kids have nothing to do with Tucker."

"You knew who I was talking about."

There's no point in arguing with him. I'm not looking for a baby mama, and if I was, I certainly wouldn't start with a married woman.

We part ways, and I tell Jag to take the long way home. After doing it almost every day for the last week, he understands what I mean. But unlike every other day, when we cruise past Tucker's apartment, there's a cab idling at the curb on the other side of the street.

"Pull over?" Jag asks.

It's a busy street, but there's a lane for short-term parking on this side. My behavior isn't normal, and even as I recognize it, I confirm that I want him to stop. The cab might not even be her, but when the rear door opens, and a head of dark hair emerges, my heart kicks in my chest. After having spent so much time with her the past few months, going a whole week without talking to her or seeing her has been a slow, unexpected torture.

When her high heel touches the pavement, something inside of me settles, and I realize part of me has been worried she wouldn't return at all. Coaching the team isn't the same as being on it, especially when all the members of the team are adults capable of training themselves. Even me, after months of training with her, could likely get by in the homestretch if I had to. After our three-day camp out, I understand how grueling the ten days in Fiji will be.

The cab driver gets out to help her with her bag, and whatever he says makes Tucker laugh. My chest tightens at seeing her so light and happy. Is it because her trip to see Enzo went that well?

He doesn't appear to be in the cab with her. Or is she that happy to be home? Or is the cab driver just ten times funnier than me?

"Are we going over, Your Highness?" Jag asks.

"No." The first time I see her again, I don't want it to be on the street when I've surprised her. She hasn't reached out to me since she left, and I won't be the one begging for a scrap of her attention. Besides, if my behavior on the camping trip threw her off-balance, turning up on her doorstep when she's just returned home would likely drive an even deeper wedge between us. While I might not be completely sure what I want from Tucker, I'm savvy enough to understand more distance isn't it.

"Have you ever been in love?" I ask Jag while we idle on the side of the road and my gaze is glued to Tucker as she tugs her suitcase toward the front entrance of the building.

"Yes," Jay says.

"What did it feel like?"

"At the start, it was all-consuming. Couldn't get enough. Needed to be with her all the time. Love is a drug, and your high is the other person."

The door closes on Tucker's building, and I settle into my seat. I just spent a whole week without Tucker, and I was fine. Missed her a bit. Same as I would any friend. Whatever this protective instinct I have toward her is, I'm relieved to hear it's not the start of something dangerous. The time I spend with Tucker is a want, not a need. A simple but important distinction. I've got nothing to worry about.

"Let's head home," I say.

# Chapter Eighteen

## MAREN

Sawyer swirls the wine in her glass and breathes out a deep sigh. I've just finished rehashing the camping trip, which led me to go to Boston for a week. I left in such a rush that I didn't explain anything to anyone, and it feels good to get my situation off my chest.

"To summarize," Sawyer says, "things are weird with you and Enzo, and it's possible things are even weirder between you and the youngest Summerset."

"Things *were* weird between me and Brice, but going to see Enzo clarified the whole situation for me." Sort of. Not really.

"How so?"

"I'm lonely," I say. "I've spent almost five years with Enzo, and it's been hard to have him gone for so long. Brice being affectionate and attentive filled a need. That's all."

"Going to see Enzo was a good choice, then?"

"Yes." Another lie. The strain that seems to live between us since he appeared at my bedside in Chile was still there, and every time Enzo tried to touch me, I tensed up. We slept in the same room, but the king-size bed might as well have been an ocean with us on separate shores.

"Great." Sawyer pours me another glass of wine. "When is he coming back to the island? Or are you two going to try for a fresh start in Boston? I'd miss you."

Enzo had floated the idea of moving permanently to Boston, but I told him I couldn't commit to that when I was in the middle of a major fundraiser for the Alzheimer's Society. When he accused me of using that as an excuse, I had a hard time defending myself. The life I want is here on the island, and I'd be abandoning all the charities I work for. Enzo can do his work from anywhere, and while I could start over elsewhere, I don't want to. Another impasse between us. The life that came together so easily after graduation is falling apart at my feet.

"I'm not being honest." I release a sigh and cradle my head in my hands. "He's not coming back here any time soon. I have no plans to go there again. I just don't want anyone pushing me about divorce. We'll figure our marriage out." I have no idea how when we seem to want different things, but I'm not giving up because things are temporarily really hard. Even though I couldn't bring myself to let Enzo too close, we enjoyed each other's company when we steered clear of any mention of what's gone wrong between us. "The Brice part is true, though. It's not him I want. He inspires feelings I miss. That's all."

"That's a contradiction."

"He's a shameless flirt, and I'm not too proud to admit I like the attention. That's all it is. I'm sure of it."

"As long as *you're* sure." The skepticism in her voice is impossible to ignore, but I'm not addressing it.

Being around Brice has become easy, and being with Enzo is hard, but that doesn't mean the easy path is the right one. In fact, when given a choice between an easy route and a hard one during training, I almost always pick the hard one. The end result feels earned, and I'm convinced that'll be true here too. I'm married to Enzo, and hard or not, that's the path I'm meant to walk.

---

After I returned to the island yesterday and spent last night drinking wine with Sawyer, today I'm back to meetings for my various charity boards and a cocktail party to drum up funds for the Alzheimer's Society tonight. InterFlix wanted to shoot some promotional material for the season, so the board opted to piggyback off their need by making the streaming service a feature of a cocktail party. Get drunk. Be on TV. It's a win-win for almost everyone. We draw in more people, and those people have a chance at possibly appearing on an international platform.

The team trained without me earlier this morning, and before I slipped into my pale-ocean-blue dress for the event, I considered texting Brice. We didn't talk while I was gone, and I've been hesitant to reach out since I returned. My life felt like it was on the edge of tipping into something I'd never want it to be when I left, and while I'm certain I've got my head in a better place now, pursing even a training partnership with Brice is a bad idea. It would be too easy to become confused.

Unlike the last fundraiser, I arrive early to help with organization and to meet with Hye Jin, the InterFlix producer who tried to prod salacious details of my life out of me last time. We greet each other like old friends because I understand how this game is supposed to be played, especially in public. I was raised on appearances. I'm facing the main set of doors, and Hye Jin is chatting to me when I catch sight of a familiar profile. My heart kicks.

*Hello, Temptation.*

The thought pops into my head before I have a chance to censor myself, but he looks sinfully handsome in his expertly tailored dark-blue suit. A hue that would go well with my lighter ocean shade, as though we'd planned it. Something of what I'm feeling must register on my face because Hye Jin turns to follow my gaze. Whatever I've shown her is a mistake, and I can only hope the cameraman who is circulating wasn't savvy enough to pick up on the shift in the atmosphere.

She rotates back to me on her heel, and I tear my gaze from Brice before he notices. I should have arranged to see him before now. Stupid. Things are going to be awkward between us, and it'll be caught on camera for the world to dissect later. Anything that helps them build a juicy narrative will be ripe for the picking. And then my husband will be forced to pick it apart. Being painted as a cheater would be my worst nightmare.

"He's delicious, isn't he?" Hye Jin smiles. "This fantastic mishmash of all the types of men women love. The rake. The tattooed bad boy. The caring family man. That photo of him and Princess Grace is enough to melt the coldest heart."

"He's worked hard for his place on the team." The reminder of the photo, coupled with Brice's admission he wants kids some day, does funny things to my stomach.

"The camera is going to eat him up on the course."

Or eat him alive. That's the only reason I'm willing to subject myself to the potential scrutiny.

"You said you just returned from a trip to Boston to see your husband?" Hye Jin says.

"Yes," I say. "I was there for a week."

"After coming off a fairly intense training exercise with Prince Brice, is that right?"

"I wouldn't call it intense. Three days of camping and hiking is nothing. Preparation everyone on the team will be doing, but as the coach, I was the right person to lead him."

"Of course," she says, with a hint of a smile. "I wasn't suggesting otherwise."

When I glance up, Brice is staring at me while someone is talking to him. I can't decide if calling him over would make what Hye Jin suspects better or worse.

"What did you say your husband is doing in Boston, again?" She peers at me with what feels like false sincerity.

I'm torn between honesty and protection. InterFlix would have no trouble digging up the truth if they asked the right people questions. Confess or deflect?

"A business opportunity," Brice says from beside me. "Some investor in one of his YouTube endeavors. Did I get that right?" Brice turns to me for confirmation, and his presence brings an instant comfort.

"Yes," I say, and his familiar scent wafts toward me, and I long to inch closer, breathe him in. One glance across the room, and he's here at my side, reading my mind. He's relaxed and either a much better actor than me, or he didn't spend most of the last week pondering what we'd been inching toward with each other. If I could get myself under control, we might be able to turn Hye Jin away from the taste of scandal. There won't be one, but I'm aware they can edit content any way they want.

"Would InterFlix consider YouTube a direct or indirect competitor? It would seem like there would be some overlap in viewership." Brice sips his mixed drink, and when he shifts almost imperceptibly closer, my shoulders lower, and the tension eases out of me. His impeccable royal training is definitely coming in handy right now.

While she launches into an explanation about the differences between the two companies and their philosophies, I tune them out. Or I try to. Brice keeps drawing me into the conversation as though it's normal for us to stand around debating such things.

One of the camera operators lowers their camera to whisper something in Hye Jin's ear, and she perks up. At the entrance are Queen Aurora and King Alexander, and tonight, they haven't brought Grace. They ooze elegance and money, even more than the rest of the people present. I suppose that's the point.

"I'll have to circle back to you two again later," she says to us. "We'd love to get some footage of the king and queen before they're otherwise engaged."

"Of course," Brice says. "My brother would love to speak to you."

Somehow I doubt that's true. King Alexander's dislike of the press is fairly well known around Bellerive, but he also allowed Brice to do this. He would have weighed the costs and benefits of having the youngest son of a dying king on an international streaming service.

Just the thought makes my heart ache for Brice.

Once Hye Jin is gone, I try to step around Brice to get another drink, but he places his hand on my lower back, and his lips brush my earlobe. It's an intimacy I never would have expected from him in public, but the king and queen coupled with the InterFlix cameras have stolen everyone's attention for a moment.

"When this is done," he says, "come climb with me."

"Brice." His name is filled with every reason I've given myself over the last week not to spend time with him alone anymore. We were getting too close and comfortable with each other. For him, it might be flirting, but for me, if I get confused, it's my marriage on the line. The stakes are nothing to him and everything to me.

"You left me for a week," he says.

"I left the *island* for a week."

Our gazes are locked, and I hope everyone is still focused on the front entrance. He won't ask again; I can feel it. If I don't agree to climb with him tonight, that'll be the end of our secret trainings, the end of whatever is jumping between us right now. The smart choice is to say no.

"Text me when you leave," I say.

He nods and steps away from me, disappearing back into the crowd and ensuring that whatever narrative Hye Jin might want to build isn't made easier by our apparent closeness. Though I hate admitting it, there's something attractive about Brice understanding this world, this high-profile life without me having to explain any of it. He inserted himself into an awkward conversation to help me, waited until people are distracted to touch me, and then he slipped away to avoid suspicion once we'd come to an agreement.

Two hours later, I watch him say his goodbyes and take his leave out the front door. From across the room, I lose sight of him, and then my phone vibrates in my clutch. I don't need to check it to know it's him.

A familiar fire lights in my belly, and I make my excuses to head for the door. My biggest concern isn't that I've given in so easily to training with him again. It's what else I'll find it easy to say yes to.

The longer I'm around him, the more dangerous the situation becomes. Feelings don't understand they can't grow unchecked in forbidden places.

But when our gazes were locked, something stirred in me that had been buried for a week, and instead of being surprised by its return, I was relieved.

In Boston, I didn't train, and I didn't talk to Brice. The edges of misery had snuck into my peripheral vision, and I'd wondered whether the happiness that had started to push out those low feelings over the last few months had been in my imagination. Thankfully, it wasn't.

Happiness can still grow in me; I just have to figure out what it looks like and tend it well.

## Chapter Nineteen

### BRICE

The conference table is full. Two days from now, my father is set to die, and today, everyone on the business side of the royal empire is meeting to go over press releases, public relations strategies, funeral arrangements, and a discussion of the king's will. We've reviewed a lot of this too many times to count, but no one wants a royal mistake on something this high profile.

The thing about being royal, the part I've never liked, is the thin line between the Summersets as a business or political entity and us as a family. We're never wholly in either category no matter what we're doing. Nick and I couldn't go to Vegas and completely ignore the implications of our actions. We weren't just two idiots going viral on a social media platform. We were representatives of the royal family, diplomats for an entire country. Where Nick and I sometimes rebelled against the weight of that, Alex mostly accepted it.

Prior to his relationship with Rory, I used to have issues with how detached and unemotional Alex was about everything. Meeting Rory and having Grace seems to have softened him in ways that were needed. Throughout my father's brief reign, he made the tough calls as a leader and a politician, but he tried to weigh the consequences with empathy.

I used to think my father was making the tough but right call in establishing the assisted suicide law. With the reality of it staring me in the face, I'm keenly aware of how hard it is to let go of anyone you love.

Everyone is talking around me. Across the table, Julia has her hand on Nick's shoulder. He drags his palms down his face, and his exhaustion is palpable. At the head of the table is Alex, and to his right is Rory. While they don't appear to be touching, they check in with each other frequently, leaning in to confer on one thing or another. Even my mother has her sister sitting next to her, clutching her hand while my mother periodically wipes away tears.

Then there's me. My friends and acquaintances dot the island and expand across the world, but I couldn't bring myself to ask to have someone in this room. Brent or Posey would have shown up for me if I'd asked, but the royal PR machine frowns on having people in the room who aren't directly related to the family. Confidentiality issues, according to those in charge of such things.

Still, as I examine my family, I think it might be nice to have someone beside me, holding my hand.

---

Since Tucker returned from Boston a few weeks ago, we've kept a polite distance. Still training together regularly, but I keep my hands to myself. She didn't want whatever was building between us, and I value her place in my life too much to push for more than she can give. Eventually, she'd hate me for it, and if there's one thing I've learned, I enjoy Maren Tucker much more when she doesn't dislike me.

We'd been planning to climb tonight for almost a week to take my mind off what's happening tomorrow. I've missed a few of the group trainings lately because of other royal obligations and spending time with my father. I've been trying to soak up as much as I can—we all have—but that's made it harder in some ways. He's had a lot of good days this last week, and we've spent a lot of time reminiscing. He speaks about me, Nick, and Alex with so much love and affection that it's hard to imagine those pieces of my history vanishing with him tomorrow.

When the door to the barn opens and Tucker steps in, I'm glad I didn't cancel. I almost did. Wallowing in a bottle of tequila and staring at the ceiling had a distinct appeal to it. I suspect I'll definitely be doing those things tomorrow.

But for tonight, the sight of her fit frame coming through the door releases the tension in my chest enough that I can breathe. She stops for a beat to examine me, and then she sets her water bottle on a table near the door before she closes the distance between us. Her cool hands slide across my cheeks, and it's the first time I can remember her touching me first, with no connection to training or critique of my form involved. She rises on her toes, and she presses her forehead to mine. I close my eyes, breathing in her faint peach scent, and I slide my hands around her waist while she loops hers around my neck. We hold each other in silence, breathing almost in sync. Neither of us moves, and I lose track of how long we stand like that, but it's a level of comfort I didn't even know I could get from a simple hug. She knew exactly what I needed, and we didn't exchange a single word.

"How did you know?" I murmur.

"Because it's what I would have needed," she says.

My heart softens and expands, and I wonder who held her when she needed it after her accident, but I can't bring myself to ask. I suspect I already know the answer, and it'll make me angry, and her sad.

I bury my face in her neck, and I give her an extra squeeze, drawing her tight against me. She sighs into my ear, and it's the loveliest sound I've ever heard. So much satisfaction and understanding in one tiny noise.

The barn door opens, and Jag and Gary wander in. Even though I don't want to, I release her. She steps away, and her normally pale cheeks are pink. I brush a strand of her hair back with my thumb, and I realize we've cracked the window between us again. Whereas I've been careful not to touch her, that long hug is going to be tough to recover from. My desire to be close to her will have to be consciously reigned in.

Maintenance changed out all the hand and footholds yesterday, and she retrieves her water bottle before going to stand in front of the wall. Unsure of what to do with myself, I sweep my own bottle off the floor.

"Where are you starting?" she asks.

I gesture to the far side as I squirt water into my mouth. There's something weird happening in my chest, and I can't decide if I like it or if it's fucking scary. But every time I glance at Tucker, a flood of warmth rushes over me. It's not the sexual kind of temperature shift—I'm very familiar with that. Instead, it's something bigger, as though I could part the seas to give safe passage only to her. This roaring protectiveness is coupled with an overwhelming tenderness that I've managed to keep in check up until now, but it won't be contained for much longer if we return to any sort of physical contact. Being close to her is fine, but there seems to be something primal awakened in me the minute we touch.

Perhaps it's a good thing we'll never have sex. This surge of intimacy even without sex can't be normal. People don't feel this way about others without the involvement of an orgasm, and not just the kind you give yourself while thinking about said person.

At least my preoccupation with her makes it easier to forget about everything else. When she's in a room, there doesn't feel like there *is* anything else.

She's at the far side of the wall, and she glances over her shoulder at me. I'm rooted to the spot where our overly long hug occurred, as though I can somehow reverse time.

"You coming?"

*Oh, I will be.* The thought causes me to stifle a grin, and she cocks her head in response.

"What's so funny?"

"Nothing." I go to her side while Jag and Gary are getting ready to belay us. "You climbing beside me tonight?"

She looks up at me, and my heart does that funny thing in my chest again. I can't resist, and I smooth down her hair and I place a lingering kiss against her temple. She wraps her arms around my middle, and we stand pressed against each other for a few beats. Then Gary coughs, and I release a sigh before stepping back. Appearances matter to Tucker, even if I don't give a fuck. No need to have Gary running his mouth, even if it's just to other staff members, about how close we've gotten.

"You okay with me climbing beside you?" she asks as she steps into her harness.

"Only if you climb slightly ahead of me too. The view is better."

She slaps my arm, and I laugh. But my comment does what I wanted; it cuts the intimacy, the tender closeness that's been cultivated since the moment she walked into the barn tonight.

Having her here makes the sadness lessen, but I don't want her presence to cause something just as dire to increase. Whatever this weird feeling is in my chest, I have to keep it in check.

For the next few hours, we navigate various routes along the wall, challenging each other and poking fun at each other's mistakes.

At the end of the session, Gary and Jag have stepped outside to get some air, and Tucker hesitates at the door. "Do you have someone for tomorrow? I mean, I know you have a lot of friends…"

"I'll be fine." The reminder causes the cloud to descend over my mood once more, and I'm sure we both know I'm lying. But I can't ask Tucker to be there. That would be insanity for so many reasons. She can't be the person holding my hand because she already gave her hand to someone else.

"If you need someone—"

"I've got lots of someones, Tucker. You don't need to worry about me."

She bites her lip and searches my face. Then she places her water bottle on the table again, and she envelops me in another hug, rising onto her toes to drag me tight against her.

"You don't ever have to pretend with me, okay? You don't have to pretend. You call me if you need me." Then she kisses my cheek, grabs her water bottle, and she's out the door before I have a chance to sink into her one more time.

The air around me contains the faintest scent of peach, but it's the loss of warmth, more than anything else, that signals her departure.

---

I'm not sure what made everyone decide some sort of twilight send-off to my father was the best course of action, but it's meant I've spent the entire day watching the clock and dreading what was to come. Breakfast with my father where I tried not to think of it as the last while also memorizing every little movement and gesture, cataloguing each expression on his face, trying to record the sound of his soft chuckle in my memory. Surreal and terrifying.

Then I went for a run. I ran and ran and ran, but one side effect of all the training I've been doing is that it's becoming harder and harder to exhaust myself.

Truthfully, the day wouldn't have been any better if the time had been set for the crack of dawn. Today was always going to be a day that felt too fast and too slow.

The leaving ceremony, as my mother dubbed it, is taking place in my parents' suite of rooms. Instead of their bedroom, an adjacent room with a spectacular, unobstructed view of the ocean has been set up with everything Dad needs. It's a massive space, but when I walk in the door an hour before my father is to be served his final cocktail via IV, I'm stunned at the number of people milling around. Maybe I shouldn't be. We've always had to share our father with the rest of the country. Why would now be any different? Likely at one of the various meetings where I only partially listened, this chain of events was discussed, but it's unnerving to have to put on my royal face when I really just want to be a boy about to lose his father.

Uncle Augustus, my father's youngest brother, spots me from across the room, and he gestures for me to come to his side. I don't know what the next hour will hold, but I understand what comes after that, even if I can't fathom what it'll feel like.

The next time I leave this room, my father will truly be gone.

# Chapter Twenty

## MAREN

I've been for a run, a swim, and a bike ride. The combination of the three activities back-to-back, given the distances I put in, should be enough to exhaust me, but I'm still wired. Everywhere I've gone today, I've carried my phone, turned to the highest volume in case Brice calls. Three quarters of me is sure he won't, but there's still that one remaining quarter that suspects he might, even if he has to drunk dial me.

Last night, I couldn't resist consoling him. When I stepped through the barn door, and I saw the expression on his face, I remembered what it was like to be that low, that in need of comfort. My heart ached for him, and I broke all the personal space rules I'd firmly established since I returned from Boston. No touching without a reason, no unnecessary close contact, no spikes of hard-to-control feelings. Impossible to be tempted when you keep temptation at bay.

Seeing his face last night burned down all those defenses. There was no way I wasn't giving him what I would have needed in his place. Warmth, love, and reassurance. But the contact has opened a valve in me, and I don't know if I can wrench it closed again.

My phone pings on the coffee table, and I snatch it up. A text from Nathaniel. When I click on it, my heart sinks. He's linked a breaking news article from the *Bellerive Bullet* that indicates the former king passed away peacefully surrounded by his family. All the funeral details are already laid out for public consumption, and although Brice and I never discussed it, I can't even imagine how much those meetings gutted him.

For most of us, King George was a, sometimes, imposing figure at the center of political decisions or island-wide controversies. A public figure who symbolizes wealth and power but who didn't rate much more thought, at least from me, until now.

Brice has told me enough over the last few months, in bits and pieces, for me to realize King George was also a loving father. An awful loss. I close my eyes and fall back onto the couch with my phone still clutched in my hand.

My miscarriage sent me into a grief spiral, but the news that came on the heels of it was really what caused me to bore so low. The harsh reality is something I try not to dwell on too deeply. Enzo and I went to so many specialists, and every single one offered the same grim reality. No amount of positive thinking can overcome something a body just wasn't meant to do. Before I can get sucked too deeply into that train of thought, my phone starts to ring.

The trill of my ringtone makes me jump, and I fumble to sit up, checking the caller ID. It's anonymous, which could mean anything. When I answer, there's a beat of dead space, and my heart sinks. Figures I'd get a telemarketer when I'm primed for someone else.

"Hello?" I try one last time, my tone hinting at annoyance.

"Maren Tucker, please," King Alexander says.

I'm stunned for a beat, and then I say, "This is she."

"My wife tells me that you and my brother, Brice, have grown quite close. As I'm sure you're aware…" He clears his throat. "Our father passed away this evening." There's another lengthy pause, and I can hear Queen Aurora in the background offering to take the phone.

"Maren," Queen Aurora says. "Hi. We're all worried about Brice. He's been telling everyone he's fine and refusing any support. As I'm sure you can appreciate, *fine* is not really something any of them are right now."

"Yes." It's the only thing I can think to say as my mind spins on Brice grieving alone. "He—he hasn't called me, if that's what you're wondering."

"He won't," she says. "Posey and Brent tried. We've all tried. Alex even suggested calling some of the buddies he goes to Vegas with—which I thought was a bad idea, but desperate times and all that. Then Nick wondered whether Brice might agree to see you?"

"He might not want to see me either." There's a tight knot in my chest. Part of me is desperate to go, but another part of me can see the danger in continuing to cultivate this closeness. On top of that, Brice isn't the one calling for help. Our private encounters are usually carefully crafted, as though neither of us wants to put a foot wrong. "I can text him and ask."

"If there's one thing I can say with absolute certainty about the Summerset men, it's that they need someone who shows up for them." Aurora groans. "That sounds like I'm advocating something I'm not. I know you're married. I'm just." She sighs. "If you text him, he'll tell you he's fine."

"You want me to come to the estate."

"If you can. If you're willing. If not, that's okay." There's a pause on the line. "I can always call one of his drinking and gambling buddies. There are—there are other options."

It's silly for me to be resistant when they're telling me he needs help, and I know from personal experience how isolating grief can be when not enough people notice.

"I'll be there soon," I say.

---

It's late, but the front entrance is bursting with press. The first time I drive past the main gates, I'm not sure I should attempt to go through the cameras and reporters. The last thing I need is a story in the Bellerive gossip pages about me and Brice. There have already been a few about our public training sessions. Nothing salacious, but it could so easily go there.

There must be a secondary entrance for deliveries or events, but I've never used it. After I've passed the estate entrance for the second time, and I'm starting to worry about appearing suspicious, I pull onto the side of the road, and I search for Jag's number in my contacts.

He answers on the first ring and proceeds to give me detailed instructions about another entrance, which has to be unlocked and opened by hand. I hang up with him, and I inch along the side road, looking for the concealed entrance that Jag assured me was in amongst the bushes. In the end, it's not the entrance I see but Jag waving his cell phone like a flashlight.

The driveway is narrow and partially covered with shrubs and bushes. I'm really hoping I don't end up with scratches across my paint job. Once I'm through the gate, Jag comes to the passenger's side and opens the door wide enough to squeeze in beside me.

"This entrance is for deliveries?" I ask once he's buckled in.

"No," he says. "It's for other things."

There's something about the way he says it that makes me think "other things" are clandestine meetings, perhaps for the princes. The idea turns my stomach. A silly reaction. The internet is rife with proof of the very colorful life Brice led before he started training for the adventure race. That life is exactly why I didn't particularly like him before. But he hasn't turned out to be anything like I expected or assumed based on what I'd seen and read.

Doesn't mean he won't go right back to being the guy I believed him to be as soon as training is done. I'm not sure how to reconcile the two versions of him that live inside my head. For now, I don't have to.

"I guess I should be glad I haven't been relegated to this entrance before."

"It was discussed," Jag says in his usual gruff tone.

"Oh?" I come to a fork in the gravel drive and gesture for help.

"Left."

"And why was that dismissed?"

"Nothing to hide, according to Prince Brice."

It should bring me a measure of comfort to hear he's told others the truth. I'm his coach, and somewhere along the line, we became friends. Nothing shameful there. But every once in a while, guilt pinches at me over how close I've gotten to him, how much I welcome his attention when I shouldn't.

"How is he?" I ask.

"About how you'd expect. Unraveling at the seams and hoping no one notices the holes."

The description, so close to how I've felt more than once, cuts me to the quick.

"I'm glad they called you. Some of his friends ... they would have tried to stitch the holes with gambling, alcohol, and women."

"That's one way to cope," I whisper, thinking of when I found him at the climbing wall on the estate, drunk on tequila.

"Used to be the only way."

This is, perhaps, the longest conversation Jag and I have had since Brice and I began training together. Most of the time, any discussions we have revolve around safety concerns or timing. It makes sense that he'd know Brice—having spent so much time with him—but I'm surprised he's offering me any of his observations. I'm tempted to ask him whether the secret entrance is still used regularly.

"Did Brice ever tell you why he wanted to do this adventure race?" The few times I've asked him, he's been evasive.

"You mean besides avoiding what was happening with his dad?" Jag stares out the side window.

My heart contracts at his honesty. I've always suspected the training was a form of coping, which is exactly like me.

"That's a good enough reason."

"The other part—" Jag gives me a slight smile. "Is that he wanted to best you. Was dying to prove you wrong."

"We didn't exactly get along."

"But now," Jag says as though I didn't say anything, "I think he wants to impress you. Two sides of the same coin—just the motivation has changed."

"I'm sure he's always trying to impress someone." My comment is flippant to combat the way his claim made my chest swell with an emotion I don't want to name.

"He's never had to work so hard for it." Jag rubs his chin. "If I had to guess, I'd say he's enjoyed the challenge."

Without meaning to, I tighten my grip on the steering wheel. There's something about being told I'm a challenge that grates on me. Enzo told me that when we first started dating. While I always say I was a puddle at his feet at first glance, he never felt like I was. The last thing I need is to start feeling any kind of anything for another man seeking a challenge.

Not that I'm feeling anything. Going to Boston established I miss love and attention and affection. None of that is about Brice, specifically.

Jag sends me to a parking spot marked for staff, even though my vehicle isn't the kind a staff member, however well paid, would drive.

Since I've never been to Brice's suite of rooms before, Jag walks with me, navigating through the maze of rooms and corridors, but he's done telling secrets, which is fine by me. All I need to know is that Brice tells people we have nothing to hide, and we don't. I haven't done a single thing to feel ashamed or embarrassed about when it comes to him. Friends behave the way we behave around each other.

Jag stops outside a heavy wooden door before drawing it open. "He'll be in his room. Third door on the right. If he won't let you in, just come back here and I'll escort you out."

"Right." I'd forgotten there was even a chance he wouldn't see me. A nervous sweat breaks out across my palms, and I slide them along my thighs as I walk.

At the third door, I glance toward Jag, but the door to the suite of rooms is closed now. Knock, and he'll either answer or not. Simple.

But my heart is threatening to pound out of my chest. It's worse than sprints up a hill. With one hand pressed against my heart, I knock with the other one. Someone approaches the door, and I hold my breath, prepared to plead my case or leave him alone. I'm not even sure what's going to come out of my mouth.

When the door draws back, my chest tightens at the mournful expression on his face. Raw, unfiltered grief greets me, and it's the sort of emotion you only show someone you trust. To realize he's not concealing this side of himself, that he'll open the door to me when he wouldn't to others, is a rush. A flood. A torrent of emotion.

I don't know what's going to happen tonight, but it already feels more profound than anything I've ever experienced with anyone else. There's a particular kind of connection between teammates when you know they'd risk life and limb to keep you safe, the same way you would for them. That's powerful, and until now, I've never known there was anything stronger than that.

But there is. I can't name it, and I don't understand it, but what's running between us is a new level of intimacy. Whatever he needs from me tonight, I'll give it to him. Without question. It's what I craved months ago after my fall, and I won't let him down the way I was let down. He might have lots of people who'd happily take my place, but he opened the door for me, and I take that responsibility seriously.

# Chapter Twenty-One

## BRICE

Even before I open the door, something inside of me senses it's her. I can't explain it, and I don't want to think too hard about what that might mean. All I know is that when I swing back the door to my room, and she's standing there with an expression that's part hope and part sorrow, I've never been so glad to see someone.

"I don't know what to say," she says. "But I'm here."

"You don't have to say anything." My throat is raw from trying to hold back my tears. "I'm glad you're here."

I couldn't bring myself to call her, and I'm not sure who told her. Even though leaning on her as hard as I'll likely lean tonight is dangerous for our training partnership, potentially lethal for our friendship, I want her here. The more time we spend together, the more I'm starting to realize I want more from her than she'll ever be able to give me. For whatever reason, she doesn't want to divorce Enzo—maybe she really does love him that much—but she can't deny there's something between the two of us too. Whatever this *something* is, it's powerful. Whenever we're together, it radiates off her, and my chest aches with it. It makes no sense, but it feels like she's supposed to be mine.

*Mine.*

A possessive, dangerous thought that's bound to lead me into trouble. The problem is, I saunter into trouble with my eyes open and a smile on my face. I might not be capable of smiling right now, but I'm definitely aware of what I'm getting myself into by letting her in the door.

She steps into my suite, and she takes my hand, lacing her fingers with mine. At the chairs near the fireplace, she eases me into one.

"I'll get you some water," she says.

But when she tries to leave, I tighten my grip on her hand. She glances at me over her shoulder, and I recognize the indecision in her expression. The right action is to let her go. She can get me a drink and sit in another chair. We can talk like adults and pretend this current between us doesn't exist—hasn't been building for months. Maybe that's what she'd prefer, but none of that will satisfy me tonight.

I tug her into my lap, and she doesn't resist. She wraps her arms around my neck and buries her face in the crook, and we both release a long, pent-up sigh. The weight of her against me somehow lessens the grip of grief that's been almost crushing since Dr. Bennett confirmed my father was gone.

Sometimes I remember what Jag told me a few weeks ago, about love being all-consuming. I'm not there yet, and maybe I won't get there. Our friendship would be so much easier if I didn't. I've been entangled with a few women before—never serious—and those obsessive feelings Jag mentioned have eluded me.

With Tucker, I didn't call her to come tonight. I didn't ask her to be there today. She's a want, not a need.

But God help me, as I breathe in her peach shampoo, I understand it's getting to the point where I don't *want* to be without her. It's going to take every last scrap of willpower I possess to keep the blurry line between us still visible when she's literally in my bedroom.

Technically, she hasn't cheated on Enzo, but would I be okay with what's been happening between me and Tucker if I was her other half? Not a fucking chance. No way. I also wouldn't be in America when my wife needed me either. Those are observations I won't be voicing. Any time I bring him up, she slides away from me, as though the mere reminder of him is enough to make her crave distance from me.

I don't want any distance tonight.

"Do you want to talk about it?" she asks.

"I don't know." I'm not sure what I'd say. How do you explain what it's like to watch someone you love die? It's not something anyone can understand until they experience it.

There's no way empathy can extend that far. The entire day has been awful and permanent and soul crushing.

"What do you need?"

Instead of telling her, I scoop her tighter against me, and I rise to my feet. On my way to the bed, her arms grow tense around my neck.

"Brice," she whispers.

The way Tucker says my name, I get the sense that if I pushed her at all, she'd give in to me, that maybe she'd want to explore what's been building between us too. The idea of burying myself in her and forgetting today happened is really fucking tempting. But I haven't had a drop of alcohol—despite the fact that I thought I'd be drunk by now—so my judgment isn't poor enough to blow up my life even more. Whether or not she'd say yes doesn't change the fact she'd regret it. Hate me for asking. Hate herself for agreeing. One night would destroy us.

The Brice I was before Maren Tucker entered my life would have been out drinking, gambling, and fucking these feelings away.

This Brice, the one who has Tucker cradled in his arms, who's going to lay her on the king-sized bed and resist the urge to run his lips across every inch of her skin, just wants to lie beside her and feel it all. I don't want to run from any of this when I've got her.

"That's not what this is, Tucker." I mean, it *could* be, but I'm not stupid enough to ask or imply. "I just want you beside me."

When I lay her on the bed, there are goose bumps on her arms, and the expression on her face is hard to read. I crawl up her body, and she runs her hands along my arms to clutch my biceps. We're face-to-face with her underneath me, and I'm tempted to kiss her. Skim my lips across hers, coax her to respond. My body aches with desire. I want to cradle her ass in my hand, press my erection against her core, and hear her moan in pleasure as I grind against her. Her breath hot in my ear, my name on her lips, the scent of peaches swirling around us.

"Brice," she says.

Except there's nothing sexy about the uncertainty in her voice this time. I'm on the cusp of fucking things up between us, and while I might be too deep in my own complex feelings to recognize what I'm so close to doing, Maren isn't.

I move to the side of her, and I lie on my stomach with my head against my crossed arms, and she turns her head to look at me, but she doesn't shift her body toward mine. We're still in the danger zone, where one wrong move might set us both on fire.

Without her body as a distraction, thoughts of my dad creep in—the room, the bed, what he said to me before they put him under—and tears prick at the back of my eyelids. I pinch the bridge of my nose hard to keep the tears at bay. Perhaps alcohol, gambling, and sex would have been the better bet. All these feelings for her and for my dad are going to wreck me.

Tucker turns onto her side, and she swings her leg over mine. While she rests her cheek on my bicep, her palm makes circles on my back over my T-shirt, but she doesn't say anything. Unable to resist, I kiss the top of her head.

I used to think reserved people were a bit boring, and I certainly didn't think Tucker's brand of quiet confidence was anything to brag about. How wrong I was. There is no one else I'd rather spend tonight with. Her ability to be in a room without demanding anything from me is actually pretty special. Rare, even. Since I'm usually so switched on, most people don't like me the way Tucker does. She laughs at my brashness, but she almost seems to relish these silent moments more, where part of me seems to speak to part of her on an entirely different wavelength.

"You won't always feel like this," she says. "But it's a long, rough road."

She probably means the grief over my father, but I've slipped into thoughts of her again, as though considering the magnitude of my father's death is too much to process. It is. My world has changed—altered forever—and I don't know what our family or my foundation looks like going forward. No matter what I've done, I always knew my father would be in my corner, perhaps with some level of disapproval, but still *there*.

"You know the last thing he said to me?" My throat tightens, and I'm not sure I'll be able to get the words out. He spent a few minutes alone with each of us before they started the IV drugs.

She gazes at me, and her blue eyes that I once considered ice chips are as open and clear as a pale-blue sky in the middle of summer.

"He said he was going to miss me." My unshed tears make her blurry. "Strange, isn't it? To think he might miss me when there's this gaping hole in my life now."

"I believe all the souls we're meant to meet never really leave our life," she says.

The way she phrases it makes me think she's talking about more than just my dad. I scrub my tears against my crossed arms, willing myself to stem the tide. If I really start crying, I'm not sure how I'll stop.

"You're going to think I have a screw loose, I'm sure." There's a hint of a smile in her tone. "Or I'm secretly some new age hippie, but I've spent a not insignificant amount of time reading about where souls go after someone dies."

"Why?" I keep my voice gentle, but I drill her with my gaze, hopeful she'll tell me.

"I just—" She flushes. "I just needed it."

"It helped?"

"Yeah." She shifts her focus to her hand that's still rotating around my back. "It helped."

Since I can't get either of my arms free to comfort her without causing her to disentangle herself from me, I give her another kiss on top of her head.

"Are you this affectionate with everyone?" she asks.

"Yes." Mostly true. I don't tend to plant kisses all over my platonic friends, but I'm quick with a hug, an arm draped around a shoulder, a high five. Not what she means, I'm sure. But I'm not admitting anything that'll cause her to move away from me. Either way, I'm grateful for the subject change.

"You aren't like—maybe I shouldn't plant kisses all over my friends?"

"Nah, the opposite actually. I'm all about free love." I give her a playful grin. "A kiss for you. Another for you. One more for you." I let my lips linger on the top of her head again. "My friends like it."

"Brent enjoys it?"

"Loves it." I almost say he isn't as keen when I do it to Posey, but that steers us in a direction I'd rather not go.

She lets out a little laugh and snuggles closer. "As long as you do this to everyone."

"My lips know no limits." She's molded so tightly against me that I can feel almost every inch of her.

"Wild and free forever."

"Doesn't sound so bad, does it?"

Tucker is quiet for a long time, and I wonder whether I said something wrong. Maybe she's thinking about how she was wild and free until she tied herself to the lead weight of Enzo. Every time I remember that, it makes me mad. I can't imagine having actually done it.

Her stomach rumbles, and I arch my eyebrows at her. "You hungry?" I don't want to move, but I'm not sure about the altered temperature between us. A chill sneaked in, and perhaps a change of scene will return the warmth to the air.

"You have enough to worry about," she says. "I can eat when I get home."

"Not a chance," I say. "It'll be my pleasure to feed you."

Or it would be if I could feed her whatever I wanted. Mutual pleasure—I'd make sure of it.

Before I can lock onto the image and embarrass myself, I clamber off the bed, and she follows behind me, straightening her clothes. I hold out my hand, and she stares at it for a minute before sliding her palm against mine. We've held hands before, but tonight is different. Seems like we both sense it.

She trails behind me as I lead her to a second door in my bedroom. It opens into a hallway that takes us directly to another hallway, which leads to the royal kitchen. As a kid, I thought my suite of rooms were the best because of this secret second door.

The kitchen is at the front but off to the side of the palace. Nick and Jules used to sneak down to the wine cellar as teenagers, and then once they were no longer friends, Nick and I did it. There's one window with a view of the front entrance where everyone important is received, which means the kitchen is often a hive of gossip.

This late at night, it'll be deserted. In the morning, Joyce will arrive at the crack of dawn to get breakfast started. Once we've slipped into the space, I only turn on one dim light to avoid suspicion or investigation by security. Then I release Tucker's hand to peer into the cupboards.

"Are you going to cook me something?" Tucker asks.

"I wouldn't do that to you." I close the cupboard door and frown. "Unless you want me to? I make a mean Mr. Noodle."

"Likely going to pass on that." She lets out a soft laugh. "I haven't had that since college. You really don't need to feed me. I'll be fine until I get home."

Except I don't want her to go home. The thought of her leaving makes desperation spider across my chest. "There must be something edible." I yank open the freezer, and there, as glorious as the sunrise, is a frozen package of Rory's scones. How they've slipped by unnoticed, I have no idea, but I'm not going to question this gift.

"Scones," I say, holding up the package, triumphant. "I bet there's jam and cream in the fridge too." I tuck the frozen treats under my arm, and I rummage around in the industrial-sized fridge until I find the toppings. "We can defrost these in my room."

"Oh," Tucker says, and she bites her lip. "I should probably get home. Maybe?"

"Eat some scones with me," I say. "Can't send you home hungry. Would make me a terrible host." The words—my father would never forgive me—die on my lips. I stare at the jam and cream in my hands, at a loss.

Tucker's fingertips skim the edges of my hair, and when I glance up, she's staring at me with such tenderness. "You gonna let me have some this time?"

"One," I say. "Two if you're lucky."

"Sounds like a deal." And then she takes the jam and cream from my hands, and she leads us back to my room as though she's been doing it for years.

# Chapter Twenty-Two

## MAREN

If there is one thing that I absolutely cannot resist, it's a wounded Brice. *God, my heart*. Every time he glances in my direction, and it's clear he's thinking about his father, my heart cracks open like a Cadbury Creme Egg. An ooey gooey mess of feeling to match his.

Until my accident, I wasn't like this. Before, I used to think bad things happened and people just got on with their life, as though there could never possibly be long-term consequences or feelings that lingered long after the physical wounds healed. Now that I know better, watching Brice struggle causes every nurturing fiber I have in me to swell in response. I want to wrap him in a big blanket of my affection and never let him go.

We've defrosted the scones in his microwave, and he's slathered cream and jam on them. When we were camping, we didn't have the spreads, and I have to admit, it makes the scones next-level amazing.

While I eat them, I occasionally catch a sheen of tears across his eyes, and he'll pinch the bridge of his nose. He ate one and now seems to be done, which isn't like him. I'm not sure if I should lay into his grief or avoid it, as he clearly wants. At some point, talking about his feelings will be important for him to process them, but it took me months and medication to get there. Hard to criticize anyone's process with my history.

In my frazzled emotional state today, I didn't eat very much, and I reach for my third scone on the coffee table between the armchairs.

"Will you come to the funeral?" Brice's elbows are on his knees, and he's staring at the carpet between his feet.

My chest tightens at the request. *Yes* comes to my lips almost immediately, but I need to be sure what's he's asking and the implications.

"As your official guest?" I know enough about royal life to understand the complications with that.

"Yes—or, I don't know. Maybe no." He glances up at me. "Obviously the message we'd be sending the public wouldn't be good."

"What if you invited the whole team? Would that—could you do that?"

He runs his hands down his cheeks and slouches in his chair. "Suppose I could get away with whatever I wanted at this point. They called you, so they're obviously worried about me."

"Alex called me."

"I'd bet on Rory being the driver behind that."

"Nick suggested me."

"Ah, yes." A hint of a smile tugs at the edges of Brice's mouth. "Truthfully, it's nice to know they considered me."

"Brice, it's clear they all love you. Why would you think that?"

He stands up and goes to the bed to sprawl across it again on his stomach. "That's not it, Tucker. They all have lives with other people now."

I leave the rest of the scones on the coffee table to stand at the edge of the bed. I fight the urge to crawl in beside him. "Doesn't mean they've forgotten you."

He rolls onto his side, and he holds out his hand to me. Butterflies take flight in my stomach, and even though I shouldn't, I give him my hand. He tugs me onto the bed beside him, so he's half beside me, half above me. With his fingertips, he tucks my loose strands of hair behind my ears.

"I've always had lots of people around me. Friends, acquaintances, but I've never had a single person I wanted around more than any other."

He spends a lot of time with Brent and Posey and even Nick. But I think I know what he's saying, what he's implying. It's thrilling and terrifying.

"Never?" I whisper, and the air around us crackles. It would be so easy to do the wrong thing here because I'm convinced, at least in the moment, it would feel *very* right.

"Never."

My heart pounds in my chest. With Enzo, I enjoyed how light and easy we were together. There was a lot of joy in our initial relationship. Nothing was ever hard between us, but with Brice, it feels like we're earning every single inch that's drawing us closer. The intensity between us causes me to squeeze his bicep, and I'm not sure if it's a silent plea for more or less of whatever this is. Naked longing for something I shouldn't desire.

"Tucker, can you tell Maren to stop overthinking it?" Brice whispers.

His comment is so unexpected, that it snaps the tension between us, and I let out a nervous laugh. "Sorry, that was silly. I thought you were saying..."

The words die on my lips because of the expression on his face, and I can't get any more out. He *was* saying that.

"You need a twin," he murmurs. "One who isn't married."

A flare of jealousy lights for someone who doesn't even exist. "You probably wouldn't have liked her either."

"I didn't know you. Just like you didn't know me. Now, I think you might be my most favorite person in the whole world."

Everything inside of me ignites, and I want to kiss him or climb him like a mountain or ride him until we both cry out in ecstasy. It's been so long. That thought snaps me back into reality.

I'm a terrible person. Oh, God. What am I doing? I wiggle out from underneath him, and I rush toward the door to put on my shoes.

"I should go. It's late, and—"

"Maren, wait," Brice says. "I'll stop teasing you or flirting with you or whatever. Okay? Just don't go. It's a gut instinct—I flirt with beautiful women. I can't help myself. I'll do an internet search right now for some sort of rehab program for shameless flirts."

His explanation immediately deflates my panic, but it also causes my chest to ache. *He didn't mean any of that?* For a moment, I'm not even sure what to say. I was contemplating cheating on my husband, and to him it was nothing.

Of course it was nothing. What was I expecting? He's told me a million times he doesn't do commitment or long-term relationships. He wants to have a baby with some anonymous woman so he can avoid being attached in that way. I'm not capable of being that woman, even if circumstances were different. We'd never work beyond whatever we are to each other now. Saying pretty things is a reflex for him, nothing to be taken seriously. His autocharm is switched on.

But he almost lured me out of my underwear, and I used to think I was so much better than that. I've become just another woman enticed by his charisma.

"Huh," he says, and he holds up his phone. "Turns out when you type in 'shameless flirt,' I'm the first result. I mean, that has to be some kind of proof."

*Proof that I'm an idiot.*

"Don't go. Please. We can—we can sit in the chairs and talk about politics. Or religion. Or some other subject we're bound to disagree on. Science, maybe? I'll bore you to death with my unproven and unresearched hot takes on whatever you want to discuss."

I'm tempted to tell him that if I stay, we have to talk about things that are real and meaningful, but after our last encounter, I don't even know what that would look like. Maybe he's not truly capable of either.

"Brice."

"Maren."

It annoys me that he's used my name instead of calling me Tucker, as though *I'm* being unreasonable.

"Fine. But I am not getting on that bed again."

"Noted. Nothing comfortable allowed."

I release a deep sigh and drop my shoe onto the mat. "And the rest of the scones are mine."

"Sounds fair," he says, but there's a melancholy edge to his voice, and I'm reminded again of why I'm here in the first place.

We go to the chairs, and as I'm taking my first bite of scone, Brice crosses his arms and slumps into his chair.

"The Advisory Council." He raises his eyebrows in mock challenge. "What do you think of them?"

His tone is already bored, but I'm going to play along. Neither of us needs to steer back into territory that confuses me. At least politics feels relatively safe in comparison.

"I'd disband it all," I say. Might as well start with anarchy. Seems fitting for a night like tonight.

---

When I wake up to an unfamiliar ceiling, I lie very still. Brice and I talked for hours about nothing of significance, and when I finally claimed exhaustion, Brice said I couldn't possibly drive home when I was so tired. He said I could have the bed because he claimed he wasn't tired.

His arm slung across my middle says otherwise.

I inch out from underneath him, and I sneak over to my shoes. As I creep out the door, I take one last look at his sleeping form, and I hate how much my heart contracts at the sight of him.

Instead of going home, I head to Caitlin's office. I don't have an appointment, but it's almost noon. It's rare for me to sleep this late, but since Brice and I were up until the crack of dawn, I must have needed the sleep.

Outside her office, I shoot her a text offering to take her to lunch. She doesn't respond right away, and I tap my fingers on my steering wheel while I contemplate going up to her office and taking my chances she'll be free. Working lunches are a real thing in her law offices.

My phone beeps beside me, and when I glance at it, my stomach drops.

*Enzo.*

Once I've opened the message, I see he's sent me a throwback photo from when we were in college. The memory of the night we took the photo rushes back to me. We were happy, once. So freaking happy. If only I could blink and take us back there.

Before I can reply to him, Caitlin texts me to grab some food and bring it to her office. A quick lunch is all she has time for. She must sense I'm desperate to talk. I am not the sort to drop in without an appointment.

Down the street, I stand in line for a sandwich I won't eat and the wrap I know Caitlin loves from here. The whole time, I keep thinking about Enzo's text, about lying in that bed with Brice last night and wishing for something I shouldn't. What is wrong with me?

Pam, Caitlin's secretary, must be gone for her own lunch when I arrive. Caitlin's office door is open, but she's on the phone. She waves me in while she talks, and I slide her wrap over before taking a seat across from her. My stomach is rioting, and I toy with my wrapped sandwich, as though that might restore the incredible hunger I had last night when I ate through half a dozen scones while chatting to Brice.

"All right," Caitlin says as she drops her phone back on the receiver. "Tell me what's going on." She undoes the wax paper around her wrap and takes a big bite.

"I'm not my father."

"Confirmed," Caitlin says around her mouthful of food. "Who said you were?"

"I almost cheated on Enzo last night." Did I? Even that I'm not sure about. But I think I would have if Brice hadn't been teasing me or flirting with me or whatever he claimed was really happening to get that electrical snap between us. Whether or not he truly meant it, the sexual tension was there.

"With who?" Caitlin's eyes have gone very round.

I bite my lip and shake my head. "That's not important."

"Yes, it is." Caitlin sets her sandwich on the desk. "There's 'I need to get laid' cheating, and then there's 'I'm starting to feel something for someone else' cheating. Which is it?"

"And then Enzo sent me this throwback photo, and I remembered how happy we used to be. So happy. I married him because I believed we'd be happy together forever."

"You went through a traumatizing experience with pretty significant consequences. Neither of you could have seen that coming."

"I'm not a quitter."

"But he seems to be." Caitlin raises her hands when I glare at her. "A few drunken phone calls and some pictures of when you used to be happy aren't a relationship."

"I feel sick," I say, and I leave my uneaten and unwrapped sandwich on her desk.

"Who is tempting you?"

"Brice." I'm sure my expression must read as pained.

"Join the club," Caitlin says. "That man could tempt all the single ladies in Bellerive and at least half the married ones. I think we both know he's not a viable option."

"Right." The tightness in my chest doesn't dissipate, and the implication that Brice can't be taken seriously leaves a sharp sting. Isn't that what he told me last night?

"Excluding him, excluding this notion you'd be a quitter or somehow like your father, what do you want?"

My heart beats an irregular rhythm, and I'm not sure what to say. Enzo is my husband, and we were happy once. But we haven't been happy for a long time. I have no idea if we can be happy again. We certainly can't be happy if he's in Boston and I'm here, and neither of us is willing to change that.

"I think I need to talk to Enzo. Tell him what I need."

"Yes. And if that's a divorce, I'm your lawyer." Caitlin picks up her wrap and takes another bite. "Brice Summerset. He's a walking sin, isn't he? Can't say I blame you with that one. As a rebound, there's no one better, as long as your mother doesn't find out. A detour off the main path for a while wouldn't be so bad."

I snatch my sandwich off her desk, even though I likely won't eat it. Concealing my annoyance is a struggle. Since Brice and I started training together, I've never once told anyone about our secret training sessions, about the nights on the estate, the long evenings in the barn. He's capable of being dedicated to something. But that doesn't mean Caitlin isn't right. He can be the man I've come to know and the one I should never for a second consider being with. As a friend, he's exceptional. He'd probably tell me that himself.

My brain is still a muddle over him. One side of it thinking all those things he said last night were serious and the other side dismissive of every single word. Maren and Tucker at war with each other.

One thing I know for sure is that I need to speak to Enzo. We can't go on like this.

# Chapter Twenty-Three

## BRICE

When I wake up, Maren is gone. Not a trace of her remains except the faintest whiff of peaches on my spare pillow. I groan when I roll over. Why did I have to fall asleep beside her? Stupid. So fucking stupid. I already scared her last night with my "you're my favorite person in the whole wide world" bullshit, even if it's true. She *is* my favorite person. I didn't realize it was true until I was saying it. Then I was glad I said it for about 0.2 seconds before her expression turned to terror, and she leapt off the bed like I'd poured a two-dollar bottle of tequila on her and set her on fire. The mention of alcohol gets my thoughts churning.

If I was pouring tequila, I definitely would have used a top-shelf brand, and once Tucker was wet with it, I would have licked it up, one inch at a time.

I groan again and throw an arm over my face.

It's unbelievable the places my mind goes around her anymore. With other women, I'd welcome these fantasies, maybe even try my luck at having them come true. Any hint of them sends Tucker running—almost literally—for the door.

Given the distance she wedged between us after my comment, it was only natural I'd want to lie on the bed with her for a teeny tiny second. Not long. Just so I didn't feel like I totally fucked things up. She looked so peaceful asleep, as though she didn't have a care in the world, and Maren Tucker never looks like that awake. I watched her sleep for a minute, maybe two, because at some point, I also must have drifted to sleep.

There's got to be something that'll get rid of this cloud hanging over my mood. Maybe I'll go hang out with Dad for a bit. Being around him makes everything—my brain short-circuits on the reality of what I've just thought. I cover my face with my hands, and I lay there as a deep, heaving sob creeps up my throat. The tears I managed to hold at bay for most of the night with Tucker here are still there, threatening to be unleashed.

I wedge the heels of my hands into my eyes, and I choke on the flood of emotion threatening to drown me. My dad is gone. God, I wish Tucker had stayed.

Once I think I've got myself under control, I climb out of bed, and reluctantly, I dress for the day. Since she snuck out this morning, I'm not even sure Tucker will talk to me later. She seems to have a soft spot for my grief, but I can't use my dad as a reason to keep her close forever.

I make my way through the palace to Alex and Rory's suite of rooms. A bit of cuddle time with Grace might cure this aching, gaping wound. Kane lets me in, so I must have somehow avoided nap time. Feels like Grace sleeps all the time.

At her nursery, I pause in the doorway. Rory is rocking her in a chair, and when she glances up at me, she looks exhausted.

"Not much sleep last night?" I ask.

"Between Alex and Grace, I got very little. How are you doing? I saw Maren's vehicle was still here this morning."

I wonder who else saw that. She'll be beyond upset if helping me out starts rumors about her cheating on Enzo. I haven't been able to help nudging her in that direction a few times, and she's resisted.

"She's good company," I say. "One of my best friends." I nod toward Grace. "Can I hold her?"

"Be my guest." Rory adjusts Grace's sleeping form to pass her to me.

I slot her into the crook of my arm, and there's something about having her gentle weight pressed against me that fills part of me that's been empty this morning.

"Should Maren be one of your best friends if she's married? I know we called her last night, but…"

"She'd never cheat on her husband, even if I'd quite happily help her do that."

"Brice."

"I'm being honest. I don't know why people always shrink away from an honest conversation."

"You've told Maren how you feel?"

"I don't even know how I feel." A lie. Sort of. I definitely feel *something*. "I just think her husband is a useless piece of shit."

"I'm glad Grace isn't talking yet."

I rock her and brush her hair off her forehead. Suddenly, I'm wondering about a baby with black hair and eyes like the sky. Maren would murder me for even considering it. But the image won't fade. If Tucker wasn't married, I think I'd ask her to consider being my baby mama. We could coparent together, I'm sure of it. Not sure how I'd broach that subject, given what she's already gone through.

"Whether or not you agree with her marriage, you have to respect it."

The idea makes my blood boil. As far as I can see, Enzo doesn't respect his marriage a whole lot, so I'm not sure why I should value it more than he does.

"Did you respect Alex's pending marriage to Simone?"

"Oh, you are grumpy today." Rory crosses her arms. "You've got a lot going on, so I'm going to let that warped truth slide. But here's what I'll say. Yes, I would have respected his marriage to her if he'd actually gotten married. Would have killed me. A piece of me would have died to do it, but I would not have interfered. It's why I went to Canada. He made a choice, and I wasn't it."

"I wasn't an available choice when Tucker married him."

"Are you saying you want to be a choice now?"

"I don't know."

"Pushing her toward something you're not even sure you want isn't kind. It's cruel. And you're not the sort to be deliberately cruel."

"I should have gone to talk to Nick instead."

"You would have liked his advice better?" Rory lets out a little laugh.

"Probably not. I think he'd murder anyone who tried to get with Jules. I just don't see Enzo as the murdering sort, given that he's chosen to be in America rather than here."

"Has Maren filed for divorce yet? Or a separation at least?"

Since talking about Enzo seems to draw her away from me, I haven't brought him up since we went camping. I have no idea what the status of her marriage is, but judging by the way she jumped off the bed last night, her marriage isn't DOA yet. When we're together, we mostly pretend like he doesn't exist. I'm sure Rory would have a thing or two to say about that as well.

"I asked her to come to the funeral."

"As your guest?" Rory narrows her eyes. "I still have a lot to learn about royal rules, but that seems like a bad idea."

"I'm inviting the whole team, but I want her there."

"Are you sure you aren't clinging onto her because she's *someone* and not because she's someone *special*? Months ago, you said you wanted this adventure race because your brothers had something or someone beyond The Crown. If you take Alex and Julia as an example, he loved what she represented, but he never loved her. Not really. Do you love Maren, or do you love the idea of her?"

"Whoa. Whoa. Whoa. Back up the love train. I never said I was in love with Maren. I said her husband was a shit, and I'd happily help her end that disaster. That's it."

"What does Maren want?"

That is a great question, and one I have not once considered. I understand what she doesn't want. She doesn't want to be labeled a cheater, and she's not the type to quit or give up on anything.

"I don't know," I admit. "We haven't really talked about it."

"Sounds like an honest conversation worth having. Even if you don't know how you feel, it's important to know what she wants. And if saving her marriage is it, then you've got to respect that and maybe consider putting some distance between you two."

None of that sounds like anything I want to do. "I'll take your opinion under advisement."

Rory laughs and then lets out a deep sigh.

---

Even though it's two days after my father's death, and the parking lot of the marina we're meeting at to go paddleboarding is packed with press, I'm holding it together reasonably well. Paxton, Riker, and Wren are teamed with my security, and they are running interference on anyone who tries to get too close or shouts too loudly some insensitive question about my father's last moments. If I didn't have this special place inside me I once created for these royal catastrophes, I'd be a mess right now. My grief is a spectator sport. The whole thing feels like it's happening to someone else. Likely not healthy, but I don't care. I just want Tucker to get her ass here so we can get on the water.

I didn't talk to her at all yesterday after she dipped out on me before I woke up. Then my conversation with Rory made me question whether I was being fair to Maren, leaning on her so hard. So, I called Seth, and a bunch of guys came to the palace last night to drink and gamble. For the first time in my life, I did not enjoy my evening of debauchery. In fact, halfway through our second poker game, I contemplated canceling it, sending everyone home, and texting Tucker to come climb with me.

Tucker wheels into the parking lot ten minutes late. She gets out of the vehicle looking frazzled, and the press descend on her, causing my hackles to rise. They'd better not fucking mess with her. I take a step in her direction, prepared to be her bodyguard if needed—after all, these idiots are here because of me—but Jag seems to sense my mood, and he immediately leaves me to guide Tucker through the minefield of questions, microphones, and cameras.

"Grab a board," she says to us as she drops her things beside the main building.

We each pick one up and cart them toward the water. The cameras and reporters are trailing behind us with only my small security detail as a buffer. A miscalculation on my part. Should have organized for more people.

Once we're past the small waves, Tucker calls out the route, but she seems distracted, not like herself. On any other day, I'd break out the dad jokes to see if I could get a smile, but I'm still too deep in my own feels about my dad and about what could have happened between us the other night. Rory's advice keeps ringing in my ears, making me irritable.

Wren paddles along beside me, and I brace myself for a conversation I'm not in the mood to have. Maybe I should have skipped training today, but I wanted to see Tucker, and I wanted to keep my mind focused on something positive.

I'm in a bad fucking mood, though. Clearly, the positive part isn't working.

"Are you hungover today?" Wren asks.

"What?" I frown and glance at her while I try to keep up with the brutal pace Tucker is setting. "No. Why?"

"Rochelle Butler posted selfies last night from the party you had at the palace."

That explains a few of the insensitive questions hurled at me by the press. It wasn't exactly a party, and if anyone is calling it that, they clearly haven't been to a real Brice Summerset shindig. Last night was deliberately mild. I needed a brain break, and my friends provided it, even if the whole time I kinda wanted to be somewhere else.

Rochelle just got herself uninvited from every event I have for the rest of my life.

We paddle for a little while in silence, and my breathing is elevated. The waves have picked up, and I'm not sure whether going back the way we came will be the best course of action. Since it's not my call, I'll keep my mouth shut.

"Tucker tell you why she was running late?"

"Got in a fight with Enzo," Wren says. "But I got the impression there were some other things going on. Not sure. She's either super specific or very vague with her reasons for anything."

Tucker and Enzo in a fight would be useful information if Wren knew why. Otherwise, I'll assume it's like any other day when you're married and living in separate countries. I'm guessing the distance isn't a choice both of them made, but maybe it is. Maybe Tucker is fine with him being gone. But then I remember the poisoned candy comment.

"That was a cute photo of you and Grace that PR posted this morning."

Rory must have snapped it yesterday when I wasn't looking. She loves making me appear like the doting uncle. I *am* a doting uncle, but I don't need it spread out for public consumption.

Fuck, I'm in a mood. It started yesterday when I woke up to find Tucker gone, and it's only increased today. Normally, I don't care how the royal PR machine paints me. Right now, my life feels like the wrong combination of things, and I can't seem to find even footing anywhere.

"Just so you know, Maren told us about you wanting the team there tomorrow. We'll one hundred percent be there to support you. I'm really honored that you've asked."

Her sincerity is genuine, and a hint of unease creeps across my chest. While I did tell Rory that I wanted them at the funeral, I never cleared it with Alex or with PR.

When we get to our outbound destination, Tucker looks at the sky and calls time on our paddle. There's a storm rolling in, which normally one of us would have checked the marine forecast for. For some reason, none of us did.

There's a house with a covered porch where we've left paddleboards one other time when the weather turned on us unexpectedly. At the pier, Tucker's sister, Sawyer, is waiting, and so is Jag. Given how fast we've been paddling, I have no idea how Tucker had enough time or energy to alert her sister about a pickup.

After we've stacked the paddleboards, Maren motions for Wren, Paxton, and Riker to climb in with her, leaving me the odd man out. Not that I don't have a ride, but it feels deliberate.

"Hey," I call to her before she can slide into the passenger's seat. "About tomorrow—"

"Desmond called me," she says. "I have the important details. We'll all be there. Don't worry."

My heart is doing somersaults in my chest at her easy-breezy attitude. Did I really fuck things up that badly the other night? Or is this about her fight with Enzo? Or something else I'm completely missing?

"I'll see you tomorrow, then?" If Desmond, Alex's secretary, called her, then Alex must be okay with the arrangement I made.

"Yep." She gives me a wave. "Tomorrow." Then she slides into the passenger seat, and the four of them are gone in a puff of exhaust.

When I climb into the SUV with Jag, he shakes his head.

"What?" My tone brims with annoyance.

"Nothing."

"Oh, come on. You've got something to say. You saw the way she just treated me. It's like we're back to square fucking one."

"You been on your social media accounts today?"

"No, not really. Didn't need all that noise on top of what's already going on in my head." I dig my phone out of my bag, and I scroll through the notifications. As I do, I start to see Jag's point. The photos Rochelle posted have me in the background of some of them either looking drunk, smoking a cigar, or with women plastered across me. All of them are platonic friends, but Tucker might not know that. "You think she's disappointed in me?"

Jag doesn't say anything. He just glances at me in the rearview mirror. My gut clenches, and my immediate instinct is to tell him to take me to her apartment. But what am I going to say? I did what I did.

And Rory's words are still tumbling around in my mind. I don't know what Tucker wants, and I'm not ready to hear Enzo might be her first choice.

Maybe it's better if she doesn't like me again, at least for a little while.

# Chapter Twenty-Four

## MAREN

I'm riffling through my racks of dresses, trying to decide what to wear for the funeral today. Bellerive Blue seems most appropriate, but I don't want to blend in too much with the family or to appear as though I'm *in* the family. I should have just asked Desmond for a color scheme when he called yesterday. But the last few days have been a hazy blur.

After leaving Caitlin's office the other day, I had a long soak in the bath and forced myself to consider what I want. If I can save my marriage, that's my first priority. Yesterday, before training, I worked up the nerve to call Enzo and deliver my terms. We can't work on our relationship when we're in separate places. I told him that if he's not back in Bellerive by the time I return from the adventure race, he should know that I'll be filing official paperwork to divorce him.

That conversation didn't go well.

Ultimatums are no way to run a relationship, and under normal circumstances, I understand that. But there comes a time when softly-softly and gently-gently don't get the results you need. He isn't here, and he has no concrete plans to return. He can't keep living off my family's dime in Boston while avoiding the hard work that has to be done between us. Either he wants to be married or he doesn't. I still want it.

Even though that's the choice I made—to try to save my marriage—I was shaken to the core when I opened my social media and found Brice plastered across it drinking, smoking cigars, and flirting with women. It made my heart squeeze so hard in my chest I wasn't sure I could get a real breath in.

Then the royal PR machine clearly tried to counteract what appears to be Brice's insensitivity about his father's death by posting a clickbait photo of him with Grace. A lovely photo, but the tender way he was gazing at her, as though he's never loved anyone more, made my breath really, really hard to catch.

Even if he was someone I could take seriously, we'd never work. I can't give him the one thing he wants above all else.

By the time I finished crying, I knew I was going to be late for practice.

I should have felt powerful after finally calling Enzo out on his behavior and giving him a firm timeline for his return. Instead, I sat on my couch in tears over Brice Summerset.

What is wrong with me?

He is exactly as Caitlin warned me. A walking sin. The guy no one can ever tame. Not that taming him would even be what I wanted—just channel that wildness elsewhere—maybe into more racing.

None of it matters. He's probably mediocre in bed because everyone loves him no matter what he does or how he behaves.

Such a bitchy thought, but I can't find my feet with him right now. The two versions of Brice I'd hoped I wouldn't have to reconcile are staring me in the face. The playboy and the caring family man. He's both, and he's neither. Best to keep both versions out of my head and away from my heart.

Frustrated, I yank a black dress off the hanger. The neckline is slanted and off-center, but the three-quarter sleeves and fitted style will work for today. On the dresser is a Bellerive Royals pin that Desmond sent to me and the rest of the team, a silent signal to the guards that we're invited guests.

Instead of feeling honored, I'm wondering if I'm a fraud. Brice and I are further apart than ever. Seeing those photos sliced and diced the closeness between us, and while I'm fairly certain it's for the best, I can't help mourning the loss. He was rapidly becoming one of my best friends, so perhaps it's okay to be a bit sad that's come to an end. It doesn't have to mean anything else.

There's a knock on my door, and I check the clock. My hair and makeup are done, but I should be dressed by now. I've wasted too much time thinking about Brice and Enzo. I slide into my dress, and I'm zipping it up as I head to the door.

I open it without checking who it is, and I immediately regret it.

"You've been invited to the funeral as a special guest." My mother's outrage is clear as she elbows past me into the apartment. "And you didn't tell me?"

"It was a last-minute choice. The whole team is invited."

"You'll be on national television." She scans me with a critical eye. "I also heard you spent the night in the prince's suite of rooms after his father died. Care to tell me what that's about?"

I purse my lips and head back to my bedroom with my mother trailing behind me. The pin I'm meant to wear is on the dresser, and I snatch it up. When I fumble with finding an appropriate place to attach it, my mother takes it from my hands gently.

"You're unhappy with Enzo. It's only natural you'd seek solace somewhere else." My mother maneuvers the pin into my dress.

"I am not my father." I meet her gaze with defiance. As much as she might want me to drop Enzo and go for Brice, that's not what's happening. It's not even an option.

My mother flinches, and the pin pokes me in the chest.

"Ow," I say as she clasps the pin together. "I can't believe you're advocating cheating."

"Your father made mistakes, and I chose to forgive them. Sometimes, that's what you do in a marriage." She gives me a pointed glare. "And sometimes it's not. Your father never abandoned me or any of you when we needed him. There are marriages worth fighting for, but both people have to want to put in the work."

"I haven't cheated on Enzo, and I won't." The notion that her and my father have worked on their marriage is laughable. Last I heard, he still had a mistress in Portugal. I double check my appearance in the floor-length mirror in my room. "Brice and I have become close friends. That's all."

There's another knock on my door, and it must be Wren. The team is meeting up to enter the church together. No hint of suspicion, especially if the news is circulating that I was with Brice the other night. A stupid mistake. The last thing I want is anyone on the island to brand me a cheater like my father. I wasn't thinking, and I should have been.

"I told Enzo if he's not back by the time I return from the adventure race, that I'm filing for divorce. There, are you happy?"

Mother trails me into the front room, hot on my heels. Part of me didn't want to tell her because I don't want her to think for a second this has anything to do with Brice. Enzo has been gone for months, and at some point, a decision has to be made. He either returns, and we figure out our marriage, or we go our separate ways. At least I won't have any regrets.

"In your circumstances, I think divorce is the smart choice. The royals don't need another scandal."

"Oh my God," I mutter, and then I spin on my mother before I get to the door. "I'm not with Brice. I'm not going to be with Brice. You can take your aspirations of having one of your children join the royal family and shove them. It's not going to happen." At this point, even if it was on the cusp of happening, I might throw on the brakes to spite her. She's infuriatingly single-minded about gaining a title any way she can. I'm all for goal setting, but they need to be achievable.

When I throw open the door, Wren is standing there looking shell-shocked, and I realize I must have spoken those last few things a little too loudly. I close my eyes and take a deep breath.

"Lock up when you leave, Mother," I say before grabbing my clutch from the side table and waltzing out the door.

---

The funeral passes in a blur of speeches, mournful songs, and my attention glued to Brice, who appears to be holding himself together in a way only someone royal can. All eyes are on them in the country and in many parts of the world. Nick looks awful, as though it's physically impossible for him to pretend right now.

Afterward, there's a reception for invited guests only. Desmond was clear that our pins would get us into the palace for the small gathering.

We enter the formal hall, which is decked out in black, white, and gray with a splash of Bellerive Blue for accents at various places.

Paxton whistles long and low. "This is small?"

"When you've been king of a country, I suppose it is," Wren says, glancing around at the lavish cocktail party.

You'd never know we came from a funeral, and I can't even imagine how exhausting it must be for all of them to keep up appearances. Across the ballroom, Brice is flanked by Brent and Posey, but the rest of his family is spread out around the room doing their royal duty of socializing.

InterFlix sent a camera crew to film pieces of the funeral and this. They must intend to lay pretty heavily into Brice's narrative this coming season. They'll be under intense scrutiny on the course, but as their race support, I shouldn't get too much airtime.

"Should we go talk to him?" Wren asks at my side as Paxton and Riker wander off together to mingle with people they recognize from another charity they're part of.

I follow her toward Brice, but there's a knot in my stomach at the idea of speaking to him. Whereas I didn't know what to say the other night, and that felt okay, I'm aware of all the people milling around us, as well as the camera crew circling.

"It was a nice service," Wren says to Brice as we approach. The two of them exchange a brief hug.

My stomach clenches at the realization it'll be weird if I don't hug Brice too, but he's already one step ahead of me, drawing me into a loose embrace as though the physical contact means nothing. His hug with Wren was tighter and longer. He is way too good at compartmentalizing and switching himself off and on.

"I appreciate all of you coming," Brice says. "It's wonderful to have my teammates support during this difficult time."

We've rarely spoken under the glare of a camera, but everything about him, from his countenance to his word choices don't feel like him. For some reason, it makes me sad.

"If you'll excuse me," Brice says, touching Wren on the upper arm, "I see someone I need to speak to about a possible donation."

And then he's gone, the camera shadowing him to his next conversation.

"It must be weird," Wren says, "to spend most of your life pretending to be someone you're not."

Brice is still an enigma, even to me. Is he the genuine, heart-on-his-sleeve guy or the incorrigible flirt who takes nothing seriously? It's almost impossible to believe both can be true.

# Chapter Twenty-Five

## BRICE

We leave for Fiji in a week, and I've been a coward about speaking to Tucker. Instead of confronting her about my little party or about what's going on between her and Enzo or any of the other thousand things floating around my head, I've been burying myself in solo training. I meet the team when I'm told to, but I don't say much.

For her part, Tucker hasn't been seeking me out either. It's as though we've both decided whatever was starting to happen between us isn't worth it. That's not how I feel at all, but I'm having trouble reconciling how I ended up in this situation. She's all I think about. If I'm not thinking about my dad, I'm thinking about her. Her laugh, her confidence, the cocky grin she gives me when she bests me. I miss all of it, and I understand the solution is to buck up and speak to her. That's the adult approach, but I've never been particularly good at taking the high road. It's so much easier to be blunt when you don't give two fucks about the outcome.

Jag and I are out on a run when the security device in his ear goes off loud enough for me to catch the incoming beep. He touches his ear while we both check for traffic before crossing the street at a slower jog. I never carry my phone when we run. Too distracting, but Jag maintains that one of us has to be connected for emergencies.

"That was Wren," he says to me once we're across the street. "Paxton has been injured. We're to meet them at the hospital."

"Oh shit," I say, and I mentally calculate how long it'll take us to get back to the palace.

"I have a car on the way," Jag says. "It'll take too long to get back to the estate."

We stop at the curb, and my mind races. If Paxton is really injured, it puts our team in jeopardy. We'd be one person short of a full team for the race, and if I'm remembering the rules right, the organizing body doesn't allow last-minute substitutions or changes. I'm sure InterFlix would if it's the difference between me competing or not. They've spent a lot of money on advance promos, trips to the island, and extensive interviews with my entire team.

"I've got a bad feeling," Jag says. "Wren sounded pretty down on the phone."

"Until we're there, I'm not speculating," I say. "Could be a twisted ankle, and people are overreacting with the race being so close."

The royal car draws flush with the curb, and Gary is driving. Jag climbs into the front, and I slip into the rear passenger seat. When we arrive at the hospital, it's clear from the minute we enter the waiting room that Paxton isn't well. Wren looks pale, Riker appears distraught, and Tucker doesn't even stand to greet me. Her head is in her hands.

"Is someone going to tell me?" I ask. The sight of Tucker so low sends my stomach plummeting. If we were in a different place, I'd sit beside her, let her lean on me.

"Paxton was on a hike. He was going through a creek, and he slipped. Tore his ACL," Riker says.

That's not good, but it's not life or death either. Everyone is acting like this is the end of the world. "But he'll be okay."

"We can't race," Riker says through gritted teeth. "We need four people."

The solution seems simple to me. Tucker takes his place, and I'll get Gary or another royal staff member to take her spot on the support team.

"This might seem insensitive, but we can replace Paxton," I say.

"It's against the rules," Wren says. "Two days ago, we could have switched it. But now? It's an illegal switch."

Sounds like bullshit to me. An arbitrary deadline. What's the difference between two days ago and now? Until we set foot in Fiji, there's room for negotiation.

"Leave it with me," I say.

"You can't royal your way out of this," Riker says.

"Watch me," I say. It's the first time anyone on the team has given me grief about my status, and it pisses me off. "Tucker, are you good to compete?"

"Maren is not competing." Wren steps in front of my line of sight.

The emergency room doctor comes out to get Tucker at Paxton's request, and she rises and follows the doctor without glancing at me. Her ability to ignore me might be the death of me. It's grating on me an unreasonable amount. The two of us blow so hot and then so cold around each other. A wildfire or hypothermia.

"We're not asking Maren," Wren says again once Tucker is gone.

"Why not?" I ask. "She's been training with us."

"Not enough," Riker says. "Not enough for her to be okay."

I shake my head, and I'm so tempted to let loose with exactly how much training Tucker has been doing with me that none of them know anything about. Doing that would betray her trust, I'm sure of it. If she wanted them to know, she'd have told one of them by now. With the way Wren is looking at me, I wonder if she *does* know.

"She's a competitor," I say. "She could do it. You both know that."

"She was..." Wren purses her lips and glances in Riker's direction. "It's taken her a long time to recover from the accident she had during the last competition. She's said she no longer wants to race."

That doesn't feel honest or truthful. It's possible that racing again scares her, but I find it hard to believe she'd never want to race again. To me, she seems happiest when she's training, and racing is a natural extension of that.

"Has anyone asked her what she wants?" Even uttering that question makes me feel like a hypocrite because I've been pursuing her, whether or not I've called it that, for months.

"She's told us," Riker says. "Asking her puts pressure on her to go against what she wants, especially in this situation."

I sink into one of the waiting room chairs. For the last six months, I've been training, attending fundraisers, doing interviews, putting my life with my father on blast to drum up money for the Alzheimer's Society. In the last few weeks, one of the only things keeping me going has been the training. This goal—finish the race, prove to Maren and everyone else that putting me on the team was a win for everyone—has been a beacon of light. All the money we'd have raised during the show to find a cure, slow down the process, or discover earlier interventions will never materialize.

To get this far and throw in the towel because they're afraid Tucker can't take a little pressure is beyond ridiculous. They might think they know her, but I know her too.

She's capable of saying no to me. She's been doing it in one way or another for months.

"You don't know the full story," Wren says to me. "Don't ask her. I know what you're thinking, and don't do it."

That's where she's wrong. I do know the whole story. The accident. The miscarriage. The antidepressants. The missing husband. All the terrible things that came out of one mistake.

But I also know about her drive and her determination. I understand that when things get hard for Tucker, she finds some well to tap into that allows her to keep going, even when other people would give up or give in.

To allow one mistake, a mistake she made with good intentions, to steer the course of the rest of her life doesn't feel like a Tucker-level decision. It feels like a knee-jerk one, a choice made under duress or when she was at her lowest. She's not there anymore, or I don't think she is.

Whatever Wren might think, asking Tucker the question is the right thing to do.

Tucker returns through the door that leads to the curtained emergency room cubicles, and she's pale. "Definitely his ACL," she says. "He's out. I'll call the race committee and InterFlix to let them know we won't be competing."

I rise to my feet, and when I open my mouth, Wren shoots me a glare. Riker rises with me, and for the first time in a long time,

I'm sure neither of them is on my side. It's a strange feeling to be on the outside for the second time in months after being treated as an equal.

Fine. They don't want me to say anything, I won't. Not here. But I'm not letting this go.

# Chapter Twenty-Six

## MAREN

In my apartment, I stare out at the dark ocean, lit only by the streetlights along the boardwalk, and I toy with my bottle of antidepressants. A few months ago, I scaled back my dose with my doctor. Lately, I've been thinking of weaning myself off them completely. My doctor said I could, but she recommended we not do that until after I get back from Fiji. At the time, she thought I was going as a crew member. There's a huge difference between being the one traveling to each base camp, keeping track of equipment and clothes, and being on the racecourse. She thought the atmosphere of the race might trigger me and cause a backslide. I can't decide if everyone else is right to be worried or if they're overreacting.

The only thing I'm certain of is that I can't slide into those feelings again. I'm not sure I'd survive it a second time.

But I think I'll be okay, at least on the racecourse. You only get the news I received once in a lifetime, and I've started to accept what my future will hold. Or not hold.

The knock on my door so late at night startles me out of my thoughts, and I set the pills on the coffee table. There are only a few people who'd dare come to my apartment so late, and when I check the peephole, my heart kicks.

I draw the door open, but I lean against the frame, not giving Brice access to my apartment. Jag stands a little distance behind him.

"Can I help you?" I ask.

"You could, if you wanted to. Depends on who I'm talking to. Is it just Maren home or is Tucker here too?"

"You're insufferable," I say.

"Sounds like Maren." He tries to peer around me. "Tucker has to be in there somewhere."

"Come search for yourself." I step back and let him enter the apartment. "Perhaps you can dig her up."

"You've buried her, have you?" Brice cocks his eyebrows, but as soon as he's in, he goes to the window to stare out at the dark view.

"Why are you here?"

"A few reasons," he says. "I don't usually have these conversations without alcohol, so I'm struggling to get these big boy pants on. They're a bit tight."

"I have no idea what you're talking about." I take a seat on the couch, and I contemplate hiding my pills, but he's seen them before.

When he doesn't say anything for a long time, I can't take the silence anymore. "Alcohol makes them looser, does it?"

"Alcohol makes a lot of things looser." He shoots me a wolfish grin over his shoulder, and my heart stutter-stops. He turns to face me, and he crosses his arms. "What do you want?"

"That's a broad question." I lean back in the couch, and I cross my arms to match his.

"Wren and Riker don't think you want to race anymore. I wasn't convinced, and when I learned you haven't called InterFlix or the race committee organizer yet, I became even less convinced."

"I don't know what I want." Which suddenly feels accurate on so many levels. With him here in my apartment after us avoiding any alone time for the last couple of weeks, everything in me is longing to be closer to him. At the window, he's too far away, and when we're in private like this, I let myself drink him in in a way I never do when we're surrounded by others. His T-shirt is stretched across his chest, and his shorts ride low on his hips. Tattoos and toned flesh lie under his clothes, and I'm not immune to those charms.

I was so sure I wanted to repair things with Enzo. Brice isn't a real option. He's not for several reasons. But it *feels* like he is.

"What's holding you back?" Brice asks, and he comes to the couch to plop down beside me as though we're still the best of friends.

There's more holding me back than I think I want to share. The trauma of the last time—if I get injured again, there's a chance I could spiral out of control. The memory of the outcome of my last race still lingers.

On top of that, I'm sure if I say yes, the death of me and Enzo is a clear consequence. If he comes home, he'll expect me to quit racing. He's only been marginally okay with me training the team, and any hint that I might return to full competition has led to a fight. Going to Fiji as a competitor is like giving him the middle finger. Since the race will be televised and dissected ad nauseum for the rest of our lives—that middle finger is writ large. I'm not sure if we can come back from my choice.

"I'm scared," I admit. It's the closest I can come to verbalizing everything holding me back. Part of me wants to go. Brice isn't wrong. I didn't call anyone to confirm our withdrawal because I've been sitting here weighing whether I'd be capable of racing if they bent the rules.

"Too scared?" His tone is gentle, and he reaches out to toy with a few strands of my hair that have come loose from my ponytail. "You never seem scared of anything."

"I'm scared of lots of things." Including the way my heart is pounding at his proximity, the way a glance from him can cause a wildfire to rage across my body. Sex with him would not be mediocre. I was fooling myself before. It would be hot and intense, and he'd probably make it impossible for me to ever want to be with anyone else. I would crave him forever. The worst possible outcome.

"Race with me," he murmurs. He takes my hand, and he plays with my wedding ring, which I put back on the other night after leaving it in a dish in my bathroom for weeks. "I won't let anything happen to you."

"That's why it's an accident. No one means for it to happen."

"If I can get the rules bent for us, will you race?"

When our gazes meet, the only word I want to utter is *yes*, but I'm not sure what I'm agreeing to. The air around us is fraught with the sexual tension that threatens to ignite. I'd also be agreeing to the dissolution of my marriage, to possibly throwing gasoline on whatever is smoking between me and Brice.

"I don't know." I stare at him, wishing my desire to race wasn't tied so closely to my yearning to be close to him.

"Can I talk to InterFlix and the race committee? No pressure. I'll just find out if it's possible."

I'm certain both of us are aware of how much InterFlix has already banked on his participation. Without a doubt, they'll land hard on the race committee to find a loophole that would allow either me or someone else, even if they aren't qualified, to step into Paxton's place.

But saying yes, at least at this level, buys me a minimum of twenty-four hours to come to grips with the reality of agreeing. Once Enzo realizes I'm a competitor, he won't come back. Tears prick at my eyes at the finality of that. I'd be throwing my marriage away for a race.

"Tucker," he murmurs. "Look at me."

When I glance up, he's blurry, but I can make out the softening of his expression. He frames my face, and he plants a kiss on my forehead. "Don't cry. Forget I asked. I'm not pushing you to do something you're not ready for."

The tenderness from him opens a similar well in me. I slide my arms around his shoulders, and I draw him into a hug. His hand slides to my lower back, and he drags me onto his lap, so I'm straddling him with my face buried in the crook of his neck. I breathe him in while he edges up my shirt to caress my bare back. The skin-to-skin contact causes a shiver of pleasure to race through me. We shouldn't be sitting like this, but I have no desire to move. As long as I keep my face buried, I don't have to face him or this or whatever is about to come to a head. My wild heart races.

"I didn't know how to cope with the loss of my dad. I still don't, if I'm honest." His voice is quiet in the room. "So, I invited a few people to the palace because I thought I'd been relying on you too heavily. That maybe I was being unfair to you. I'd never want to put you in an impossible situation. But I wanted to call you that night. I wanted to call you so badly."

I love the rumble against my ear and the sincerity lacing his words. I clutch the back of his head. He tugs me tighter, and there's no doubt our closeness is affecting him. In return, he'd find me warm and wet if he slid his hand between my legs.

Hearing and feeling how much he wants me is exhilarating. Even though I shouldn't, even though it's wrong, I want him too. I've been fighting these feelings for so long.

"You can ask them if I can take Paxton's place," I murmur, my lips grazing the sensitive skin of his throat.

"Are you sure?" His voice is thick and raw.

When I draw back to look at him, he slides his hands into my hair, dislodging my ponytail. We stare at each other for a beat, and then he brings my forehead to his.

"I always try to balance what I'll regret more," he says. "And I think I've finally decided." He tilts my head, and his lips are a hair's breadth from mine. "What about you, Tucker? What will you regret?"

*Not this.*

Then I tug on him so his lips connect with mine, and he meets and matches the intensity of my kiss. We slide against each other, feast on our pent-up hunger. His lips are soft and pliable. He dips his tongue into my mouth, and I welcome the connection, the feel of any part of him inside me. He tastes like mints and tequila as though he took a shot before he walked out his door.

Or maybe he always tastes like this—like intoxication. When I rock against him, he groans, and his hand grips my ass, squeezing my cheek, encouraging me. Neither of us says anything. We kiss and grind and gasp, lost in a haze of feeling. I can't remember the last time I wanted anyone the way I want him. I'm so wet and hot that I think I could probably come from this alone.

*More. More. More.*

When my phone rings, I block out the noise. If we stop kissing, I'll realize this is a mistake. Brice was right to reference regret, except he seemed to know which side his regret would fall, and with him hard underneath me, all I know is that I don't want this to end.

After the second ring, the internal sound system picks up the signal, and an automated female voice announces my caller ID.

*Call from: Enzo, husband.*

The reminder that I still have a husband, that I shouldn't be doing this with Brice, that I'm a terrible person, is like being dunked in a tank of ice-cold water. Years ago, I thought putting Enzo in my contact list like that was cute.

I spring off Brice's lap, and I avert my gaze while running my hands through my loose strands. Somewhere along the way, my hair elastic vanished, but it's better because I can use my hair as a shield. My breathing is ragged, and the dampness between my thighs is embarrassing. What have I done? What would I have done?

The phone keeps ringing, and Brice rests his elbows on his knees with his head bowed toward the floor.

"I don't know what I was thinking," I whisper. I wasn't thinking. This time, I let my body lead the way, and guilt is already eating at me. No matter what, I shouldn't have kissed Brice. The other day I gave Enzo an ultimatum about returning home. My choice felt clear—save my marriage.

"It's my fault," Brice says. "This isn't your fault. It's mine. I knew where you stood, and I—and I selfishly went after what I wanted anyway. I'm sorry, Maren. Truly."

To hear him say he wanted me, even if the evidence was literally underneath me only a moment ago, sends a shot of warmth through me. It shouldn't be warmth shooting through me; it should be guilt.

The phone stops ringing, but my voice message system is about to click in. I frantically search the coffee table and the surface of the couch for my phone, but I can't find it. In a panic, I rush to the wall to hit end or to pick up or to do anything but have to hear Enzo over the speakers in the house after I've just made out with Brice. The disconnect is way back by the kitchen wall, and I'm not going to make it in time.

"Hey, M. I know we haven't spoken since our fight. But I heard you. I understand what you need."

I smack the disconnect on the wall.

"He understands what you need?" Brice scoffs from the couch. "Does he? What the fuck does he know from Boston?"

"Brice."

"No, seriously. You want to be married to that? Someone who doesn't *understand* that he needs to be here when his wife is hurt and suffering and sad? Someone who has to be *told* that? Likely repeatedly. I just—" He lets out a frustrated noise, and he heads for the door.

I'm at a loss about what to say to him. We've never talked about Enzo, so I don't know how to defend him or whether I even should. He has been a terrible husband for getting close to a year now. But he wasn't always. Was he? We used to be good together.

At the door, Brice opens it and stands in the frame for a moment. "I'm making the calls, and I'm getting our team to Fiji. I'm sorry I kissed you. If it makes it easier for you, we can pretend like this didn't happen. You're not your father, and this truly will stay between us. I won't—" He rests his forehead against the edge of the door. "I won't let it happen again." Then he tugs the door shut behind him as though I couldn't possibly have anything to add to the conversation.

What would I have said, though? *I kissed you*. Super mature, and not at all the point. I wanted to kiss him, and I want to go on this race. Part of me is terrified of both of those realities, but it doesn't change them.

From the minute Brice tugged me onto his lap, Enzo never crossed my mind. Maybe that's all I really need to know. Enzo isn't here, and there's a chance he won't even be here when I get back from the race. He's given me empty promises before.

I find my phone stuffed between the couch cushions, and I stare at my contacts before searching one out and hitting dial.

# Chapter Twenty-Seven

## BRICE

For the rest of the week while I make phone calls to the race committee and InterFlix to get Maren on the team, all I can think about is how badly I fucked up with Tucker. Epic-level fuckup. That phone call I overheard from Enzo makes it clear she's still trying to patch up her marriage. I convinced myself she couldn't possibly want to be with someone who was so careless with her heart. How wrong I was.

The truth is, it's not like I'm prepared to offer myself as a better option. While I might never do what he did, I can't see myself getting down on one knee and declaring my undying devotion for anyone. That means I'm asking her to abandon a relationship she intended to have forever for a few hookups with me. It pains me to realize Rory might have been right. I had no business trying to wedge myself into something I didn't understand.

As a result, other than a text message to the group to confirm we're still on for Fiji, I haven't spoken to Tucker. She suggested we all do our own training, which used to be code for her and I training together, but neither of us messaged the other. We're both avoiding whatever the fuck combusted between us the other night. Definitely confirmed that sex with her would be next level if that brief make-out session was any indication. Not that I'll ever know for sure.

The way she moved on top of me was the best kind of torture. Seems criminal to never get a follow-through. All that heat. All that desire. Wasted.

Not completely wasted, I suppose. Late at night, the memory of that make-out session has gotten me off over and over again. Not helpful in the grand scheme.

If she's determined to make her marriage work, I really do need to stay away from her. Even if the thought makes me vaguely sick to my stomach, and the minute I allow myself to veer off the rational path, I want to bang down her door and offer myself as an alternative. Irrational me is completely on board with doing anything I can to sabotage Tucker's relationship, but rational me understands that's a recipe for disaster. Eventually, she'd hate me. I can give her better than she has, of that I'm confident, but I might not ever be able to give her what she wants.

None of that matters because the phone call made it clear she's trying to work on her marriage, and I'm an unwelcome distraction.

But if I was going to pursue something, the whole knocking down her door thing would be pretty easy in a few hours when our last plane lands in Fiji. Jag, Gary, Riker, Wren, Tucker, and I are spending two days in Fiji getting acclimatized and adjusting to the new time zone before the race begins. Two days was the maximum covered by our competition fee, and given the last-minute scramble to get Tucker organized after Paxton was out, I'm glad we get a couple days to regroup.

InterFlix sent a camera crew to travel with us. Seems like a waste of money to me, but I'm starting to realize InterFlix's goal is to get me to cry on camera. One hundred percent, they are determined to crack the royal facade. I've got news for them. My twenty-eight years of experience tell me it won't happen. A person I've never met before asking me deeply personal questions is just like every other public event I've ever attended.

Now if they convinced Tucker to ask me the questions, the rivers would run. I have a hard time pretending with her for very long in any direction. Indifference and a lack of feeling don't mix or mingle around Tucker. I care a lot, and I feel a lot. Too much, maybe.

If the cameras are dogging me, it'll be impossible to talk to Tucker. I understand the value of a narrative to an editor on a TV show, especially an unscripted reality TV show. My family has had enough documentaries and history pieces done on them that I'm aware how right and wrong filmmakers can get it. They can create a story out of nothing, and I don't intend to give them something that would embarrass Tucker. Keeping a polite distance is the responsible choice. Hopefully I'm capable of making that choice enough days in a row to get us through.

When we deplane, Jag offers to deliver my things to my hotel room. I'm not appearing entitled when I'm front and center on camera, so I shake my head and grab all my own things. Tucker hitches her backpack onto her back, and she shoots me a shy smile. My chest threatens to cave in, and I want to throw my arm around her shoulders and draw her into my side. At one point, before anything happened between us, I would have.

It's annoying that one kiss—okay, many kisses and some sexy grinding—have led to this awkwardness between us. But she doesn't have the air of guilt around her that I would have expected. Maybe she doesn't consider what we did cheating, but I would. If I was her husband, it would fucking destroy me.

For the next day and a bit, Tucker sticks close to Wren's side, and the two of them are social butterflies with all the other teams. It's only natural, since they've raced so many times that they'd know a lot of people, but the number is stunning. They seem to know at least one person from every team. While they have genuine conversations with people, I seem to be on the same introductory loop with a camera crew so far up my ass I wonder whether I should have purchased a family-size container of lube.

Of course I realized I'd be a focus, but this almost feels like a documentary. At the briefing meeting the night before the race, it becomes apparent there are several camera crews. The others are rotating through the fifty-some-odd teams, but the one we have only orbits around me.

When Iris, the camera woman, gets called away by a producer before the organizer begins speaking, Tucker slides into the empty space beside me.

"Are you enjoying your personal videographer?" she asks.

"Immensely. Wish I'd thought of documenting every nanosecond of my life earlier. Course, that would have caused massive problems for my parents. Social media was bad enough." I slide her a glance. "Not to worry, I'm on my best behavior." I've skimmed over the reference to my father, but when she looks up at me, I see she didn't miss it. There are few things I love more than the expression of tenderness Tucker gets when she thinks I'm sad. Not sure I'll ever tire of watching the shifting emotions drift across her lovely face.

"Are you okay?" she whispers.

"Okay enough." I search her for a sign of something negative between us. Her attitude is a lot more relaxed than I expected. We've avoided each other this week, and part of me assumed we'd continue to avoid each other as much as possible here too. "Are you okay?"

The camera woman who wasn't gone nearly long enough is headed back to us with the camera on her shoulder. She's probably already running the damn thing. Tucker follows my gaze, and she purses her lips.

"I'm great," she says.

Although I don't expect to, when she meets my gaze again, I almost believe her.

---

Riker is snoring softly on the other bed, and Gary is outside the door standing guard. He and Jag are our crew members, and while they can't follow me through every step of the race, they're here to protect me. Jag is in an adjoining room resting up for the grueling adventure ahead. I should be sleeping too—we're rising before the sun—but it's the first time I haven't had a camera within hearing distance all day.

I creep out of bed and head to the balcony. A few deep breaths of fresh air might settle me. It's been unnerving to be so close to Tucker the last two days and not feel like I can be myself around her. Every time I've wanted to touch her or tell a joke or check in with her, I've been hyperaware of how it might seem when edited. If she's trying to save her marriage, I can't appear closer to her than anyone else.

I'd really love for her to wave the white flag on her marriage, but I can't wave it for her. For the first time in my life, I've got big, scary feelings for someone, and I can't pursue them without doing the other person immeasurable harm. If there's one person in the world I'd never want to hurt, it's Tucker.

I slide open the back door, and I suck in a deep breath of the Fijian air. So many air fresheners and perfumes claim to smell like here, but I'm convinced none of them get the fruity-flowery-salty combination right.

"Can't sleep?" Tucker's voice is rusty from the balcony beside mine.

"First time I haven't had a camera up my ass since I arrived. Quite liberating. Very awkward to have it shoved so far up there." I give her a slight smile. "You?"

"I can never sleep well the night before a race." She's sitting on one of the deck chairs, a blanket wrapped around her.

I judge the distance between the two balconies. We're only one story up. Would I really do that much damage if I fell? I check the ground below and see it's covered in shrubs. Good enough. At the edge of the balcony, I hop onto the metal rail, and Maren rises to her feet, the blanket pooling at her ankles.

"Brice," she says.

"Your balcony looks much better than mine," I say, and I step from the top of mine to the top of hers, and I jump down with grace. Not going to lie—I'm a bit impressed with myself. Last time I tried that, I fell. Of course, I was drunk. "All those hours of climbing amounted to something, I guess."

"Almost amounted to a heart attack for me."

But instead of smacking me or drawing me into a hug, she sinks into her lounger and motions for me to take the bottom. She gathers the blanket from the ground and drapes part of it over herself and then offers some to me.

"How are you really doing?" I ask after I take the offered blanket, and then, even though I know better, I draw her legs across my lap.

"Okay," she says, and she lets out a deep sigh. "Are you being weird with me because of the cameras or because of what happened in my apartment?"

Normally, I'm all for blunt, but she's shied away from it before, and her upfront attitude takes me by surprise.

"I just have to know how you want me to behave around you," she says.

"Any way you want," I say. "But you need to be aware that they'll edit the shit out of everything. What seems innocent might not after it's been sliced and diced." I pick my words carefully, like I would do if I was being a royal and not if I was being Brice. "I don't want you to go home to a difficult situation because I overstepped." I hesitate. "Again."

"You didn't overstep. I did." She drags her fingers from her temple to her chin. "Voicing this next part is terrifying—"

"Your Highness!" Gary comes storming out the balcony door across from us. "Your Highness!" The third balcony door is thrown open, and Jag appears.

"Did you find him?" Jag asks.

"Find who?" I try to keep the irritation out of my voice. Clearly, they're looking for me, but Tucker and I were about to have a moment.

Gary releases an audible breath, and Jag grumbles before heading back into his room. The sliding door closes with a bang.

"Your Highness," Gary says. "If you're leaving the hotel room, you need to notify one of us."

"Last-minute decision," I say, and I run my hand along Tucker's bare leg under the blanket. Her skin is so soft. "What's wrong?"

"Your mother is on the phone," Gary says, and he holds up his cell phone.

All our devices have already been collected. We aren't allowed any technology on the course. Jag and Gary, for safety reasons, have been allowed to have them. But the GPS trackers and map apps all had to be deleted or disabled. Not as though my teammates are likely to condone cheating, and it would be a PR nightmare for The Crown if I was caught doing that…in any capacity.

My hand stills on Tucker's leg. Every time I promise myself I won't slide back into this easy affection with her, I can't help myself. Someone needs to put a shock collar on me.

I get off the lounger, and when I go to the edge of the balcony, I shoo Gary away. "I need space."

"Your Highness," he says in an uncertain voice.

Then I'm on the metal railing, across the gap, and on my own balcony before he can formulate a reaction. I take the phone from him and press it to my chest before turning back to Tucker.

"I'll just be a minute." I hold the phone to my ear, and as soon as my mother starts talking, I realize I won't be a minute. The conversation starts with her wishing me luck and then quickly morphs into her worrying about my safety. This is going to take more than a minute.

When I glance across at Tucker's balcony, I realize she's gone, and whatever she was going to tell me, the opportunity is lost.

# Chapter Twenty-Eight

## MAREN

There's something about being up before the sun rises that I genuinely love. It might be the quiet or maybe it's that so many of my best memories have started on days like today—a group of people, an organizer making announcements, a sharp chill in the air while I hoist a heavy pack higher onto my back.

Beside me, Brice is jittery, but Wren and Riker are calm and focused on my other side. There's a camera crew behind us, and they've hovered near us since we left the hotel room. I have a feeling last night on the balcony is going to be my final chance at any alone time with Brice without the glare of a camera in one of our faces. Maybe it's better I didn't get a chance to talk to him for longer; I might have said things it would be hard to take back. Could have made for an awkward ten days on the course.

We're less than five minutes from rushing toward the tiny sailboats we'll use as the first leg of the race when Jag wedges his way in between me and Brice.

"I just got a text from Caitlin. Said you needed to know. The package has been delivered to Boston."

The weight that's been sitting on my chest dissipates. I thought the heaviness was about my decision, but maybe it was more about whether my wishes would be carried out in time. Caitlin said she was prioritizing me, but she had some sticky and time-sensitive legal situations crop up this week.

"Package?" The look of puzzlement on Brice's face is cute.

I'm keenly aware of the camera rotating around to the front of us, but I want what I'm about to say to be present in whatever narrative InterFlix builds.

"I asked Caitlin to serve formal separation papers to Enzo in Boston."

"You're getting a divorce?" The expression on Brice's face is priceless. He's clearly forgotten about the camera and his royal training because his level of shock can't be faked.

I want to stare into the camera when I confirm, but instead, I tip my head in its direction. "Likely, yes."

The subtle reminder about who's watching seems to snap him back to himself, and he glances at the camera before dipping his head. "I'm sorry to hear that."

There's a smile in his voice, but his tone is pitched low enough, the camera might not even catch it. He's not sorry, but he doesn't want InterFlix, and consequently the world, to bear witness to his glee.

"Oh," Wren says from beside me. "I'm so sorry, Maren. He's been off-island for months, and I know things have been really rough, but I didn't think you wanted to get divorced."

I didn't tell her this was coming, but her reaction is exactly what I would have wanted. She's framed the issues between me and Enzo, and she's made it seem like divorce was a last resort. All true, and every single word is on the digital record. There's no way to know what the next ten days will hold, but I want everyone who watches this show to realize I was on the path to divorce before the starting gun went.

Brice isn't leading a married woman into a compromising situation, and this married woman has already made a choice about the state of her marriage. After I cheated on Enzo the other night, I could hardly justify any other outcome. I won't be my father.

On top of that, when I gave Enzo the ultimatum about returning to the island, he balked at my request. We fought over whose needs were most important. If neither of us is willing to put the other person first, willing to compromise, then maybe there isn't anything worth saving. It's not as though he showed up on my doorstep after our fight and said he was willing to do the work. He left me a voicemail.

For the next ten days on the course, I'm unreachable, and I don't intend to turn on my phone until I've returned to the island. Legally, and as far as the show is concerned, I've filed for separation from my husband. If he has something to say about that, he can talk to me when I get back. Assuming I'm even willing to hear him out at that point.

"It was a difficult choice," I say to Wren. "But it finally feels like the right one."

And when Brice slings his arm around my shoulders and drags me tight to his side, the sense of rightness in me solidifies.

The announcer comes over the loudspeaker, counting us down from ten. Brice lets me go to double-check the straps on his bag. Jag has already retreated into the crowd, likely to make sure we get away safely before getting a ride to the first rest area with Gary. There, they'll set up everything we'll need for the end of our first fifty-kilometer trek. Nerves flutter in my stomach. The thrill of anticipation never gets old.

"You ready?" Brice asks me.

"For anything," I say, and he grins.

---

Anything turns out to be getting lost. Riker is the team captain for this race. In the past, we've taken turns, and he's never been the strongest navigator, but I've never had him get us *this* lost before. The shortcut he suggested, and that none of us double-checked, has turned into a disaster.

To top it off, we're in the middle of the rain forest, and with the dense foliage around us, it's incredibly hot. We're all dripping, and we're going through water faster than we should be. The sailboat and biking portions of our day went smoothly, and I was pretty sure we were likely in the top ten out of the fifty or so teams. This mistake is costing us time and energy.

"Give me the map and the compass." I try to keep the annoyance out of my voice. Up until now, I've avoided contradicting him or causing friction. On the course, it's almost impossible to avoid getting on each other's nerves at some point. Exhaustion sets in, and people's tempers flare. For it to be happening on the first day isn't setting us up for success.

"How much does our race position matter?" Brice asks. "We're raising money either way."

"If you're Maren?" Riker's frustration is clear. "A lot."

"You want to be wandering around the rain forest lost?" I glance up at Riker while I reorient the map and trace paths to get us back on track. Somehow Brice missed the memo on how competitive I am. To me, there's little point in racing if you're not attempting to win. I've done enough of these that the *experience* isn't why I'm normally here. For Brice, maybe that's enough. The prize pot for coming in first is sizeable, and now that we're here, I think we've got a chance. None of us need the cash, and it would be great to add it to the other donations.

"Does this happen often?" Iris asks as she points the camera at Wren.

"Not usually," Wren says. "A bit of bad luck to start us off."

And stubborn pride because if he admitted to being lost almost an hour ago when I asked him, we wouldn't have continued this aimless, pointless wandering. I take my pack off my back and dig around until I find a highlighter. Carefully, I outline the route that'll get us on track the fastest, and I stare at it again to memorize the junctions that might throw Riker off. After I've done that, I pass him back the map and compass.

"Let's go," I say.

We fall into single file through the dense bush, and I wonder how well Iris trained for this grueling race. She seems fit enough with the camera either slung on her shoulder or dangling from her body, but this would be quite an assignment to take on.

Once we're on the right path, Iris says she needs five minutes to do a couple individual interviews that they'll intersperse in the shows when they air. She takes Brice over to stand in front of some trees, but they're too far away for me to hear what he has to say. Next, she calls me over.

She has an earpiece in, and I'm assuming someone is feeding her the questions. Instead of wandering back to Riker and Wren, Brice stands off to the side, out of the camera shot.

"Tell me about your divorce," she says as an opening.

"My husband, Enzo, moved to Boston months ago while I was still recovering from the accident I had on the Chilean racecourse. We've been separated for a while. This just makes it official." According to Bellerive's laws, Caitlin's separation filing will backdate to the day Enzo left the island. He hasn't returned since, so she said that date was as good as any, and if the press got hold of the documents somehow, the length of time makes me look sympathetic.

I can't believe I even have to consider how my separation will look to the public in Bellerive and beyond, but I'm aware of who I'm on this race with. People will care. By the time the race is done, people might care a lot. His brand of charm is hard to resist, and I imagine it'll translate just as well to the small screen.

Brice has his arms crossed and his head is lowered while I talk. Having him so close while I discuss this, given we haven't had a chance to talk in private, is uncomfortable. I feel like a failure.

On the one hand, divorce was a necessary step after I kissed Brice, but on the other, I didn't go into my marriage thinking this outcome was an option or even a likelihood. Certainly not when we've only been married a few years.

"Do you still love him? Is there any hope for the marriage?" Iris asks.

With Brice standing so close, I want to say no to both, but the reality is a lot more complicated. If Enzo were willing to try, really try, I would find it difficult to abandon my marriage, one I once wanted so much. Given the right memory, it's easy to remember why I fell in love with Enzo, the qualities I still find attractive. It's just that those memories and feelings have faded over the last year. Faded doesn't mean gone.

"I'd rather not answer that question," I say.

Brice drops his crossed arms, and he runs his hands through his hair in a gesture that looks a lot like frustration. He turns away from me and heads back to Wren and Riker where he slings his pack back over his shoulders.

"Winning is important to you?" Iris asks.

"Always. There's still time to make up our team's mistake, but we'll have to sacrifice sleep."

"You don't think that might put some of your teammates in danger? Wasn't your accident in Chile partially attributed to exhaustion?"

Her question is meant to raise my hackles and get a sharp response from me, I'm sure. I've already proven myself to be competitive and a tad bitchy. She can't have this one, though. "Exhaustion? On a challenge racecourse? Can you imagine?" I laugh. "You'll see, Iris. It's impossible to make it out of this race without being exhausted. My accident was overconfidence."

"Any regrets?"

"I don't have regrets. I learn, and I move on."

"What have you learned from your failed marriage?"

I've walked into this narrative with my eyes wide open, but I still hate it. If she keeps circling back to Enzo for the next ten days, I'll be miserable. My arc on the show should be about overcoming tragedy to race again, but none of them truly know what I'm overcoming. Instead, my narrative is about a broken marriage.

"To be more discerning about my life partners." I check my watch. "We really do need to get moving again."

Iris lowers her camera and follows me back to the group. When I glance at Brice, his gaze is averted, and I can't help feeling I've disappointed him.

# Chapter Twenty-Nine

## BRICE

There are checkpoints roughly every twenty-two kilometers. We make checkpoint one in twentieth place, and we make small gains at the second one on the first day. Tucker, not Riker, sets a punishing pace on the second day, and we hit tenth. With Maren coleading, I think we likely have a shot at being one of the top finishers, but Riker clearly isn't pleased with her attitude. Wren seems resigned to the unspoken conflict, and maybe this happens often on the course or between the two of them during a race. I haven't asked. No point in stirring the pot.

Despite the huge number of kilometers we're accumulating, and the faster than comfortable pace, I've got too much time to think.

When Tucker said she was getting a divorce from Enzo, I was euphoric, and I'm positive I didn't hide it very well. My expression, if captured on camera, will likely become a gif for the ages. I will become the international symbol for shocked and impressed. Chris Pratt in his *Parks and Recreation* role will have nothing on me. If I was the type to care about winning the lottery, I'm sure hearing she was getting a divorce was better than that.

Then I listened in on her interview with Iris—which I shouldn't have done—and her answer made me feel like shit. As though maybe she's filed for divorce because we kissed last week and not because her husband is a waste of space or because she's developed real feelings for me. Of the three reasons, I'm good with two and three, but I'm royally pissed if it's number one.

We haven't had a single second alone, and I'm contemplating a bold move to resolve the underlying uneasiness between us. Patience isn't my thing, and if Iris is going to shove that camera in my face every chance she gets, she's about to get an earful.

We've stopped for lunch, and I gesture for Tucker to follow me. Iris clambers to her feet and shadows us with the camera, which is what I expected. My goal is to make this conversation hard to edit smoothly.

Once we're far enough away from Wren and Riker, I turn on Tucker, who has a concerned frown on her face.

"Are you okay?" Tucker asks. "Did you forget to pack something? Do you need more water or food?"

"InterFlix is looking to build a narrative," I say. "Their goal is to get viewers and to lure people in to watch the show."

"I'm aware."

"Right now, InterFlix has a story about my father and your divorce."

Iris lowers her camera and takes a seat on a rock not far from us. "Carry on," she says, switching the camera off. "I don't care about your plot for airtime or to fool the world, and InterFlix will want people to believe that whatever they see is real. This isn't *Survivor*. No one needs an alliance."

"You could always grab some individuals with Riker and Wren," I suggest. Inside, I'm smiling because this is exactly what I wanted.

"Good idea." She heaves herself off the rock and wanders back to the other two.

As soon as she's out of earshot, I rub my face and try to gather my thoughts.

"You wanted her gone," Tucker says.

"Are you definitely getting a divorce?" It's the closest I'll come to asking her what I really want to know.

"I filed the paperwork for the separation. Divorce comes after that, I guess. It's not like I've done it before."

"I know I said you could behave any way you wanted with me, but now I'm second-guessing how I'm supposed to be with you."

"If it helps, I'm fine with you being how you normally are."

"Normal me is very flirty and affectionate."

"Hard to believe, but I've been in the room for those interactions." She gives me a teasing smile.

"InterFlix will make it appear as though you and I are…" I fumble for the best way to phrase my concern. "I'm not the kind of guy women settle down with. I'm a fling. I'm not a relationship."

An unfamiliar expression clouds her face, but the emotion is so swift, I can't catch it.

"I'll look like your rebound. Like you're rebounding out of your marriage with me," I say.

"Maybe or maybe we'll just look like good friends who have spent a lot of time training together. We won't be alone on the course. Iris and the rest of the team will always be with us." She crosses her arms. "But if you want to be my rebound, I would be fine with that."

No woman has ever described a relationship with me so dispassionately and with so little care. I started this conversation with Tucker, but somewhere along the line, we've switched to Maren, and I'm not sure what I said wrong to get us there. Last week, Tucker was grinding on my lap and murmuring my name with so much intensity I thought she might come all over me. That's the level of enthusiasm I wanted this conversation to have. More of a fuck me than a fuck you, energy.

"To recap, I can behave any way I want around you. If InterFlix edits everything to make it appear as though you've rebounded into my bed, you're completely cool with that."

"There are no beds out here." She flushes and glances away.

"Maren."

"What do you want me to say?" Maren asks, stepping closer. "I gave you the answer you wanted, didn't I? A fling, a rebound, nothing serious."

"That's not—"

"I'm getting a divorce, so it's not as though I'm looking to jump from one relationship into another."

I cross my arms and stare at her while I take in her claim. Something about her attitude doesn't sit right with me, but I can't put my finger on which part. Her words sound true, but to me, it doesn't *feel* true. Not sure if that's a *me* problem or a *her* problem.

"We need to get moving again, or we'll lose time and positions." She walks away from me. "I'll take my lead from you," she says. "You know this aspect of things better than me."

Her decision should make me feel better. I can go back to flirting and affection, and she's given me permission to do both on camera. Her marriage, which is currently on life support, will be dead. Guaranteed. I should be happy about all that.

Except I always pictured her agreeing to be with me, any version of being with me, with a hell of a lot more enthusiasm. Her begrudging acceptance doesn't feel like a win at all.

---

Luckily, I am not easily deterred, and since she agreed, I have slung my arm around her with planned casualness, kissed her temple and dropped a few well-timed dad jokes that almost got a smile. Maren is still in charge, but I'm warming her up one degree at a time. Soon enough, I'll have Tucker back. If I was the manipulative sort, I'd bring up my dad, but that would betray them both.

Two hours later, we're climbing onto bikes, and Iris is slipping into the vehicle that will ride along beside us while Iris films. It's a smart move on Iris's part because it's starting to drizzle. The claylike surface of the road is going to become impossible to navigate, even on a mountain bike. Tucker warned me, whenever I complained about doing Mount Juniper in the rain, that we were racing in Fiji during the wet season. She forgot to mention the red dirt paths.

We secure everything on our backs and bikes, and then we're single file up the path. Rain falls at a consistent sprinkle, but I can see from the bikes ahead that it's becoming muddier, and the mud is beginning to stick to places on the bikes. The rain isn't strong enough to wash any of it away; it's merely creating more of a mess.

Maren is just ahead of me, and her back tire is saggy.

"Tucker," I call out. "I think you've got a flat."

Wren and Riker, who are leading, stop with us. Tucker crouches down to peer at her tire, and she sighs.

"It's flat. I've got the tools to fix it. You three go ahead. I'll catch up."

Riker and Wren climb back on their bikes, but I'd rather stay. She glances in my direction and then says, "Riker, tell Brice to stick with the team."

"Come on, Your Highness," Riker says. "Maren has this covered."

"You sure?" I ask her, even though her dismissal was rude, at best. Whatever I've said to create this distance between us, I'd really like to undo it.

"Yeah," she says.

I climb on my bike and let out a deep breath. Leaving her doesn't feel right, but it's pretty clear she doesn't want any of us around. Maybe she just needs some space. The constant filming makes it tough to truly be yourself. None of us have gotten to the point where we've forgotten Iris is there.

I follow Riker and Wren, and our bikes get progressively more gummed up. Iris followed me, but when Riker has to stop to clear out his chain, I glance behind us.

"At what point are we supposed to expect her to catch up?" I ask.

Wren checks her watch and frowns. "Maybe I should double back to check on her."

"No," I say. "If anyone is, I'll do it. We'll meet about a kilometer from the next checkpoint. Does that work?"

"We don't normally split up that much," Riker says with a grimace.

"This mud is only going to get worse," I say. "Better to have at least half the team through it before we're all pushing our bikes instead of riding them."

"You don't have a map or compass," Wren says.

"Tucker checked the map earlier, and I was looking over her shoulder. Seemed like a straight shot down this road. Then we switch to water of some sort." Or I think so.

Riker has the map out. "You're right. We'll meet at the river."

They both get on their bikes and pedal onward, and I'm surprised when the vehicle with Iris in it doesn't turn around to follow me. But the path is narrow, and it's probably easier to stay the course.

Returning to Tucker is slow going, but when I arrive, she's struggling to get the new tube in the tire, and there's blood dripping from her hand.

I drop my bike and crouch at her side as the rain increases a notch. "What happened?"

"Sliced my finger," she says, showing me the gash.

My first aid kit is in my bag, and I ease it off my back and dig around until I find it.

"Then I couldn't get the tube in and the tire back on without making my cut worse."

"Should have let me stay," I say with a hint of a smile as I clean her wound with an alcohol swab.

She winces at the contact and glances up at me. "An 'I told you so' was exactly what I was hoping for."

"That's surprising," I say. "I would have thought it would be the last thing you'd have wanted. Not to worry." I tap my temple. "I'm locking that in for future reference."

"Where's your appendage?" She gazes over my shoulder.

"Would you believe Iris and her camera ditched me to follow Wren and Riker? I feel betrayed."

A hint of a smile touches her lips, and I grab a bandage from the first aid kit, trying to keep the contents from getting too wet. I wrap it around the slice on her finger.

"Thanks for coming back for me," she says.

"I'd never willingly leave you behind," I say, and I take the tube and tire from her, and I slot it in as though I've done it many times before. And I have—too many. Jag and I spent a whole afternoon taking tires apart and putting them back together after Maren mocked me for my lack of perseverance.

"I've been blowing a little hot and cold on you, huh?"

Her comment catches me by surprise, and I let out a snort. "A bit?"

"We can label whatever we do in front of the camera as a fling or a rebound or whatever." She takes a deep breath. "I think I just—I just." She huffs out a breath. "I mean, do you actually care about me? You're fire and ice with me too. One minute I think you might have some sort of feelings toward me, and the next minute, I feel like I could be any woman anywhere."

"Can you handle the truth, Tucker?" Can I? We run forward and retreat on each other all the time, but I don't want to do that anymore. If she's done with her husband—if I can convince her to be completely and forever done with him—then there are things I'd want to have with her. Labeling those half-baked ideas seems impossible, but they're there, in the back of my mind, percolating. I remember staring at Grace and picturing a baby with dark hair and pale-blue eyes.

I finish the tire, and when I glance at her, there are tears in her eyes. The sight causes a twinge of hesitation in me over whether I should be completely honest. I'm not sure why she'd crying. We can't keep dancing around each other, and I've got nothing but my pride to lose by confessing.

"I don't know if I can handle it," she says. "But tell me anyway."

"I meant what I said in my room the night my father died. You are my most favorite person in the world. There is no one else I'd rather spend time with. Truly. Not a line, not a joke. The complete truth." The rain has soaked through our clothing, and I'll probably wish I'd worn better layers. "I don't want to run hot and cold with each other anymore. I want to let the fire burn."

She runs her thumb along my cheekbone, but I can't read her expression. I'm throwing myself out into the void, and I have no idea if she'll meet me there. But I won't keep doing this back-and-forth with her. I want what I want, and if I can have her, I'm damn well going to take this slice of happiness.

"What do you want?" I ask.

# Chapter Thirty

## MAREN

Whatever is between us can burn until it burns out. Hot and fierce and out of control. But I don't say that. Coherent thoughts are impossible when he's looking at me as though he wants to lap me up. Instead, I kiss him. The bike tools fall out of his hands and plop into the mud. Brice grabs my ass, dragging me up his body while he rises to his feet, so my legs are wrapped around his waist. My hands are in his soaked hair, and just like last time, I'm completely lost in him.

An earthquake could hit, and I'm not sure I'd notice. Was kissing always this good? Unlike last time, his kisses quickly turn from frantic to sensual and slow, as though we've got all the time in the world. His tongue slides into my mouth, and I tighten my legs around his waist. I wish we were anywhere but on a muddy dirt road in the middle of Fiji. Everything in me is yearning to be closer, to shed my wet clothes and rip off his, and live in this moment forever.

Earlier when he said he was only fling material, my chest ached. It shouldn't have. I only decided to end my marriage a few days ago. Something brief should be exactly what I want, and maybe it's what I need. No strings. No attachments. Even if he wanted something more serious, I can't give him the one thing he's already told me is of the utmost importance. It's presumptuous to think he'd want a baby with me, but I can't help going there as he backs me up against a tree, under the cover of a denser canopy, and grinds against me. The desire to be with him overwhelms me, knocking out all logical sense.

How risky would it be to let him fuck me here in the middle of an adventure race being streamed by an international conglomerate? I wish I cared. All I can think about is getting him naked, feeling every inch of him against me, inside me, racing toward a different kind of finish line.

"How fast can you be?" I gasp.

"Tell me you did not ask me that, Tucker." He chuckles against my neck. "Aren't you the same person who told me passion is overrated, once?"

"That was Maren," I say, and I try to steer his lips back to mine. I'm only sort of joking. Over the last few months, I've come to see Brice's point. Maren is guarded and prickly around him, but Tucker—she's the part of me my mother claims is wild at heart. The risk-taker, and God knows, Brice is a risk.

My admission that he's right about me being two people sets off another laugh from him, and when our gazes connect, so much warmth floods me that it's hard to think straight. He's such a beautiful man, and right now, the way he's looking at me, it feels like I'm precious, irreplaceable. I'm not sure anyone has ever looked at me with quite so much reverence.

Brice is cut in two like me—the happy-go-lucky guy who couldn't care less about most things and the man who's staring at me now as though there is truly nowhere else he'd rather be.

The mix of silly and serious is far more appealing than I ever gave him credit for. I don't wonder anymore how women have been sucked into his orbit over and over again. The pull is magnetic, impossible to deny, a curved path that keeps leading them back to him. And here I am, not repelled, just as caught up in his gravitational field.

He runs his fingertip over my brow and down the side of my face before giving me a gentle kiss. "I want you, Tucker." To emphasize his point, he brushes his hard length against me. "But not in a rush against a tree." Then a slow smile spreads across his face. "At least not the first time." He nuzzles my nose with his, and then he kisses me again.

We kiss a thousand different ways. Softly, deeply, tongues dipping in, half smiles on our faces, and with a mixture of tenderness and passion that makes everything in me ache for more. I haven't spent this much time kissing someone in years.

"You," Brice says, digging his hands under my ass to keep me up. "Are." He tilts his head to the side to skim his lips across mine. "An excellent." And he brushes another kiss against my temple. "Kisser." He breathes heavy in my ear. "And if we don't stop, I'm going to come in my shorts."

"If it makes you feel better," I say, "I came ten minutes ago."

He nibbles my earlobe and then slowly lowers my legs but keeps me pinned between him and the tree. "Unless you came while watching me change the bike tire, you're a liar."

"It was incredibly sexy," I say. "A man who can rise to a challenge is a beautiful thing." His diligence with training and learning new skills has been impressive.

"I've been rising for you for a while now." His lips are tipped up in amusement. "I didn't want to disappoint you a second time."

Pinpricks race across my skin at the notion my opinion matters to him. Instead of saying anything, I draw him into another kiss, and he slides his hands under my damp shirt. At least beneath the tree's canopy, the rain isn't hitting us as hard.

In the distance, an engine rumbles, and Brice releases a sigh.

"I can't decide if Iris is saving me or extending my torture." He steps back, and he bends at the waist, taking a few deep breaths with his hands on his knees. "Might need a minute."

"You going to see how fast you can be after all? A little solo trip to the finish line?" I say with a small smile before I plant a kiss on his temple. When I try to step away, he snakes an arm around my waist and draws me against him. I lean into him, but I'm aware there's a chance Iris is filming. "I need to go. Or you need to go. One of us needs to meet her."

He scrapes his teeth along my earlobe, and then he lets me go so I can leave the trees to return to the bikes. As soon as I step out from the canopy, the rain hits me with force. Brice was smart to guide us under the cover of the dense foliage.

"I'll think of you the whole time," he calls.

"I hope it's good."

"It always is."

When I glance back, he's got the cheeky grin I've come to expect, and he's standing upright now while rain sheets around me.

"Where's the prince?" Iris asks when the SUV is close enough.

"Bathroom break." I gather the tools Brice dropped in the mud, flick them as clean as I can, and slot them into my emergency repair kit. When I do, I notice that blood has seeped through my bandage, and that reminds me of the last time I was on a course. Blood never used to bother me. Earlier I was too focused on the bike tire, and then on Brice, to really absorb my sliced finger. A chill streaks through me, and I shiver.

Brice emerges from the tree line, and his presence pushes out the cold edging over me, but guilt pinches me at what we just did. I sent the separation paperwork, and Caitlin confirmed that Enzo received it. Coming to Fiji as a competitor was as good as dooming us, anyway. But after so many years with Enzo, it's hard to believe we've truly reached the end of our marriage, that what I just did with Brice wasn't a betrayal.

Who am I kidding? I've been betraying Enzo for months. Whether I was actually kissing Brice or not, there's been an undeniable connection between us. Perhaps all the hate was never hate at all. The thought, like so many lately, makes me both happy and sad.

I lift my bike out of the mud where it fell. Brice must sense my mood because he comes over to me and rubs a hand along my back before leaning in close enough for me to feel his breath on my neck.

"You okay?" he calls above the rain.

"I'm good," I say, keenly aware of the camera over his shoulder. "Thanks for circling back to help me fix my tire."

"Did you know," he says as he gets on his bike, "that it gets more expensive to buy a tire pump with every year that passes?"

He's setting himself up; I can feel it. But the casualness with which he always presents his terrible jokes does amuse me. "Oh," I say, playing along. "Why's that?"

"It's all that inflation."

I grin and shake my head. Not for the first time, I'm grateful for him. He's gotten so good at reading my moods, and a lot of the time, he seems to understand what I need to be drawn back to the present. The here and now is the best place for me to live. Nothing in the past can be changed, and if I keep looking back, I might miss what's right in front of me.

We both get on our bikes, and we begin the hard pedal through thick mud that will get us back to Riker and Wren. Hopefully, we haven't lost too much time.

That night at dusk, when we roll into our checkpoint where we'll crash for a few hours after white water rafting and rappelling down a cliff face, I'm not as tired as I expected. Part of it is what I know still lies ahead on the course, but the other part is what happened with Brice and me earlier. The memory is enough to light my body up again, but I also have this lingering guilt I can't quite get rid of.

Once we're settled, Iris says she needs some individual interviews with Wren and Riker. In response, Brice claims he's headed to the bathrooms, and he raises his eyebrows at me before leaving.

"I'm going to talk to a few other teams. See how the race is with all this rain," I say. Perfectly plausible. I know a lot of the competitors, but Jag's eyes narrow slightly. The guy doesn't miss much.

There are tents and other shelters dotted along the field being used as this checkpoint and base camp for racers. Brice is ahead of me, and a few people call out to him to congratulate him on our great standing. Top ten is okay, but we're capable of so much better. Likely, the other experienced racers are surprised he isn't just a pretty face and a dead weight. Makes me a bit proud to realize he's proven me and them wrong at almost every turn since we started training.

Brice disappears into the portable bank of bathrooms, and I wonder whether I misinterpreted him. I was sure we were headed for the bushes behind here.

When another racer I've known for years from Australia hobbles over, we fall into a discussion about the mud and the amount of rain. None of us expected an easy course during the rainy season, but it seems like an unusually high amount of precipitation, even for that. Without our phones, we don't have a search engine at our fingertips, so it's all speculation. The one thing everyone seems to agree on is that it's impossible to keep any kit we wear dry for long. Despite changing socks and shoes as often as we can, we're all on the lookout for the start of trench foot.

Brice comes out of the washrooms, and he stands on the little platform for a beat. Our gazes connect, and then he slips behind the unit. I make my excuses to my friend, and I go around the building. As soon as I'm past the edge, he sweeps me into his arms and pins me against the wall. His nose brushes against mine, but he doesn't kiss me. There's a soft glow from the bathroom windows, which lights the area around us.

"What is this sorcery?" Brice mutters.

"You make me sound like a witch who should be burned at the stake."

"Never. I'd hunt anyone who hurt you to the ends of the earth."

Then he kisses me, and my heart is singing, intoxicated by his words and proximity. He sneaks his hand up the back of my damp shirt, and the skin-to-skin contact sends another jolt of desire through me. The rest of this adventure race is going to be torturous for reasons I've never encountered before. Lust. So much lust.

"Are we sneaking around?" Brice murmurs against my neck.

"Aren't we?" I cling to his biceps, and coherent thought seems to have vanished from my mind.

"I don't want to sneak around."

His whispered words are like having a bucket of ice dumped on me, and I draw away from him, turning my face when he tries to kiss me again.

"I don't want this"—I gesture between the two of us—"on camera."

"You're getting a divorce."

Saying what's caused this streak of panic inside me doesn't feel right, but I can't discount it either. Brice said it himself—he's not the commitment guy. Putting whatever this is on blast across the world could ruin both of us. How would I look to everyone when he moves on to someone else? Perhaps even before the show airs.

"I don't want to answer those questions later," I say.

"It's not like you'd go back to him." Brice pins with me his gaze. "Tucker, tell me you wouldn't take him back."

"I cheated on him," I whisper. "I couldn't go back to him now."

He pushes off the building and strides away from me and then paces back and forth. He runs his hands through his wet hair before putting his hands on his hips and staring at me.

"I feel like you should have more self-respect."

His statement sets my teeth on edge, and I mirror his pose. "Self-respect? In what regard? Are we talking about this flirtation or fling or whatever you want to call it between you and me? Or the breakdown of my marriage?"

In the muted light from the bathroom window, his jaw tics. "Every time he comes up, we take ten steps backward."

"How many steps forward are you and I actually going to take? Let's be real."

He closes the distance between us, and he backs me against the wall again, his lips connecting with mine with so much force that our teeth scrape before we're devouring each other. There's nothing tender or gentle about these kisses. They're filled with our mutual frustration and desire.

When Brice breaks the kiss, we're both breathing hard. "No more steps back. You want this—" He kisses me again, slow and deep. "To be a secret. Fine. But I'm not pretending, whether there's a camera present or not, that I don't care about you."

He's a jumble of mixed signals, but I'm not sure I want to sort them out right now. On the racecourse, we have to stay focused, or accidents happen. Wondering what I mean to him, questioning what I feel for him will only push us into emotional territory I'm not ready for.

"Stolen moments," I say.

"I will gladly become a thief for you."

There's such a mix of sincerity, and that teasing quality I've come to love, that I kiss him again. I don't know where this road of stolen moments will take us, but I don't doubt that I want to walk it, even if it leaves my feet bruised and blistered.

# Chapter Thirty-One

## BRICE

At every checkpoint and every area that has an out-of-the-way nook or cranny, Tucker and I snatch moments with each other. A kiss. A flick of a tongue against an earlobe. Her ass pressed against my pelvis, a delicious tease. Her fingers sneaking under my shirt and dancing along the small of my back. Each point of contact is carefully coordinated and crafted, and she's driving me wild. Who knew delayed gratification could be so intoxicating?

Being around Tucker and not being *with* Tucker is such a fucking tease. I've never wanted a woman the way I want her. Every move she makes draws my attention, and if I have any moments in the day where I'm not focused on getting ahead in this race, my thoughts wander back to her. It's like my brain has been rewired, and each wire leads to Maren Tucker. If I didn't enjoy how she makes me feel, I'd be worried about my mental health. The intensity of my feelings for her cannot be normal, but right now, I really don't care. In life I've always been one to do what feels good, and being around Tucker is an incredible high.

At tonight's checkpoint, Tucker leaves for the washrooms before me. Without discussing it, we've fallen into a pattern of staggering our exits from our teammates to make it less obvious something is going on. I've seen the looks Wren has been throwing us, though. She knows something is up, even if she isn't sure what that *something* is. Likely she isn't the only one.

Our flirting has become progressively less subtle, and I couldn't be happier. The exhibitionist in me would love to grab Tucker and let our make-out sessions be for public consumption and inspection. People can think what they like, judge me in any way they want. Most of the people who don't like me don't know me. I've learned that nothing deters someone determined to think ill of me and my family. Besides, I know my truth and my worth.

Tucker isn't like that, though. She puts up a front like she couldn't care less about other people's opinions—she used to be like that with me—but now that I know her, I realize her attitude is a decoy. Her parents' poor morals and ethics seem to have created this intense desire to be *better*. If I dragged her down, she'd never forgive me, so I keep my lips to myself in public and my dick, mostly, in my pants in private. Part of me is a bit surprised she's even allowed us to get this far. She is a puzzle I'm slotting together one piece at a time.

At the edge of the washrooms, I wait for her. The bathroom door bangs, and someone close to me calls Maren's name. Her steps stutter, and I can't see her yet, but I sense she's close. Just out of reach. If I appeared out of the shadows right now, I'd give too much away.

"What's up, Emery?" Maren says, and there's wariness in her voice.

"Wanted to congratulate you. Rumors all over the racecourse about you and the prince concocting an affair for ratings and donations."

"That's what people are saying?"

My heart kicks at the notion of people talking about us. Despite what we've been doing, Maren will hate being a source of gossip.

"I notice you didn't deny it. Careful the pretend doesn't become real for you. I heard you're getting divorced, but Prince Brice is not the kind of rebound anyone needs."

"Oh? You know him, do you?" Maren's tone is acidic. I've been on the receiving end of that burning sting.

"He's been all over the gossip pages since he was a teenager. It's not like it's hard to see where this scheme is likely headed." Emery scoffs. "I never thought you'd be the type to be swayed by glossy charm."

"I'd be a lot more inclined to listen to your opinion if you actually knew him. You're talking out of your ass."

"He has an on-off fuck-buddy princess in Denmark, so I wouldn't go pinning your hopes on landing a prince. You and I both know that lots of people confuse the camaraderie of teammates on a racecourse for something else only to realize later they're wrong."

I'm half tempted to emerge from the shadows and give Emery a piece of my mind. What's happening between me and Tucker isn't what she's trying to label it. While I might not have a tidy label for the attraction we feel, it's not what she's calling it. I take a step before Tucker speaks up.

"I'm not pinning anything on anyone except my team thoroughly demolishing yours once again on the course. Shame you've tried to resort to some sort of inept rumor warfare. I'm not defending him to you, because you don't deserve to know him."

"I was trying to warn you. He's a fuck boy."

"Your ignorance is noted."

Footsteps retreat from the edge of the washrooms.

"I would say enjoy the view of my ass on the course, but your team is so far back, you probably can't see it without selling your soul to the devil," Maren calls. "Assuming she hasn't already done that," Maren mutters.

When Tucker doesn't immediately come around the edge of the washrooms, I lean against the corner of the building. "Tucker."

She spins on her heel, and she walks toward me, but she doesn't reach for me like she normally does, as though we can't wait to get our hands on each other.

"You heard all that?" she asks.

"I did. You okay?"

"Am *I* okay?" She frowns. "Emery just made you seem awful, and you're asking about me?"

"Haters gonna hate." I shrug. "She's not worth my time, but whatever you're feeling is." The tenseness in her frame is worrying. "You're upset."

"I hate that people are gossiping about me, and I hate that anyone thinks I'm naïve. I know what's going on between us. They don't, but *I* do."

Suppose it's good one of us knows because I don't have a fucking clue what's happening between us anymore. She's top-shelf tequila, and I want to suck up every drop.

"Do you want me to explain Denmark?" I ask.

"You have a past, and I have a past. Given how I've been behaving, I don't have much of a moral leg to stand on, do I?"

"Tucker, come on." Unable to resist, I loop my arm around her middle and tug her against me. As far as I'm concerned, her morality hasn't been comprised. The temptation to remind her what a shitty husband Enzo has been is almost more than I can bear, but I've learned from past experience. I don't need more frost to coat the air between us, so I nuzzle her neck instead, and she bends into me.

"Denmark?" I suggest again. Technically, what I do in Denmark is a royal secret. Alex offered me up in a deal when he practically ditched Princess Simone at the altar. At the time, I didn't care how the situation was represented to outsiders or how Freja and I might appear. One favor has turned into multiple, so our two monarchies keep up the appearance that what happened between Alex and Simone was carefully orchestrated rather than a giant "Oh, fuck."

She shakes her head, and she draws my lips to hers. I tighten my embrace, and when she hops into my arms, I back her against the building while I kiss her. Letting this conversation go is probably the wrong thing to do, but I only get so many minutes with Tucker pressed up against me, and I'm not ruining them with unimportant details. Denmark is insignificant, has never come up in all our conversations. I knew there was gossip, but it had never touched our bubble before, and unless Freja calls me, the arrangement tends to slip my mind. The truth is complicated to explain, and no one outside the royal families would understand.

"She doesn't know you," Tucker says when I tug on her earlobe with my teeth before kissing a line down her throat.

I bring my lips back to hers, and I kiss her deeply, pouring every ounce of my certainty into her well of uncertainty. Of all the people I know, I'm not sure anyone but my family has seen the sides of me Tucker has. Maybe she even understands me more because I've never had to hide any part of me from her—never wanted to. In so many ways, she's been privy to me at my worst, and we're still here.

When I break the kiss, I place my forehead against hers, and we're both breathing heavy. "Tucker," I say.

"I don't want to talk," she says. "None of it matters."

She doesn't give me a chance to respond before she kisses me again, and when her hand sneaks under my T-shirt to slide against my skin, all coherent thought vanishes. But in the back of my mind, unease lives. All of it matters where she's concerned.

In fact, I'm starting to worry she matters too fucking much. Maren Tucker has tattooed herself across my skin, and I've got no desire to scrub her out or erase her. I'm not sure what's going to happen when this race is over, but I'm sure I don't want what's between us to stop.

# Chapter Thirty-Two

## MAREN

It's an hour before dawn on day eight out of ten, and I'm exhausted. We've just waved goodbye to Gary and Jag. All of us aren't far off zombies, sleeping as little as possible and moving through obstacles with as much speed as we can, safely. Between the cameras and brisk pace, Brice and I have been only able to snatch moments here or there—mostly behind the bathrooms when we reach a checkpoint. Every interaction is rushed, and sometimes I'm so paranoid about being caught that I can't quite get swept away.

Ever since my confrontation with Emery, a little voice in the back of my head has been cautioning me against enjoying Brice too much. He's been very upfront about how casual we are, and I don't need more from him than his honesty. A level head where he's concerned is a must because whatever is happening between us is temporary.

Our team has managed to climb into third position in the ranks, and first is within our sight. If we manage to top the leaderboard, we'll have an extra two hundred thousand to put toward the Alzheimer's Society. We never discussed winning when Paxton was part of the team. Wren, Riker, and Paxton were content to finish, raise some money on the island through a donation push, and ensure the youngest prince didn't get injured. None of us thought we had a chance at winning.

Once we started the course, and Brice proved himself not just capable of succeeding but determined to keep up with any tempo we set, our perspective shifted.

We're so close now that we've all got the hunger. We're calculating hours of sleep and negotiating where we can sensibly cut time. The biggest issue is the rain, which has been much higher than seasonal norms, and is both a blessing and a curse. Since we've trained so many times in poor conditions in Bellerive, it's not slowing us down or depressing us the way I imagine it is for some less experienced teams and fair-weather racers. The mud, though, is making any biking sections almost impossible. It cakes the spokes, wheels, and tires to the point where we eventually have to carry the bike or drag it along the road.

Hours after we've left the checkpoint, we're standing at the edge of a cliff, staring down the ravine at a river we need to navigate along for the next six kilometers, and I'm so tired of being wet that I want to collapse in a puddle and cry. Everything

I own smells musty, and despite Jag and Gary's efforts at the base camps, nothing gets one hundred percent dry before I need to put it back on. Of all the weather conditions I've raced in, extended rain is the worst. Snow or heat have their own challenges, but I much prefer them over this constant chilly dampness.

As though he can sense the change in me, Brice slides his hand along my shoulders and rests his fingers at the base of my neck. It's a gesture I didn't even realize I needed, and when I glance in his direction, his lips tilt into an almost smile.

"What did one raindrop say to another?" he asks.

On instinct, I rise on my toes and kiss his cheek. He draws me tight against his side and places a kiss on top of my head.

"Two's company. Three's a cloud," I say.

"I've already made that joke?" He grins.

"Two days ago, also when it was raining. You running out of material?"

"Going to have to hang out with some dads and get some new jokes."

"Or just get better jokes," I suggest. The casual mention of fatherhood causes a brief tightening across my chest.

"Who could have predicted I'd need ten days of rain jokes?" He chuckles and gives me another squeeze before releasing me.

"Right," Riker says from beside us after surveying the ravine below. "Down we go."

According to the directions we received, this river is supposed to be shallow enough for us to wade in some places rather than swim. The water is freezing—so cold I worry about hypothermia if any of us stop moving—and we haven't been able to touch the bottom at all.

Riker says we'll reach the checkpoint in another kilometer, and there, we should be able to touch in order to collect the talisman we need. Night is beginning to fall, and I'm concerned we'll be stuck in this ravine in the dark. We've got headlamps, but unknown water at night is a safety concern.

At the checkpoint, we gather on the wrong side of the river by accident. Rather than crossing the river, we find a spot to sit and eat something before carrying on. We have another two kilometers before we're out of here, and it's the tail end of dusk. While I'd rather not stop, I understand that our bodies need some fuel, especially with the cold temperatures in the water.

Since I finish first, I stand up and rub my hands along my arms, trying to warm up. "I'll get the talisman."

"Not alone," Brice says, dusting off his hands and stepping down to the edge of the river beside me.

"It actually is shallow here," I say. "I'll be fine to cross, grab it, and cross back. There's enough light."

"Not alone," he reiterates.

An unnecessary waste of energy. It's not as though there are any spots across the river where we could even snatch a single moment of time alone without the camera seeing us. Iris has been wielding that thing like a weapon. Still, I'm so cold and tired that I can't bring myself to argue with him. Instead, I grab my pack in case of an emergency, and I sling it across my back.

As I wade through the water, Brice is a couple of steps behind me. It's deeper than I thought in the middle, and the current is so strong that I have to be very deliberate about where I place my feet. We're coming up the other side when a blast of water hits my knees, as though someone released a tiny dam right behind me. The sudden rush dislodges the grip my shoes have on the river floor.

"Oh!" I cry out as I go down, and a sharp pain slices into my upper thigh.

Rather than being propelled down the river like I expect, I'm brought up short and sharp, and there's a grunt behind me.

"I've got you," Brice says through gritted teeth. "Can you get your feet underneath you?"

My leg that isn't throbbing with cold and pain is able to scramble for purchase and find some. When I ease myself into a standing position, Brice changes his grip from my backpack to my elbow.

"Jesus," he says. "You fucking scared me." He drags me against his chest, and we stand clutching each other on the edge of the river.

Truthfully, I thought I was going for a swim in the wrong direction, and if he hadn't insisted on following me across, I would have. The current is faster and stronger on this side, or maybe the current is changing. It wasn't that hard to swim against it a little while ago, but now looking at it, I'm not sure how we'll navigate the last two kilometers to get the team out of the ravine.

He starts to lead us the last few feet to the shore, but I'm hobbling, and my uneven gait catches his attention.

"Tucker, are you hurt?"

"Sliced my leg on a rock, I think." I'm not checking, but it definitely hurts. We just need to grab the talisman and get back to our teammates. We didn't work this hard, deny ourselves rest and sleep, for me to go down in the last few days.

"Your pants are ripped," Brice says.

I reach for the cliff face holding the talisman, and I grab the gold circle we need to prove we made it this far. We have our own personal videographer to document every second of our day, so the proof feels more of a formality than during a normal race. Brice slips it into my pack, and my leg pulses in pain. If I prod it or baby it, Brice will realize how much it hurts, and I don't want him to know. But the ache is incredibly distracting.

"Maren! Brice!" Iris calls from across the river. "They've called time on the race. We're paused."

Iris carries a walkie-talkie to communicate with the producers and the race organizers. Overhead, a helicopter circles, and it makes hearing difficult for a moment.

"The river is flooding. You need to get to high ground." Iris points to the cliff face behind us. "There's a crew cabin up there."

"We'll stay here!" Riker yells and gestures behind him to the cliff we initially came down. "When the race resumes, we'll meet at the talismans."

"Ten-four," Brice calls back.

Unable to resist anymore, I glance at my legs, and my pants are dark. Wet from the water, I'm sure. I run my hand along my thigh, and when I draw it back, my palm is bright red in the glow of my headlamp. Then my brain clicks on the sticky texture between my legs, and my vision blurs.

"Brice," I murmur.

He glances down at me, and our gazes connect for a beat before his slides to my hand, which is framed in the spotlight of our headlamps. "You hurt yourself?" There's an edge of panic in his tone.

"I don't know," I say, and my voice cracks. My brain is stepping back to the last time this happened—all the blood—what all the blood meant. "I don't know."

"I've got you," Brice says, and he takes my pack off my back, slings it over his in one fluid movement, and then he picks me up. He scales the cliff with me in his arms, a testament to how much time we spent on the wall at his property that he can pick his way through the rocky face and find the logical places to climb without having to put me down. I curl myself into him, and I try not to think about what the blood means.

*It can't mean that. It can't mean that. It's not possible. It's not. I'm fine. It's nothing. A scratch. A scratch.*

At the top of the cliff, he's breathing heavy, but he doesn't set me down. He seems to get his bearings, and he presses his lips to my temple before striding forward.

"As soon as I get you to the cabin, we'll get you fixed up. A scrape, that's all. You're going to be okay." There's so much determination in his voice that the panic welling in my throat stops rising. He'll look after me, and I believe that with every fiber of my being.

At the cabin door, Brice fumbles with the handle before swinging it wide and getting us inside. He sets me on the couch, and I curl into a ball, and it's only then that I realize I'm sobbing. Heaving, gasping sobs. How long have I been crying this hard?

He appears crouched in front of me with a first aid kit in his hand. "Tucker, sweetheart, I can fix this, but I need to get your pants off to assess the damage."

Any other time, I might laugh at him offering to take my pants off, but right now, I'm so caught up in whatever this is I can't breathe. I cover my face with my hands, and I focus on getting my breathing and crying under control. My head throbs in time with my leg, and my chest is tight. So unbearably tight. My breath hitches, and I fumble with the waistband of my pants. I need them off. I want them off.

Brice covers my hands with his, and the contact stills everything inside of me for a beat, centers me. I meet his gaze. One of his hands strays to my hair, and he brushes aside some pieces that have come loose from my ponytail. He leans forward and presses his lips to my forehead, breathing me in. Then he returns to the waistband on my pants, and he gently eases them down my legs.

The gash on my leg is jagged and ugly. Must have been a rock, but seeing the evidence of where I hurt myself calms me another notch. This isn't the same. A cut. I'll be okay. I take a deep, shuddering breath, and Brice squeezes my hips with one hand while he digs through the first aid kit with the other.

He cleans the wound with enough alcohol to make me put a death grip on the couch. Then he applies a long, thick bandage and secures it in place with medical tape. Not ideal, and it'll likely come off in the water when the race resumes.

"I have waterproof bandages in my first aid kit," I say, my throat raw.

"When they restart the race, I'll change it out. No point in wasting those if this bleeds through." He glances up at me, and then he runs his thumb along my cheekbone. An increasingly familiar gesture.

"I probably look a mess," I say.

"A gorgeous mess," he says. "I'm going to get the cabin organized. Take advantage of these clotheslines to dry things and crank the space heaters. Practically the lap of luxury."

The cabin is more like a shack with two space heaters, a single oversize couch, a walkie-talkie set, and a fridge. But Brice is right. Hanging our stuff to dry with the heating cranked is a good idea. Although the dampness will feel even colder when we eventually have to go back out there.

"How long do you think they'll delay the race?" Brice asks as he putters around hanging things up.

"Likely until morning," I say, and my teeth begin to chatter.

"I once missed class because of hypothermia," Brice says as he digs around in my pack.

"Really?"

"I was too cool for school," he says as he drags out my tightly bundled sleeping bag from the dry bag I keep it in. He urges me to lift my arms as he removes my soaked shirt. My bra and underwear don't leave much to the imagination, and if I wasn't so cold, I might be more self-conscious. He unzips the sleeping bag and lays it around me, tucking it in tight as though seeing me almost naked is no big deal.

"Do you have a joke for everything?" The sleeping bag isn't warm yet, but the space heaters are starting to kick off some heat.

"Spent a lot of years having to entertain everyone from diplomats to bored society women." He winks at me before unearthing more things to hang up. "Court jester, at your service."

"You don't have to entertain me."

"I don't like seeing you sad."

"You're not the only one." I draw the material up to my chin, but my teeth are still chattering. All the times Enzo tried to cajole or force or threaten me into a better mood spring to mind.

Even before my accident, he didn't just hate to see me sad. He resented it. "People are allowed to be sad."

"Yeah, I—" Brice huffs out a breath. "I vowed that I wouldn't be the cause of it anymore." He runs a hand through his damp hair. "You can be sad. Of course you can be sad, but I'd never want to be the reason for it—not anymore."

"A vow?" I try to catch his gaze, but he's hanging things on the various clotheslines and drying racks. "Why would you make a vow?"

The walkie-talkie set on top of the fridge makes a static noise. "Prince Brice or Maren Tucker. Please confirm you're in the cabin."

Brice crosses the room and speaks into the walkie-talkie, confirming they'll radio when the race restarts and the plan to stay put until the water levels recede. He doesn't mention my injury, and if I wasn't so cold, I'd breathe a sigh of relief.

"We should probably take advantage of being able to sleep somewhat comfortably." He flicks out our rolled foam mattresses onto the floor, and he arranges his sleeping bag.

My teeth haven't stopped chattering, and I'm afraid to shift the blanket at all in case the chill creeps in.

He takes off his shirt, and his muscles ripple. After he undoes the top button of his shorts, they fall to the ground with a soft thud, and he places both items near the heaters.

"W-wh-y d-do you have so many tattoos?" I ask. They litter his skin, but I wouldn't say they cover it. A few are overlapped, but most of them have their own space carved out on his body.

"That's like asking why I've drank so much tequila." He stands at the edge of the couch with his hands on his hips.

"W-w-why have you drank so much tequila?" If that's the question he'd prefer to answer, I can ask it. Anything to keep my mind off his hot (mostly) naked body and my freezing one.

"You're still cold. Body heat, Tucker, or I'll have to use the walkie-talkie to get a medic in here."

"No. No medic." My teeth chatter through each word. A medic could end the race for me and for us. This chill will pass; I'm certain of it.

"Scooch," he says, and he tugs on the edge of the sleeping bag.

As I shift more toward the back of the couch, I try not to wince at the pain in my leg. That's another reason I don't need a medic. By morning, I'll be able to walk on it again. Physical pain is temporary.

Brice eases onto the couch, and with him comes the initial nip of opening the sleeping bag. But as soon as his body is pressed against mine, and the sleeping bag is snug around us, I remember why body heat is so beneficial. He's so warm, and I can already feel the deep freeze seeping out of my bones.

He loops his arm around my waist, and he presses me flush against him. We fit together in ways I never would have imagined, and I release a sigh of relief at the close contact. There's something about being close to him that causes the last vestiges of panic to dissipate. Without the watchful gaze of other people and a camera crew, it feels like I can be myself. Turns out

Maren Tucker loves being glued to Brice Summerset. Color me surprised.

"Will you tell me why you got so upset about your leg?" Brice asks. "Was it the blood?"

I stare into his light-brown eyes, and there's so much tenderness in his expression, my heart expands. How did I ever label him superficial? So much depth he hides behind jokes and bravado and charm. He is an ocean that I would drown in, every day, forever.

"I've heard some of the questions Iris has been asking you about your dad." I tiptoe my fingers across his temple, and he closes his eyes in response to the caress or maybe the mention of his father. There's so much warmth between us now that my teeth have stopped chattering. "That must be hard."

"It's not so bad if I focus on the things my father was able to see and experience with me. With us." He swallows, and he doesn't open his eyes. "I can't consider what will be missing when I go home. What will be absent—" He clears his throat. "From now on."

I snuggle into him, and I press my lips to his cheek. He sucks in a shaky breath, and I whisper, "You can be sad with me." They are words I wish anyone offered to me after my accident. I needed permission to grieve, and instead, so many people expected me to rebound as though I'm made of rubber and not flesh and bone. I suppose most of those people had no way of knowing it wasn't just my ankle that cracked wide open.

"You are a gift, Tucker," he says in a hoarse voice. "An absolute treasure."

Then he kisses me, and I mold myself to him, seek the heat that's thawing my heart and the frozen wasteland of my life one degree at a time.

# Chapter Thirty-Three

## BRICE

No one has ever given me permission to be anything other than my best self. As a royal, my high visibility means I'm on constant red alert. While I haven't always obeyed the societal norms my parents would have preferred, I've learned to keep a tight lid on my emotions in public. Too much of anything is bad for business. Nick and I tested that piece of wisdom many, many times when we were younger.

Now that I think about it, I've spent most of my life juggling the whims and wishes of other people. My parents, Nick, Alex, and an entire country—all have had certain expectations about who I am or what I'm capable of. So much so that I ignored as much as I could, often taking whatever path seemed easiest or the most fun.

Before Tucker entered my life, if someone had asked me if I was happy, I'd have said yes. A superficial happiness compared to whatever this is, on the couch, with her. Or maybe I was merely content, and I didn't know any better. She's pressed against me with her lips sliding over mine, and I'm the most alive I've ever been. After eight physically grueling days, I'm still ready to take on the world. It feels like I could conquer anything as long as I could look over and see her at my shoulder. Such a strange feeling to need someone with this intensity.

If I could rewind time and experience this again with her, I'd do it in a heartbeat. My world is in bloom, and she's the bulb that started it all.

"Are you warm enough yet, Tucker?" I murmur against her neck.

"Getting warmer," she says in a breathy voice. "I can take it hotter."

"You sure you can stand the heat?" An invitation to more of anything with her is one I'll gladly take.

"Why not? It's not like I'm getting out unscathed." Tucker dances her fingertips along my spine, and I harden in response.

"I promise I won't burn you." I feather kisses along the edges of her face before planting a gentle one on her lips. "I don't want to be the cause of your pain, Tucker. I want to soothe it."

"Pretty words," she murmurs, exposing her neck for my attention. "You always have such pretty words."

"You don't think I mean them?" I nip at her earlobe and then brush my nose against hers before angling another kiss across her lips. Her lack of faith in me should be offensive, but I understand that Enzo gave her the biggest promise of all—a ring, a life, forever, and he left. That has to make even the most open heart more closed, and Tucker is far from unguarded. What does that sort of misplaced faith do to someone who is already wary?

"Do *you* think you mean them?"

"I'm trying not to be offended here, Tucker," I say as I shift her farther underneath me, taking care to be gentle with her thigh. "Do you really believe I'd say things to you that I don't mean?"

"No," she whispers. "I think you mean them all." There's a strange sadness in her voice, but I'm so turned on it's hard to think straight.

"I do." I brush my length against the heat between her legs, and she moves with me. Her fingernails dig into my biceps, and she raises her hips to force contact again. I slip my hand under her to cradle her ass. "Your thigh—"

"Don't stop. It doesn't hurt. Just. Don't. Stop." Each word is punctuated by the drag and retreat of my erection grinding against her most sensitive parts.

I bury my face in her neck, and I move against her. Her breath is hot and heavy in my ear, and my breathing becomes elevated at the realization of how switched on she already is.

"I want you. I want to feel you inside me."

Those words are a sweet, sweet torture. There's nothing I want more than to tug her panties to the side and bring us both to the height of ecstasy, but I didn't exactly expect anything like this to happen on the racecourse.

"Tucker, I don't have—I've got nothing."

"My first aid kit," she says, drawing my face to hers, kissing me deeply. "Check my first aid kit."

"Are you sure—I—I need you to be sure." Even as I say it, I'm struggling to keep myself in check. Touching her, pressed tight against her, hearing those breathy, turned-on sounds in my ear, is undoing any hint of willpower I might have possessed where she's concerned.

"Yes," she says against my lips. "Yes."

Instead of leaving her, I cradle her close, and I rock against her. She drags her nails down my back to clutch my ass, and she keeps me tight to her. I'm stalling because this feels so good, but also because I'm not sure we should go further. I want to—I really, really want to—but I already feel so much for her, and sex hasn't been completely meaningless for me in years. Being with her might crack something open that I'll never be able to shut again. Rather than mocking my brothers from the sidelines, I fear I'll become them. Be so deeply immersed in my emotional connection to her that I won't be able to see straight. Everything already feels blurry, as though I'm uncertain where she ends and I begin. Solidifying that connection, putting it into sharp focus, is dangerous.

But I'm here—standing at the line—begging myself to both step over it and run for the hills. I want her so fucking much.

"Brice, please," she moans. "Please."

Fuck it. If I'm doing this, I'm doing it right.

"I want to go down on you."

She shakes her head. "You don't have—"

"I want to." I smooth her hair from her face, and I roll my hips against her most sensitive spot again. "Let me lick your pussy. I want to make you come."

"Orgasms are like magical unicorns for me. You'll be down there forever."

"Sounds like a hell of a way to pass the time in this isolated cabin—searching for a magical creature between your legs." I keep my tone light even though inside I'm pissed off. It's obvious her husband made her feel as though her pleasure wasn't worth his time and energy. Given all the other things I know about him, I shouldn't be surprised. The only good news is that I'm certain if we do this, she'll never go back to him.

"If you're sure..." She bites her lip.

I don't need a second invitation. Sliding down her body, I keep the sleeping bag on her while I discard her panties, and I cradle her ass in my palms. "Tell me when it feels good," I say, and then I slide my tongue up her center. She's wet and sweet on my lips. "I want to make you feel good."

She moans, and her hand strays to my shoulder, squeezing while I start a gentle rhythm. "That's—oh, oh, wow."

Her other hand is clenched around the couch cushion beside me, and when she rocks her hips against the slide of my tongue, I'm know I'm onto a winner. Patience and consistency are the keys. I'm careful to keep her thigh with the bandage out of the way. The pleasure-pain threshold is something we can discover together later. I could see Tucker getting off on that, but right now, all I want is to give her an orgasm she'll never forget. Me, between her legs, my tongue pressed to her core.

When I slip my tongue inside her, and I use my thumb to caress her nub in slow circles, her short nails dig into my shoulder.

"Tell me," I murmur.

"More," she says. "More. I think I'm—" She lets out a breathy sound that's an incredible turn on, and my dick twitches in response. "I'm close." Her hand flexes on my shoulder. "A little…a little faster."

I follow her directions, and I can feel her body tightening.

"How are you so good at this?" She sounds almost offended, and I release a soft chuckle at Maren coming out at the last minute.

The vibration of my laugh has an unexpected impact, and her hips rocket off the couch while she cries out something indistinguishable. She pulses around my tongue, and I lap her up, relishing in my success. One magical creature discovered.

I kiss a line up her body, and when I reach her lips, she drags me tight to her.

"Now give me your horn," she says next to my ear.

I chuckle against her neck. "You still want it?" I peer down at her, and there's a softness around her eyes that causes warmth to spread across my chest.

"I need to verify that the magical unicorn is you." She frames my face and places a gentle kiss on my lips.

Her bag is beside the couch, and I draw back to dig through it before coming to her first aid kit. Instead of opening it right away, I sit with it in my hand. It's been years since I've experienced this strange sensation in my belly, and I think it might be nerves.

"Need some help?" Tucker's tone is teasing.

"No, I—" I glance in her direction, and the hope and uncertainty are bare on her face for me to witness. We're not pretending with each other, and her expression is a good reminder. We take each other just as we are. "I think I might be nervous." I wince.

"About being with me?" A slow grin spreads across her face. "Really?"

Her delighted reaction is enough to smother my nerves, and I unzip the first aid kit to discover an entire string of condoms. "Tucker, how much sex were you planning to have?"

"First rule of adventure racing—always be prepared." Her grin is saucy.

"And for that, I am grateful," I say, and I smooth her hair back before ripping off one of the packages. I tap it against my thumb. "Your thigh, though. I don't want to hurt you." But I'm stalling because there are a hundred ways I could enter her and never come near her injury.

Tucker lets the sleeping bag slide to the floor, and her naked body is pure perfection. The only light in the room is the glow from the space heaters, and she's ethereal. Slowly, she turns onto her stomach, and she glances at me over her shoulder.

"Are you going to make me beg?" she asks.

I fear the only begging that'll be happening will be mine from now on. I slide my hand along her lower back, and she arches into the contact. After this, I'm convinced there will be no going back. The minute I sink into her, I'll never want to be anywhere else.

"You're sure?" I ask her, but it's really for me. Am *I* sure?

She grabs my hand and slides it between her legs where she's wet with need.

Before I can second-guess myself, I rip open the condom with my teeth, and I roll it over my shaft. She rises onto her knees, and I'm poised at her entrance with one hand on her hip and the other braced against the arm of the couch. Her palm covers my knuckles, and the last of my hesitation, my willpower, vanishes.

I slide into her, and I lose myself completely.

# Chapter Thirty-Four

## MAREN

In the past, sex has been good. Good enough that I was happy to do it again, but it's never crossed that plane into whatever is occurring between me and Brice. We're so in sync as he moves inside me that I'm trembling. It's terrifying and exhilarating to be so full of want and need. That's what it feels like—I don't just want this connection—I *need* him. All of him. That's the exhilarating part. The terrifying part is that I can't imagine this sensation ending. At this point, it would be like having a piece of me ripped out.

His hand smooths down my spine, and then he circles around to flatten his palm against my stomach, driving deeper into me. For the first time in my life, I think I might come from sex alone. Something is building inside of me again, a volcano ready to erupt, and I'm loving every second of the escalation. I'm floating on a plane of heightened awareness. It's too much and not enough.

*Overwhelming.* But so, so good.

"I don't understand why this feels... Why does this feel so good?" I gasp as his fingers slide between my slick folds.

"Magic," he murmurs before planting an open-mouthed kiss on the curve of my neck. "Witchcraft." His breath is hot in my ear, and his chest skims against my back.

Sensations course through me, hard to decipher, but the experience is definitely otherworldly. I grip his hand on the couch, and his thumb latches onto one of my fingers, locking it against him.

The second orgasm rushes through me with unexpected force, and I cry out, arching into Brice, and reaching for his hand that's between my legs to still his movement. Too much. Not enough. I already want it all over again even as I squeeze the length of him over and over, trying to catch my breath.

"Magic," he whispers, before latching on to my hip, and following me over the edge.

---

Brice is curled around me on the couch, his relaxed breathing in my ear, and guilt is creeping across me, insidious and unwanted. I have no reason to feel guilty that I just experienced more pleasure with Brice in one night than I did in five years with Enzo. After a few faltering attempts at oral sex when we first started dating, he never bothered pursuing it again. No boyfriends before him had much luck either, so I didn't blame him or his lack of perseverance. As far as I knew, it wasn't a way I could achieve an orgasm.

That's not to say I went completely without during our relationship, but climaxes were few and far between. A happy accident rather than something either of us expected me to achieve.

Sex was usually pleasurable and fun, but it never reached the intensity of what happened between me and Brice tonight. That's where the guilt and confusion seeps in. I've never felt this kind of connection with Enzo, despite the fact we got married. I didn't even know a bond could be this powerful, and to realize I might never experience this all-consuming high again makes me sad.

We're a fling. A rebound. An on-set romance that'll end as soon as the director calls cut. All the pretty words in the world don't change the hard truths Brice has also given me. He's not the forever guy. He doesn't want to be a happily ever after for me or anyone else. The baby he craves I can't easily give him, unlike most women in the world. I'll never carry a child, let alone his. To realize that what's divided me and Enzo is also what'll drive an impossible wedge between me and Brice makes my stomach clench.

"You're so tense." Brice kisses the back of my neck.

I was so wrapped up in my own thoughts, I didn't realize he'd woken up.

"What's got your brilliant brain in knots?" His voice is rough with sleep.

The silence thickens between us, and he tightens his arm slung around my waist, drawing me flush.

"Talk to me," he says. "Is your leg sore? Something else?" He draws in an audible breath. "You can talk to me about *anything*."

The way he says it makes me think he's inviting a discussion about Enzo, but it's better if I give him part of the truth, just in case his thoughts are wandering in a direction it's best they don't go. I'm not the woman he wants, the one he's seeking for what he *really* wants. There will be no babies or arrangements made between us. My sad heart hardens a little at the thought.

"Last time, when I was racing, I hurt myself. When I fell." I haven't said these words out loud to anyone. The doctor told Enzo and my family, and I've never had to get them past my lips. Brice splays his hand across my stomach. "I miscarried."

There's no sharp indrawn breath behind me, but he goes very still against me. We aren't facing each other, so I have no idea what he's thinking. Maybe it's better I can't see. I hate when people look at me with pity. It's not an emotion I can tolerate.

"I already knew," Brice says. "Posey found out by accident and told me."

"By accident?" My tone is acidic, and I throw the sleeping bag off us to sit on the edge of the couch. The heaters have made the hut warm, and the sleeping bag was becoming claustrophobic.

The cooler air on my skin is a relief. "How does Posey Jensen find out something like that by accident?"

He shifts to sit beside me, and when he tries to lay his hand on my thigh, I brush him off.

"You admitted you asked her to dig up dirt on me." I drag my hands down my face. "What were you planning to do with that information?"

"Nothing," he says. "She told me because... because I was having a hard time letting go of my preconceived notions of who you were."

His admission only makes the tightness in my chest worse. I always attributed, whether I really thought about it or not, his change in behavior toward me to his father's illness and my empathy. Instead, he found out about the most traumatic thing that's ever happened to me and softened because of that.

"If you hadn't found out, you'd still hate me."

"No," he says with conviction. "No."

I stand up, and my leg that's bandaged buckles. Brice rises and catches me about the waist. He tips my chin up when I refuse to make eye contact.

"Maren," he says.

"Don't treat me like I'm being unreasonable. You went behind my back. You wanted to hurt me."

"I don't know what I wanted back then. It was months ago. A lifetime ago. Neither of us are exactly the same person, are we?" He tries to draw me closer, and I hold my ground. "I was wrong. Really, really wrong. About you. About my approach to you. Learning that piece of your history shifted my perspective a little faster, that's all. I would have gotten here, to this place with you, regardless."

"How can you be so sure?" When I gaze up at him, my heart contracts at the remorse reflected there. I won't soften toward him. For the first time, I actually wanted to share some of what happened to me, and he already knew. He's been keeping that knowledge from me for weeks or months.

Since I won't step closer to him, he closes the distance between us, and he searches my face. His knuckles graze my cheek, and then he tucks a strand of hair behind my ear. "You didn't become my favorite person on the planet by accident, Tucker. Call it whatever you want, but what's between us has been inevitable."

Combustible chemistry. I want to scoff at how superficial that is, but I can't deny that what happened between us earlier on the couch didn't merely skim the surface. A deep and meaningful connection, but it's hard to believe he'd feel that way too given all the other things he's said before. I keep having to remind myself that he's not the one. Doesn't want to be. Can't be. Won't be. It makes me sad and angry that I'm even thinking like this when I'm not divorced yet. Even if he did want those things, going from one relationship right into another is wrong.

"And I'm honored," he continues, "that you trusted me enough to tell me what happened."

"I wish you'd trusted me enough to let me tell you my secrets when *I* was ready." I snatch the sleeping bag off the floor. "I'm taking the couch. Make yourself comfortable elsewhere."

"Maren."

"Stop doing that!" I turn on him, my leg unsteady, and when his hand snakes out to grab my elbow, I wrench myself away. "My name is not a weapon. You can't like one part of me and still dislike the other."

Before I can step away, he loops his arm around my waist, and he drags my naked body against his. The skin-to-skin contact immediately ignites the flame that always flickers between us.

"I don't dislike *any* part of you," he says next to my ear. "There isn't a single inch of you that I don't worship completely."

"More pretty words." My tone is breathless with betrayal. I hate that I want him even when I'm mad at him.

He turns me in his arms, and our lips connect with a mixture of frustration and something else I'm not even close to naming.

"Your skin is so soft, Maren." He trails a line of kisses along my jaw and down my throat. "Your body is so warm, Maren."

"Don't mock me." I clutch his shoulders as my knees threaten to give out. All the same sensations as before threaten to overwhelm me.

He eases me down on top of the foam cushions on the floor, and he slants his body over mine while his fingers begin their brand of magic. "Maren," he groans. "You're so wet for me."

"Stop it," I say. "Just call me Tucker."

"No," he says as he slips a finger inside me. "Not until I convince you that whether I call you Maren or Tucker or Maren Tucker, I want all of you. The good and the bad. The happy and the sad. I want it all."

More pretty words, but I'm so high on a cloud of intense physical pleasure that I let his words seep over me, sink into my unconscious to be dissected later. No matter what he says in this moment, I understand the truth. We're temporary. Today I am his favorite, but when the race is over, it may very well be someone else.

At the first swipe of his tongue against my core, I can't think straight, don't want to. I clutch his shoulder with one hand and the sleeping bag underneath me with the other, and I let myself get swept away.

# Chapter Thirty-Five

## BRICE

The sunrise is creeping in through the curtains, and Maren is beside me, still sleeping. After I confessed I'd known for a while about her miscarriage, a frost crept in between us. While I tried to thaw it with my tongue and hands and multiple orgasms, she fell asleep curled away from me, unwilling to talk.

At least now she's snuggled up beside me with her head touching my shoulder as though I didn't ruin what might have otherwise been a critical moment between us. Maybe I should have sealed my mouth shut. But I'd kept that truth to myself longer than I normally would, and it felt wrong to have her confide in me and not confess in return. The number of times hindsight has bitten me on the ass should have told me this would be the outcome. Of course she'd see it as some kind of betrayal, and I can't blame her. My initial motivation was... not good.

When I look at her now with her dark hair partly concealing her face, I can't even remember how I used to feel, who the guy was who asked Posey for intimate details I had no right to seek. She was hurting, and she was sad. Now that those same emotions live in me, I understand why she'd have looked at my seemingly carefree lifestyle and scoffed.

Since my father died, it has amazed me that anyone can walk around upright with that loss draped over them, an invisible weight. Without Tucker, I'd be stooped over with it, struggling to cope. I imagine losing a child, even one you never met, would have a similar impact. To face that alone must have been crushing.

When Tucker stirs beside me, I run my hand along her back as a test, and rather than moving away, she scooches closer.

"You're so warm," she murmurs.

I kiss her temple, and I decide to give her a truth I glossed over yesterday. "I got my first tattoo in a fit of rebellion. Mom and Dad gave Nick and Alex a speech about being respectful and respectable. They didn't talk to me. I thought someone would care when they found out. But no one did, and so I just continued. Each one more outrageous."

She opens one eye to peek at me, and then she crosses her arms to lay her cheek against them. There's a hint of amusement in her blue depths. "Did I ever tell you that I can speak and read Mandarin?"

"Never came up, actually." I release a deep sigh. "That one was a mistake for obvious reasons."

"What was it supposed to say?"

"Live free. Die young."

"Brice." She shoves my shoulder.

"It was on my back, and Nick and I were drunk." I kiss her temple again. "I'm surprised you didn't go for the jugular on that months ago. It literally says, 'translation error.' Might as well read World's Biggest Dumbass."

"Too easy," she says with a sly smile.

A comfortable silence settles between us, which is surprising, but I'm fucking grateful she doesn't seem to hate me this morning. I was certain I'd be navigating the trust mountain all over again.

"Will you tell me about your accident?" I trace a line down her shoulder and along her bare back. The space heaters have made this hut toasty warm, but I'm waiting for the chill to hit with my request.

"You don't want to call Posey and ask her? I'm sure she could tell you all about it."

I lick my finger and draw an imaginary line in the air. "Point for Maren Tucker."

She stares at me for a beat with her jaw tight, and if I had to guess, there's an internal battle waging in her about how far she wants to push me away over my mistake. "I don't want to trade points or keep score. You shouldn't have gone behind my back, and once you did, you should have told me you knew."

"Finding out was an error in judgment. One I regretted almost immediately." I mirror her pose, leaning my cheek against my arms to stare into her eyes. "I wanted you to decide if I truly deserved to know, so I never said a word."

She fiddles with an edge of the foam mat we're lying on, and I'm certain she's determined I'm not worthy. I can have her body but the rest I don't deserve.

"I didn't know I was pregnant," she whispers. "Whenever I go into intense training mode, my cycle gets all weird. In the helicopter—the bleeding—I didn't realize what it was. At the hospital, once I knew, it was…" She shakes her head, and her voice is thick with tears. "Up until then, I wasn't even sure I wanted a baby. Isn't that stupid? I spiraled over the loss of something I wasn't even sure I wanted."

I rest my hand on her arm, and she lays her cheek on top of it.

"But it wasn't the *experience* I was mourning. Seeing the blood, and realizing what was happening, what it meant. I don't think I've ever wanted to reverse time more in my life." She takes a deep breath. "Since I'd always been on the fence about kids, Enzo didn't believe me when I said I hadn't known I was pregnant."

The anger sweeps through me so quickly, I don't dare open my mouth. She'd been in an accident bad enough to require an airlift to a hospital, broken her ankle, and miscarried while her husband sat at her bedside laying blame at her feet. If she married him, he must have some good qualities, but I have yet to discover a single one.

If I got a call that Tucker had been injured that badly at a race, my first thought would be relief that she was alive, not to blame her for going. To get through this conversation without adding to Maren's load, I may have to employ some royal training.

"I would have sat beside you and held your hand and been so grateful you were okay," I say, because "I'm sorry that happened to you" is inadequate for the depth of my feelings.

Tears leak out of the corners of her eyes, and she raises her head to brush them away with her fingertips. "I would have been really grateful for someone like you too." Her voice hitches on a sob.

"Oh, Maren. Come here." I roll onto my side, and I tug her tight against my chest. She wraps her arms around me, and she lets the tears come. And while she cries, I think about what a privilege it would be to have someone like Maren Tucker decide you're worthy of her love and attention forever. To throw that away is truly unfathomable.

I can't even imagine the lengths I would go to if I was her husband to keep her safe and happy and satisfied. There's nothing I wouldn't do—climb a mountain, lay beside her in silence, walk through hell with her in my arms. Anything. Whatever she needed. How do you marry someone and not feel that way?

The walkie-talkie crackles over by the fridge, and then a male voice announces, "The water has receded. The race will resume in one hour. All contestants should be at the place they left off when the race recommences."

When Maren sniffs and tries to draw away, I tighten my embrace, and I kiss the top of her head. The race is secondary compared to what's happened between us over the last eighteen hours.

"We need to eat and pack and get dressed." Maren's lips move against my chest. "And I need to fix my leg."

Where the other things didn't grab my attention, the mention of her thigh does the trick. I can't have her going back onto the course with any chance of getting an infection. I leave the mat to grab her first aid kit, and I rummage through it until I find the waterproof bandages. Easing off the previous patch, I frown at the bright-red wound, and I try to remember from my wilderness first aid course whether this color is normal.

"It's fine," Tucker says, reading my mind.

"You'd say that even if it wasn't." I get out the wipes to clean it. "You like pushing yourself to the limit."

"Guilty," she says. "But it really is fine. That looks normal."

Rather than arguing with her, I decide to take her word for it as I patch her up. She hobbles around the cabin while we repack, and I worry the next two days are going to be hard on her. She's not hiding the pain she's in right now, but I know her well enough to understand as soon as Iris and the camera are within view, Maren will grit her teeth and mask her pain.

The whole time we're getting ready to leave, a lingering question dogs me, but I'm not sure I want to ask it. Or more accurately, I'm not sure I want the answer. We're at the doorway, getting ready to head back out into the cooler, damp air of the early morning when I decide I need to understand before we're back with everyone else.

"Do you know why he left? I can't understand it." I hate saying his name, but she'll know who I mean.

"It's complicated," she says, but she doesn't look at me. "A lot of reasons. Not enough reasons."

"Tucker."

She rubs her cheeks and opens the cabin door. "Once the dust settled," she says over her shoulder, "I told Enzo I didn't want to have any kids. One miscarriage was enough."

Before I can respond, she ducks out the door and starts walking toward the cliff face we'll need to navigate down to return to the water's edge. Her revelation is a stone dropping into my stomach, weighing me down. The intensity of my sadness is a surprise. My ideas about me and Tucker were only half formed and definitely not something I could pursue with her right now. But they existed.

I stand there, watching her walk away, and I replay the way she threw the comment over her shoulder like an afterthought. She didn't make eye contact, and there was a false note to her words. The part I'm not sure about is where the falsehood or inaccuracy lies. Is it simply how she boiled down something she claimed was complicated to a cut-and-dry answer?

I draw the door closed behind me, and I trail Tucker toward the cliff. Maybe her claim is accurate, and maybe it's not. The one thing I know is that, at least for now, I've got Tucker, and I'm not throwing away one more minute trying to puzzle out why her marriage failed. What we have isn't what she had with him. There's no doubt in my mind *this* is better.

Someone who was so unsupportive and victim blaming wasn't a good husband, and he would have been an equally bad father. With him in the rearview mirror, I have time to show her that what I can offer is exactly what she needs.

# Chapter Thirty-Six

## MAREN

I didn't lie to Brice, but I didn't tell him the complete truth either. Knowing what he wants out of life, I had to be clear that I'm not an option. I thought telling him I didn't want kids, rather than the truth, that having kids is extremely complicated for me, would drive a wedge between us. But that hasn't happened. Instead, he's the same fun, flirty guy. As though I never told him that our futures weren't aligned, and in some ways, as though our time in the cabin never happened either. His ability to flip himself to the other side of a coin is impressive and unnerving.

We've met up with the rest of our team, and he's fallen back into the race mentality faster than me. Where can we cut time? How can we inch ahead in the final days?

Maybe he's the same because he's never considered having anything with me beyond this race. Perhaps I'm flattering myself. Sex might always be magical when you're Brice Summerset.

Just because I've thought about what a boy with brown hair and light-brown eyes would look like doesn't mean he's done the same for me.

My reaction is odd, though. This morning I told him I didn't want kids, and all I've done while we struggled to get out of the ravine, while we rode our bikes almost a hundred kilometers and while we ate at the final checkpoint, is think about babies. *His* babies. Babies with Brice.

Before Enzo and even with him, I was never sure I wanted to have children. Mostly, I was indifferent until I miscarried. Once it became clear I couldn't have children the way most people do, I was certain fate was telling me something. Motherhood wasn't meant for me. The accident, my inability to carry a child, and Enzo's reaction sent me on a headfirst dive into oblivion. I've spent the better part of a year in a fog because my body, which had never betrayed me before, let me down in such a massive way. Then my husband, instead of blowing away the haze, only contributed to the thickness.

I'm beginning to wonder whether my previous apathy about children was because I wasn't sure I wanted *Enzo's* babies. Such a strange realization to have when I *wanted* my marriage. Despite filing for divorce and what's materialized between me and Brice, there's still a tiny part of me that considers giving up on Enzo to be a failure, a character flaw, as though I could have singlehandedly saved our marriage if only I'd tried harder. I've never been one to give up, which is what made the news about babies so hard to take as well. It's not an outcome I could change through sheer force of will.

I'll never have children without significant medical intervention and a surrogate. I'll never carry a child to term, never hear a heartbeat thrumming inside me, and never feel the flutter of movement in my belly. None of those things will ever be mine, the same way Brice will never be mine.

Those thoughts are prying open the chasm in my chest, and I can't afford to let the fog descend again.

After dinner at the checkpoint, we plan out exactly how many hours of sleep we'll allow ourselves before our final push to the end. There will be no more sleeping after tonight until we're resting our heads on hotel pillows, hopefully fresh off a victory.

My thigh aches, but I'm too afraid to take the bandage off to check for infection. When Jag offered to change the dressing earlier, I made up excuses to avoid it. But when I head to the bank of bathrooms, I sense my shadow behind me.

Sure enough, when I come out, Brice is waiting for me, but not in our usual spot. He's right in front of me, and his annoyance is clear.

"If you won't let anyone else check your leg," he says, "then I'm checking it."

"We have one more push. By the end of the day tomorrow, none of this will matter," I say with a wave of my hand, trying to step around him. "I'll be fine."

"Tucker," he says, and there's a warning note in his voice I've never heard before. "Your body, your choice, and all that, but I'm not taking you home in worse shape than when you arrived. When you agreed to come, I said I'd watch out for you. If I ignore your pain, I'm not doing what I said I'd do. Pretend for everyone else, but don't pretend with me. We don't do that with each other."

I *wish* we didn't do that with each other. We've been pretending for so long—all day, all week, for months—that I don't know what's real or not real between us. The thing is, even if I asked him, I'm not sure what I'd want him to say.

Last night was real and raw, but today has been disconcerting, as though I can't quite get my feet under me.

"I'll let Jag take a look when I get back to the team," I say, and I try to step around him again.

He loops his arm around my waist, and he draws me tight against him before dipping his head to nuzzle the curve of my neck. There are other people milling around us, but as soon as his skin grazes mine, I'm so hyperaware of him that we could be on another planet. Up until now, we've been focused on where Iris is at any given time, but the truth is there are cameras with other teams and in other places. We could have been caught a thousand times doing things I'd rather not have an international audience see.

"Brice," I murmur.

"I don't know why you're trying to resist me." His voice has the now familiar rough texture, which tells me I'm not the only one who's caught up in the close contact. He raises his head to meet my gaze, and he keeps his palm on the small of my back while his other hand smooths a tendril of my hair behind my ear. "Let me help you."

"I don't want to rely on you for this," I say.

"Too late," he says. "This is what we do. We rely on each other. You're my favorite person, and I'm yours."

I can't help my soft laugh at the certainty oozing out of him. This cool confidence used to be the version of him I disliked, but now that I've discovered so much more under his veneer, I find I like every side of him.

"You're that confident, are you?"

"Your lack of denial just gave me another ten confidence points."

"Oh no," I say. "No one needed you to have another ten points of cockiness."

"Trust you to turn my positive self-talk into a negative." But there's a teasing glint in his eyes. "If it makes you feel better, I'll distribute my extra confidence to other people on the way back to the tent to check out your leg."

I open my mouth to tell him that I really will let Jag administer some first aid if I need it, but he must sense a protest on my lips because he cuts me off.

"Let me take care of you, Tucker." He frames my face with his hands. "I want to take care of you."

Given the year I've had, those words mean more than they ever have, and my eyes fill with tears. "Okay." I can barely get the word out around the lump in my throat.

He wraps his arms around me, and he holds me tight against his chest. We stand like that, soaking each other in for longer than we should. Whatever everyone else on the racecourse might think, what's between Brice and I isn't a game or a ploy for airtime. This unexpected affection is real.

When he steps away from me, he runs his hand down my arm to lace our fingers together. Part of me wonders if I should pull away and keep that inch of distance between us around other people. I hate the idea of being the source of gossip, and walking back to the tent like this with Brice will only feed the mill.

As we wander past my South African friend, Brice calls out, "Yvette, great job on the bike today."

Yvette beams at him, likely surprised he knew her name. I didn't realize he did. Then he leans down close to my ear and says, "One cockiness point in someone else's hands."

"I'm really not sure you should be putting your cockiness in so many other people's hands."

"If you're offering to put your own hands all over my c—"

I press my palm to his open mouth, and he chuckles against it. He turns his head away, and my hand falls. My body is lit with amusement at his joke and our easy comradery.

By the time we get back to our tent, Brice has given up every one of his extra confidence points to other people—people I didn't even realize he knew. Their joy at being recognized for whatever small thing Brice noticed about them was infectious.

In a corner of the team's tent, as I ease off my pants for Brice to tend to my wound, I'm still buzzing from the kindness he showed other people. Nearing the end of a grueling race, his comments clearly lifted other people's spirits. Even my mood has completely shifted.

He takes some salve out of the first aid kit, and he smears it across my injury with incredible tenderness. When he glances up at me, I'm forced to acknowledge that Brice has been taking care of me, in one way or another, for a lot longer than I ever realized.

# Chapter Thirty-Seven

## BRICE

I've looked out for and after other people before. Sort of. Truthfully, mostly just Nick and a bit with my father toward the end. No one lets me have Grace unsupervised.

But the concept of caring for others isn't foreign, even if most of my life other people have been doing those helping pieces for me, I understand how it works. As the former third in line to the throne, there was always someone to clean up any mess I made or guide me through any crisis. I've been on the receiving end more often than I've been the one providing care. When I have helped others, it's been predominantly financial, or I gave a bit of my time, and overall, these ventures required little from me.

Which is basically what Maren accused me of months ago, and I denied it. My emotional investment in caring for others was virtually zero before my father got sick, and even then, I joined this team largely to avoid my own helplessness and inadequacy. Watching him deteriorate was gut wrenching, and I've never felt so inept.

However, aiding Tucker during our last two days on the course has given me the weirdest sense of satisfaction. The trust she's placed in me by coming on this trip, by opening herself up, by relying on me for support gives me a strange sense of power. As though it's impossible for anyone else in the world to know Maren Tucker, all the sides and angles of her, the way I do. Where I might have skimmed along the surface with my other commitments, I'm in so deep with Maren that I can't see the light above me, and I have no idea where the ocean floor is. I'm completely lost, suspended in a sea of feeling, with the strangest, most satisfying stillness in my soul. Whether we win or lose the race, I already feel like I've won.

According to Riker, we're ten kilometers from the finish line, and we're just about to descend a cliff to get on an outrigger to sail to the final talisman and then on to the end. We're in second place, and we haven't slept in over twenty-four hours. Adrenaline is our fuel, and I'm amazed at Tucker's stamina. She keeps telling me her thigh is fine, but I'm not convinced. Wren asked to look at it, but Maren refused. That alone tells me she's not being honest about how much pain she's in, but I also realize she wouldn't forgive me for seeking help when we're so close to the end. Maren's stubbornness is admirable and frustrating, and I wonder how many times her obstinate nature has led her to places she never had to go.

Like hating me, for example.

Though I don't know if we would have had *this*, whatever this is between us, if we hadn't battled to start with. As much as I hated our relationship initially, being around her has changed me in ways I never could have anticipated.

We pick our way down the cliff in the early morning sun, and ahead, the Australian team in first place is just pushing their outrigger into the ocean. We're setting a brisk pace with our main competition within sight. When Maren steps onto the sandy beach, her ankle buckles, and I loop my arm around her waist, practically carrying her as we rush toward the outrigger.

Wren climbs into one of the seats in the boat, which is a combination between a canoe and a sailboat. Riker glances at Maren and gestures for her to take the other seat, leaving him and I to propel us into the water before hopping on.

"I can push," Maren says.

"Get in the boat," I say, and I lift her off her feet and ease her into the seat, mindful of her leg.

"Brice!" Tucker yells at me before catching a paddle from Wren.

I'm already stepping behind the contraption, and Riker is beside me. "I'm surprised you've managed to keep all your limbs, manhandling her like that," he says.

"Tucker likes it when a man handles her," I say, loud enough that I'm sure she can hear. Her body rises and falls with what's likely a huff of annoyance, but when she turns to glare at me over her shoulder, all I can think about is how she looked in the cabin, lit by the glow of the electric heaters while I entered her from behind.

*Fucking hell. What an image.*

After the race, we've got two nights at the hotel, and I'm already trying to figure out how to convince Riker and Wren to share instead. The cameras will still be running at the after-party, so I'm not sure I'll be able to persuade Tucker that a room change is for the best. But I can't stand the idea of not being with her. Our time in the cabin solidified my feelings, and I'm done pretending they don't exist.

Riker and I propel the boat into the water, and we hop onto the back, both of us settling into makeshift seats. Wren tosses us both paddles from where she had them wedged in beside her. The nice part about being on this team, aside from all the time with Maren, has been how fluid and effortless their planning is. No one told Wren to shove enough paddles in beside her. Years of experience and numerous races guided that instinct. Neither Riker nor Maren asked where the paddles were—they knew.

We don't gain much on the Australian team as we make our way to the talisman, but once we're there, I don't wait to discuss who will swim to the ocean floor to get the final disc. Instead, I dive off the side of the boat with Brent's advice ringing in my ears. When my chest tightens, I release a little air, which lets me get to the bottom. With the talisman in my hand, I kick and pull my way back to the outrigger, hoping the Australian team wasn't as quick.

Riker is at the surface, and he grabs my shorts, yanking me out of the water and into paddling position.

"Go!" he yells.

I tuck the medallion into the closest bag, and I fumble for my paddle with water still streaming down my face. The saltwater stings my eyes. Maren, Wren, and Riker are already in sync, paddles dipping in and out of the ocean at a frantic pace. Beside us, the Australians are only half a boat length ahead of us.

My heart kicks at how close we are to being the first to cross the finish line. For months, the emphasis was on finishing the race injury free, and I don't think Tucker ever considered we'd be here, together.

Beside us, a gust of wind catches the Australian outrigger, and it lifts the vessel. They all cry out with surprise, and I can't help glancing in their direction while the other three are focused ahead. The Australian boat wobbles but rights itself. The fluke wind has allowed us to inch ahead, and the muscles in my arms are burning from the strain of pushing my body to its absolute limits. When this race is over, I'll be able to say I put my whole heart into it—in every way.

None of us are talking, and we're all focused straight ahead. The shoreline comes into sight, and out of my peripheral vision, I can sense rather than see the Australian ship. They're definitely behind us now but not by much.

"We're paddling into shore," Riker says. "Paddle hard up onto the sand, and then we need to grab our kit and run."

As we near the shallower water, Riker instructs everyone to bear down and paddle. Adrenaline must be the only thing still making my muscles work. They're wobbly from exertion, but I won't be the weak link.

The outrigger shoots up onto the shore, and as it glides to a stop, everyone is scrambling for bags, grabbing whatever they can, and then we're all running across the sand.

Behind us, the other boat makes contact with the shore, and the Australians are barking at each other. Feet pound on the path, and ahead, I can see the cameras, the host, and the finish line. We're so close, I can taste it. Beside me, Tucker is wincing in pain, but I'm not sure if it's from the run, the exertion on the outrigger, or her leg. I'd ask her, but I suspect she'd hit me if I talked to her right now when we're so close to winning.

"Keep focused," she says to me.

"I'm focused on the right thing." Her. Always her.

Riker crosses the finish line, then Wren, and just before our feet cross, Tucker takes my hand, and we cross the red line on the path together.

"Holy shit," I huff out with my hands on my knees. "We won?"

Tucker laughs from beside me. One of the cameras is likely zoomed in on both of us, but they could be a million miles away right now. Her leg has bled through the bandage, and there's a trail of blood running down her leg.

"Medic," I call, standing up to look around.

"Who's hurt?" The show's host appears at my side.

"Maren," I say.

He points us toward the medical tent, and I draw her against my side while we walk there.

"Prince Brice," the host calls to me. "Can we get an interview?"

"Once I know Maren is okay," I call back.

"I'll be fine," she says, but I notice she hasn't looked down to check her wound. She's been focused on the path ahead of us the whole walk.

"The medic can be the judge of that," I say as a tall, lithe woman emerges from the tent ahead.

"Got an injury?" she asks.

"Leg," I say. "We patched it, but I wonder if she needs stiches or a visit to the hospital."

"Let's have a look." The medic gestures for Maren to enter, and when I try to go in as well, the medic raises her eyebrows at Maren, and she shakes her head.

I take a deep breath and put my hands on my hips. Deep breathing my way through this is the only way I won't lose my shit on television over Maren refusing to let me be with her when she's injured. What's it going to take to finally crack her shell wide open? I thought I was there, but clearly, I'm not.

While I'm standing outside the tent, Jag arrives with my phone in hand. "Your brothers have been trying to get in touch with you. Change of plans."

Another flare of annoyance ignites, but I tamp it down as I scroll through my messages. Instead of returning to Bellerive,

I'm to head to Denmark right away. The eighteen-hour delay on the course means I've lost my Bellerive window. At least Nick is meeting me there now. Something has shifted behind the public relations curtain if Alex and PR are sending both of us to this climate change fundraiser. Of course, only one of us is acting as Freja's date. Not that it's a real date, despite what the tabloids tend to print.

Still, the idea of getting into the complexities of what I've been doing for a year in Denmark when Tucker is already starting to pull away from me is not appealing. Now that the race is over, she has no reason to spend time with me other than because she chooses to.

"We're headed to Denmark instead of home?" Jag asks. Gary is just behind him with the car.

I have no idea what proper race protocol is. Other teams might take hours to reach the finish line, so I'm assuming we go back to the hotel and wait for the rest of the teams to trickle in.

"Denmark," I agree. "Nick is meeting me there with everything I need."

"Julia too?" Jag asks as he checks his phone.

"No, just Nick. He must have had Jules surgically removed to be able to take a flight without her." That joke used to be funnier before I wanted to fuse someone to me as well. Now, I'm fairly certain I'd do anything to tie myself to Tucker, force her to drag me around like a literal ball and chain.

The zipper on the tent opens, and I rush forward to hear the outcome.

"I'm fine," Maren says. "Stitched up with some antibiotic cream." She waggles the small tube at me.

"She doesn't need actual antibiotics?" I ask the medic. "The cut looked okay?"

The medic glances at Maren, and she nods her consent.

"The wound had reopened, but it seemed to have been healing fine. Would have been a jagged scar, and it's fairly deep, so I put in a few stitches. I have recommended that Ms. Tucker see her own doctor when she returns home as a precaution."

Since I won't be in Bellerive to make sure Tucker does that, I'll have to call Sawyer or Nathaniel and ask them to check on Maren. They seem to be the only people she half listens to.

"Prince Brice," the host calls to me from near the finish line again. "Can we get that interview now?"

Maren makes a shooing motion with her hand when I hesitate. "I'm fine. You heard her. Go. I'm going to congratulate the Australians on a great race. We'll all need some sleep soon."

At the mention of sleep, I become aware of just how exhausted I am. We're pushing thirty-six hours without so much as a nap. I rub my face, and I head to where the host is waiting. Royal persona activated.

---

When we get back to the hotel, I shower and then crash. Riker, Wren, and Tucker talked about trying to set an alarm to see more teams finish, but knowing I'm leaving here and going straight to a royal commitment, I need my sleep. By the time I wake up, night has fallen. Outside my open balcony window, people are talking and laughing below on the patio. Sounds like quite a crowd.

Riker was either very quiet when he left or I was that tired because he's gone, and I have no memory of him leaving. Whatever alarm he set was useless for me.

After I've gotten dressed, I wander out to the balcony on the off chance I can catch Tucker alone. Fate is not my friend when I notice her on the patio, surrounded by everyone, a massive grin on her face as the guy beside her recounts a raucous story.

Jealousy, hot and irrational, streaks across my chest. Feels like I wasted the time I have left with her by sleeping. I'd like to believe she'll still see me when we get back to the island, but I have no idea what's going to happen. Only what I want to happen.

Rather than standing there letting someone else soak up Tucker's attention, I text Jag that I'm awake and going to the party downstairs. For the last ten days, I haven't had to alert security about anything, and the absence of my phone and my normal life was a welcome relief. Now we're back to business as usual. My family comes first, and everything I want is second.

It doesn't take me long to get down the one flight of stairs, but the patio seems even more packed than it did from above. As I try to make my way through the teams to Tucker, I keep getting stopped by people who want to congratulate me, tell me how proud my father would be, or ask how I ever convinced Tucker to have a showmance. That one boils my blood, but I'm enough of a professional to answer without really answering. Growing up, I learned to ignore the opinions of people who don't matter in my day-to-day life. Once I leave Fiji, the majority of these people won't be on my radar.

When I get to where Tucker should be, she's nowhere in sight, and I turn in circles trying to find her dark head in the crowd. A few times I think I see her, and then I realize it's not her.

"You looking for Maren?" Wren asks from beside me.

"Have you seen her?"

"She went to the beach." Wren gestures behind us. "As soon as the race is done, she likes some alone time. I was surprised she was down here as early as she was tonight. Normally, she needs to decompress."

It sounds like Wren is telling me that Tucker wants to be alone, but I'm going to ignore that piece of advice. Maren won't have any problem telling me to take a hike if she doesn't want me around.

On the beach, lit only by the moonlight, is Tucker with her knees drawn up to her chest. She's not far from where the waves are washing onto the shore, and if she hears me coming, she doesn't let on.

"Is it safe to be out here by yourself?" I ask.

She turns to rest her temple on her knees, and she gazes at me before releasing a deep sigh. "Safe enough."

"You okay?"

"Just a bit sad. I'm always like this when a race ends. The adrenaline rushes out and, in its place, at least for me, is a strange melancholy. I've never been good at goodbyes or having things end." She holds up her phone. "I haven't even turned it on. As soon as I do, I have to go back to reality."

"Reality has already hit me in the chest. I turned my phone on." I take a seat beside her.

"Royal obligations abound," she says with a hint of teasing in her tone.

Now is my chance to tell her about Denmark, to give her the full story, but I like the vibe between us right now, and I don't want to ruin it.

"I've always found marking an occasion with a tattoo to be therapeutic," I say.

She reaches out and draws a line across one of my tattoos on my bicep that peeks out of the edge of my sleeve. "What occasion did this one mark?"

"One tequila shot too many in Vegas with Nick. You'll find quite a few of them mark the same occasion."

"Shouldn't a tattoo mean something? You have to burn it off or cover it over if you make a mistake."

"Some of mine mean something." I raise my shirt and I point to an inscription near my hip. "Nick and I both got this one when our gran died."

"Alex didn't get one?" She traces the tattoo with light fingers.

The contact undoes the little willpower I've managed to maintain around her since we left the cabin. She's so close the scent of peaches surrounds me, and I slide my hand into her hair to draw her lips to mine. When she doesn't pull away, I shift closer to her to deepen the kiss. That I can get turned on so quickly from one kiss is a testament to how into her I am. Any time I touch her, I can't help wanting more.

"What does it say?" she asks against my lips.

"Love hard. Love well," I murmur as I find the spot on her neck that makes her squeeze my biceps. "From the last speech she made to the country before she retired. She was speaking about our fellow Bellerivians, but it struck a chord with Nick."

"Because of Julia?"

"Because he's Nick, and he's a soft, soft boy."

"Oh, and you're so tough, are you?" She cups my cheek, and there's a playful tilt to her lips.

"Used to be." I take her hand and lay it over my heart. "Used to be a lot of things that I'm not anymore."

A heavy silence settles between us, and I'm not sure what else I should say or what I want her to say. Somehow I need to figure out a way to tether her to me. Another race or something else. She lets me into her head, and then she pushes me back out. Once we return to the island, I fear it'll be far too easy for her to keep me out.

"If you got another tattoo right now, what would you get?" she asks.

"That's easy. Something for my dad. It just—I wasn't sure I could do it. With the race, and I didn't want more questions." I lie on my back to stare up at the stars, and Tucker peers at me from above before laying her hands on my chest and resting her chin on top of them.

"We could get one tonight," she says.

"We?" If she offers to share a bottle of tequila with me while we get them, my heart may never recover.

"I could go with you."

"Are you going to get one?"

"I might," she says. "Do you think anything is open?"

"Without a doubt, I can get us a tattoo." I dig my phone out of my pocket, trying not to dislodge her off my chest. With my free hand, I tug her around so she's flush against my side with her head on my chest, and it's easier for me to use two hands while I search for somewhere to go. As a bonus, she's snuggled in tight. I love the weight of her against my side.

Ten kilometers away there's a place with good reviews. I call them to confirm they take walk-ins, and when I'm off the phone I say, "Are we doing this?"

"Yeah," she says. "Let's get tattoos."

I help her to her feet, and I wonder what's weighing on Tucker's mind with such heft that she wants to remember it forever.

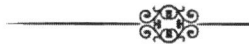

The tattoo artist is finishing up my sands of time with purple sand near my hip, next to the tattoo Nick and I got for my gran. Tucker is in a different area with another tattoo artist. When I suggested she might want to think about whether she really wanted to do this, she held my gaze and said that too much thinking leads to inaction. Fairly certain that's a racing philosophy she's poorly applying to this experience, but I wasn't going to contradict her. After all the impulse tattoos I've gotten, who was I to criticize?

In the SUV on the way over, she was the one who suggested the purple for the sand in honor of the Alzheimer's Society after I mentioned my initial idea. A reminder for me to seize every memory, every moment, every grain of sand while I've got the chance. The urge to ask what she planned to get hovered at the edges of our conversation the whole time, but she didn't offer, and I didn't ask. Part of me is afraid it'll have something to do with Enzo or her divorce, and although it's none of my business, it would gut me for her to have a permanent reminder of him.

In the lobby, she's already paid for both our tattoos by the time I'm done. At the edge of her collarbone, just under her shirt, I catch the shine of the protective tape covering whatever design she got. It'll be visible more often than not, and I'm surprised she didn't go with somewhere more discreet. My curiosity is piqued, and I curse the fact that Riker is my roommate and not Tucker.

"Get what you want?" I ask.

"Yeah," she says, but her response is subdued.

I'm now convinced the tattoo must be about Enzo or her divorce. That's the only time she's like this. Why she'd get anything on her body that would make her feel *less than* forever, I have no idea, but I've realized that Tucker's stubborn streak doesn't always serve her best interests.

Jag is driving us back to the hotel, and Tucker has been quiet since we left. I glance over at her as the streetlights streak across her face. "Can I see it?" I ask.

She tugs down the neck of her shirt, and a flower or vine of some sort follows the line of her collarbone. It's tiny and delicate, so it makes more sense that she wouldn't mind people seeing it, unlike some of my more garish choices. Should have known Tucker would have enough taste and common sense to pick something beautiful.

"What is it, exactly?" I ask.

"Baby's breath," she says, and she lets her shirt go, so it slithers over it. "Next week is one year since my accident."

With everything going on with my dad and then the race, I lost track of the dates. But I remember when I first found out, I realized this race and her last one were almost a year apart. The end of this race and how the race before ended must be triggering some bad memories. Never occurred to me when I asked her to compete, though. I was too deep in my own feelings about my father's death, needing a purpose, and my growing desire for Tucker. It's a huge thing for me to have ignored, and I'm surprised when Wren and Riker were warning me off, they didn't say something. Of course, they'd have risked having to tell me *why* racing was so potentially devastating for Tucker, and neither of them would have wanted to betray her trust.

We're driving into the parking lot of the hotel, and I realize I need to say something in response. "I should have been more sensitive when I asked you to come here. To race."

"I wanted to race, but I was scared," she says. "I've got no regrets, so you shouldn't either."

She makes it sound so simple, but her tattoo says otherwise.

When we get out of the car, Jag leads the way to the rooms, giving us some space. I sling my arm around Tucker's shoulders, and she wraps hers around my middle. At the door to her hotel room, Tucker turns to me.

"Wren is staying with one of the Australian team members tonight," she says.

"A whole hotel room, all to yourself?" My heart kicks, and I lace my fingers with hers. Sounds like an invitation, but I don't want to push my luck.

"Stay with me?"

"Fuck yes," I say, and I pluck the keycard from her fingers, swipe it, and have us in the door before she can take back her request.

She laughs, and I swallow it with my kiss. We're shedding clothes before the hotel room door has even clicked closed. The scent of peaches is all around me again. Her hands are in my hair, and I've got mine cradling her face, trying to figure out how to merge us together. It's impossible to be close enough to satisfy this feeling inside me.

Never in my life have I experienced this combination of lust and respect and something else I'm still not sure I want to name. The rest of my life could be spent here in this hotel room with her, and I wouldn't regret a moment of it. So much makes sense that never did before. I get how Nick could pine for Jules for years; how Alex could almost give up becoming king, a title he'd wanted since we were kids; how friendships are ruined or families torn apart; why wars are waged—this feeling is that monumental. Being with her feels as necessary as my next breath.

Maren meets me, kiss for kiss, touch for touch, and I wonder whether she's as far gone as I am. Is it possible? Coming off a divorce and a disaster of a marriage, would she ever truly give me a shot? Is that what I'm seeking? She's said she doesn't want kids anymore, but that tattoo of baby's breath makes me long to dig for the truth. Her reasoning didn't ring true then, and it doesn't now either.

When we come up for air, I trace my fingertip around the edge of the protective tape. The temptation to ask is strong, but I know if I do, I'll ruin tonight. She'll tell me when she's ready, and if I learned anything from getting Posey involved and the fallout in the cabin, giving Maren the space to decide is critical.

"I feel like I've hardly seen you the last couple of days," Maren says, and she's staring at me with the same reverence I feel.

We've spent the whole time beside each other, but I know exactly what she means. With the cameras and other people, I spent a lot of time pretending I didn't want to be where I am right now.

"When we get back to Bellerive," I say as I ease her onto the bed, and I trail kisses down her body. "I don't want this to be over. We're not over."

"Brice."

Her tone suggests she doesn't think that's a good idea, but I've said my piece. Even if I don't know what things between us will look like, even if being together is complicated, I can't let her go. I don't want to.

"I don't need an answer," I say as I slide my fingers along her slick folds, and she rocks her hips against me. "I just needed you to know."

She wraps her hands around my neck and drags me down for a kiss, and the minute our lips reconnect, there's no more talking about anything other than our mutual pleasure. We're gasps and moans and murmured pleas until I'm so deep inside her I don't know where I end and she begins. The best feeling in the world. As we both race toward the finish line, all I can think about is how I never want this to end.

Tomorrow I'll tell her about Denmark, and tomorrow I'll figure out some way to keep us connected beyond this race.

# Chapter Thirty-Eight

## MAREN

We're slow to get moving the next day, and I spend most of the morning basking in Brice's undivided attention. He even has Jag bring us breakfast so neither of us have to leave the room and risk being caught in yesterday's clothes.

Last night, Brice said he wanted whatever this is to go beyond the race, and I didn't know what to say. I've spent the last ten days convincing myself that we can never be more than a fling. Even now with the offer of more on the table, I can't wrap my head around what that would look like or whether it's a sound decision for me to go for it.

The ink on my separation papers is still fresh. Yes, Enzo and I haven't lived together in almost a year, and I can't even remember the last time I felt as close to Enzo as I do to Brice, but appearances matter in Bellerive and soon across the globe.

Brice will be front and center for InterFlix, which means I will be too. I'm already a little panicky about how we'll be portrayed, questioning whether I made the right decision in forging ahead on camera.

I jumped into my marriage with Enzo, and I didn't care whether it was the smart choice or the right choice. At the time, I wanted what I wanted. Enzo and Bellerive, and the only way to get it was by getting married.

Coming to Fiji, I filed for separation because I knew I'd developed feeling for Brice, but my decision to end my marriage was largely an impulse. I can't make the same mistakes with Brice. He's not an interloper in Bellerive who people will forget, and a scandal with him will follow me forever. Every time we're at a function together, enter the same room, speak in passing, people will talk. A fling in Fiji we could explain away as a showmance or the dreaded rebound, and people might have a short memory. Going beyond this race, back to Bellerive like this, is risky.

No matter how Brice thinks or feels about me now, I'm well aware of his track record with women. He doesn't do serious. He doesn't date exclusively. That means what he really wants is to keep having sex, and that feels dangerous to my heart. A small part of me, that I try not to acknowledge, already considers him mine in ways I shouldn't. If I let myself really believe in what's between us, I'll never find my way back out.

My separation and divorce haven't been easy, and there were some really hard days, but I've never questioned whether I could survive them. With Brice, I'm connected and in tune with him in ways I've never been with anyone else. To have him, really, truly have him, and to lose him would devastate me. So much easier not to want what he's offering at all.

Just before lunch, Wren texts me that she's coming back to the room, and we reluctantly get dressed.

"Tomorrow," Brice says as he tugs on his shirt, "I'm not going back to Bellerive. There's a climate change summit in Denmark that I'm scheduled to attend. I thought I'd have a bit of time at home, but with the race delay, I lost it."

*Denmark. Freja.* Though I'd never paid any attention before, I did a search for her yesterday, and there are several photos of them at events in Denmark looking comfortable and, in some, downright cozy. Another reason I shouldn't be pinning any hopes on Brice. It won't work. He doesn't want a long-term relationship with anyone, and I can't give him the children he wants.

"Okay," I say while I tie my hair back at the mirror. "I hope it's a good trip."

There's a heavy silence between us, but if he expects me to pry for more information, I won't. His royal life is none of my concern. Every time I inch toward believing we might work as a couple, something reminds me we can't. At some point, I need to not only acknowledge those roadblocks but remember them. The last year was hard, and giving myself another hard year when I can prevent it would make me an emotional masochist.

"I'm hanging out with Wren this afternoon, but I'll see you at the after-party," I say.

"Are we—" Brice runs a hand through his hair and takes a deep breath. "Are we okay? We felt solid this morning, but now there's this weird distance between us again."

I close my eyes and run my fingertips along my temple. "My mind is just a bit muddled," I admit.

"Doesn't have to be," Brice says, and he sits on the edge of the bed. "Talk to me."

There's a knock on the door, and I'm sure it's Wren. The window to get Brice out the door without being seen might be short. It's one thing for people to believe Brice and I are sleeping together, but it's quite another for anyone to have photographic proof.

"Later," I say as I check the peephole. "You should go while you have the chance."

When I step away from the door, he's at my side. He loops an arm around my waist, and he buries his face in my neck before placing a lingering kiss there then my temple and a quick peck on my lips. "Later," he says with an unexpected firmness before slipping out the door while Wren slides in.

"How was your night?" Wren asks as soon as the door clicks closed.

"He definitely knows his way around a woman's body." I keep my voice deliberately light, even though I'm sure she's not asking what the sex was like.

"Not a shocker," Wren says. "Charm oozes out of him. He's a tube of toothpaste that can't be capped." Wren goes to the mini fridge and takes out her water bottle. "What are you two doing once this is all done tonight?"

"He's going to Denmark," I say, "and I'm going back to Bellerive."

"You know that's not what I meant."

"I don't know what to tell you." I sit on the edge of the bed, and then I flop back to stare at the ceiling.

"The two of you clearly have feelings for each other, but you're fresh off a divorce, and I mean *fresh*. I was all for a rebound, but the way he looks at you doesn't feel very rebound-like."

"He's also been clear from the start that relationships aren't his thing." I twirl a strand of my ponytail around my finger while I'm lost in thought. "I think I miscalculated this whole thing. I'm *so* confused. The only thing I'm sure I don't want is a scandal. At some point, he's going to move on from me. It's inevitable, and I can't be the woman he left behind. I can't." The Tucker family is used to managing public perception. While I don't want anyone to believe I cheated on Enzo, even if I did, I also don't want people to think I was just another notch on Brice's bedpost... even if I am.

"The woman Prince Brice left behind? Yeah, that would not sit well with you."

I've tried to keep my expectations realistic where Brice is concerned, but I know they've slipped several times into desires that are a lot bigger and deeper than we likely warrant. "Nothing about us has been simple."

"Does it need to be?"

"Everything with Enzo felt simple."

"Until it wasn't."

"But I don't think any relationship should feel this hard to navigate, should it? Look at me. I just used the word *relationship*. You know who hasn't used that word? Brice. Not once, except to directly refute the idea that he'd ever want one."

"With you?"

"With anyone. He said, and I think this might be a direct quote, that he doesn't understand 'the point' of marriage."

"Would you want to marry him?" Wren's tone brims with surprise.

"I don't know, but I wouldn't want the option to be off the table, you know?" The thought of marrying Brice calls to mind my mother's ambitions, and I cringe. "With my divorce not even finalized, the last thing I should be thinking about is whether I want to marry someone else. But I can't help it with him." That's the crux of the matter. Right now, I think I could walk away, and I'd be wounded, but it wouldn't be fatal. If I let this continue, though... "He wants kids. Badly. And you know..." I gesture with my hand.

"He wouldn't just want to be the fun uncle?" Wren twists the lid off her water and takes a long drink.

"Nope." He's been the most open man I've ever met when it comes to children. Enzo claimed to be fine with either having kids or not having them, until I miscarried. Then my trauma over the loss of our baby and my former indifference to starting a family became huge things looming over our fractured marriage. He resented that I'd never cared about having children, and he couldn't comprehend my grief when he felt he'd been the one with the dashed hopes and dreams.

"Maybe having him go to Denmark will be good for the two of you. Put things in perspective. You've spent a lot of time in close proximity, and you and I both know how easy it is for training relationships to morph into something else only to fall apart later."

That's almost word for word what Emery said earlier. Once we aren't seeing each other anymore, not locked in a common goal, these feelings might fade. A training romance has never happened to me before, but I've seen it many times in others.

"Am I overthinking this? Maybe I am. I should just go with the flow tonight. Enjoy our last night on the team together. Have a few drinks. Accept our big, fat check for winning. Worry about the rest when he returns from Denmark." It might be easier to say no to him once I've got my bearings. Here, on the racecourse, he feels too much like *my* Brice and not Bellerive's Brice.

As the afternoon wears on, and we visit with other teams, I expect the anxiety in my stomach to stop sloshing around at my easy-breezy decision, and when that doesn't happen, I can't help wondering what my subconscious is seeing that I can't when it comes to Brice.

When I arrive at the after-party in my short, tight Bellerive Blue dress, the first thing I notice is a whole table of tequilas set up with shot glasses, lemons, salt, and various other cocktail-making concoctions. InterFlix's last hurrah must be to get Brice drunk on film, since there are cameras everywhere. Charming.

"Tucker," Brice calls from the middle of the dance floor where he is already the life of the party. "Come celebrate!" He raises his tequila sunrise in the air. "Get a drink."

I can allow my uncertainty over what is or isn't happening with Brice to get a foothold, or I can grab a drink and join the chaos. The cameras already have plenty of footage to prove Brice and I are close. What's one more night of demonstrating that?

At the tequila table, I take a shot of the top-shelf brand, and as it slides down my throat, it reminds me of kissing Brice. I wiggle and tug on the hem of my dress at the memory. If I close my eyes, I bet I could feel him.

A hand eases around my waist, and when I'm towed gently backward, I connect with Brice's hard chest. Tequila, mint, and orange juice mingle in the air, and I let my head fall against his shoulder.

"You look amazing," he whispers in my ear before flicking his tongue against my earlobe.

He still has his ten days' worth of stubble, and it grazes my neck, sending a shiver racing down my spine. I'm surprised he hasn't shaved, but I did run my fingers through it the other day and tell him how much I liked him in an almost-beard. Irresistibly sexy.

"Wren sleeping with her Australian friend again tonight?"

"I haven't asked her yet," I say with a throaty chuckle.

"Wren!" Brice calls, stepping away from me to search the crowd with his hand perched on his forehead as though the sun might get into his eyes, even though it's dark.

"Brice!" I grab his arm and rotate him back to me. "Don't make a scene."

"I was born to make a scene, baby." He kisses my temple and pours himself a shot. "Play Truth and Tequila with me," he says. "One round. I've got like…three hundred questions I want to ask you. But only three are actually important. We can start there. You get to ask me anything too."

"You don't need tequila to talk to me." I give him a light punch in the arm.

"I really do," he says. "I don't say the sorts of things I want to say to you to other women."

"And that requires—"

"Liquid courage. It's a thing. A real thing. Ask any of my brothers."

"You already seem a bit drunk." By "bit," I mean "very."

He reaches behind me to pour me a shot to pair with his. Before picking them up, he drains his tequila sunrise and sets it on the table. Then he passes me a shot, and he clinks his glass with mine.

"To being unexpected winners," he says before throwing the drink back.

"Unexpected?" I smile and follow his lead. "Speak for yourself."

He runs his knuckles from my shoulder down to my elbow, and it's a move other men have made, but it's never ignited my body the way his touch does. A shiver races through me, and when I glance up at him under my lashes, his pupils are dilated. He lowers his head, so his lips are next to my ear.

"Everything about you is such a fucking turn on," he rasps.

"Everything?" I let my thumb glide across his cheekbone, at the edge of his beard. There is nothing about him I don't find attractive. "Funny where we've ended up, isn't it?"

"My life will be forever split in two. BMT and AMT."

"Those sounds like sandwich combinations," I tease, but my heart is thumping in my chest at his drunken sincerity. The intensity in his words and his gaze hits me in my gut.

"Something like that," he says with a wry smile. "More alcohol." He pours another shot and takes it. "You gonna get wild with me, Tucker?" He points his empty shot glass at me.

"Yeah," I say because I promised myself I'd go with the flow, even if the idea doesn't do anything to dissipate my anxiety over what we will or won't be to each other after tonight. "I'll get wild with you."

He lets out a crow of delight and pours me a shot along with another one for himself. When I go to drink, he stays my hand.

"Wait, wait. Before I get too drunk," he says, and he motions to my collarbone and to my thigh. "Did you look after both of those like you were told?"

"Yes, Dad." I roll my eyes and take my shot.

"You can call me daddy, but we'll save that for later." He winks at me, and then he slides his hand into mine and drags me onto the dance floor.

The rest of the night passes in a blur of shots and shouted conversations and Brice slow dancing with me every chance I'll give him, even when the music doesn't warrant it. If my head was in a different place, his attachment to me would be cute.

When people start to leave to go back to their rooms, claiming early flights or overtiredness after the grueling ten days, Brice links his hand with mine, and we stumble back toward our hotel room.

Wren said she'd sleep in another room again to give us space if I wanted it. Part of me desperately wants to seize the alone time, and another part of me thinks lingering in this limbo with him will only make ripping the Band-Aid off later that much harder.

At the door to my hotel room, Brice stretches across the doorframe, pinning me against it, and he kisses me. Given his level of drunkenness, his restraint up to now has been admirable. He came close a few times to forgetting we were in the middle of a dance floor or at a party with lots of cameras, but he caught himself at the last second every time.

To avoid my own drunken mistakes, I switched to water many, many shots ago because I'm not-so-secretly a lightweight, but I'm not sure he noticed.

"Tucker," Brice says, rubbing his nose against mine before kissing me again. "I want you to have my baby."

"What?" My heart sinks to my feet as though it's made of lead. I'd almost convinced myself he'd never ask, and if he never asked, there was a chance we could continue on, together. "Brice, you're drunk." If this is the alcohol talking, maybe I can ignore this conversation.

"No, no. Listen. I'm serious. It'd be perfect. We get along. You understand my life like no one else does. We've got lots of money so neither of us cares about any of that shit."

"Brice." When he tries to kiss me again, I turn my head to the side.

"Sorry. God. My timing is terrible. I don't mean right away. You've got things to sort out, and you're still grieving, and I probably sound like an absolute asshole right now. But I can't stop thinking about it. I haven't been able to stop thinking about it."

His words are slurred, and when one of his hands slides around my waist to land on my abdomen, I wish the floor would open and swallow me. Anything to escape this conversation.

"I'm not the right woman for you." I shake my head, and because of the alcohol coursing through my system, I can't keep the tears that spring to my eyes in check. "I can't. I don't want to. Please don't. Just don't."

"Tucker." His voice is gentle. "I didn't mean to upset you. Shit. I'm sorry. When I'm sober, this will sound a lot better and smoother."

"I'm not the woman you need." I sniff and straighten as I dig my keycard out of the tiny pocket on the outer thigh of my dress. Falling apart in front of him would lead to questions I don't want to answer. His priorities are clear, and they aren't about me.

"You're exactly the woman I need. It'd be perfect, I swear. When I'm sober—"

"I won't change my mind," I say, and I let some of the old steeliness I used to show him creep into my voice and posture. "There are hundreds, if not thousands, of women in Bellerive who'd gladly have your baby. You don't need me." The keycard beeps on the door, and I turn the handle, backing into the room.

He tries to follow me, but I put my hand on his chest. "When you get back to Bellerive, you should start looking. If that's what you really want, you should start looking for someone who can give that to you. It won't be me."

Then before he has a chance to argue or charm his way in the room and deeper into my heart, I close the door in his face. Any uncertainty I had about what I meant to him and what we could be is gone.

It's not me he wants. He wants what he assumes I can provide him. The one thing he wants more than anything, I'm incapable of, and I won't rake myself over the coals about it again, not even for him.

Even if we could have a baby together, his proposal is so much less than what I'd need to be happy. In an ideal world, if I looked five or ten years down the road, our relationship wouldn't be shared parental duties and two separate houses. His idea of perfect would never be mine. Complete emotional detachment might look nice from the outside, but it's a lonely existence, and it's not a life I want to lead forever, not even after what happened between me and Enzo.

That, in some ways, is the hardest thing to reconcile about his request. I want the relationship and love, and Brice only wants the baby.

# Chapter Thirty-Nine

## BRICE

I wake up to Jag standing over me with a coffee in his hand. My mouth is full of cotton balls, and a raging headache pounds my brain. Worst fucking hangover in a long time. Of course, it's been ages since I drank that much. All the training and hanging out with a teetotaling Tucker made sure I lost my tolerance.

Thinking of Tucker, so often the first person who comes to my mind, causes what I said to come back in a rush of word vomit followed by actual vomit when I dash to the toilet just in time.

"Good night, then?" Jag asks from the other room.

"Quite possibly the worst night of my life," I mutter into the toilet bowl. What the fuck was I thinking asking her to have my babies? Should have known better than to get that drunk around her. Surprised I didn't fall to my knees and beg her to never leave me. Likely would have been a better outcome than suggesting she bear my children after she just got a tattoo marking her miscarriage. I'm a colossal fucking idiot.

When my legs seem like they'll hold me, I get up and stare at myself in the mirror. I'm clad only in boxers, and there are dark rings under my eyes. Even drunk me didn't sleep well. My subconscious must have realized how badly I fucked up. Terrible. Absolutely terrible.

Sober me would have never done what drunk me did last night. While this isn't the first time I've stared into a mirror and had that same thought, I've never regretted anything as much as blurting out my insensitive request to Maren last night.

I'm not even sure what my drunken self was hoping to accomplish. Her response was never going to be an enthusiastic "yes" under the circumstances. Not sure I expected quite that firm of a dismissal, though. Given how close we've gotten, having her suggest I find, quite literally, *anyone else* for the job seemed a tad extreme.

As I brush my teeth, I try to come up with ways to fix things between us once I'm back in Bellerive. There's not much I can do for the next five or six days while I'm in Denmark for their climate change summit.

After I'm done in the bathroom, I sit on the edge of the bed, and I scroll through my phone.

Jesus. I'm a stalker. I must have sent Tucker a hundred messages last night of varying degrees of cringe. Some of my jokes are funny, but the majority of them are decidedly not. All of them sit unread. At least she hasn't turned on her phone yet.

There really needs to be some sort of breathalyzer for operating a phone when you're drunk and upset. Perhaps that'll be my next venture. Figuring out a way to save myself from myself.

"Have you ever wished you could suck words back into your mouth or somehow rewind time?" I ask Jag as I keep scrolling through the obscene number of messages I sent Tucker.

"What'd you say to Maren?" he asks.

"Nothing." There's no way I'm speaking those things out loud to anyone. They'll bury me with them. I check my outgoing calls.

Or perhaps they won't be buried with me. Other than speed-dialing Tucker obsessively, I also drunk dialed Brent, Nick, and Posey. I close my eyes when I catch sight of the last number. Rory. I drunk dialed Rory.

Alex is going to fucking kill me.

Why do I always need witnesses to my idiocy?

"You all right, Your Highness? You've gone pale."

"Next time I pick up a bottle of tequila to drink, can you just, like, tap me on the shoulder and say, 'Your Highness, tequila is no longer your friend,' and I'll know. I'll know exactly what you're talking about."

"If you and tequila are in a fight," Jag says, "I can't even imagine what happened last night."

"We're not just in a fight. We may very well be mortal enemies." Of all the stupid things I've done in my life, last night takes the top spot. "When do we need to leave?"

"Thirty minutes." Jag consults his watch.

I'm throwing on clothes and trying to block out the pounding in my head. In my bag, I find a package of aspirin, and I throw them into my mouth before taking long gulps from my water bottle.

"I have to go talk to her," I say more to myself than Jag.

"I'll load the vehicle."

Somehow, my drunk self managed to half-ass pack last night, so I only need to stuff a few last things into my bags before Jag can start taking them out.

At Tucker's door, I knock, and when there's no answer, I knock again. It's early. Maybe she's still sleeping.

"Tucker?" I say, and I press my forehead to the door. "I need to talk to you."

"She's not there, mate." One of the Australian team members stands in the doorway of his room, bare chested. "She woke Wren up to go for a run. Does she ever stop?"

I run my hands through my hair, and I sink down to sit beside her closed door. One of my favorite things about Tucker is that she never stops, never quits. I just hope she forgives.

If she returns in the next forty-five minutes, I'll be waiting.

What feels like only a few minutes later, Jag appears in front of me. "Your Highness, if we don't leave now, you'll miss your flight."

I stare up at him, and I release a deep sigh. Intentional or not, I won't have a chance to explain or apologize to Maren today. Truthfully, I'm not sorry I asked, but I do regret my timing and delivery. Not sure if that apology would have made things better or worse. I guess I'll find out when I get back to Bellerive.

---

I'm holed up in one of the guest suites in Denmark's palace, regretting almost all my life choices, when Nick arrives with a smirk and a bottle of tequila. At least my headache is gone.

"Hair of the dog?" he suggests.

"I drunk dialed Rory," I say from my position sprawled on the bed. While I've had my phone with me since I arrived a few hours ago, I haven't heard anything from Tucker. Every time I check, my messages are still unread. I wouldn't put it past her to read them all and then mark them all unread again just to teach me a lesson.

"I heard," Nick says, sliding the bottle and shot glasses onto a side table. "Alex told me he was concerned about you this morning before I left. I told him he'd gone soft on me." Nick scoffs and throws himself into one of the recliners across from the couch. "Though the shitstorm you and Maren Tucker have kicked off on social media is impressive."

"What?" I say, sitting up and snatching my phone off the bed beside me. "Please tell me I didn't post anything on my accounts."

"Not you," Nick says. "You weren't that stupid. But to say you and Maren weren't discrete at the end-of-race party is an understatement. Holding hands. Grinding on the dance floor. Pressed up against the door of her hotel room. Hell of an introduction for the Bellerivian elite to your relationship. Celia Tucker already called Desmond to suggest the families should get together soon."

As he provides the running commentary, I see the stream of photos plastered all over social media. We're both tagged, and I should feel bad. It's a disaster. Sure to send Maren into a tailspin. Depending on how we handle it and how royal PR handles it, this has scandal written all over it. The problem is, I don't have a clue how to respond to any of it. We agreed to a fling, a rebound, and then I asked her to have my baby.

"At least it seems to be public knowledge that Maren filed for a separation from her husband," Nick says. "Whoever leaked that did you two a favor." He gives me an exaggerated wink.

"You leaked that."

"Gotta look out for my younger brother making poor decisions. You're probably wishing I was with you last night to tape your mouth shut."

"I told you," I say in a flat voice.

"I think you told everyone." Nick chuckles. "It's a good day to be me today. Know why? Because I am not you."

"Fuck off." I toss my phone onto the bed beside me again, and I flop back. His smugness is not helping my mood. I cover my face with my hands, and I breathe out a deep sigh.

"I realize you're new at this, but the traditional way to ask someone to be in a relationship with you is to ask her to be your girlfriend or go steady or whatever. Not suggest she bear your children."

"I don't want her to be my girlfriend," I say. "I want to tie her to me forever. A baby does that."

"That's called marriage, then."

My heart thuds at the mention of marriage. Seems ridiculous that I haven't even considered that option, but I haven't. "Bellerivian royals can't get divorced."

"Is that why you've always been against relationships? Had that weird opinion that the other person should love you more?"

Not weird—smart. Means I've never felt this dread spiral before over anyone. Tucker is all I can think about, and there's an endless, gaping hole in the pit of my stomach.

"I need out of this Denmark deal," I say.

"That's up to Freja. You know that," Nick says. "But Alex did tell me to tell you that he's prepared for any fallout. He's sensed this coming, I think. Sent me here for crisis management."

"He sent *you* for crisis management?" I bark out a laugh. "How are *you* crisis management?"

"*You're* the crisis," Nick says. "He sent me here to manage you."

"How the mighty have fallen when you're the sane and rational one," I say while I stare at the ceiling.

"You've never been the sane, rational one."

"Neither have you."

"Fair point. Together, Alex would have argued we still made up half a brain."

That makes me laugh despite myself. A perfect Alex comment. Silence falls between us again, and it's thick with my anxiety.

"I'm terrified I've ruined any chance I had with her." The thought has been on repeat in my brain since I woke up.

"You've only ruined it if you stop trying to make it right. Trust me on that." Nick sinks deeper into the recliner.

"Honestly," I say, sitting up, "I expected more gloating from you. I'm fucking miserable."

"Oh, I'm gonna gloat," Nick says with a grin. "I've got days, though. Can't waste all my best material out of the gate. My baby brother is finally in love, and it's the biggest mess I could have ever hoped to see."

*Love.*

I let out a deep sigh. It's the word I haven't allowed myself to attach to this feeling, but it can't be anything else. I've fallen off my aloof emotional perch and straight into the depths of love with Maren Tucker.

We have the opening speeches for Denmark's Climate Change Summit in less than an hour, and I know I have to speak to Freja before the event is in full swing. The schedule is packed with appearances from one or both of us on a variety of climate change issues. While our schedules were created to line up almost exactly, nothing I want to say to her can be said in public.

I knock on the door to Freja's suite of rooms, and she calls for me to come in. There's a woman putting the final touches on her makeup and a man finishing the updo of her brown hair.

"Did you win?" she asks.

"Bound by an NDA not to answer."

"Those photos on social media certainly seemed celebratory." There's no bite to her words. Things have never been like that between us. She checks her appearance in the mirror and gives a satisfied nod.

"Everyone was celebrating," I say. "We survived."

"Can you both leave us?" She tips her head toward the door to her suite, and the makeup artist and the hairstylist slip out. "What's bothering you? You're never so serious."

I wander the room, picking up framed photos and setting them down again. There's no easy way to broach the subject, and even suggesting it makes me feel like a bad person. But if I'm going back to Bellerive to give it my best shot with Maren, I can't have any dangling threads that might embarrass her or make her uncomfortable. Considering how skittish Tucker is, any excuse to say no to me will be all she needs.

"I'm wondering whether you feel like you've made enough progress that you might not need me anymore."

"This is about Maren Tucker?" She rotates on her stool to face me rather than watching me through the large mirror. "There was a lot of heat coming off those photos. Made me blush."

Not surprising. Part of the reason I've been summoned to Freja's side the last year was due to a sudden onset of social anxiety. Simone thought I might be able to help ease Freja's mind since I've never met a person I can't charm—according to Simone, not me—though, I wasn't exactly going to refute that. She equated me to a golden retriever but not nearly as loyal.

I've been turned into Freja's emotional support animal for charity functions, diplomatic dinners, and bigger things like this climate summit where Freja is expected to be there but needs someone at her elbow in case the room starts to close in. Her family reduced her obligations as much as possible, which has allowed me to be here when necessary.

Anyone could do the job I'm doing. They could, quite literally, buy and train a golden retriever to take my place, but I'm aware of the larger picture. Simone's ability to dictate my fate and lord it over Alex is a big piece, and my frequent appearances feed the narrative that our families are closer than anyone ever realized. Alex embarrassed her, and her family and I became the consolation prize.

For the most part, I haven't minded. Throw on a suit, let the royal facade descend, and work the room. Simple. Keep Freja from losing her chill in public. I've only had to step in to get her out of a room once or twice. The fact that people and members of the press have assumed some sort of relationship exists between me and Freja allowed her real issues to remain private, and neither of us or our respective PR departments have corrected those assumptions.

"It's about Maren, yeah," I admit. "The press has created this whole narrative about you and me that we both know isn't true."

"And what does Maren think? Did you tell her?"

"Signed an NDA for what I'm doing with you too, didn't I?" I grimace. Had Tucker pushed for more information, I would have broken it. Admitting that here would be foolish. "Not that she cared to know, anyway. But when I go back to Bellerive, I can't have her doubting me."

Freja crosses her arms, and her brown eyes scan me from head to toe. "A year ago you showed up here all jokes and swagger and easy-breezy charm. Do you remember you told me to be careful not to fall in love with you because you weren't romantic-lead material?"

"Did I say that?" Sounds like something I'd have said a year ago. Advice that appears helpful. Mostly bullshit, or maybe not bullshit so much as careless. Now I understand those feelings don't play by any rules. Falling in love isn't a choice. It's a free fall off a cliff with no safety net and no idea how far away the water is or whether you'll hit the rocky face on the way down. Chaos. The best and worst feeling in the world. "I didn't go looking for this."

"Isn't she married?"

"Getting a divorce. Separated."

"That's not an issue in your country?"

"If it is, Alex will change it." My certainty is absolute. After what he went through with Rory, I know he won't make me suffer needlessly.

"I never asked for this arrangement between us," Freja says, "and if Simone had asked me, I would have said no. When you showed up that first time, I was horrified." She turns to check her appearance in the mirror again. "But she was right, in the end. You're so good with people and so easy to be around. Having you beside me at all these functions *was* a comfort when I needed it most." She gazes at me for a beat and seems to be weighing what she wants to say next. "My doctor found a medication that works for me a few months ago, and I'm feeling much better. This summit will be the real test."

"You don't need me anymore."

"Not really, no. I would have kept you." A small smile tugs at the edges of her lips, and there's a fondness around her eyes that makes me wonder whether I was right to give her the warning when we first met. "One last hurrah this week?"

"I'll stay. I'm not leaving. If you do need me, just give me the signal." Even though I'd really like to walk out and return home right now. If everyone is going to let me out of this arrangement without a fuss, there's no reason to create one. "But I think it would be better if we kept our distance in public. With the photos out of me and Maren..."

"You want to protect her and her image."

"In any way I can. I wouldn't want to embarrass her."

"Look at you," she says with good humor lighting her eyes, "becoming the romantic lead in someone's story."

I hope so, and when I get back to Bellerive, I intend to do everything I can to prove to Maren that, despite my numerous mistakes, no one will ever love her more or better than me. For the first time in my life, the idea of forever with someone isn't scary. It's exhilarating.

## Chapter Forty

## MAREN

Since I returned from Fiji a few days ago, I've been sleeping a lot. The kind of deep, dreamless sleeps I had when I came home from Chile and sank into my depression. In an effort to be proactive, I asked for my medication to be returned to pretraining levels. My body feels like it's being dragged under, and I'm worried my spirit will be next.

I can't get a handle on Brice's request and the race being over and him being gone.

Maybe I need to get back out on a bike or have my feet pound the road, but I've just been so tired. Impossibly tired.

On top of that, pictures of me and Brice from the after-party broke over social media, and I haven't been able to face anyone. None of my friends or family because I don't know what to say about those photos. We aren't a couple, and we'll never be a couple.

That hasn't stopped my mother from calling me at regular intervals to find out whether we should be "getting the families together" as though Brice and I are a foregone conclusion based on a few scandalous photos.

He's in Denmark with Freja—though I haven't seen a single snap of them together—and I'm here in Bellerive sad and angry that I found another man who wants a baby more than he wants me.

While I unpack, I can't seem to figure out the temperature in my apartment. One minute I'm sweating and the next I'm shivering. It's taken me days to have enough energy to get organized, so as I'm sorting laundry and putting things away, I'm constantly increasing layers of clothes or taking them off.

My final pieces from the trip are in the washing machine when a dull throbbing begins behind my forehead. I've been living off aspirin for my aches and pains from the race and now this headache too.

In my pocket, my phone rings, and when I take it out to see who it is, the name is a little blurry. I blink to refocus. Brice?

My initial instinct is to answer, but I have no idea what I'd say. Pretend he didn't ask me to have his baby? Pretend we're totally fine? Ask how his trip is going? Pretend I don't wish I'd asked about Denmark? There's a good chance I'm not capable of faking anything anymore where he's concerned. I've gotten so used to having him around that I'm likely to beg him to come back from Denmark, and where will that land us? I can't give him what he wants physically or emotionally. Pursuing anything with him would be a mistake when we won't last.

Over the last year, I've had enough heartbreak for a lifetime.

I send him to voicemail knowing he'll call back. If there's one thing I can say with certainty—Brice has perseverance down to a science. At some point, he'll force me to talk to him, but I'm hoping I'll be ready when it happens. Full of steel and certainty rather than this soft confusion that's been clouding my thoughts for days.

When my phone starts buzzing again, I brace myself to see his name. Instead, it's Caitlin, and I answer the call hoping she's heard from Enzo, who has gone MIA since the papers were filed.

"What have you heard?" I ask once we go through the regular pleasantries.

"He's been contacting divorce lawyers on the island, and a few acquaintances in Boston contacted me to say he visited them too. He hasn't signed the papers yet, though."

The aspirin I took hasn't touched my headache, and I massage my forehead while I try to figure out what those two pieces mean. He hasn't tried to contact me at all, even though he must know the race is over. We spent enough years together that he understands the patterns of my competitions. Maybe he's still fuming that I competed at all.

"If you hear anything else," I say, "let me know."

"Are you okay?" Caitlin asks. "Have you heard from Brice?"

"I'm not taking his calls," I say.

"From what I've heard, he's not with Princess Freja," Caitlin says. "Despite what the press is printing about him jetting off to soothe her hurt feelings."

"He told me about Denmark before the photos broke." While he and Freja might have been a casual thing at one point, he would have mentioned her over the last few months if they'd ever been in a relationship. His solitary commitment to Presley Cook wasn't exactly impressive, and if he could have given me another example back then, I'm sure he would have. He had no reason to lie. Even with how complicated we've become, he isn't the type to withhold that information. I don't understand why he's been to Denmark so much, but sometimes the obvious answer isn't the right one, despite what the tabloids like to believe. Although I hate how the situation looks to outsiders and how a sliver inside me buys into the appearance of something more, that isn't my main issue. It runs so much deeper than some made-up affair with another royal.

"You didn't sound like yourself, so I thought I would mention it. Both Nathaniel and Sawyer said Brice called them to see if they'd check on you. He's obviously concerned about how things would look to you."

"I can't—" I press my fingertips into my forehead again. "I can't talk about him right now. We're not sustainable, so there's no point." Sawyer and Nathaniel both stopped around when I first got home, and they tried to talk me into seeing a doctor about my leg. But I've been monitoring it, and it's healing fine. Going to a doctor would be a wasted trip, and I'd be exposed to all sorts of questions about me and Brice from everyone I encounter. I just can't face any of it.

"For what it's worth," Caitlin says, "I haven't seen you look as happy as you were in those photos in a really long time."

My stomach churns at the realization that I *have* been happy. The last few months, despite the disintegration of my marriage, despite my body's betrayal, I've been happy. It would be such a gamble to let Brice in all the way only to discover I was right all along. So much easier to keep my expectations low to nonexistent.

"Tell me if you hear from Enzo," I say, and after Caitlin hangs up, I wander down the hall to my bedroom.

In my room, I stare at myself in the mirror. I'm flushed and glassy-eyed. A nap. If I can get enough sleep, I'll start to feel better.

---

I wake to the doorbell ringing, and I'm disoriented at first. In my dream, Brice had a cool hand pressed to my forehead and a worried expression on his face. Seeing him, even in my dream, felt like the warmest, coziest blanket.

At the edge of the bed, I sit for a minute, getting my bearings. My headache is still there, but it doesn't seem as urgent. A gentle reminder that I'm not myself.

The doorbell sounds again, and I go to the front entrance, a vague sense of dizziness causing the room to feel slightly out of focus. Without checking the peephole, I open the door.

There, with two suitcases at his feet, is Enzo. His shoulders are still as broad as the last time I saw him. His waist is just as tapered, and his dark wavy hair is glossy with product. The jeans he's wearing are designer, and his polo shirt clings to his muscles. I take him in, but I can't process that he's on my doorstep after being gone for a year.

He's got a manila envelope clutched in one hand, and he raises it. "I'm not signing this," he says. "Not without a fight."

"What are you doing here?" I whisper. "Why didn't you sign them?"

"You said I had until after you got back from Fiji. Imagine my surprise when you sent these and then made yourself impossible to contact." He grimaces. "I'm here to save our marriage."

I stare at him, dumbfounded. My brain can't seem to process anything.

"You had the locks changed on our house. I went there first, and I had to ask Gage where you were holed up."

Of course my younger brother would sell me out. He always liked Enzo, probably the only one in my family he truly connected with. Should have known that was a bad sign, but for the longest time, I thought my family and everyone on the island hadn't given Enzo enough of a chance.

"I've been here for almost a year," I say, and I lean against the door, my energy trickling out. "Look, I'm not feeling great. Can we—can we do this later?"

"I knew you shouldn't have gone on that race," he says, and his tone is laced with bitterness. "You never know when to quit."

"I don't want to fight," I say. "I don't have the energy."

"If you give me the keys to the house, I'll get myself set up there. You take a nap. I'll come pick you up for dinner, and we can talk. Or I can stay here, or you can come home with me."

"No." I shake my head, and I leave the door to grab the keys from a drawer in the kitchen.

Enzo is at the windows, which offer a full view of the ocean, and he glances at me over his shoulder. "I can see why you'd come here."

It's surreal to have him in my space after so long, and it causes a dreamlike sensation, as though I'm still sleeping. Or maybe I'm actually sick. Everything is slightly out of focus. I keep my distance from him, the keys to our old house in my hand.

"I don't want to go out for dinner," I say. "I'm not feeling well."

"M, I came. You said if I was here when the race was over, we'd have a chance."

Feels like months rather than weeks ago that I said it.

"We're still married. You owe me an opportunity to talk."

The reminder causes my blood to run cold. For the last two weeks, I've been acting as though I was separated, but if he never signed the papers, the truth is much murkier.

"You should have signed the papers," I whisper.

"Maybe. But I didn't, and I won't until we have a chance to talk. Get some rest, and I'll pick you up for dinner." He plucks the keys from my hand before heading for the door.

---

When I wake up later, the half-light of dusk is filtering in my bedroom window, and I lie in bed for a moment, assessing how I'm feeling. The headache is still there, but it's so dull I can almost ignore it. I've been doing so much sleeping, I probably haven't been drinking enough water. Dehydrated. That's likely all it is.

In the shower, I lean against the wall and let the water wash over me. Shampooing my hair and getting myself ready takes a monumental effort, and in the end, I don't wrestle with my hair. It sits in a messy, damp bun, and my makeup is minimal. Enzo has seen me at my best and my worst over the years. We're in solid middle ground tonight. My dress is long and loose, but it's the same light blue as my eyes.

The doorbell sounds right on time, which is like Enzo when something is important to him. He's never early or late, and after so many months of not thinking about him very much, it's strange to have him occupy my thoughts. At the door, he takes my hand, and for a moment, I let him, testing out how it feels. But it's not his hand I wish was pressed against mine. The reminder of Brice causes a spike of guilt and sadness to zip through me. Brice and I don't want the same things, but I'm not sure Enzo and I do either.

Outside my apartment complex, there are photographers, and I hesitate at the exit. They're obviously here because of the photos of me and Brice. Enzo grips my hand a little harder, and he steers me out the door, forcing me to face my uncertainty.

He's hired a car and driver, which is an extravagance I wouldn't normally indulge in. For security reasons, Brice has the armored car and driver, but I can't understand why Enzo and I would need one. Flashes go off as we get into the Bentley, and I realize I forgot my phone and purse in the apartment. My brain is sluggish, and my skin feels clammy.

"I didn't bring my purse," I say in the back seat.

"I can cover dinner." A heavy silence falls over the car. "You were always so adamant you didn't want to be your father."

"I'm not him."

"Those photos of you and Prince Brice indicate otherwise. All those questions the reporters just hurled at you that you didn't bother answering suggest otherwise. The comments he's made in Denmark about how the two of you are very close say otherwise. That tattoo on your collarbone says otherwise. You hate tattoos—you used to call them tacky. Does he make a habit of going after other people's wives?"

"You've been gone for a year." I have no energy or desire to explain the baby's breath that lies on my collarbone. He wouldn't understand.

"And you gave me a timeline to come home, and I was coming. Instead of waiting, you start an affair with, quite frankly, the last guy I would have expected."

His comments are hitting me where it hurts, and that's the thing about being with someone for years. They know exactly which buttons to push, what things to say that'll drive home whatever point they're making. He's setting out to turn me into the villain, and maybe I am. Being with Brice was a selfish decision. I could have waited to see whether Enzo would turn up after the race and then come clean about the kiss Brice and I shared. If I'd been sure Enzo would come home, it might have been different.

"If you think I'm such a terrible person, why are you back here? Just sign the papers and be done with it." I press my fingers into my temples. They're throbbing and making it hard to concentrate. My nap lulled me into a false sense of wellness, and whatever is plaguing me is roaring to life.

The car draws flush with the restaurant, and I cringe when I realize Enzo has brought us to the same place he proposed years ago. Back then, this building was a Mexican cantina, but it's since changed hands, and it's now a tapas restaurant. Perhaps I'll actually be able to stomach some of the tiny dishes.

Reluctantly, I get out of the car. He seems determined to make me feel bad, and maybe I deserve it. The last few months, both he and our marriage have been further from my thoughts than they should have been.

As we walk in the door, my vision blurs, and I stumble. Enzo doesn't catch me, the hostess does. I give her a grateful look, and she merely smiles before sliding a questioning glare in Enzo's direction. She stays by my side as she shows us to our seats.

The waitress arrives with menus, but my stomach is gurgling and rolling.

"I think I—" I rub my forehead. "I need the bathroom." Since I returned from Fiji, I haven't been anywhere, so whatever is wrong with me, I must have picked it up on the plane. I weave my way to the bathroom, and once I'm there, I stare at myself in the mirror.

My earlier claim that my appearance was solidly in the middle ground seems like a brag now. I'm pale with overly rosy cheeks, and my eyes are still glassy. When I lay the back of my hand across my forehead, I'm hot to the touch. Does that check work? Do I have a fever?

My stomach clenches, and this time, I rush into one of the stalls. I'm on my knees praying to the porcelain god just before my stomach empties into the bowl. For a beat, I clutch the toilet as my stomach releases its contents over and over again. Once I've got nothing left, I sit on the floor, trying to remember if I've been this hot all day. Sweat has soaked through the armpits of my dress.

Unsteady on my feet, I wobble to the counter, and I turn on the tap to splash water in my face. When I glance up at the mirror again, my vision blurs, and I can't keep myself upright. As I fall to the ground, everything goes black.

# Chapter Forty-One

## BRICE

Nick and I are on a private plane back to Bellerive. Tomorrow is the one-year anniversary of Tucker's accident, and even if she hasn't taken a single one of my calls or responded to any of my text messages, I'm showing up at her door, and I'm begging for forgiveness. My request was poorly timed in the extreme, but I can walk it back. I'll walk it back as far as Maren needs me to.

There's a bottle of tequila sitting between me and Nick on the armrest, but I'm ignoring it. The last thing I need is to show up at Tucker's door plastered. Liquid courage just led to liquid stupidity last time.

Nick shifts in his chair to check something on his phone, and the way he does it makes me think he's trying to hide something from me. Without asking, I flip to his favorite social media platform on my device, and it doesn't take me long to see what he was trying to conceal. Some assholes have already tagged me in the photos.

Enzo arriving at Maren's apartment with two oversized suitcases. Maren and Enzo holding hands as they exit her apartment building.

What. The. Fuck.

"Are you kidding me right now?" I say to no one in particular. My chest is so tight I can barely breathe. "I totally understand now why I always thought the other person should love me more. Being the one who loves them more fucking sucks."

"Yeah, it does," Nick agrees. "Been there. Done that. Would not recommend. You saw the photos?"

"Was very helpfully tagged in the photos by the people posting them. So kind." My voice drips with sarcasm.

"We both know one photo or even two photos don't tell the whole story. Look at what the press built about you and Freja, and that was very far from the truth."

Part of me wonders whether the Freja thing is to blame for Maren giving Enzo a look in. If so, that's my fault for not breaking my NDA to tell her everything. But the other part of me knows that if Enzo is getting another shot, it's got far more to do with me suggesting she bear my children. For someone who was already skittish about any sort of commitment, I dropped the motherload on her. Literally.

"I have this intense desire to fly to Vegas," I say. My instinct is to flee from these emotions, and I turn off my phone so

I don't stare at the photos obsessively, dissecting hand placements, body language, and eye contact. If she chooses Enzo after the awful way he's treated her this past year, I don't know what to think. She deserves better, and for her not to realize that is truly baffling. "If she's getting back together with him, I can't be there."

"You want my advice?" Nick asks.

"Will it be helpful?"

"Hard-won experience tells me that if you regret anything in this situation, it'll be avoiding the tough conversation. If she loves him more, then she loves him more. Trust me when I say that *assuming* she loves him more and then finding out years later she *didn't* love him more is its own particular brand of heartbreak. Years wasted for nothing."

I snap off the cap on the tequila, and I pour myself a shot. While I've got no intention of getting drunk, there's a certain comfort in doing something familiar when I'm so out of sorts. Five minutes ago, I was headed back to Bellerive, and I was determined to do anything to make up my mistake in Fiji. Now the calls sent to voicemail and the unread text messages make more sense. Maybe she said no to me because she already knew she was going back to Enzo. Maybe the vibe I thought I was getting off her was just me, so into her I couldn't see that she wasn't there with me.

"If you go talk to her, and she picks him," Nick says, "I'll catch the first flight to Vegas with you. Might even force Alex and Brent to tag along."

He makes heartbreak sound slightly more appealing, but I'm still not sure I can stand in front of Maren and have her admit she would rather be with Enzo. For her to pick him over me is unthinkable, and yet there's a part of me that realizes it's possible she will. Maybe even likely. She married him, and they've been together for years. She hates failure, and I have no doubt she'd see divorce as the biggest one.

There's also her stubbornness, and I need to account for that. Whatever way she decides to go, her heels will dig in deep.

"What sort of man do you want to be?" Nick asks. "The one who runs from hard things or the one who faces them?"

It's the type of question our father would have asked me, and it pulls the situation into tight focus. Nick spent years running from important and necessary conversations with Jules, and so I know he's coming from a place of experience. On top of that, Enzo ran when Maren needed him the most. To be worthy of her, to make myself worthy of her, I can't shrink away from a straightforward conversation. This one just might be the most important one we'll ever have.

"I'll talk to her." I tip back the shot of tequila, and then I screw on the top. One shot for courage.

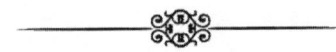

---

We've just passed through the royal customs protocol when I remember I switched off my phone earlier.

"Julia just texted me," Nick says as a series of texts pop up on my phone. "I'm not sure how to tell you this..."

There are three missed calls, and I've got half a dozen text messages. "Tucker's in the hospital," I whisper as I scan the messages from Posey, Wren, Riker, Paxton, Sawyer, and Nathaniel. The thump of my heart is so loud I'm not sure I can hear anything else. "I need to get to the hospital." My stomach has dropped to my feet, and my body is as cold as ice. Something is wrong with Maren, and I haven't been here. She didn't go to the doctor when she got back, and now she's got an infection. If I hadn't gone to Denmark, had told Alex earlier that I was done with the deal he made, I'd have been here, seen the signs she would have hidden from everyone else.

Jag is there waiting with our car, and I climb into the back seat, numb. He catches my gaze in the mirror.

"You've heard?" he says.

"What do you know?" I ask as Nick climbs into the car beside me.

"Leptospirosis is what I heard through the grapevine. The cut on her leg combined with the flood waters." He holds my gaze. "A fluke."

Exactly one year after Tucker's last accident, she's back in the hospital, and this time, it's my fault. I must not have cleaned the wound well enough in the cabin or in the days after. While Jag navigates the streets to the hospital, I spend the time reading about leptospirosis. The common symptoms sound like a million other illnesses, and knowing Tucker, she likely tried to tough it out longer than she should have. Untreated, though, it's a nasty bacterial disease. How long was she sick before she collapsed in the restaurant bathroom? Days?

At the hospital, Nick gets out of the car with me and Jag. "I'll be fine," I say to Nick in the elevator. "You can call Kane or Jules or someone to come get you."

"Enzo is going to be there. You realize that, right? None of us needs a brawl in the hallway or her hospital room on top of everything else."

Truthfully, I've never been much of a physical fighter. Of the three of us, Nick's the most likely to throw a punch, whereas I'm typically a heckler.

My emotions are so turbulent as I wait for the elevator to open on Tucker's floor that I think Nick might have a point about me going for Enzo's jugular. Posey heard Enzo wasn't even the one who found Tucker in the bathroom. It was the hostess who worried Maren had been gone from the table too long. The idea of her collapsed on the bathroom floor, alone, bleeding from a head injury makes me clench and unclench my hands.

"Does this feeling fade?" I address Nick, but I'm keenly aware of Jag's silent presence too.

"What feeling?" Nick raises his eyebrows.

"Like I—" I fumble for the right way to phrase it. "Like I could tear people apart with my bare hands for hurting her, or I'd use myself as a human shield to keep her safe." Never in my life have I experienced such an intense surge of protectiveness.

For a while, I've suspected this feeling lay underneath what I allowed myself to show Tucker, but there's no hiding its ferociousness now.

"Not for me," he says. "And you've seen the lengths Alex will go to for Rory. We love hard, and we love well."

His reference to gran's tattoo has never resonated more. "You probably shouldn't leave me alone with him."

"One step ahead of you on that one, little brother." He flashes me a grin. "Jag and I will pull you off him if you go for his throat."

When we get to the nurses' station on Maren's floor, they tell me that her husband has requested no visitors other than her family. I stand in the middle of the corridor with my hands on my hips, trying to deep breath my way out of this. Under other circumstances, I'd try to charm my way past the rules, but I'm not feeling particularly charming.

"Is she awake?" I ask. "Can someone ask her if she'll see me?" Still a gamble, but at least she'll know I'm here, even if she decides she's still too mad or disappointed in me to let me in.

The nurse leaves to check on Maren, and Nick takes his phone out of his pocket. "Do you want me to call Nathaniel? He might be able to get you into the room."

"Nathaniel is too nice." I've been contemplating another option if Tucker is sleeping or Enzo insists that I can't go in. Before I go nuclear, I text Wren to see whether Enzo has let any of the team in to visit. She gets back to me right away, confirming what I suspected—he hasn't. He's isolating her from anyone who might point out that her absent husband shouldn't get to be controlling her recovery.

There's one person I can call who'll get me in, but I'm not sure Tucker would forgive me for doing it. "Celia. If Enzo won't let me in, I'll call Celia."

"An AK-47 to a knife fight," Nick says drily.

"I'm not messing around. If he won't let me in, I'll find someone who will."

The nurse returns with a frown on her face. "She's not awake, but her husband has offered to speak to you outside her room to update you on her condition."

Pretty sure the only thing he wants to update me on is that he's back in Bellerive and wants to resume his place in her life, as though that's going to deter me from going after what I want. He's been gone a year, and he doesn't get to come back here and lift his leg all over her life as though he has a right to mark anything as his. She sent him separation papers. She slept with me—more than once. Pretty clear signals about where she falls on the idea of their marriage.

Or where she did fall. The handholding as she came out of her apartment is still throwing me off. Could he have said something to sway her?

She wouldn't take him back, and if she did, it wouldn't be that quickly. Her stubborn streak runs deep.

As I follow the nurse down the hall, I can't get my thoughts straight. The only thing I know for sure is that I'm not leaving this hospital until I get to see Maren with my own eyes.

Outside the hospital door ahead is a tall, broad-shouldered, well-built man. He looks athletic, but the fact that he never got into adventure racing with Tucker makes me think he can't be much of an athlete, in the same way he hasn't been much of a husband. Appearance versus reality.

An irrational surge of anger goes through me that he's the one who's been sitting beside Maren when he's done nothing in that last year to earn that place in her life. He shouldn't be the one in that room; *I* should be.

"Brice—" Enzo begins.

"Your Highness, actually. As is the custom in Bellerive, *my* country, when you address royalty." I come to a stop in front of him, and I can sense Nick and Jag behind me.

"Hmm," he says, and we stare at each other. "I hope *my* wife hasn't given you the wrong impression about what's happening between the two of you."

"Not the wrong impression, no." I cross my arms.

"She's married."

For now. Maren already decided to let the marriage go, and now it's merely a matter of sticking to that decision. "I want to see her."

"She's not up to having any visitors. The race took a lot out of her, and this infection has taken even more. She's asked not to see anyone."

"If she said that, she wouldn't have meant me." There's a fifty-fifty chance she meant me, but I've never had a problem with bluffing. "One way or another, I'm getting in to see her."

"It'll have to be another, then." Enzo gives me a smug smile. "As far as I'm concerned, you've got no business being here, no matter what's been going on since I've been gone." He grips the door to her hospital room. "I have to say, your influence on her hasn't been good. She's back in the hospital on another road to recovery, and you've turned her into the one person she never wanted to be. Her father. If you wanted to knock her down, you did a hell of a job."

He slips inside the hospital room door before I can formulate a response. I whirl on my heel, and my jaw is so tight, it's aching. Whatever it takes, I'm going into that room. He's not getting a chance to guilt her into staying with him or to convince her that I'm a bad influence.

"Jag, I want you to make some calls to private investigators in Boston. I want to know what Enzo has been up to for the last year."

"I know a guy," Jag says, taking out his phone.

"Is that a good idea?" Nick asks.

I ignore Nick's attempt at being the voice of reason for once in his life. Whether or not Maren wants to be with me, she deserves the truth about Enzo, whatever that might be. No man stays away from his wife for a year with unlimited freedom and unlimited cash and keeps his nose clean. Guaranteed there are some skeletons lurking somewhere. I slide my phone out of my pocket, and I make the first call that I hope will get me to Maren's side.

"Alex," I say when my brother answers. "I need a favor."

# Chapter Forty-Two

## MAREN

The white walls, stiff sheets, and the scent of antiseptic are dead giveaways that I'm back in the hospital even before I open my eyes. But the person fast asleep in the chair beside my bed is a surprise. Warmth floods my chest.

*Brice.*

He's dressed in a Brioni suit, expensive but rumpled, and all the pieces are askew. His ten-day racing beard is gone, but in its place is a light layer of stubble, and I wonder how long I've been drifting in and out of consciousness. This is the first time I'm aware he's here, and it's almost too good to be true.

My mind is still fuzzy on how I ended up here or why Brice would be sitting at my bedside, but I'm grateful, after the way we left things in Fiji, that he came.

Someone clears their throat on the other side of the room, and I turn my head so fast my vision blurs for a moment.

*Enzo.*

My heart kicks with an instant spike of anxiety, which is mirrored on the monitor next to me.

"I forgot you were here," I say.

"Clearly," he says, and his response is filled with so much vitriol that heat invades my cheeks. In contrast to Brice, he's dressed in the same jeans and polo shirt as the other night.

The last thing I remember, now that I've been reminded Enzo is here, is arriving to the restaurant where we got engaged. Once the car was flush with the curb, I can't recall anything else.

"What happened?" I ask.

"You collapsed on the bathroom floor," Brice says, his voice rough from sleep beside me. "The hostess found you."

"You're back from Denmark?" There are too many things happening in this room for me to keep my head straight. Brice is here. Enzo is here. I passed out in a bathroom.

"A day and a half ago," Brice says. "Came straight here." He rises to his feet to lean over my bed, and he smooths my hair back. "Do you need anything?"

Confusion swirls in my brain over the right thing to do with either of them. Last time Brice and I spoke, he asked me to bear his children. The last time Enzo and I were in the same room, we were fighting about almost exactly the same thing—my ability and desire to have children.

"What's wrong with me?" I try to read Brice's expression when he withdraws from hovering over me.

"Leptospirosis," Enzo says. "Someone didn't clean your wound thoroughly enough in Fiji. The antibiotics they're feeding you should clear it up."

"I'll take the L on the infection," Brice says. "If I'd been here, I would have noticed you weren't well. At least I didn't leave you lying on a bathroom floor for so long that the *hostess* became worried."

"The only reason she was on that floor was because you coerced her into competing again when she'd told everyone she was done."

"Stop!" I hold up my hand. "He didn't coerce me. I wanted to go, so don't try to blame him for a decision I went into with my eyes wide open." That's true for pretty much everything that's happened between me and Brice. I understood the consequences of my actions, and I did it all anyway. My wild heart beats faster around Brice, and it turns out, I like it. If only that had been as far as things went.

"I'd like to speak to you alone." Enzo's jaw tics, and he crosses his arms.

"I'm not leaving," Brice says.

I close my eyes and throw my forearm over my eyes. The two of them are exhausting, like squabbling children.

"Are you okay?" Brice asks. "Should I call a nurse?"

"No," I say. "No. Can you give me and Enzo a minute?" I lift my arm and crack an eye to see how he's taking my request. His expression tightens, but he gives me a curt nod.

"Celia wanted to know when you woke up. I'll step outside and call her."

He's been talking to my mother? It doesn't seem like the right time to ask, but to say I'm surprised is an understatement. The Tuckers and Summersets don't have that sort of friendly relationship, mostly because my parents have always been too eager to cultivate it. My mother must be gleeful that my involvement with Brice has given her an in with them, even if I'm in the hospital.

The door clicks closed behind Brice, and I realize I'm still staring after him.

"I'm not giving up on our marriage without a fight," Enzo says. "Whatever has been going on between you two, it stops now."

I drag my hands down my face, and I try to gather my thoughts. If we stay together, I'll have cheated on Enzo, and I'm not sure I can stomach that. Beyond that, I don't know if I'm capable of recovering my feelings for Enzo. When I look at him now, I can acknowledge that he's an attractive man, but the butterflies and the softness I once felt when I looked at him are gone. Can people fall out of love and then back into it? Would I even want to?

"I'm back, and I'm okay with the terms you laid out in your ultimatum." He swallows. "You don't want to put yourself through any of the emotional or physical turmoil to have kids, and I can—I can accept that."

That is what I told him, what I've been telling him for months, and it was the argument that led to him leaving. Not just that I couldn't physically have kids but that I didn't want to pursue any of the options to have them. Not surrogacy, not adoption, not anything. Granted, I was not in a good place physically or emotionally when I made that decision. But I've stuck to it with him, even as I've contemplated other options or paths in my head with someone else.

It occurs to me that we may have gotten married too young and for the wrong reasons. For months I've avoided that exact thought, but there it is.

"No kids. Just you and me," Enzo says. "I want our marriage. But no more competing. I can't do this"—he gestures to my hospital bed—"over and over again."

"Enzo, I—" I stare at my nails, unable to make eye contact. "I filed for a separation. In my mind, we were getting a divorce."

"You slept with him." Enzo's voice is flat.

My heart thuds, and I don't know what to say. Saying the truth out loud feels cruel when he's standing here asking for us to make our marriage work.

"I wasn't perfect in Boston," Enzo says. "We were going through a rough patch, and we both made mistakes."

"What?" My blood runs cold.

"After I got the separation papers," he says. "Once, and as soon as I did it, I realized I didn't want another woman. I want what you and I can build together."

His revelation is hard for me to process. Although he didn't do anything differently than me, the conclusions we've drawn are divergent. The idea that we can go back when we've done what we've done doesn't make sense. Wouldn't we be just like my parents? Ignore the indiscretions and forge ahead? For me, cheating has always been a hard line. The fact that I did it when I kissed Brice was the moment when I realized my marriage had to be over. If I wanted my relationship with Enzo, really wanted it, I would never have let anything happen with Brice.

"I don't know what to say," I admit.

"We can get what we had back, M. I wouldn't be here if I didn't believe that. Neither of us has to quit this marriage. We don't have to fail."

Before I left for the race, I would have said there was no way we could salvage our marriage. It seemed like neither of us wanted to stay together badly enough to make it work. His conviction that we can recover is throwing me off. The words "quit" and "fail" bounce around my mind, but I'm no longer sure that a fear of failure should be what drives me.

"He's got a different woman in every country, just like your dad," Enzo says. "Do you really think he can give you what you want? That he's capable of giving you what you need? You've never been one to be swayed by a bit of charm before."

Not entirely true. At one time, I was swayed by Enzo's charm. I'm not finding him particularly charming right now. "That's not who Brice is," I say, and it comes out with a surprising amount of conviction. There are pressure points Enzo could hit, but Brice is loyal, and he's taken care of me in ways Enzo never has. "Don't slander him to make your offer look better."

"Fine. But he's a fling not a future."

There's a knock on the door to my room before I can formulate a response. I don't know what I'd say anyway. Based on everything Brice has told me, Enzo's statement is true, even if it feels unfair for reasons I can't pinpoint.

My mother pops her head in the door. "Brice said you were awake." She doesn't wait for me to invite her in and instead comes to my bedside, pointedly ignoring Enzo. I also noticed she called Brice by his first name rather than by any of his formal titles, and I wonder if she's already given him half of a heart necklace that says "best friends" in bold letters.

"You had us all worried," she says, and she lays a cool hand across my forehead. The scent of her hand lotion takes me back to my childhood. "I'm glad you're on the mend. Brice was beside himself when Enzo wouldn't let him in here to be with you."

"What?" I turn toward Enzo.

"Forgive me if I didn't welcome the man my wife's been fucking deeper into our lives. Being face-to-face with the man my wife cheated on me with has been enough already." Enzo holds up his hands, but his tone is bitter.

"Cheating?" My mother raises her eyebrows. "You're mistaken. According to Bellerive laws, the minute the separation papers were filed, regardless of whether *you* sign them, you're separated. That legal designation only changes if *Maren* withdraws the application. She didn't cheat on you. She moved on from you, and if she'd listened to any of us, she'd have done it even sooner."

"Mom," I say. This whole conversation from Enzo admitting his own indiscretion to him asking for a second chance to him accusing me of cheating to the realization we really are legally separated is putting me into a tailspin. But I don't want to be cruel, and my mother, probably hoping for a seat at the royal table, won't have a problem ripping Enzo to shreds. I'm old enough to realize her attitude is less about me and more about who she believes will be taking Enzo's place in my life.

"I'd really like some space. To be alone for a little while." Then when neither of them leave, I continue, "I'm still really tired."

"I'll go to our house to shower and change. I haven't left the hospital since you were admitted," Enzo says, and he rakes his hand through his dark hair. "I'll be back in a few hours, but if you need me, just call."

He's saying all the right things, and I would have given anything to hear them a year ago, but I don't understand how we can go back. Brice might not be an option, but it doesn't mean I should stay with Enzo either.

Enzo leaves first, and my mother is lingering even though I made myself clear. If she's going to stay, there is something I want to know.

"Is the legal stuff you said true?"

"Should be," my mother says. "Caitlin is the one who told me after Enzo was being a prick about letting Brice into your hospital room."

"Where is Brice?" Since he left the room, I've been antsy. His presence makes me feel safe and secure in a way I've never had with anyone else. It's part of the reason I didn't question how much I was sleeping after I returned from Fiji. When I was asleep, I wasn't missing Brice or worried about what he was doing or questioning whether I'd made the right decision in pushing him away.

"In the cafeteria waiting for me to tell him the coast is clear," she says. "I was supposed to come up with some reason why Enzo couldn't be in here any longer. Do you want me to get him?"

I do. So much. But my brain is a muddled mess, and I'm not sure seeing Brice will give me the clarity I need. Before I see him alone, I have to be sure whether my marriage is definitely over or if it's worth trying to rebuild with Enzo. For months I told myself that if Enzo returned to Bellerive, we could figure out our relationship. My gut instinct already has an answer about whether that's still true, but for everyone's sake, I should consider every angle.

"Can you ask him to come see me in an hour?" I ask. "I just need a little time to process my life."

"I'll tell him." She gathers the Valentino purse she placed on the foot of my bed when she came in. "For what it's worth, you looked really happy in the photos Ava sent me from that party in Fiji. It was nice to see you so happy again."

"I was happy," I say, and then just before my mom is out the door, I continue, "but I don't think Brice and I want the same things out of life."

"Have you asked him?" She stands at the door with her designer purse slung over her arm.

"He told me months ago what he wanted, and it's not what I want. It wouldn't be enough for me." We've never had the type of relationship where we confide in each other, and it feels strange to be so honest with her.

"You know what'll keep you up at night years from now? When you're old like me?"

I shake my head.

"The questions you never had the guts to ask. Maybe he doesn't want the same things you do, but I've spent the last day and a half in constant contact with him. He's got big feelings for you, whether he's acknowledged them or not. Your heart is already on the line, so you might as well show it to him."

I swallow and nod, shocked that a conversation with my mother is snapping my life into sharp focus.

"Here's the other thing," she says, clearly on a roll. "You always thought I was surprised you got married because I've called you my wild-hearted daughter. But I wasn't surprised you got married. I was surprised you got married to *him*."

Her hand is on the door to leave, and everything she's said is seeping into me, like a long drink after a drought. I did love Enzo once, but not in the same way I love Brice. It might not be fair to compare, but I can't help it. Things were easy with Enzo because we never pushed or challenged each other in any way, and maybe that's a relationship other people would value and enjoy. I did for a while, until things got hard, and neither of us understood how to navigate it.

Brice and I have been the opposite—challenging each other, propelling each other into unknown depths, but being there to support one another when we stumble, and I've loved it. Loved every minute of it. I never knew a relationship could run *this* deep, but I don't know if he sees us like I do.

"Can you tell Brice I want to see him?"

"Now?" She glances at me over her shoulder.

"Yeah," I say. "I'm ready."

# Chapter Forty-Three

## BRICE

I haven't left the hospital in two days, hoping for a chance to talk to Maren alone, and when Celia delivers the message that not only is Tucker on her own but she *wants* to talk to me, trepidation beats a drum in my chest. This conversation will either go very well or very poorly. There's no middle ground.

Outside her hospital door, I mentally recap all the things I need to tell her during this conversation. It's a lot, and there's a chance I'll scare her off, but I've spent the last two days hoping for this chance, and I'm not going to waste the opportunity.

Sweat dampens my palms, and I wipe them on my dress pants. I'm still wearing parts of the suit I had on for the flight from Denmark. My tie and jacket were abandoned long ago, and I've rolled my shirt sleeves to the elbows.

When I open the door, Tucker meets my gaze from the hospital bed, and my gut clenches at her still so pale. There's a bandage on her temple from where she hit the vanity in the restaurant when she collapsed. It still makes me angry and does funny things to my heart to think of her lying on the floor, unconscious. If I'd been the one to find her, my heart would have been on the floor beside her while we waited for help.

"I don't even know where to start," I say, which is not how I planned to start.

"Me either," she says, and she holds out her hand.

I shut the door behind me, and I cross to her bedside to take her hand. She shifts over to leave enough room for me to sit on the bed beside her. This feels like a good sign. If she was going to choose Enzo, she wouldn't let me this close. Unless she wanted to let me down gently.

"Enzo asked me to try again," she says.

"Are you going to?" My chest tightens almost unbearably, and it takes everything in me not to drop to my knees and beg her not to.

"We're beyond that, I think," she says. "And so that's—that's my decision regardless of how the rest of this conversation goes."

My breathing is shallow, and hope, rather than dread, starts to stir in my stomach.

"I wasn't completely honest with you in the cabin," she whispers, and she's staring at our linked hands. "After my miscarriage, we found out that I'm not able to carry a baby to term. It'll just—it'll never happen for me. We went to all kinds of specialists and experts, you know, before you offer some sort of solution. My uterus doesn't function properly, and giving birth will never be something I can do. Saying it out loud is really hard." Her voice is thick, and when she glances up at me, there are tears in her eyes. "And I know how important a baby is to you."

Her admission causes a flood of heat and cold to rush over my body. The realization of exactly how badly I fucked up in Fiji hits me like a Mack truck. "Maren," I breathe out.

Tears trickle down her cheeks, and she gives a little shrug. "You didn't know, but it's why Enzo left. Or one of the main reasons." She closes her eyes, and more tears slide to her chin.

Her sadness is cracking my heart open, and I don't know what to say, but I can't stand seeing her cry. I catch them with my thumbs and brush them aside before planting my lips on her forehead and breathing her in. How she can still smell like peaches after being in the hospital for days is a mystery. Enzo left her alone in her grief, and then I prioritized a baby over her too. No wonder she didn't want to talk to me after my *have my baby* bullshit.

"I told him that I didn't want to have kids. Even if there was a way, I didn't want them."

It's almost, but not quite, the line she fed me in the cabin. The one that rang false to me, but I'm not sure if the falseness was because she physically can't have kids or whether she's trying to convince herself she doesn't want them. Some of my friends have gone through fertility troubles, and I've seen the strain it can put on relationships. This time, it's contributed to the breakdown of her marriage. Her reluctance makes sense.

"Is that really how you feel?" If I'm taking Nick's advice, I can't leave any stone unturned, any question unanswered.

"Honestly? I don't know. I thought so." Her voice is thick with tears. "But then lately..." She searches my face. "Lately, I've been thinking a lot about a baby with brown hair and light-brown eyes."

There's a good chance I've stopped breathing, and I scan her expression to see if I'm reading her right. "Tucker, are you saying you've thought about having *my* baby?"

"I can't do the arrangement you want. Coparenting with no attachments. It would gut me to see you with someone else. Just the thought of it is a knife to my heart." Her chin wobbles, and her bottom lip trembles.

"Oh, Tucker. Jesus, what have I done?" I gather her to me, and she cries against my chest. "There's no one else. I've been running from commitment my whole life because it's the one place where I don't get a do-over. Can't finesse my way out of it. No divorce for the Summersets. Used to be fucking terrifying," I say into her hair.

She sniffles against my shirt and squeezes me. If I don't go all in with my feelings here, I'll have the regrets Nick warned me about.

"But I didn't see you coming. Never knew I could love someone with this much depth and certainty. I'm not afraid anymore, Tucker. I have no doubt we'll grow together—grow older, grow wiser, grow to love each other more. Whether we have kids just changes the view from the mountain. If I've got you, I'm already at the peak. I don't need anything else."

She wraps her arms around my neck and buries her face in the hollow, hugging me tight. "You always have such pretty words."

"That's all you're going to give me, Tucker?" My voice is hoarse.

"God, this is scary." She inhales a shaky breath. "While we were training, I tried so hard to keep you out, and I couldn't do it. It was impossible." She draws back to meet my gaze. "I love you too," she says. "I love you so much." She places a gentle kiss at the edge of my mouth. "I want the view with you, but I'm just so afraid we'll never get it."

"Another challenge for us to overcome together. But if we do walk that path, and it ever gets too hard or rough, I need you to tell me because you mean so much more to me than a 'what if.' Do you understand? I won't have you miserable when we can be perfectly happy just the two of us."

"I hear you," she says, and she searches my face before pressing her lips to mine. "Can you lie with me for a while? Enzo's supposed to come back, and I'll need to tell him my decision, but I just want to be with you for a bit. Feels like you were gone forever."

"Longest five days of my life," I agree as I ease down and draw her tight against my side.

"Can you tell me about Denmark, or is it top secret royal business? I'm assuming it's got something to do with the mess Alex made?"

A smile tugs at the edges of my lips that she understands enough about how my world works that she's made the correct leap. "I signed an NDA, so I'm trusting you to keep this between us."

"Your binding, legal contract is safe with me."

Technically, it's not safe with anyone, hence the NDA, but if I want to go the distance with Maren, I need to let her in all the way, in places I've never let anyone else, and give her a level of trust I wouldn't normally bestow. We were teammates, and now we're a team. Her thoughts and feelings have to be my priority.

"Freja developed social anxiety. Princess Simone required me to be Freja's emotional support animal."

"Aww. Like a Labrador retriever?" Tucker's tone is delighted. "But also, that must be terrible to be that high profile and anxious about it. I can't imagine."

"Simone equated me to a golden retriever, actually. But less loyal."

"Shows what she knows." Maren scoffs. "You're very loyal."

"To you," I say. "Always to you."

She snuggles tighter and squeezes me.

"We're about to be very high profile soon, I suspect," I say. "The first episode of the InterFlix show airs next week. Do you think Enzo is going to be a problem?"

"He slept with someone else," she whispers. "After I sent the separation papers. Claims that was his moment of clarity."

"His moment of clarity happened when he was dick deep in someone else? He and I are clearly opposites. If I ever even wanted to do that, there's my moment of clarity. Not *doing* it. *Considering* it." I don't even try to keep the scorn out of my voice. "And I'd never fucking do it."

"He didn't see it that way," she says. "But he didn't blame me for what happened with you either."

Definitely nothing alike. If I were in his shoes, I would not take Maren being with someone else well either. That sentence might be the biggest understatement of my life.

"I asked Jag to hire a private investigator to look into what Enzo's been doing this last year."

"Brice."

"I know. Not my place. Or it wasn't, then. But I wasn't sure if you were going back to him, and I didn't know how else to protect you."

"You thought I'd go back to him?"

"There were photos of you coming out of your apartment holding hands. Others of him carrying suitcases into your apartment."

"None of him carrying those suitcases back out?"

"Strangely, no." Though it's not strange. I've been a victim of selective photography and editorial decisions on what to print many times.

"I don't know why I was holding his hand," she says. "I was sick, and I didn't want to go. But he hadn't signed the papers, and I felt guilty over what had happened between you and me."

We curl up in the single hospital bed together, and I run my fingers through her hair in soothing motions, a little in awe that I can do this whenever I want from now on.

"Want to move into the palace?" I ask. "I could get used to lying like this with you in a slightly bigger bed."

She laughs, and her breath skims across my neck. Yeah, I could definitely get used to this.

"For appearances sake, don't you think we should wait until I'm actually divorced?"

"Sounds boring. Come live on the edge with me, Tucker. We'll keep each other from tipping over." If she says yes, I'm all in, but if she stills says no, I'll let it go for now. I get that everything is more complicated than either of us would like.

"Can I think about it?"

"As long as you want. It's an open invitation that never expires."

"I really do love you," she says as she traces figure eights on my chest. "In a way I didn't even know it was possible to love someone."

There's a knock on the door, and the attending physician enters without waiting for a response. She stops short when she sees me in the bed with Tucker.

"Your Highness," she says. "I didn't realize you were in here."

Jag must not be right at the door, but I'm sure he's somewhere in the hallway keeping watch. He's never far.

"I've come to update Ms. Tucker on the plan of care."

"Update away," I say, making no move to leave.

"Ms. Tucker?"

"He can stay," she says with her head still on my chest. "He'll want to know."

The fact that we're finally at this point sends a shot of warmth through my body. She trusts me enough to let me stay, and she's sure enough about my feelings to know I'll care. As I listen to the doctor detail Tucker's recovery plan, it really feels like everything is falling into place.

# Chapter Forty-Four

## MAREN

With things between us in a good place, Brice went home to shower and change. I'm being released from the hospital tomorrow morning, but Brice says he's sleeping here tonight. Now I just have one last difficult conversation before I can look to the future.

Sawyer and Nathaniel stopped by to check on me, and Ava and Gage both called to make sure I wasn't dead. The difference between older siblings and younger siblings has never been so clear. My dad came too, but he didn't stay long.

I'm starting to wonder whether Enzo is going to make an appearance like he said when the door to my room opens, and he enters with his hand behind his back. He reveals a bundle of peonies with a flourish.

"Your favorite." He brings them to the bed and sets them on the table beside me. "I saw them, and I couldn't resist picking them up."

Peonies are actually his mother's favorite flower, not mine, but I didn't correct him the first time he made the mistake and then didn't feel I could after that. For the three or four times he's bought me flowers over the years, it wasn't worth creating an awkward situation.

"I had some time to think away from all this." He gestures to my hospital bed as though my being in here is an inconvenience. "And maybe we should sell the house and have our fresh start in the apartment. We should look beyond everything that's happened this last year."

"Enzo," I say, keeping my voice even. "I'm going through with the separation and divorce. It's too late for us."

"I don't accept that." He shoves his hands into the pockets of his jeans. "You spent a year asking me to come back, and now that I've come, I'm too late?" He scoffs.

"A year," I say. "A whole year I asked, and you chose not to return until it was too late." He's not going to make me feel bad about this when I even went to Boston, whereas he never came back here. Not once.

"I'm not agreeing to a divorce," he says.

"That doesn't mean we won't get divorced," I say. Talking to Caitlin earlier prepared me for this response. "All it means is it'll be drawn out."

"Then I'll draw it out. I've made mistakes, but I always said I wanted our marriage to work. I never once said I didn't."

That's true, but his words weren't followed by any actions that reinforced his claims. "I fell off a cliff, had a miscarriage, and I was struggling with depression. You left me, and you left the island. Did you really think I was going to wait here forever to see if you'd decide I was worthy of your love and attention?"

"You were always worthy, M. I was blindsided by you saying you never wanted to have kids. That's not the understanding we had when we got married."

"We never talked about it before getting married. What understanding did you think we'd come to?"

"You never said you didn't want them."

"You never said you *did*. We can go in circles, but we didn't talk about it. After the miscarriage and how you—how you blamed me for not being able to have children—how did you think I'd react? Not an ounce of support from you. Of course I didn't want to have children with you when that's your response."

Enzo and I met young and married young, and maybe we didn't have enough life experience between us to commit to forever with our eyes open. Marriage isn't always going to be easy, and oddly, I have zero expectations that my relationship with Brice will be constantly filled with heart eyes and flowers. But I have faith that he won't walk away when things are rough.

Whatever the path is, he'll walk beside me, carry me, or let me carry him. I'm certain we won't let each other down. The last few months with Brice have taught me that we take care of the people we love, always. Even when things were exceptionally hard with his father, he never shirked his duty or tempered his love, and he's been at my side every step of the way through training. On the course, when I stumbled, Brice was, quite literally, at my elbow to keep me on my feet.

With Enzo, I fell lower than I've ever been in my life, and his response was to leave the island. For a long time, I wasn't emotionally ready to acknowledge how awful it was for him to abandon me given that we were supposed to be partners.

"We didn't get married for the right reasons," I say, "and we can't stay together just because neither of us wants to fail. The truth is, our marriage failed a year ago when we couldn't figure out how to steer our way through tragedy together. You can't come back now and say we should act as though the last year didn't happen. We're not the same people we were."

"You're punishing me for needing some time and space to sort through my feelings."

"That's not what I'm doing." I sigh. He's not listening.

"You can push through the divorce," he says. "Apparently I can't stop you. But the prenup is void because you cheated on me. If you don't want to stay married, I'll seek half of everything."

"Nothing happened with Brice until after we were separated." Almost true. I'm not sure how he'd be able to prove otherwise.

"You can have what you want, M. But it's going to cost you." He strides toward the door. "I guess we'll see how all those InterFlix viewers feel about you and Prince Brice once I'm done telling my side of the story."

He's gone before I have a chance to respond, and I stare at the closed door, a sense of dread bubbling in my stomach. I made sure the cameras caught my declaration that Enzo and I were legally separated, but I have no idea how the show will be edited.

Later when Brice appears at the door, I'm still out of sorts. He's got a round tin in his hand, and he climbs into the bed with me without hesitation.

"Scones," he says, "courtesy of the queen. I resisted eating one on the way over just to let you have first pick." He cracks open the tin, but when he glances up at me, he grimaces. "Talk with Enzo didn't go well?"

"He intends to try me in the court of public opinion. He's going to tell everyone I was cheating on him with you, and I'm sure the race will only feed that narrative."

"Anyone can look up the separation document and dates to discover the truth."

"How many people will bother with that when Enzo will be hollering foul play from the rooftops? People don't dig for the truth anymore. They go with the facts presented to them by whoever shouts the loudest. He's trying to nullify the prenup."

"No tears? No begging to save the marriage?" Brice purses his lips.

"No, not at all. He seemed... angry."

"I'm not going to let him drag you through the mud. You care what people in Bellerive think, and he's trying to use that against you. I'll abuse my royal privileges and status and start calling in favors to suppress his claims," Brice says, plucking a scone out of the tin.

I'm not surprised he can do that, but warmth spreads across my chest that he wouldn't hesitate to go as far as possible to protect my reputation.

"This abrupt switch from 'I want you back' to 'I want your money' just makes me even more certain a little sniffing around in Boston will turn up something foul," Brice says. "The money shouldn't be the important thing, but I suppose that's been his problem from the beginning. He never valued you the way you deserved."

"I love you," I say. Everything I once thought about him seems so out of touch. When Brice cares, he cares so deeply.

"Enough to agree to stay at the palace until we take care of your divorce? If I can't suppress Enzo's lies, I want to make sure you're protected from the fallout."

"Will you be upset if I move out afterwards? If it's temporary?" The idea of being with him constantly is more appealing than I would have thought. But I don't know that I should be going from one relationship straight into another one with that level of seriousness.

"I mean, I intend to make things so great for you at the palace that you'll never want to leave." He takes a bite of scone and chews. "But I'll respect whatever decision you want to make once you're divorced. You're a little skittish, and I'm a patient man." He grins. "You're the only person who gets to set rules and expectations about what's best for you, Maren. You dictate how you live your life. If you want to move into the palace with me and that's what feels right for you, fuck anyone who doesn't understand. They don't matter. I love you, and you love me. We don't have to answer to anyone if we don't want to."

He makes it sound simple. The royals bow to public perception and opinion all the time, but they also buck it when it suits them. Bellerive society's opinions matter to me, and I may have to work on letting that go in favor of what makes me happy.

"I never asked, but how did you get into my room if Enzo wasn't letting you in? My mother?"

"Your mother, in a roundabout way. I had Alex call her to offer brunch with the royals in exchange for an entry pass. Then Caitlin confirmed that Enzo shouldn't have been the one controlling entry, anyway. That left Celia firmly in charge."

"My mother would have let you in if you'd called and asked."

"Couldn't take the chance she might actually like Enzo. Even if she did, Enzo is no match for my brother's power and influence. Celia wasn't going to say no to that, was she?" Brice polishes off the final bite of scone. "No matter what, I was getting in here, so I wasn't taking any chances."

Warmth swells across my body at how nothing deterred him from being here for me when I needed him. What I've longed for in a partner for the last year, I've got with him. Why do I care what anyone else thinks when he loves me like this?

"I'll move in with you," I say. "The public perception thing might be a bit of a learning curve."

Brice tilts the tin of scones toward me, and I pluck one out. "I'll hold your hand every step of the way."

The best part is, I know he means it.

# Chapter Forty-Five

## BRICE

Three days later when Tucker walks into my suite of rooms after seeing Dr. Bennett, my heart kicks. She's dressed in workout tights and a sky-blue T-shirt, but I've never seen a lovelier sight.

"How did I get so lucky?" I ask from my seat on the couch.

She comes over to me and straddles my waist, her chest pressing against mine. "Did someone say something about getting lucky?"

"In another life, I did something very right to get you in this one." I tuck her dark hair behind her ear, and she nuzzles my neck, squeezing me tight.

"In another life, I think you must have written poetry. You're spoiling me with all these poetic, romantic thoughts."

"Not spoiled," I say. "Loved. The universe gave me a gift in you, and I intend to admire it every day."

She draws back to gaze at me, and she runs her fingers through my hair lightly. "Only three more days until the whole world gets to dissect our relationship."

"You're nervous?"

"You're not?"

"However they edit us or whatever it looks like to other people, I know what I've got with you. I don't need anyone's approval to be happy." I give her a gentle kiss on the lips. "And if I have to summon a press conference to call the media and the public a bunch of dickheads like Alex does from time to time, then I will."

"I think we'll come off okay on camera. But I'm worried Enzo will use our closeness to paint a very different picture. Caitlin says if he can somehow prove I cheated on him, then the prenup will be void, and I'll likely owe him spousal support."

Not in a million years am I going to let any of that happen, even if I have to play dirty to make sure it doesn't.

"We spent months training together before we left," she says. "I'm sure there will be people willing to speculate."

"Let 'em. They can't prove anything because there's nothing to prove. His accusations won't have any weight in a court of law." I hold up my phone from the cushion beside me. "Jag says his contact in Boston has a lead on a few things, but we won't know anything until the details are firm and irrefutable."

"We had a lot of problems, but I hate the idea that I got him so wrong." She runs her hands through her hair.

My instinct is to comfort her and offer placating words, but if he was a good husband at some point, he wasn't this past year. Doesn't mean she got him totally wrong, but she didn't get him right either. He turned out to be the kind of man who flees from conflict and takes advantage of people who love him.

"You were still footing the bill for all his activities in Boston?" I ask.

"We were married, and he kept saying he wanted us to work." She flushes. "I wasn't going to cut him off."

"You don't have to justify those choices to me, Tucker. Any criticism isn't landing on your shoulders. You were coping the best you could, and he was taking advantage. Money is a powerful motivator in all kinds of directions."

Her hair falls across her cheeks, and she's focused on her hands, which rest against my chest. I press my lips to her forehead, and she sighs.

"What did Dr. Bennett say about your concussion and illness?" Now that the race is over, I'm back to a full slate of royal duties, so I couldn't go with her to the doctor. Not that she had to go far, since Dr. Bennett's office is on the estate.

My packed schedule has made me wonder whether I need to evaluate what I genuinely want to be involved in. For years, I've let my parents and now Alex push me into various endeavors that weren't close to my heart. As a royal, I might not be able to have a connection with all the charities and causes I'm linked to, but I think I should prioritize my efforts.

"Not in the clear yet for going back to exercising, but I can return to using electronic devices and television. Just in time to watch our debut." She gives me a wry smile.

"No exercise, huh?" I feather kisses along the side of her face.

"No *strenuous* exercise. He said long walks on the beach are fine." She catches my lips with hers, and she draws tight against me, deepening the kiss. "There are probably other slow and steady activities I could partake in." She rolls her hips against my erection. "Are you up for the challenge?"

"I've got no problem rising to that challenge." I cradle her face and search her expression. "You're sure it's okay?" The last thing I want is to have her push herself too hard when she was in the hospital a few days ago.

"The good doctor gave me the okay," she says. "I just want to be close to you."

Any chance to be connected to her, I'm taking it. I slide my hands up her sides, dragging her shirt with me, and I've got her bra unsnapped with a flick of my thumb and forefinger. She yanks my shirt over my head, and we're bare from the waist up.

We tease and toy with each other, fingers skimming across flesh, tongues dipping in and out of mouths. She rocks her hips against me, and when she arches, I draw her nipple into my mouth, swirling my tongue around the bud before grazing it with my teeth. There's nothing rushed or hurried in any of our movements, but her pants and moans of pleasure coupled with her sliding along my length are going to do me in.

"I want to feel you inside me," Tucker murmurs against my lips.

In the table beside the couch, there are condoms in the drawer, and I dig one out while Tucker strips herself, and then she undoes my jeans before tugging them off. Her efficiency is impressive.

When she goes to straddle me again, I grip her hips to hold her off, and I trail a line of kisses across her abdomen before flicking my tongue along her hot, wet center. She digs her fingers into my hair, and my name brims with pleasure when it falls from her lips. I could listen to her say my name like that all day.

"I need you," she says. "Please."

And because I also need her, I roll on the condom and guide her over my shaft. As she lowers herself onto me, she grips the back of my head, and we're cheek to cheek.

"I love you," she whispers. "I love you so much."

"I don't know how I got so lucky," I say. "I love you, Maren Tucker, more than I ever thought possible." I drag her mouth to mine, and I kiss her deeply.

While the two of us move together, for the first time in my life, I truly understand why someone would call this making love. Everything inside of me is straining to be closer, more connected, and the big emotions I've had for her for months are rotating around us, making every touch, every kiss, every slide of our bodies feel bigger and better than it's ever felt before. Sex was always pleasurable, but it was never *this*.

When she cries out with her orgasm, I swallow her cries and follow her over the edge. And while her forehead rests on my shoulder, an immense gratitude radiates through me that I get to have her and this feeling for the rest of my life.

---

Later that night in bed, I lie on my stomach with the pillow propped under my cheek, and Maren is facing me, her hand on my back and a soft expression on her face. We've just spent the last hour talking about our childhoods, and it amazes me how much she's giving me now that we're both sure and secure in our feelings. There are no barriers, and I didn't think it was possible to love her more, but it feels like every conversation we have lately tips the scales a little further.

"How did you pick your charities to support?" I ask because it's been weighing on my mind since we returned from the adventure race. The Alzheimer's Society is staying, and it'll likely always be one of my passion projects, but I think it'll also be a cause tinged with sadness, and I want something that'll bring me joy too. Like Nick and Julia's project in Tanzania—I want something where I'm capable of making a difference.

"Four of the five I picked because I have a genuine interest. The Alzheimer's Society approached me—well, Cheryl did, actually—when they had a vacant spot and they wanted someone they knew could bring in the fundraising dollars."

"What's your favorite one?"

"No Child Hungry. Working with Bellerive families who are less fortunate has been really rewarding. The BAS asked me to work with them just before we went to Fiji. I haven't said yes yet, but I'm actually really excited about that opportunity."

"Bellerive Animals Shelters?"

"I love animals, but my mom always said they were too messy when we were kids."

"You're an adult now, and you don't have any pets."

"No." Her expression turns sad. "Enzo wasn't a fan."

"When you fall in love with one, you let me know."

"There are no pets at the palace."

"Not yet, but I like animals, and I love you." I lean over and give her a quick peck. "Now I need to figure out a cause that gives me that kind of joy."

"What are some of your favorite things?" Maren nuzzles closer to me, tucking herself into my side and lying close enough that her lips could graze my arm.

"You, tequila..." I hesitate to say the next one, even though it's true. "Kids."

"When Paxton came to see me at the hospital, he mentioned that the Bellerive Youth Sports Committee was looking for another member. You sit on the committee, but you also help match kids with sports they're interested in. Develop new sporting opportunities across the island. Take disadvantaged kids to pick out equipment and other essentials with fund money. He was angling for me, but it might be a good fit for you?"

I let the idea sit between us for a beat, and it settles over me with a surprising rightness. There's one more thing I want to broach with Tucker, but I'm not sure now is the right time when she's still recovering.

"I'll talk to Paxton," I say. "That sounds like something I might really enjoy." I press a kiss to the top of her head. "Do you think the team would be up for fundraising for another race?"

"Yeah?" Maren perks up and cradles her head in her hand, resting on her elbow. "You want to do another one?"

"With you," I clarify. "I'd want to do another one with you, if you're up for it."

"Yes. One hundred percent." A wide grin spreads across her face. "I love that it's something we can share."

My phone goes off on the nightstand with a text message, and I contemplate ignoring it. Between Denmark, Maren's illness, and my stupidly busy work schedule, I haven't had many moments like I'm getting right now with my lady love. But I also know that Jag wouldn't text this late if it wasn't important.

I roll over and snatch my phone off the nightstand. After scanning the message twice, I write back to let him know I received it. Then I take a deep breath.

"Jag's friend in Boston uncovered a few things, and he's flying to the island tomorrow to go through his results with us."

"Oh," Maren says, and it sounds like a mixture of surprise and disappointment. How one word can be so loaded, I'm not sure, but it is.

"Tomorrow," I say, "we'll find out what Enzo has been up to in Boston for the last year."

"I don't know how I'm going to handle it." Maren cuddles back into my side and rests her head on my chest.

"You won't be handling it alone," I say. "That much I can guarantee. Whatever you find out, I'll be with you every step of the way." I just hope that whatever is revealed doesn't make her question her instincts where men are concerned. My gut tells me that whatever Enzo was up to, Maren is going to feel blindsided, and that's never a good feeling.

I draw her tight against me, and I kiss the top of her head. No matter what, I'm not letting her lump me into the same category as Enzo. His choices will never be mine. I understand that what I've got with Tucker is rare and precious, and I'd never do anything to jeopardize her faith in me. Whatever we learn tomorrow, I hope she's able to keep it in perspective.

# Chapter Forty-Six

## MAREN

The private detective concludes his slideshow of all the pictures and evidence he gathered of Enzo's deceit, and I'm numb. It feels like I've been dropped into someone else's life or a nightmare. Brice is beside me, holding my hand, but I can't wrap my brain around what I've just been told.

"He did not cover his tracks very well." Caitlin sits opposite me, and she rocks back and forth in her chair. "Good for us. Makes the divorce and settlement with Bellerive's laws a lot cleaner."

"Explains why he went to the divorce lawyers in Boston and then contacted some here too," Brice says. "He must have been trying to figure out how badly he'd screwed himself."

"And he must have believed those leaked photos of you and Maren together at the race were a gold mine. Suddenly, he could prove she'd been the one cheating all along."

"I feel really dumb," I whisper into the room, not sure who I want to respond.

"As I said," the private detective says, "from what I could discover, it appears as though he was faithful for the first three years of your relationship. But over the last two years, he broke his vows repeatedly."

The private detective had text message exchanges, emails, and even photos and videos of Enzo's indiscretions. The timeline makes some sense, but I'm not sure which came first. There was definitely an increasing amount of distance between us even before my accident.

"He told me about this one," I say, picking up the final photo, which shows him kissing a bartender at a bar just after the separation papers were delivered. "Why would he admit that if there was so much more to discover?"

"Happens more often than you'd think. Confess to a small crime and hope no one discovers the one that's much worse," Caitlin says.

"Why would he want to stay married with all this?" I ask. Though I should be familiar with the concept since my father did the same thing with my mother. But while I was building walls between me and Brice and resisting our growing closeness, Enzo was getting close to anyone and everyone he could in Boston.

"Finances," the private investigator says, sliding a file across the table to me. "His are a mess. He's spent recklessly, and he doesn't have a penny to his name. Without you, he's practically homeless."

"I suspect that's why he came to the island after talking to lawyers," Caitlin says. "He found out he couldn't break the prenup easily, and he risked his own activities being discovered by going after spousal support. The photos of you and Brice must have seemed like a gift. Come back and either guilt or blackmail you into staying together."

I can't discount my own privilege because money has never been a concern, but I can't imagine resigning myself to a relationship I don't respect for financial reasons. At least with Brice, I'll never have to worry that he's with me for my money.

"All this evidence means Enzo gets nothing, right?" I check with Caitlin, and Brice squeezes my hand.

"According to Bellerive law, when a spouse is found cheating, they cannot seek spousal support. You didn't have joint bank accounts, so that's good. The monthly sum you'd been floating him will be cut off. He'll get half of any profits from the sale of the marital home, but that's it. No other settlements or spousal support will be awarded, no matter how long he fights. None of our laws work in his favor."

"Do I need to meet with Enzo to go over all this with our lawyers?"

"No," Caitlin says. "Not unless you really want to be there. I can meet with him and his lawyer and clue them into how this is going to go."

Although I'd insisted on the prenup and the cheating clause when we got married, I never thought I'd need it. Even when he was gone for almost a year, I never suspected he was cheating. The Enzo I met in college was a flirt and a tease, but he knew how much my parents' relationship had screwed me up. As the years went on, we drifted pretty far from the people who met in that campus bar. I guess he evolved into the type of man who *could* do those things, and I didn't notice.

"Do you think he would have stayed married to me and off island forever if I'd let him?" A terrible thought, but it's there in the back of my brain. Every conversation we had, he assured me he'd be coming back eventually. How long would I have let him drag that out? His opinions on my racing almost had me miss out on the Fiji trip.

"You gave him a very long leash," Caitlin says. "And he chose to hang himself. That's not your fault. You were far more understanding than I'd ever be."

"I don't want to see him." The lies he told and the way he manipulated my depression and my desire not to fail at our marriage will never sit right with me. "He'll try to convince me that everything is my fault and that I owe him something as a result."

"If he needs to see someone," Brice says beside me, "I'll happily have that conversation."

I glance at him for the first time since the private investigator stopped laying out all the evidence. His jaw is tight, and although he gripped my hand reassuringly any time I faltered or something particularly egregious was presented, he hasn't said much until now.

"While I appreciate the gesture," Caitlin says, "it wouldn't be beneficial to Maren's case and claims to have you too involved."

"Do you need anything else from me?" I'm still in a bit of shock over everything I've learned.

"I can take it from here," Caitlin says. "If he and his lawyer understand they have no recourse, I might be able to fast-track this through."

I rise, and Brice stands with him, his hand firm on the small of my back. As we leave the office, Jag sets out in front of us, leading the way back to the car.

"That must have been pretty fucking hard to hear," Brice says, and he gathers me close to his side as we walk, kissing the top of my head.

"I don't know what to think." In some ways, I can see how this all came about—the distance, the lack of communication, my unwavering desire to never fail at anything. At the same time, the Enzo I was presented with in Caitlin's office doesn't bear any resemblance to the man I thought I married.

"When you want to talk it out, I'm happy to listen."

I squeeze him tight while Jag opens the rear door to the car. Once I'm settled, I lace Brice's fingers with mine, and I stare out the window. "Can we swing past Sawyer's clinic on the way home?"

"Do you want us to wait, or do you want me to send Jag back to get you when you're ready to come home?"

His unwavering support is a gift, and his casual use of "home" for me at the palace is more thrilling than I would have expected. It really feels, despite the terrible news about Enzo, that I'm moving in the right direction. Closer to him and a future and further away from everything that's been holding me hostage in the past.

"I can take a cab," I say.

"I'd be more comfortable if Jag circled back for you when you're ready. The press is still milling around, you've got your concussion, and I don't see the point in putting you in an awkward situation we can avoid."

His media training and inherent savvy at dealing with challenging situations might be the sexiest thing about him. When we get to Sawyer's building, instead of getting out, I unbuckle my seat belt, staddle him, and I give him something to think about while I'm gone.

He doesn't even question what I'm doing. He grips my hip with one hand, and the other digs into my hair, drawing me deeper into the kiss.

Jag clears his throat, and Brice chuckles against my lips.

"I like you, Jag," Brice says. "That's the only reason you're getting away with a suddenly scratchy throat." He plants another quick kiss on my lips. "And I love you, Maren Tucker. Call Jag when you want picked up, and he'll come get you."

Having someone want to take care of me is going to take some getting used to, but the flood of warmth across my chest at the realization that Brice cares so much is a welcome rush.

"I love you too," I say before scrambling off his lap and out the door.

Sawyer is with a client when I arrive, and I sit in the waiting room, hoping I've come close to calculating her lunch break. The receptionist picks up her stuff to go for lunch as Sawyer's client comes out, and she flips the closed sign as the two of them walk out the door.

"How are you feeling? How did the meeting go this morning about Enzo?" Sawyer asks as she clicks the lock on the door and goes to the fridge behind the desk to grab her lunch. "I've got an extra salad, if you're hungry?"

"I'll take the salad," I say, and I hold out my hand. While we eat, I fill her in on everything that happened in Caitlin's office.

"Does any of this impact what's happening with you and Brice?" Sawyer sets her empty salad container to the side and cracks open a package of cookies, offering me one.

"No," I say, carefully, "not really. My issue with Brice has, at least since we've gotten close, been about him wanting kids. Enzo and I never talked about it, and we should have. Brice says he's fine if we never end up having any." I take a deep breath. "I guess I'm just worried he'll resent me at some point if we don't."

"There are all kinds of ways the two of you can create a family. It's going to be whether both of you have the stomach for those processes. Did you change your mind about wanting them?"

"I want *his* kids. My desire is very specific to him. I don't know if I'd want them if I wasn't with him."

"You want them because he wants them?"

"No, it's like..." I let out a self-conscious laugh. "Biological or something. It's him. It's one hundred percent the idea of sharing that with him that appeals to me. In some ways, it makes the reality of not being able to carry a baby worse."

Sawyer reaches out and rubs my arm, but she doesn't try to invalidate my feelings.

"I just need some kind of sign," I say, "that makes me one hundred percent sure he's not going to regret being with me if we don't have kids." I toy with the remaining pieces of lettuce. "Or maybe I just need to get over myself. I don't want to live through the disintegration of another marriage, and maybe I'm being overly cautious."

"It's an important question, and it's definitely one where you don't want a partner to have regrets."

It's clear that talking about it with Sawyer isn't going to somehow magically make me feel better about the situation, but I needed a neutral third party to bounce ideas off, and Sawyer is my most levelheaded sibling.

"How's everyone else?" I ask.

"Nathaniel has decided to dip his toes into producing television shows. Wants to represent the underrepresented in Bellerive."

I don't say anything out loud, but he's been preoccupied with the disadvantaged in Bellerive since he was in high school. His relationship with Hollyn Davis was, according to my mother, a scandal, but in a lot of ways, it seems like Nathaniel never quite moved past whatever happened between them. She's been gone from the island for years.

"Caitlin's been fielding strange calls from some woman in America who has been trying to contact Gage, but he's been avoiding her," Sawyer says.

"One thousand dollars says he got some one-night stand pregnant," I say. My comment is mostly a joke. Where Sawyer and Nathaniel are cautious, Gage and Ava are train wrecks, leaving swaths of destruction in their paths. Not sure how I'd feel if he actually got some girl pregnant by accident.

"It's possible," Sawyer says. "Though he's back together with Abby."

"Again?"

"Like a light switch."

They've been on and off since freshman year of college, and Gage just recently graduated. My brother's running joke is that they break up whenever one of them gets the urge to fuck someone else. Not exactly romantic. Why they keep getting back together mystifies me. But that's Gage. Nothing he does makes sense to me despite the fact he's only a couple years younger. Our nanny wasn't equipped to raise five children, and my mother's lack of interest once they became toddlers meant Gage and Ava got away with far too much, despite Sawyer's best efforts. They still do.

"Is he coming back to Bellerive soon?" I ask.

"Mom said he's asked for the beach hut so he can surf and figure out next steps. Not like he had four years to figure out a next step." She rolls her eyes.

The beach hut is actually a two-thousand-square-foot cottage on the only part of the island that gets decent waves. After going to college in California, Gage took on a bit too much of the casual billionaire lifestyle. Despite getting a degree, I'm not convinced he'll ever use it, content to surf his inherited wealth.

"You sticking around?" Sawyer asks, checking the clock on the wall. "I have a client in ten."

"No." I take out my phone to send a text even though I feel a little guilty asking. "Jag is picking me up."

"I hope whatever you need to set your mind at ease about the kids thing happens," Sawyer says. "That ball of uncertainty in your stomach is never fun."

No, it's not, and I'm not sure talking to Brice about it again will ease my fears. It's something I need to come to grips with on my own.

Brice straightens his tie in the mirror, and he catches my eyes in the reflection as I put on another coat of mascara. He grins and kisses my temple before leaving the bathroom.

The premiere of InterFlix's series is tonight. Unlike some of their programs, which drop all at once, they've opted to release two episodes a week for five weeks to capitalize on the hype around Brice's involvement. The photos released by people at the after-party have only stirred the pot more. InterFlix decided to ride that wave, and several of their promos have included footage of me and Brice that I didn't realize they'd gotten. Doesn't bode well for whatever else they've caught on camera. Brice isn't nervous, but he's navigated far more scandals than I have.

As part of their "After the Race" episode, they've sent a camera person to record our dinner tonight—the first time I'm eating with the entire royal family, including extended relatives. No pressure. Brice asked me before he agreed to it, and I've met everyone who'll be seated around the giant table before, but I've never met them with the implication I'll be joining the family at some point.

When I come out of the bathroom, he loops his arm around my waist, and he tugs me into his embrace. My long blue dress swirls around my feet. Tanya, the woman who normally dresses

Rory and Julia, selected my Bellerive Blue attire. We're definitely making a statement.

Instead of kissing me on my lips, which would ruin my lipstick, he trails a line of kisses up my neck to just under my ear, and then he takes my hand and leads me through the maze of palace hallways to the formal dining room.

There, everyone else is mingling, not yet seated, and there's Iris with the producer, Hye Jin, circling the crowd and occasionally stopping to ask someone a question. I can only imagine what dirt InterFlix is interested in learning about me and Brice.

As soon as Hye Jin catches sight of Brice, she grabs Iris and makes a beeline to drag him away for a solo appearance, and as I watch her interview him, a burst of pride springs forth. He's so easy on camera, but she must ask him about his dad, because I can see his whole demeanor shift, as though he's having to hold himself together. We talk about his dad a lot when it's just the two of us. Our commitment to each other has made us open in ways I don't ever remember being with anyone else. Then he flashes her a grin, one that exudes genuine happiness at her next question, and I wonder if she asked about me. The change in him is the same one I see when I walk into a room and we lock eyes. The prospect of watching this show isn't so distressing anymore.

Rory appears at my side with Grace on her hip, and her gaze is trained on Brice, where mine was moments before. "I was worried about him when George died," she says. "But I don't worry about him anymore because I know he's got you."

It's probably the nicest thing anyone could ever say to me, but I've come to expect those sorts of comments from Rory in the short time I've lived at the palace. There's a warmth to her that counters Alex's coolness with remarkable effectiveness. She is the embodiment of keeping the home fires burning.

Soon, I'm surrounded by Julia, Nick, Alex, and Helen too, as though someone planted a bug in his immediate family's ear about me being nervous to appear here tonight. The room is brimming, and my parents are here somewhere, but I imagine they're loving the chance to bump elbows with so many Summersets. With Brice occupied, his family has gravitated here. The show of solidarity causes a sheen of tears to rise to my eyes, and to conceal my emotion, I ask Rory if I could hold Grace.

She doesn't hesitate in handing her over, and I cradle her against my body. She's big enough to sit up comfortably. Her eyes have turned a greenish hazel, and her previously blond hair has darkened slightly. I can't help marveling at how children can be such mixes of their parents.

Brice reappears at my side, and he presses a gentle kiss to the top of Grace's head before pressing one to my temple. When I turn to meet his gaze, I expect sympathy or longing or some emotion over me holding her, but he's looking at me exactly as he always does, as though I'm the only person in this room worth seeing.

A shiver skates across my skin, but it's not from the cold, it's from realizing that this might be the sign I wanted. He meant what he said, and I have to trust that he'll mean it long after tonight, no matter what happens.

A leap of faith, and I make those all the time on a racecourse without second-guessing myself. Trust my instincts and go for it.

He leans in, and his lips graze my ear. "I love you too." His hand settles on the small of my back, and then he strikes up a conversation with his mother as though this whole scene is the most natural thing in the world.

When I look around the room, I see that Iris likely captured that whole thing on video, and it doesn't bother me. I don't care. This happiness that I'm finally allowing to bloom in me won't wither and die under the glare of public opinion. My love for him only seems to grow stronger the longer I let myself feel it.

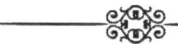

---

Brice sets a bottle of tequila, two shot glasses, and a bowl of popcorn on the coffee table in front of me. "First two episodes. Are you ready?"

"Why have you got tequila?" I take a handful of popcorn.

"In case we need to get drunk after watching them and scrub our memories clean." He plops into the seat beside me, and he puts his arm across the back of the couch, his fingers grazing my shoulder.

I cuddle into him as he clicks on the streaming service, and a giant banner of our faces with dirty, stressed expressions appears. "Oh no," I mutter.

"We look like we're in an action movie. I love it." Brice chuckles.

"I guess there's no question what their marketing strategy is. To be honest, I'm curious to see how we'll come across on camera, whether it'll be obvious we were falling in love."

"I was in love with you long before we ever stepped onto Fijian soil," Brice says as he clicks on the first episode.

"Part of me knew I was in love with you the night you asked me to go to Fiji, and I kissed you. I'd just been fighting it for so long."

He presses a kiss to the top of my head, and we settle into watching the episodes. As the scenes we lived play on the screen, it's the strangest sensation. I've been interviewed for things before and watched myself on television, but it's a whole different experience seeing myself competing.

Toward the end of the first episode, I have to admit that InterFlix seems to have portrayed us accurately so far, and in the dying minutes, I reveal that Enzo and I are separated. The camera catches Brice's expression, which causes him to groan.

"If everyone in the world doesn't know I'm crushing on you hard after seeing that look on my face..." Brice covers his eyes. "I just became a meme, a gif, and that'll trend on all my socials. Guaranteed."

"There are worse things." In the moment, I knew his response was significant, but watching it back with the editing and music, it truly feels like the start of something epic. "Do you think people will like us?"

"Of course. I'm funny, highly attractive, and a prince. The trifecta of awesomeness."

I slap his chest, and he chuckles.

"And you're gorgeous and smart and so driven to succeed that I get turned on just thinking about it." He clicks off the TV and tosses the remote over the back of the couch. "We can watch the second episode later. I've got a little Maren Tucker appreciation to conduct."

I laugh as he draws me underneath him. "I do love your Maren Tucker appreciation moments."

"You're in luck," he says, tenderly brushing my hair off my cheek. "I've got a supply fit to last a lifetime."

Then he kisses me, and nothing and no one else in the world matters except this man and these moments with him. Forever.

---

**Can't get enough of Brice and Maren? Sign up for my newsletter to receive their bonus content.**

**Maren's family is next! Grab Temporary Love, the fake dating, marriage of convenience story of Gage and Ember, here: https://mybook.to/TemporaryLove**

# About W Million

W. Million is a high school teacher whose award winning contemporary romances about strong women and troubled men have captivated her loyal readers. Writing as Wendy Million, she is also the author of the romantic suspense series *The Donaghey Brothers*, the contemporary second chance romance, *When Stars Fall*, and the NA sports romance *Saving Us*. When not writing, Wendy enjoys spending time in or around the water. She lives in Ontario, Canada with two beautiful daughters, two cute pooches, and one handsome husband (who is grateful she doesn't need two of those).

# Also By W. Million

**Bellerive Royals Series – Interconnected standalones**

Fake Crown

Scarred Crown

Heavy Crown

Fallen Crown

**Tucker Billionaires – Interconnected standalones**

Temporary Love

**New Adult Sports**

Saving Us

Fake Crown

**Donaghey Brothers Series – Romantic suspense**

Retribution

Resurrection

Redemption

**Adult Contemporary Romance**

When Stars Fall

Miss Matched

# Acknowledgments

As always, thank you to my husband, my children, and my dad for their constant support as I write these stories.

A special thanks to Tiffany, my PA, who is trying to keep me organized as I navigate a full time job and this writing career. I appreciate all your help. Social Butterfly PR has also been an asset as I try to figure out how to get these books into readers' hands.

My street team and ARC team are honorary Bellerivians. Your enthusiasm for these characters and stories is truly appreciated.

To everyone reading this, thanks for being here.

Here's to the next one!